ROUSTABOUT

The Traveling Series, Book 3

JANE HARVEY-BERRICK

HARVEY
BERRICK
PUBLISHING

DEDICATION

To James
A reluctant cover model who is willing to be bribed to take his shirt off
for charity.
And to Lily
For helping him.

James' model fee was donated to www.felixfund.org.uk

PROLOGUE

Spring

TERA

It was my brother's party, a going-away party, I suppose you could say. But it was more than that: it was a celebration of life and love and living.

Kestrel was my half-brother and had been brought up in a traveling carnival. Our father certainly had some explaining to do when the news broke, not only to his constituents, but also to me since I was unaware that I had not one, but two brothers. This past year of getting to know them had been a revelation in so many ways. I loved my new brothers. My relationship with my father was strained.

Kes's friends stared at me curiously. They weren't unfriendly, but it was clear that I wasn't one of them. I felt prim and proper in my $300 jean skirt and silk top. I clutched the warm beer in my hands and tried to look like I was just chilling out.

My brand new BMW stood out among the rusting trucks, trailers and RVs. I didn't fit.

If it had been a cocktail party or one of my father's political fundraisers, I'd have been fine, schmoozing with the best of them. But these people didn't care about any of the things that I'd been brought up to think were important: the right school, the right job, the right clothes, all the trappings that came with my father's success.

Just as I was considering making my excuses and driving back to the hotel in Arcata, a man's laugh rang out, a sound of deep joy echoing through the twilight. I looked across and saw him: his head thrown back, his eyes sparkling, his hands on his hips. He was still smiling when his gaze met mine. I saw his eyes darken with a predatory expression that made me feel as if his gaze alone could strip the clothes from my body.

Tucker McCoy.

I knew who he was—Kes's brother, not by blood, but certainly in every other sense of the word. A stunt rider, like my brother, and the biggest manwhore walking God's green earth. His prowess with women was almost as legendary as his prowess on a motorcycle.

He'd been traveling all the times I'd visited Kes and his fiancée Aimee before, but I couldn't help thinking that even when he had been around they'd decided to keep me away from him. For my own good, no doubt.

That was probably Aimee. I liked her and we'd become close.

Even though we were the same age, she sometimes treated me like a little sister, and honestly, I felt immature when I compared myself to her. All I'd ever been was a student with an allowance and a black American Express card provided by my father. I didn't even have to take some low paying, part time job while I went to school. But Aimee had a career as an elementary school teacher before falling in love with my brother ... although the way she tells it, she'd been in love with him since they were children. I think that's why she'd decided to give up her entire life to travel his road. I couldn't imagine doing that for a guy. Kes was great and I could see how in love they were, but she'd given up her whole world. Not that she saw it like that.

"Love is in all the small gestures, TC," she said to me. "But sometimes it all adds up to something bigger. I can't imagine my life without him—and I don't want to."

I envied her—but I pitied her, too.

I straightened up fractionally when Tucker started to approach me, his walk loose-limbed and confident.

"Hey there," he said, giving me a sexy half-smile as he casually propped a shoulder against the coffeeberry tree where I was slumped in a deckchair. "Tell me why a beautiful woman is sitting all by her lonesome."

His accent was warm with a touch of Southern that melted like honey on his tongue.

I raised an eyebrow and gave him one of my father's patented campaign stares, the one he used with reporters who asked dumb questions.

"I'll take the compliment of being called beautiful," I said, "but really, is that the best line you have?"

The light of challenge sparked in his eyes and his grin grew wider.

"Not even close to my best," he said with a cocky edge to his voice. "I thought I'd start off easy."

"Oh, but I'm not easy," I replied. "I'm complicated and difficult and it takes a lot of work to impress me."

I was lying. His long, lean build, deep-set eyes and model-pretty face were impressing the hell out of me. His hair was curling to his chin, the ends bleached to a dirty blond by the sun. And what color were those amazing eyes? Gray? Green?

Almost a light olive color—I'd never seen anything like them before.

Close up, the air seemed to spark and crackle around him. There was an intensity hidden in his lazy gaze and laidback smile that made me uncomfortable. I didn't want to feel the heat in his eyes, and I definitely didn't want to feel the attraction pulling at me.

Feeling twitchy and starting to squirm under his penetrating gaze, I did the opposite: I leaned back, crossing one leg over the other, smiling to myself as his eyes followed the movement.

He glanced up and grinned again.

"I've never been afraid of hard work," he murmured, hooking a thumb through one of his belt loops.

"Good to know that you like a challenge—that makes it easy for me."

"How d'you figure that?" he asked, his lips curving upwards.

"I just keep saying no to keep you interested."

"So you want to keep me interested?"

"I like a challenge," I threw back at him.

He leaned a little closer and it felt like a bolt of static electricity zipped between us. I glanced out toward the ocean, wondering if a storm was brewing, but the waves were silky ripples under a purple sky.

"I'll work for my supper," he said, his tongue flicking out to wet his lips as he spoke, looking at me as if I was on the menu.

It sounded so dirty, the way he said it, the way his gaze roved over my chest. But I wasn't going to let him know that.

"Now you want me to cook for you, too? Wow, you're sure of yourself."

He gave a husky laugh. "Is it bad that I'm sure of myself? It's you I'm not sure about."

"What makes you so sure of yourself?" I asked, looking him in the eye.

"What you see is what you get."

"Hmm, so no hidden depths. That's disappointing."

He grinned at me, his eyes crinkling with pleasure.

"Nope, absolutely no hidden depths. As shallow as the day is long. But that means no surprises, right? Just lil ole me— everything that you've been checking out for the last two minutes."

My cheeks flushed as I met his eyes.

"Not that I mind," he went on. "I like the way you look at me ... pretty much like the way I'm looking at you."

"Slightly annoyed?" I suggested, pretending to be bored of the conversation.

He grinned and shook his head.

"Uh-uh, pretty lady. The look you've been giving me says that you're interested." He leaned closer. "I'll be hitting the road tomorrow, but we could make sweet music tonight. It'll be worth your while—I'm a guy who knows how to use his ... hands."

"I'm more concerned with your mouth ... more specifically your tongue ... especially if you keep mixing your metaphors."

He gave a startled laugh.

"I think you're teasing me, beautiful, or maybe that's a challenge?"

"Not at all," I said, being serious for a moment. "I know you're good with your hands. I was told you did most of the repairs on Kes and Aimee's cabin. Did you work in construction before you joined the carnival?"

Tucker looked taken aback. "Who told you that?"

"Aimee mentioned a few things."

Tucker lifted a shoulder and leaned back against the tree, his face hidden in the shadows.

"Just some stuff I picked up," he said, sounding wary now.

"More than a few things from what I heard."

He shrugged again, noncommittal, then his eyes made a slow appraisal of my body. I should have been insulted by the way he let his hot gaze roam every inch of me, but I was enjoying returning the favor.

His jeans hung loosely from his hips, the rips in one knee caused by hard usage not designer tears. He wore an Eagles t-shirt that had been washed so many times it was impossible to read the words that ghosted over his firm chest. His biceps bunched as he propped himself against the tree, and his tanned skin was turning from gold to light brown in the first months of spring, but he was no gym rat. Everything he had was from hard, physical labor. I'd been brought up with men who pushed papers for a living—this man was not from their world. And that excited me.

"Why's a class act like you hanging with a bunch of carnies?" he asked.

His voice had turned edgy and his question felt like a test.

"What do you mean?"

His tone was still lazy, but there was a tightness that hadn't been apparent before.

"Sweet cheeks, you're wearing a designer skirt that must have cost two hundred dollars and there's nothing cheap about your perfume."

Determined not to show my chagrin that he'd read me so easily, my reply was calm and level.

"Three-hundred dollars. And I'm visiting friends."

"Guy friends?"

"Jealous?" I asked with a light laugh.

He grinned. "Maybe I just don't feel like kicking anyone's ass tonight."

"Maybe you'd be the one getting your ass kicked."

He leaned closer, and I caught the scent of soap and clean sweat.

"If you're the one doing the kicking, it would be worth it."

He whispered the last words, making me lean towards him,

but when we were close enough to touch, he pulled away at the last second and winked at me.

Annoyed, I sank back into my chair. "I think I'd like to kick your ass."

"I think I'd like to let you."

I couldn't help laughing. "Very smooth, Mr. McCoy."

His expression showed surprise.

"Well now, that just doesn't seem polite that you know my name but I don't know yours. You gonna tell me your name, sweet cheeks?"

I stood up and smiled at him. "Well now, it isn't 'sweet cheeks'."

I lifted my beer in a salute and walked away, hearing his laughter follow me.

I knew myself well enough to know that I was minutes from falling for his obvious charms. I needed to get right away before...

The hell I did!

I almost stumbled as my steps faltered. What on earth was I doing? Why was I running away from a man that I was deeply attracted to, whose eyes promised as much sin as I could take in a single night?

I'd never had a one night stand; never been brave enough to choose gratification over being sensible.

But maybe I wasn't that girl anymore. Not since I'd learned a few hard truths about my father, about my family.

I turned around, determined to enjoy everything that Tucker McCoy had to offer. Even if all I'd end up with was a pleasurable soreness between my legs and something memorable to write in my diary.

When my eyes found him again, he was still leaning against the coffeeberry tree, talking to Zef, the other stunt rider in Hawkins' Daredevils.

I guessed they were talking about me because Tucker's eyes

met mine as he laughed at whatever Zef had said. But then his laugh died away and for a second another emotion flittered across his face. He seemed surprised, maybe even a little angry. Then he looked away and it felt deliberate.

Two others joined them: Zachary and Ollo. Now, I was even more surplus to requirements.

I knew the guys were tight; after all, they spent most of the year traveling together, but they looked out for each other, too.

No one knew how old Ollo was. He was born with dwarfism and was less than four feet tall, but in many ways he was a tribal elder, a grandfather to the carnie family. I loved to sit and listen to his tales of the olden days. Aimee was writing them down, afraid that they'd be lost forever if she didn't.

I had friends from home in St. Paul, and friends from UCLA, and I was even making friends up in San Francisco, but they weren't family—not the way the carnies were family.

Everyone was accepted, regardless of race, color, creed or sexual preference. Zachary's boyfriend, Luke, was playing his guitar by the bonfire, loved and protected—one of them.

Well, everyone who was a carnie was accepted. So that ruled me out.

I studied Tucker out of the corner of my eye, watching, assessing. He stayed beneath the tree, chatting with Zef, but didn't look my way again. After a few minutes, Ollo climbed onto Tucker's shoulders and they all headed back to the bonfire as Tucker's laughter echoed through the still air.

Disappointed, I sipped my flat beer for something to do. I felt self-conscious by myself, so I headed toward the cabin and joined the short line for the bathroom.

But as soon as I was back outside again, I couldn't help looking for Tucker. And I found him.

He was walking away from the bonfire, a brunette wrapped around him with one hand in his back pocket, the other sliding up inside his t-shirt.

I combed my fingers through the ends of my straight fair hair and watched as the other woman fawned all over him. I guess he wasn't into blondes. Why couldn't it have been my lucky night instead of hers?

Something shifted inside of me, something that had been holding me back broke open. I *didn't* have to live by my parents' rules, I *didn't* have to live the life they had preordained for me. I was 27 years old. *What was I waiting for?*

I gazed wistfully after Tucker and his conquest.

He did what he wanted when he wanted. He did *who* he wanted, and I envied him. It wasn't that I particularly wanted to be a notch on his belt, but I wanted to be free of all the guilt, all the bullshit that had stopped me from living my life so far.

Until I met this crazy carnival family, I hadn't understood.

To protect my dented pride, I told myself that Tucker had been warned to stay away from me because I was Kes's sister, and therefore off limits.

I was used to that: my father had guys warned off of me all the time. He didn't do it himself, of course, but he had 'people'. Only eligible men were allowed anywhere near me—men who wore suits, worked in upscale offices and had the right family connections.

I was relieved when Aimee strolled across, her pet monkey clinging to her neck.

The little animal chattered softly, then swung himself into my arms, surprising me with his affection.

"Hello, Bo."

His small, leathery hands tugged my hair gently then he nestled against me.

"He's going to miss you," Aimee said with a quiet smile.

"Do you think so?" I asked, nuzzling the warm fur.

Aimee chuckled.

"Well, I was talking about Kes, but yes, Bo will miss you, too."

"I'm going to miss you all so much," I said truthfully.

"We'll be back after Thanksgiving," she said, her voice kind. "And you can visit us on the road anytime."

"I know, thank you. And I'm really happy for you. Kes is in his element tonight."

We both turned to look at my brother. He was standing by the bonfire, the flames throwing dancing shadows across his face that did nothing to dim his obvious joy. His eyes flickered across to Aimee and his smile widened.

Then he dragged his t-shirt over his head and tossed it to the ground.

I had to admit my brother was a good-looking guy. All the women—and a few of the men—had their eyes all over him.

"Do you ever get used to that?" I asked.

Aimee shrugged. "No, not really." Then she looked at me closely. "Are you alright?"

"Sure, just annoyed with myself."

"Why? What happened?"

I groaned with frustration.

"This guy was hitting on me ... and I walked away. Now I'm really wishing I hadn't. That's all. Stupid, I know."

She cocked her head to one side.

"This is about Tucker, isn't it? I saw you talking earlier."

I gave an embarrassed laugh. "I don't really know if anything would have happened..."

"Did you want it to?"

That was a good question.

Aimee stared at me appraisingly and opened her mouth to speak, but whatever she was going to say was swallowed by the crowd's roar of approval as a three-foot jet of fire flew from Kes's mouth.

Bo hid his face in my hair, upset by the noise and flames, but I couldn't tear my eyes from the performance.

When it was over, I glanced across at the coffeeberry tree

where I'd had my close encounter with Tucker McCoy, but then I wished I hadn't looked.

His back was pressed against the rough, silvery bark, while the brunette was pressed against his chest. His hands loosely cupped her ass as she ground into him.

His eyes were closed, but it was almost as if he felt the weight of my disappointment because his eyelids slid open and he stared back at me, even as the woman assaulted his neck with her tongue.

Then he blinked, and his hands gripped the woman more tightly, lifting her up so her legs wrapped around his waist.

Definitely my cue to leave.

I sighed again, then smiled as Aimee hooked her arm through mine, following the direction of my gaze.

"Well, I'd say he's made it fairly obvious he isn't interested. That's never much fun."

"You should take it as a compliment," Aimee said quietly.

"Hmm, not sure I follow you," I admitted.

"Tucker respects you and he let you walk away, otherwise that would be you right now and he'll be gone in the morning. Believe me, he leaves a trail of empty beds and broken hearts wherever he goes."

I laughed lightly. "I can believe that, but I think it's Kes he respects, not me."

Aimee was silent, which I took for her reluctant agreement.

"He's not a complete asshole," she said at last. "I used to think he was … when I first met him: always a different woman," and she shook her head sadly. "But he's a lot of fun to be around, too. He's always happy, always smiling. And even though he's a total slob," she said, shuddering, "he's always ready to help me out with anything. Doesn't matter what, whether it's cleaning, cooking or laundry. He flirts all the time, but that's just Tucker. He doesn't mean anything by it."

I sighed. "That's what I was afraid of."

Aimee shook her head. "What I mean is that he's never once made me feel uncomfortable to be alone with him. He's respectful ... well, when he's not walking around half-naked. But they all do that. They're so used to living in a men-only environment, their manners get rusty." She shot me a sly look. "He does have a great ass."

"Are you trying to make me jealous? Because it's working!" Aimee laughed.

"He makes a great roommate. And you've seen what an amazing job he did on fixing up the cabin. No one could have worked harder. The people he cares about..."

Her words trailed off and she took a deep breath.

"When Kes was so badly injured, Tucker said something. I couldn't forget it, but I never really understood it either. He said, 'It wouldn't have mattered if it had been me'. At the time I wanted to agree with him," and she shot me a rueful glance, "but it made me realize that he wasn't as shallow as I'd thought." She paused, staring unseeing into the roaring flames of the bonfire. "He's never mean to women. He lets them know that he's not looking for anything more than one night, or two at most. It makes me think that somewhere in his past, someone hurt him badly. Men who treat women like disposable objects are either running from something..."

"Or...?" I prompted.

Aimee grinned. "Or he really is a douchey manwhore." Then her smile faded. "Tucker is always laughing and joking around. I could be wrong, but I'd say the river runs deep with him. The women who get hurt are the ones who think they can change him."

I felt her looking at me and knew she was sending a message.

"It's hard to know him well, but he's like all of the Daredevils in some ways: always chasing the next adrenaline rush. He seems so laidback when you meet him, but he's got that hunger driving him ... but like I said, he's hard to know."

"Kes changed for you," I pointed out.

She nodded slowly. "But that was because he found out that I hadn't abandoned him, that I'd been just as miserable as he was."

"I wasn't trying to change Tucker," I sighed. "I just really, really wanted to get laid by someone who looked like they knew what my clit was for and where to find it."

Aimee choked out a startled laugh.

"Oh my God! That's so funny. Or not but ... my last boyfriend before Kes, he, well, he wasn't very dynamic."

I nodded in sympathy.

"You mean he couldn't have found a clit with a road map."

Aimee laughed and shook her head while we shared an expression of commiseration.

"So why did you turn Tucker down when you had the chance?" she asked.

I shook my head. "Ugh, I'm regretting that so much. I'm just not ... I don't ... I mean, I never have ... you know? I just wanted ... to live a little."

Aimee smiled knowingly.

"Sorry, but I don't think Tucker will go near you now that he knows who you are. He loves Kes like a brother."

We stood in silence for a moment and I felt the disappointment settle inside me.

I watched Kes's carnie family, their wildness, their willingness to accept whatever life threw at them, the tight knit community forged in the fires of society's disapproval. An invisible line separated me from them—and it always would.

"I think I'll get going now," I said quietly.

Carefully, I unpeeled Bo's tiny fingers from my shirt, trying to ignore the hurt I saw reflected in his black button eyes. He latched onto Aimee quickly, winding his paws into her dark hair.

"I'd better take him inside," she said, nuzzling his furry head. "It's past his bedtime." Then she looked up. "Will we see you in the morning? We leave at five."

I smiled and shook my head. "No, that's a bit too early for me. But you'll email, won't you?"

"Of course I will! But don't forget—you can use the cabin whenever you want. You're family."

Her words brought tears to my eyes.

"God, I'm going to miss you all so much."

Aimee smiled sadly.

"We'll miss you, too. Are you going to say goodbye to Kes?"

I shook my head. "No, I hate goodbyes."

CHAPTER ONE

August: three months later...

TUCKER

"C'mon, sweet cheeks. Don't be like that."

Mandy ... or it might have been Mindy ... pouted at me. She was trying hard to be pissed, but couldn't quite get a hold on it.

I'd leave her smiling. I always did, because life is too short to spend your time being miserable. I wanted a woman to enjoy me as much as I enjoyed her.

"You are just the hottest lil thing I've ever seen. My God, woman, you have ruined me. I'm wrecked. Look at me—I'm on my knees!"

I crawled up the bed, kissing her belly and the space between the edges of her silicon valley.

"You rode me hard and put me away wet, honey. A man needs time to recover from that."

I sighed against her neck, tickling her skin with my hair.

She giggled, which was what I'd been aiming for.

"You're such a liar, Tucker!"

"You wound me," I murmured into the pillow.

She giggled again and wrapped her free hand around my dick.

"*That* doesn't feel like you need time to recover."

I grunted in surprise because I was genuinely trying to leave. I was running late, and Kes was going to kick my ass.

Mindy ... or Mandy ... fluttered her eyelashes hopefully and I figured it would be just plain rude to leave without a final encore.

"Sheathe me up, sweetheart. One for the road."

"Two," she smirked.

"Two," I agreed, winking at her.

A gentleman never argued with a lady.

I had to book it back to the fairground. Even at midnight, the faint breeze felt too warm against my damp t-shirt. My helmet was so hot that sweat trickled into my eyes making them sting.

I groaned when I saw the train of trucks already pulling out and moving on, kicking up clouds of dust that made me cough, my eyes watering even worse as I rode past.

The sideshows had been stripped from the midway already and the owners were on the road, traveling through the night. Takedown for the bigger rides took longer and meant hours of work under the hot spotlights, then loading into the rigs, leaving a torn patch of bare earth as the only sign that the carnival had been there.

By tomorrow morning, the early-birds would be in Minnesota: a new town, another state, and for me, a different woman. That's just the way it was.

I winced when I saw Aimee pacing up and down in front of the small arena that held our display ramps and stunt bikes. She was pissed, and had every right to be. We should have been further on with dismantling everything by now.

She saw me and shook her head slowly, then shrugged, a gesture that clearly meant, *you're on your own.*

Kes was shirtless and bathed in sweat, scowling as I drove up.

"What the fuck, Tucker? We should be on the road in four hours! We've gotta make Waconia by nine!"

I swung a leg over my Duke, taking a moment to appreciate her smooth lines, white trim and red wheels. She was the only female in my life that I cared about—well, apart from Aimee, but she was like a sister to me. Mindy/Mandy wouldn't have been happy to hear that, but it was true. A Ducati 899 Panigale was a Super Sports bike—way different from the stunt motorcycles that I rode in Hawkins' Daredevils. She had carbon fiber covers, heel guards for the foot-pegs, an aluminum tank plug, and carbon and aluminum alloy number plate holder. It was love at first sight.

Kes looked at it longingly and I felt a pang, knowing that he couldn't afford one for himself. When he had his accident 18 months ago, it left him and Aimee with next to nothing. I'd tried to give them some money, but I thought Kes was going to punch me in the face—and that was when he was still in a wheelchair. Then I tried to loan them some money, but Kes flat out refused. Stubborn asshole.

So the Duke was twenty-five thousand dollars of giving the finger to the past, and maybe the future too. Plus, I let Kes ride her. It was the most I'd ever spent on a bike and it left me living from pay check to pay check again for the first time in four years, but I'd done it before and I'd probably do it again. Yeah, not the smartest way to carry on, but there are no certainties in life. Don't worry, be happy—like the guy in the song said. Dude knew a thing.

I grinned apologetically at Kes.

"Just keeping a promise to a lady."

"Whatever, dickhead," he replied, shaking his head, a smile sneaking through his annoyance. "Just park that piece of Italian shit and get to work."

"Sure thing, boss!"

I saluted him and rolled the Duke up the ramp, securing her into a stall at the back of the rig so she wouldn't get knocked around as we drove.

I didn't hear Zef come in behind me, but I damn sure felt the kidney punch that he landed on me. None too light, either.

"Fucker," I muttered under my breath as I rubbed the sore spot, knowing I deserved worse for holding everyone up.

"You should try thinking with your big head instead of your little one," he snorted, flicking me on the ear.

"Nothing little about either of my heads, bro," I grinned at him.

"Dream on," he laughed loudly, heading to work, a large monkey-wrench in his hand.

I followed him out and joined the two other roustabouts who were helping to take down the jump-ramps. They worked for all of the shows, lending a hand wherever was needed. It had been the first job I'd had when I left home at 17. It was a hard life, but I wouldn't have changed it for anything.

"Sorry, guys!" I called out, grinning at the amused faces. "Lost track of time."

"Lost track of your dick, more like," snorted Carl, and I heard Buddy laughing his ass off.

"Nope, still attached," I shouted back, climbing to the highest part of the ramp and started loosening the bolts that held it in place.

There were upward of 100 pieces of metal and wood that held the ramps together. Some of the sections weighed nearly 300 pounds, and everything was moved by hand. The five of us could do takedown in less than six hours, but I'd held everyone up. Yeah well, it was hard to regret the satisfied look on Mindy/Mandy's face when I'd let myself out of her place.

We worked through the night, and the last things to dismantle were the huge spotlights that we used for the show and to see what we were doing during takedown.

I pulled on a pair of thick leather gloves, careful not to let the hot metal touch any part of me as they were stored away.

Aimee joined us bleary-eyed an hour before dawn with coffee and snacks. We were all tired and dirty, but there was no time to wash up.

"I'll take first shift at the wheel," Zef said, drinking his coffee standing up. "Something tells me you didn't get much rest last night *before* we started takedown."

"I'll get all the sleep I need when I'm dead," I said solemnly, dodging his next punch.

"Yeah, yeah. I'll wake you up when we hit Fargo."

I really needed to shower and wash off the scent of Mandy/Mindy. But I'd missed my window. I jumped into the cab of the rig, folded my leather jacket into a pillow and got comfortable.

"Man, you stink of cheap perfume," said Zef.

"Nothin' cheap about Mindy," I lied.

Zef laughed again. "Her name was Linda, you douche!"

I cracked an eye. "Serious? How come you know that?"

"Because her friend Melissa told me."

"Bummer," I yawned.

Too soon, Zef was shaking me awake.

"'Sup?" I asked, rubbing a knuckle into my eyes.

"Man, your cell has just about been ringing nonstop. Someone really wants to get ahold of you."

He raised his eyebrows.

"Don't tell me you slipped up and gave your number to Linda?"

I had to smile at that. "No way. I gave her yours. Thank me later."

He muttered something I didn't need to hear. Zef knew my rules as well as I did. Hell, he used to joke that I should get them tattooed on my junk to save repeating myself.

The rules were simple, and they kept me sane.

1. Never give a woman my number. *That's smart.*
2. Never sleep with them more than once. *Why only eat the red M&Ms when you could have all the other colors too?*
3. Always leave her satisfied. *That's just polite.*
4. Never look back.

If you keep moving, you can't get caught. Right?

Still grinning, I pulled my cell out of my pants pocket.

My mind went blank when I saw the 423 area code: four missed calls, one voicemail and three texts—all from the same number. I had a strong suspicion that whoever was trying to reach me wouldn't say anything I wanted to hear. I deleted the voicemail without listening to it, then casually deleted the texts.

Zef frowned but didn't ask any questions. After living with the guy for three years, he knew me well enough to know that questions wouldn't get him anywhere. I turned my phone off and shoved it back in my pocket. As far as I knew, only a handful of people had my number and all of them were carnies. Whoever was calling had no business knowing where I was. I was happy here and I just wanted to be left alone.

With that thought, I tried to go back to sleep, but the best I could manage was to rest my eyeballs.

When we hit Fargo, Zef took a break at a truck stop we used when we were over this way, and headed for the restaurant. I loaded up on eggs, bacon, biscuits and gravy. I loved truck stops out here—none of that organic, gluten-free, dairy-free, taste-free shit that you get in California—just good, honest food for hard-working men. Just like momma used to make. Well, not my momma.

I took a cup of coffee from the waitress, winked at her as she blushed when she served us, and filled another cup to go, before heading out and hauling ass eastward.

I loved the Midwest—friendly people and wide-open spaces. My kind of place.

Our destination was the Carver County fairground in Waconia, about 20 miles from St. Paul. Aimee was excited because she'd be near enough to visit her family. Kes was less thrilled, knowing that his asshole father was also close by, but he'd get to see his sister.

Thank Christ I hadn't hooked up with her last spring before I found out who she was. Shit would have been more than a little uncomfortable.

My gut twisted at the thought, but I did my best to ignore it.

The county fair took place later in the year, but several traveling shows like ours used the empty lots from Easter onwards. I'd visited for the first time the year before when it had been just me and Zef as Hawkins' Daredevils. We'd done okay, putting on a pretty good show, but there was no denying that Kes was the star attraction, and without him we'd struggled to make the big bookings.

I was nearly as good a stunt rider as him, because I had no fear—not of dying anyway. I wasn't trying to kill myself, I just didn't care either way.

But I couldn't do that extra shit he did—the fire juggling and what Aimee called 'being a showman'. Kes had spent his whole life in the carnival; I'd done 12 years, and I still didn't know everything there was to know. Along with the freedom, that was one of the things I loved about this life: every day was different, and I didn't have to stay still.

With Kes back in the game, we were packing them into the

smaller showgrounds and with luck, we'd be able to get back to some of the bigger, better-paying arenas next year. Kes and Aimee needed the money badly. I didn't care for myself, but they deserved more.

It was nearly 11AM by the time I pulled into the fairground two hours behind already, thanks to me. The pin for the Ferris wheel was in place, stark against the pale blue sky. All around, there was a buzz of activity as families settled in and the roustabouts started to erect the games and slides, sideshows and rides.

I inched the rig toward the faded grandstand where we'd be setting up and put the rig in park, letting the diesel engine stutter and die.

Zef and I both jumped out and I stretched my back to work out some of the stiffness. Zef was already around the back unlocking the trailer's doors.

"Welcome to Minnesota."

I turned around, surprised to see Kes's sister sitting on a bench in front of the grandstand, hiding a smile.

"Well, if it isn't Miss Hawkins. You're lookin' prettier than ever. You sure you're related to Kes?"

An arm hooked around my neck as Kes dragged me away, folding my arm behind my back painfully.

"No hitting on my sister, motherfucker!"

"Wouldn't that make me a sister-fucker?" I asked.

I regretted my words immediately when Kes punched me in the ribs.

"Your mouth is writing checks your body can't pay, asshole," he grunted.

He let me go, and I stood up, rubbing my sore ribs.

"Sorry, Miss Hawkins," I called out. "But you call me anytime you want, sugar."

She laughed as Kes started to chase me, and I had to make like Usain Bolt.

I jogged back to the showground to get started on emptying the rig with Zef and Luke. Kes was pretty well healed after breaking his back eighteen months ago, but he wasn't supposed to do too much of the heavy lifting. Aimee would get on his case if he did, and man! That woman had a set of lungs on her once she started.

We'd gotten it down to fine art, hauling out the ramps and setting up in the showground, but it was hot work and I was sweating like a pig. I wiped my face with the bottom of my shirt, then concentrated on tightening the bolts on the jump ramps.

The humidity was a bitch, so we were all relieved when set-up was finished too many hours later. Luke and Zef went to grab showers while I decided to do a quick walk-through before I lost the light.

I was surprised to look up and see Kes's sister watching me. I thought she'd be hanging with her brother.

I was amused to see that her eyes were glued to my chest where my shirt clung to my skin, damp in the June heat.

She sat in her little summer dress, and with her long, blonde hair pinned up, she looked sexy and classy.

But off limits.

Tera

I'd been watching Tucker for a while, probably like some creepy stalker, except I wasn't trying to hide. He'd been so absorbed in his work that he hadn't noticed me. I let my mind wander, imagining how I'd go about executing a hookup with my brother's best friend.

I sighed, staring around me at the scrubby field and the carnival slowly rising skywards.

As a child, my parents had never let me near a fairground. Not that many of the girls from my school visited fairs either, but those that did talked about awesome rides, scary tattooed carnies, too much cotton candy and funnel cake. I'd had to stay home and pretend it didn't appeal.

Now I understood the reasons why my father wouldn't take me—but as an adult, I wasn't sure I saw the fascination anyway. The rides looked tired and dangerously worn; the carnies were hard-eyed and clannish; and the fatty, sugary, over-priced food was a stroke waiting to happen.

And yet ... there was no doubt in my mind that when my brother performed his amazing stunts, there was magic in the air. The looks on the faces in the crowd, men, women, and children—you could see in their awed expressions that they were witnessing something special. I'd seen some of Kes's videos with the Daredevils on YouTube: they were absolutely terrifying!

Aimee said he wasn't able to do all of the big stunts—yet—but I'd seen some of his practice runs before they went on the road. Few people were allowed close enough to see the blood, sweat and tears. I'd seen all of those things, and I knew the cost.

But watching Tucker check the ramps, his worn, ripped jeans clinging to his sculpted ass, I had to admit that sweat had never looked better.

If I was going to branch out from my safe, boring life, he'd be perfect: one night of mindless pleasure—it sounded good to me. I'd thought about him a lot since the night we met, but this was the first time I'd been able to get away to visit. My imagination hadn't let me down—he was just as hot as ever.

He'd changed in the three months since I'd seen him. His skin was more tan now, but the most noticeable difference was he'd cut off his hair so it was shaved around the sides and only slightly longer on top.

I imagined running my hands over his smooth skin, tangling my fingers in his hair.

If only.

I'd never done anything like this before, but I figured that a man I was powerfully attracted to like Tucker ... this was the place to start living my life.

But then I also wondered if sleeping with my brother's best friend was such a smart idea after all. I'd have to see him every time I visited: awkward. I'd just about convinced myself it was a bad idea and was losing my nerve when he finally spotted me. A huge smile spread across his face and he seemed genuinely pleased to see me. A small shiver traveled up my spine as he let his eyes wander across my body.

"Lookin' good, sugar. Real classy."

The hairs on the back of my neck stood up as I slowly turned, as if I'd only just noticed him, my head cocked to one side.

Tucker walked right up to me and was standing so close, I could see every one of the golden hairs that stubbled his cheeks and chin. His t-shirt clung damply to his chest and he was carrying a red helmet.

"Do I know you?"

He grinned at me.

"Aw, don't be like that after all that time we spent together—you and me, alone under the stars."

I snorted dismissively. "That's not how I remember it. We had a two-minute conversation..." *and then you left to hump some other girl,* "with fifty other people present. And it was twilight."

He smiled broadly. "See, I knew I was unforgettable."

I chuckled quietly. "Hello, Tucker. How are you?"

"All the better for seeing you, Miss Hawkins," he said flirtatiously.

Then he seemed to think better of his behavior and took a step away from me.

"Nice t-shirt!" I said, raising my eyebrows.

A picture of a woman was printed on the front of the worn

cotton. A naked woman. Reading a book. All she was wearing was a pair of glasses.

He glanced down, as if he'd forgotten what he was wearing.

"Oh, yeah," he grinned at me.

"Big fan of reading, I take it?"

"Big fan of brainy chicks," he replied with a wink.

"Hmm, well, it's sexist and it objectifies women."

"I could take it off," he said, his voice low and suggestive. "Then you could objectify me all you want."

I shook my head, even as a smile overtook me, but then Tucker smiled and stood up straight.

"Well, better get back to work or the boss will kick my ass."

He turned to leave, and I called after him impulsively. "Will you have a drink with me later?"

He hesitated, a questioning look on his expressive face, and ran his fingers through his hair which was curling up at the ends from the heat.

"That's probably not a good idea," he said at last.

"Because?"

Tucker sighed. "Kes wouldn't like it."

"He doesn't have to—it has nothing to do with him."

Tucker frowned and I saw his eyes dart to my lips before he looked up.

"Why is Senator Hawkins' daughter inviting some carnie to have a drink with her?"

I stared straight back.

"Maybe the Senator's daughter chooses her own friends."

"Your dad wouldn't want you talking to me, let alone having a drink with me."

"I'm not inviting my father; I'm inviting you."

He gave a low, quick laugh. "That's the kind of answer Kes would have given—except you say it prettier."

"Look," I said, my voice no nonsense as Tucker continued to

dance around the issue, "I'm in town for a few days because I'm helping my dad with a couple of things, as well as seeing Kes and Aimee. I've got appointments lined up during the day, but my evenings are my own."

I raised an eyebrow, challenging him to wimp out.

"I'm staying at the Inn on Cherry Drive. There's a separate bar with a restaurant attached to it. I'll see you there at 8PM. You can buy the drinks—maybe dinner too, if you get lucky."

He leaned one shoulder against the railing and stared at me.

"Kes and the Senator don't agree on much, but neither of them would want you having drinks with a guy like me, let alone dinner."

For once his tone was serious and his ever-present smile had vanished.

"A guy like you?" I laughed, rolling my eyes. "Oh! You mean your *reputation*. Don't worry, you're not that cute. I think I can resist you for one night. I just want to have a couple of drinks, eat dinner, and I'd like some company while I do it."

The lies fell from lips with surprising ease.

"How come you're not having dinner with Kes and Aimee?"

I rolled my eyes. "They seem to be ... busy."

He laughed softly, his beautiful smile lighting up his whole face.

"I don't reckon it would be right to make a lady eat by herself, and I can hardly say no when she begs."

"Oh, get over yourself. And for that, you're definitely buying dinner, too."

He looked worried for a moment and I could have kicked myself. I knew how hard it had been for the guys to get work over the last year. Maybe Tucker couldn't afford a nice meal in a hotel. But then he smiled again.

"You drive a hard bargain, Miss Hawkins, but seeing as you begged so nicely, I'll see you later."

"Tucker?"

"Yes, ma'am?"

"I don't beg."

He raised his eyebrows, his smile growing wicked. "You sure about that, Miss Hawkins?"

"Call me Tera or TC."

He rolled the words over in his mouth then gave a quick nod.

"See you later, TC," and he walked away.

Damn. His ass looked fine in denim.

As I drove back to the hotel, I had second- third- and fourth-thoughts. I didn't have Tucker's number so I couldn't call him to say I'd changed my mind. I almost turned around and drove back to the fairground to cancel. *It's just dinner,* I told myself; just friends sharing a meal. Yeah, right.

Nervous and excited, I dressed casually in jeans and a t-shirt with a good pair of heels and subtle makeup that didn't look like I was trying too hard.

To be honest, there was no game plan. Tucker didn't seem interested in me beyond a mild flirtation; Aimee had already said he wouldn't go near me because of Kes, and I would be pissing off my dad just by talking to Tucker, not that he'd ever find out. I ran my hands through my long hair in frustration: what the hell was I doing?

Unable to answer that question, I made my way down to the bar and found a corner booth where I could see the entrance. The waitress brought me a glass of water and a menu, and I ordered myself a bottle of beer.

I shifted around in my seat, torn between irritation and disappointment as the dial on my watch showed 8:15PM. I reasoned that Tucker wasn't the kind of guy who thought too much of the time or being a few minutes late. But when it reached 8:30PM and the servers were throwing sympathetic looks my way, I had to admit that I'd been stood up.

CHAPTER TWO

TERA

I'd just slunk out of the bar, ignoring the pitying looks of the servers, when I heard a motorcycle roaring down the high street. I glanced over my shoulder, feeling relief and irritation in equal parts as I confirmed that Tucker had finally arrived.

I was fuming that he was 30 minutes late—and pleased that he hadn't stood me up. But what kind of guy was that late for a first date? *An asshole*, replied one half of my brain.

The more reasonable half reminded me that it wasn't a date, and that I'd all but bullied him into having dinner with me.

I stood in the covered entrance, watching as he dismounted, surprised to see unguarded emotion on his face as yanked off his helmet. He stood for a moment, his hands on his narrow hips, staring down the road he'd just driven along, then he took a deep breath, squared his shoulders and strolled toward me carrying his helmet.

When he looked up and saw me, something flashed in his eyes, but it was gone too quickly for me to name, and immediately his confident grin was back.

"Well hey! A pretty girl is standing in a bar waiting for me. That's almost too many good things in one place to be legal."

I folded my arms and glared at him. "This 'good thing' is pissed that you're late!"

He was still smiling as he strode up

"Don't be mad, sugar. I was thinking about you the whole time—that's gotta count."

"Not even nearly."

His grin widened. "How 'bout I buy you the biggest piece of chocolate cake they have and call it nearly even?"

"Huh, it's a start. Why are you so late?"

He rubbed a finger across his eyebrow.

"I would have called, but I don't have your number. And I didn't think it was a good idea to ask Kes for it."

He raised his eyebrows, a half-smile hovering on his lips.

"I waited half an hour! You'll have to try harder than that!"

He was within touching distance when he replied.

"You want me to be harder, TC? Because I think that can be arranged."

I knew I wasn't imagining the smolder in his eyes before he suddenly backed off.

"How about I buy you dinner *and* chocolate cake with a cherry on top?" he said teasingly.

"Hmm, I don't know. Those waitresses in there have been feeling sorry for me because they thought I'd been stood up. And that pisses me the hell off!"

A surprised laugh rattled out of him.

"You're somethin' else, TC."

"The 'something else' is hungry and fed up with waiting," I pointed out as I turned to walk back into the bar.

Then I felt his strong hands on my shoulders, pulling me to a halt as he darted ahead so he could open the door.

"Why, thank you, kind sir," I simpered, batting my eyelashes at him. "Because I'm too weak and feeble to open the door for myself."

"There's nothing weak and feeble about you," he said as I pushed past him. "A gentleman should do right by you, Miss Hawkins."

Aimee had told me manners could get rusty when it was just a bunch of guys, so something about Tucker's behavior warmed my heart.

Not that I was going to tell him that.

"Now you're getting it," I said coolly. "I'll need at least an hour's groveling before I'm satisfied."

"I'd like to see you satisfied," he whispered in my ear.

I felt a warm heat pulse through me at his suggestive tone.

But once again he didn't follow through.

"I'm going to feed you until you have to go find a quiet corner to sleep it all off," he said with a wink.

I didn't know whether he was attracted to me, or whether flirting was his default setting with all women. Either way, being Kestrel's sister was clearly a mixed blessing when it came to Tucker. I was certain he didn't back off when he was with other women.

God, all those other women. What the hell was I doing? Scratching an itch? Playing with fire?

All of the above?

I glanced at the hostess as I headed back to the table where I'd sat before, and she walked across, seeming to withhold a heavy sigh as she carried her notepad in front of her like a weapon.

"Are you and your friend ready to order?"

"He's not a friend—just a bum I found on the street," I smiled sweetly.

The surprised server glanced at Tucker.

"What she said," he added with a grin. "I guess the lady isn't all that fussy."

The server shook her head, smiling slightly.

As Tucker scanned the menu, she scanned him, her eyes so gratified that I thought she'd paste a sticker on him saying 'passed inspection—USDA Grade A'.

And he did look better than anything I'd seen on the menu. His washed-out t-shirt was tight across his shoulders and chest, damp from the warm evening and leather jacket he'd been wearing. His ripped jeans would be a disgrace at one of my mother's cocktail parties, but hugged his butt and toned thighs. I know because I'd looked.

As he turned the pages of the menu, a small frown notched between his eyebrows, I could see long lashes, much darker than his dirty blond hair. The smooth skin of his forearms and muscled biceps caught and held my attention.

"What?" he asked, glancing at the exact spot where my eyes had been burning holes. "I got something on me?" Then he looked up and raised his eyebrows. "Or are you checking me out?"

"I thought I saw a spider," I defended. "My mistake."

He laughed softly. "A spider? I knew I felt something crawling all over me. I thought it was your eyes. My mistake."

I slammed my menu shut with a huff. "I'll have the vegetarian lasagna."

"Steak," said Tucker, looking straight at me. "Burn it. I like what I put in my mouth to be heated all the way through."

The waitress fanned herself with her notepad before writing down the order.

Tucker grinned at me, then used his hands to rake a lock of misbehaving hair out of his eyes.

Even though his hair was shorter than I'd seen it before, it remained untamed. Almost military length at the back, the stubborn, longer section at the front refused to stay in place. I wouldn't be surprised if one day he decided to shave it all off.

His whole body was sculpted to my idea of near perfection,

but he wasn't vain—his body was like an extension of the bikes he rode, a highly calibrated, powerful machine. He cared more what his Ducati looked like than how he was dressed. His clean but ripped jeans and ragged t-shirt were a testament to that.

He settled back in the booth, his arms spread wide, as if inviting me to carry on checking out his honed, toned body.

Since attack is the best form of defense, I forced myself to relax and speak pleasantly.

"Thank you for coming tonight. I wasn't looking forward to having dinner alone.

He gave me a small smile.

"You're a lot like Kes," he said.

"How so?"

"He can turn on the charm when he wants to get his own way."

I wasn't sure I liked *that* comparison, and really, wasn't that an example of double standards?

"And you don't?" I asked, more harshly than I'd intended.

His amused gaze softened. "Naw, I'm just full of shit, shine and hot air."

I suspected that Tucker was smarter than he let on. He was never lost for something to say, and he made me laugh with his witty replies. But for some reason, he preferred people to think he was a dumb hick. I didn't get why he wanted to be underestimated.

I decided to change the subject.

"How did you and Kes meet?"

This time his eyes smiled along with his mouth. I realized I was in danger of becoming addicted to that expression.

"I was working as a roustabout..."

"I've heard the term, but I don't really know what a roustabout does. I'm assuming it's not like working on an oil field."

He grinned and shook his head. "No, in the carnival a

roustabout is a jack-of-all-trades, a laborer. Doing whatever needs doing."

"Such as?"

He shrugged. "Pitching the tents for the sideshows, hanging the lights and electric cables, working with the ride owners to put up the Ferris wheel or the rollercoaster, set up the dodgems or the carousel. Feed the animals if you have them or clean out their cages. Sometimes I'd set up a temporary corral for the rodeo acts. One time, I had to take care of a two-ton elephant called Phoebe. Man, that was some shit-shoveling."

"I don't know if you're being serious or not."

Tucker grinned. "I'm never serious. Except when it comes to three square meals a day."

"Hmm. So how did you end up in the Daredevils?"

He scratched his eyebrow with his forefinger, as if contemplating the question.

"Well, one of the ride owners had a wall of death show: one of those stunts that takes place in a silo-shaped cage and you ride your motorcycle around it—you're held in place by centrifugal force. I didn't have a regular slot—I just kind of helped out sometimes. Kes saw me doing that and said he was going to start up his own stunt show. He offered me a job—I was ready for a change so I said yes." He smiled again. "And here I am."

"How old are you?"

He held his hand to his chest. "That's a mighty personal question, Miss Hawkins."

I shook my head in exasperation. "I'm 27. The same age as Kes. But you already know that."

"I'll be 30 on my next birthday," he admitted with a grin.

"Wow, so old!" I laughed.

He closed his eyes, letting out a sigh. "And she aimed straight at my heart."

I threw my napkin at him.

"Seriously," I laughed. "The big three-oh. Any plans on how you're going to celebrate that?"

"Me and Daisy will take a trip some place," he said, an impish smile on his face.

I'm sure my expression said it all. "Daisy? Is she your girlfriend?"

"Is that a bit of green-eyed jealousy there?"

I cocked my head to one side. "Maybe. But I don't hit on guys who have girlfriends."

His smile deepened. "Is that what you're doing? Hitting on me?"

I leaned back in my chair. I don't know why I was so disappointed: Aimee had warned me that Tucker was the biggest manwhore out there. I'd seen the way he operated with my own eyes. I could just add 'cheat' to the long list of reasons why Tucker McCoy was a dog.

I took a sip of water and made my voice casual.

"I *was* hitting on you, Tucker. But it won't happen again. I don't like cheats."

His eyes widened. "Hey! I'm not a cheat. I never promise a woman anything except..."

The words trailed off and a dull red crept across his unshaven cheeks.

"Except a night of unforgettable bliss?" I teased.

He smiled, but it was off—not the usual full wattage.

"I don't cheat," he repeated.

I stared at him. "That sounded almost serious. I thought you didn't do serious."

"I don't," he said simply. "I'm not serious about women—I don't do relationships, so I never cheat either."

"Just a series of one night stands."

"Sometimes two," he said with a wink.

"And what does Daisy think of your philosophy?"

He grinned. "She always plays along."

Disgusted, I stood up, laying some bills on the table.

"Where are you going?" he asked, surprise on his face.

"I seem to have lost my appetite," I said calmly.

Tucker was on his feet in a flash.

"Don't go, TC. I was just messing with you. I don't have a girl; I don't have anyone. Daisy is my motorcycle. It's a Ducati, or a Duke. So I call it…"

I laughed with relief at his explanation.

"Daisy Duke—I get it!"

"Will you stay and have dinner with me?" he asked, his smile so sweet I could have gotten diabetes on the spot. "Please?"

"Fine, I'll stay. But only because you begged me," I snorted, taking my seat again.

Tucker laughed out loud. "Girl, you are a hard ass."

I leaned closer, and Tucker automatically mirrored my stance.

"Woman," I said softly.

He licked his lips, the same small frown tugging his eyebrows together.

The moment was broken when the server brought our food.

Tucker's salad had surrendered before his enormous steak arrived and he dove into it with relish, attacking the slab of meat with a knife and fork until it had disappeared and the accompanying baked potato was a distant memory.

"Hungry?" I asked, raising an ironical eyebrow.

Tucker looked almost guilty, as if I'd caught him doing something illicit.

"I just don't like wasting food," he said, with a casual shrug of his shoulders.

He grinned quickly, but his eyes darted away, another secret hidden behind his smile.

I hadn't expected to find Tucker McCoy so intriguing.

Damn.

. . .

Tucker

I'd been surprised as hell when Tera asked me to have dinner with her.

I couldn't remember the last time I'd done something as ordinary as eat a meal with a woman ... other than Aimee.

I knew Tera was attracted to me, and I was definitely attracted to her, but that was the problem. She was Kes's sister: she wasn't someone I could fuck and forget. But I also suspected that she wasn't a woman I'd be able to stop thinking about anyway, which made it doubly stupid for me to agree to have dinner with her.

I enjoyed her sass, the way she gave it back to me, and I admired her honesty, too. She wanted to have dinner with me so she just asked. No dropping heavy hints, no pouting and whining—just straight to the point.

Seeing her like this after all these months, it had knocked me off balance. I should have walked away, but I couldn't ignore Kes's sister completely. After all, I'd be seeing her several times a year for as long as I was a member of Hawkins' Daredevils. It would make it easier if we could find a way to spend time together without me wanting to bend her over the Duke.

But talking to her, hearing her laugh, I wanted it even more.

Not good.

Kissing Tera would be a mistake.

Dinner had been more than fun—it had been exciting. She teased me and challenged me. It had been a long time since a woman had given me the same rush as pulling stunts on my bike. Why the fuck did she have to be my best friend's sister?

But every time I tried to push away from Tera, her laughter, the glint in her eyes, the intelligence she showed with every sentence, it all pulled me back.

It didn't help that she was on her fourth beer.

"My, it's warm in here," she said, holding the chilled bottle against her neck.

I was mesmerized as droplets of water rolled down her chest, disappearing into the deep vee of her t-shirt. And she knew it, the witch, a small, cat-like smile tugging at the corners of her mouth as I yanked my thoughts out of the gutter.

A minute later she was moaning and groaning again, rolling that damn bottle over her throat before taking a long swallow.

It was getting harder to remember why I couldn't have this woman. Yeah, and that wasn't the only thing that was getting hard.

"It's late," I said, nodding at the streetlights outside.

As if we needed them to know that twilight had come and gone, and stars were sprinkling the sky like fireflies.

"I'll walk you back," I said decisively, standing to make my point.

Tera grinned up at me, her eyes a little unfocused. "All the way across the parking lot? What a gentleman!"

Then she leaned forward, her elbows resting on the table, giving me the money-shot view down her t-shirt.

God had given her beautiful tits—she could make a sucker out of me any time.

My eyes darted up to hers when she spoke again.

Damn, she could make jogging a spectator sport.

"Tucker, I like you, and I can tell you like me. We're both single. I'm not asking you for a commitment." She smiled and cocked her head to one side. "Let's just see how this goes."

I sat down heavily. She was so damn fearless—just like Kes.

"TC, it's not a good idea."

She rounded the table and sat next to me, her thigh pressed to mine, leaning her head against my shoulder so her silky hair tickled my cheek.

So damn soft.

I could feel the heat of her skin burning through my t-shirt and my dick swelled, trapped sideways, the seam of my jeans pressing painfully. I'd had a chubbie all evening, but now it was trying to climb through the denim.

"I think it's the best idea I've ever had," she said, her voice quiet but clear.

"You didn't think that at the bonfire last spring," I reminded her. "You walked away from me then. Why aren't you walking away from me now?"

"Because."

I waited, but that seemed to be all the answer I was getting.

"Because what?" I prompted her.

"Because ... because that's what I've been taught to do. I'm supposed to wait for the right guy, then marry him and give up my career to make perfect little babies that my dad can kiss on his campaign trail."

"Doesn't sound so bad," I hedged.

She shook her head fiercely.

"No, it doesn't, but it's not me either. I've met a lot of *right* men," and she rolled her eyes, "but it seems as if it's the wrong man that I'm attracted to. There's something there, something between us." Then she smiled brightly. "And I haven't gotten laid in ages."

My head dropped into my hands.

"You can't say that to a guy!" I groaned.

Her arms wrapped around my neck, pulling my head down with a fierceness that surprised me. Her pink lips flattened against mine, demanding, insisting, until her tongue was in my mouth.

Stronger men couldn't have resisted her, and dammit, I'd always been weak.

I kissed her back, stroking my tongue against hers, my hands tangling in that glossy hair the way they'd wanted to all night.

Tera's hands were at my waist, tunneling under my t-shirt,

tracing her nails over skin that was suddenly sensitized.

She hummed against my mouth, then nipped my lower lip.

"Let's take this somewhere private," she whispered.

I glanced up to see the servers whispering together in the corner, and Tera giggled.

I nodded quickly and tossed down a pile of bills onto the table.

I stood up to leave, but Tera grabbed the money and shoved it back in my pocket. I would have argued, but my brain was numb from the moment she touched my ass.

"I invited *you*," she said.

"And told me I was paying!" I called after her.

But she ignored me, walking away swinging her hips.

"Damn it," I grumbled to myself.

I grabbed my leather jacket and held it in front of me so my boner was hidden.

Once she'd paid, I followed her outside, her heels clicking across the parking lot as she strode at a rapid pace. I had no idea how she walked so fast in heels that high after four beers. Maybe she practiced.

As we approached the entrance to the Inn, she suddenly veered left toward a stand of pine trees, until we were hidden from prying eyes.

"TC, I don't think we..."

But then she shoved me hard in the chest so I flailed backward, the breath whooshing out of my lungs as I thudded against a broad trunk. She was on me before I could take a breath, her hands were everywhere—one hand pushing up under my shirt, the other was shoved down the back of my pants, gripping my ass.

My body felt like it was on fire, and every argument in my brain shut down, wanting only this moment with this woman.

I spun her around, pressing her into the rough bark as the thin wall of my control exploded apart.

Without needing to look down, I knew my dick had grown even harder and was pushing against her thighs like a greedy fucker, trying to get closer.

Her tits pressed against my chest, and my breath caught in my throat. She was all soft, all woman, but aggressively taking what she wanted. I was in heaven.

I was in hell.

I pushed away, taking a step back, breathing hard. It was just enough room for her to cup my dick over my jeans.

Her chest was rising and falling hypnotically and I damn near had to tear my eyeballs from my head to look away. This woman was turning me inside out, lust making me crazy.

"This can't..." I began, waving my finger between us.

Her eyes turned glassy and for a horrible moment I thought she was going to cry. But then the blue turned to ice, and the temperature dropped a dozen degrees.

"Is it because of Kes?" she asked, her voice accusing. "That's why you won't let this happen?"

"Shit, Tera, he's my *brother!*"

She pulled her clothes straight and tossed her long, shiny hair over her shoulder. "No, he's not," she snapped. "He's *mine*." And she stamped away, her hair glowing silver in the moonlight.

Before two seconds had passed, she'd disappeared through the darkness and into the hotel's wide, glass doors.

Wow, I really managed to fuck up that conversation.

My cock was so depressed I thought he was going to whimper. But instead I was left with one hell of a boner and only myself to blame.

Fuck it! I had two really good things going on in my life: Hawkins' Daredevils and now Tera. Of all the fucking luck that I couldn't have both.

I rubbed the back of my neck, the tension from the last twenty minutes leaving me with a motherfucker of a headache.

I headed back toward where I'd parked the Duke then

remembered that I'd left my helmet in the diner. Cursing myself for being such a dumbass, I walked back inside, smiling at the server who was clearing our old table.

I pointed at the helmet still laying on the bench seat in the booth.

"Any excuse to come back and see you," I said, grinning.

"Oh, get on with it!" she laughed.

I winked at her and strolled back outside, allowing my smile to slip.

After this evening's clusterfuck, I was looking forward to going back to the RV and having a quiet beer with Zef before…

"Nice bike. I always appreciated Italian design."

I ground to a halt, staring at the beautiful blonde smirking at me from the Duke's pillion seat.

"TC, what are you doing? We already had this conversation."

She looked at me seriously.

"I know you think I'm a little princess, Tucker, but I'm not a virgin. There have been quite a few guys. In fact more than a few—maybe even a lot."

She underlined her words with a swift look. A sliver of jealousy speared through my gut. I didn't like the idea of that *at all*.

She raised her eyebrows.

"But I've never been kissed the way you kissed me. And you know? I've been thinking what Kes would say if knew about this … *thing* … between us…"

My stomach twisted.

"…he'd say life is too short. You really want to spend the rest of your life wondering 'what if'? Because I don't. Maybe I'm wrong. In fact, why don't you tell me I'm wrong? Tell me that life is easy, and that second chances are a dime a dozen; that third chances are more common than pennies. Go on, Tucker—tell me what you think I should hear."

Her crystal blue eyes sparked with defiance and the words I should have said dried in my throat. She leaned forward, hooking her fingers into my belt loops and pulling me forward until her lips were on mine again.

This kiss was soft, sensual, and the wanting and needing that I'd been pushing away all evening flooded open. I crushed her body against mine, almost lifting her out of the saddle.

"Are you finally agreeing with me?" she gasped.

CHAPTER THREE

Tera

I opened my mouth in a gasp. Tucker didn't need a further invitation. His tongue slid in and he was no longer gentle.

One strong hand gripped my hip and the other was on the nape of my neck, controlling my body as his mouth angled over mine, his greater height and strength pulling me up from the seat of his bike.

Then he tore his lips from mine, panting against my neck, his warm breath fanning my hair.

"One night," he grit out. "One night and then..."

"Shh, don't say it. You don't need to. You're on the road and I live in California. I get it."

"Kes will fucking kill me," he groaned.

"Kes will never know," I whispered, stroking my hands over his butt and the back of his thighs.

The moan that came out of his mouth was more animal than human, and God help me, I wanted to hear that sound again.

"Let's go to my room," I said, my voice urgent.

He shook his head softly. "We can't be seen together. If word gets out that the Senator's daughter..."

"We'll go in separately. Room 837," I said. "I want you to tuck me in, Tucker. Now give me your bike keys."

"What?"

"I said give me your bike keys—I'm not giving you the chance to wimp out on me again."

He choked on a laugh and shook his head. "You are something else."

"So you said," I agreed, pushing my hand into his jeans pocket and pulling out his keys.

His smile was heated and amused as I grinned at him over my shoulder.

I was 27—not a teenage virgin on her first date. Although I had somewhat exaggerated my experience to Tucker: I'd had three serious boyfriends, all long-term. The sex had been nice, pretty good in one case, but nothing that had turned me on as much as kissing Tucker. Nothing that burned.

I am in so much trouble.

I reached my room in a couple of minutes. And then I had a metaphorical stumble. Should I wait by the door? Should I wait in the bed? No, I had to open the door to him. Should I leave the door ajar? Oooh, bad, bad idea.

Should I...?

But then I heard a quiet knock outside—Tucker must have been less than 30 seconds behind me.

I yanked open the door without checking the peephole—rookie mistake—but Tucker was leaning against the wall, looking more sinful than a triple chocolate cake with whipped cream and sprinkles. Waaay more.

"Last chance to be a good girl," he said, his voice low and resonant.

I shook my head slowly. "We're a long way past that, Mr. Roustabout."

"Good," he said, pushing the door wide open and stalking into the room. "Because I want to see you being bad."

"Back at you," I laughed, my voice more breathless than I'd have liked. "You're going to come so hard..."

He stepped closer, his body looming over me. Suddenly 5'7"—or 5' 11" in my heels—felt petite.

"Is that a fact?"

"Yes," I challenged. "That's a fact."

There was a moment when promise and power and the weight of every mistake hung in the air. A moment when I could have, should have stopped it before it started.

Then he kissed me—a kiss so intense, so deep, so demanding, that I forgot my name; forgot my lungs needed air; forgot that blood should wash through my brain.

I felt his body shaking as the kiss intensified, and then with a low moan he pulled back, cupping himself over his jeans with one hand, his lips trembling against my neck.

A pause. A breath...

And then our bodies crashed together again.

There was no slow seduction, no tender moment; this was possession—mine, his. It didn't matter.

Our teeth clashed, hot breaths panting into each other's mouths. I grabbed his hair, my fingers slipping through the short locks, nails biting into his scalp. I angled his head, tugging his lips to my neck, where he licked and sucked so hard I knew that I'd have hickeys. He fisted my hair and pulled my head sharply, his mouth urgent and demanding.

While his hands were occupied, my roaming fingers skated over his torso, once, twice and for a third time, greedily tracing the ridges and dips of his muscles. I watched, fascinated, as he sucked in a sudden breath.

Then he yanked his shirt over his head and my eager hands were thirsty, stroking and sliding over his satiny skin, pulling roughly at the smattering of soft hairs on his chest.

When his hands tugged on the hem of my t-shirt, I took the hint, yanking it up and tossing it over my shoulder. Immediately, his head dipped to my chest and I felt his warm, wet mouth fastening over the lace of my bra, his tongue working under the material, his teeth pulling the cups down.

As he licked and sucked and bit my nipples, I arched into him, pressing his face into my boiling flesh, suffocating him against my breasts, watching him gasp and drown.

Then he was on his knees, kissing and sucking my belly, working his hands into the waistband of my jeans. The tight fabric bit into my flesh as he forced his hands inside, lower, lower and lower again, until his fingers were brushing against my clit.

I scrabbled frantically trying to find the button to open my jeans, fighting those possessive, knowing fingers as they fucked me where I stood.

An orgasm flamed through me, taking me out at the knees and we stumbled backward toward the bed. When I fell, Tucker's hard, heavy body crushed me into the mattress.

I gasped and shoved at his shoulder and he rolled suddenly, pulling me on top of him so I was splayed across his broad chest, the hairs tickling my exposed skin, as I gasped and wheezed and tried to fill my lungs.

He snapped open the clasp on my bra with one hand and pulled it from my body with brutal strength.

But he didn't let up. He grabbed and pushed and forced the denim from my legs as I lay on top of him.

I broke a nail as I struggled to pull the zipper down and he growled as the broken edge scored a red line across his stomach.

I was naked and lying on top of a man made of muscle. He was satin-hard, iron-soft, polished stone and silky skin.

He rolled again and this time I was underneath him and I thought he'd fuck me through his jeans, the rough material abrading the smooth skin of my thighs.

"Off!" I gasped. "Take them off!"

I scrambled with shaking hands to undo the button and zipper of his jeans, and he let his cock spring free from his briefs, the blunt head poised at my entrance. I shoved him hard and he swore, lifting his body to push the denim away so his jeans fell into a pile at the bottom of the bed, his black briefs still tangled on one foot. He kicked again, and his clothes disappeared onto the floor.

I thought this was it. I thought this was the moment when Tucker McCoy would fuck me for the first and last time.

But I was wrong.

His body slid lower and lower down the bed, the scruff of his cheeks and chin harsh on my sensitive flesh.

I whimpered as his head pushed between my thighs. Unapologetically making room for himself, he hooked my legs over his shoulders and opened me wide.

Heat that was part embarrassment, part arousal, flooded through me. When his tongue touched me, stroking me, probing me, I cried out, grabbing his hair and forcing his face deeper.

His fingers tightened against my thighs hard enough to leave bruises as he spread me open again, the pressure of his talented tongue undoing every molecule of restraint, every fiber that made me who I was.

He needed to stop. It was too much. Too much! God, I didn't want him to stop. A thousand lights sparked behind my eyes and fireworks exploded through my body.

I think I must have screamed, because his hand clamped down on my mouth. I didn't mean to bite him, but he cried out and I tasted his blood.

"Goddamn it, TC," he ground out.

I tried to apologize, but my body was limp and boneless, liquid from tip to toe.

And that's when his long, hard cock entered me. Against

49

any reason, my exhausted body reacted, my back arching to meet him as he surged against me again and again, his thrusts deep, even, controlled.

He pulled out halfway, then pushed back in over sensitive nerve-endings.

My mouth dropped open as I watched him, intense, controlled.

He was an incredible lover—I'd expected nothing less. But he was holding back.

"Don't do that," I gasped against his shoulder as he moved inside me. "Don't hold back."

His eyes seemed black with lust and his jaw clenched. And then he let go.

My faint whisper broke him. He thrust into me so hard, so unexpectedly that a hoarse scream left my throat, but he didn't stop and I didn't want him to. I angled my hips upwards, encouraging him to go faster, harder, deeper.

The real Tucker fucked like a force of nature—fierce, unstoppable, powerful.

"You like that? You like it when I fuck you hard?"

He gave me everything he had. And I was beyond speaking.

A thousand explosions, a megaton, a nuclear reaction blew my body apart. I'd never climaxed so hard or for so long.

His hips slammed against me, sweat slicking us together, until his own body shuddered and stilled. His orgasm was silent, the only sound his harsh breaths as he slowly collapsed against my chest, his face softening as his cock throbbed inside me, his expression dazed.

I winced as he pulled out, immediately bringing my legs together and rolling onto my side, my thighs sore, bruises sure to show on my skin from the punishment of his hipbones against me.

I curled into a tight ball, but Tucker's insistent hands pulled at my shoulder, until I relaxed and rolled onto my back.

My eyes slid open to find him staring down at me, his expression a mixture of concern and fear.

"Did ... have I hurt you?" he grit out. "Was I...?"

My smile was weak but real. "So good," I whispered. "So good."

I was 27 and Tucker had just set the benchmark for pleasure for the rest of my life—it was a depressing thought.

And then I passed out.

Tucker

It was a mistake. The whole fucking night had been a mistake.

I shouldn't have had dinner with her, shouldn't have kissed her. I definitely shouldn't have fucked her. And I shouldn't be here now.

Being with Tera, kissing her deep, being inside her sweet, sweet pussy, it made me forget all the shit, happy amnesia.

I should go. I knew I should go.

But I couldn't make myself leave either.

She fell asleep the second I pulled out, her eyes closed, her sweat-damp hair tangled across her cheek. I reached out to brush it away from her face and was shocked to see my hand was shaking. I'd hit it hard, that was for sure. I thought for a moment I might have gone too far, but she said it was good and she'd smiled.

It had felt amazing to me. Sex was sex—whether I did it with one girl or two, drunk or sober, high or straight, from behind, on top, underneath. In a bed, on the floor, with the sky blind above—it was all the same. Different woman, different scent, different taste, but all the same—just sex.

And now my hands were shaking and I wasn't dumb enough to think it was just the last drops of adrenaline leaching out of me. I wasn't sure what it was—probably because I knew it was *wrong*.

Fuck, Kes was going to kill me. Jeez, right now I would have helped him. His *sister*, for crissake!

Everything Tera said about life being short and all that shit made sense at the time, but *now* ... now I knew I'd fucked up. I didn't think I could look at Aimee every day and lie to her face. And Kes ... he was family, my brother—the only family I'd ever had that mattered. I'd fucked this up and now he'd beat the shit out of me, plain and simple. What's more, I'd let him. Hell, I'd kick my own ass if I could reach.

I rubbed the palms of my hands over my eyes.

Fuck, I was probably out of a job the second Kes found out. I was going to lose everything. Again.

Dumb shit!

But looking down at Tera, her breathing deep and contented, I couldn't regret it either. It was the best sex of my life, and there had been a lot of women. For the first time, I was ashamed that I'd lost count. It had seemed pointless to keep adding to the notches after I'd gone past ... well, I stopped bothering with numbers sometime in my late teens.

It still surprised me how many nice girls from good homes got their rocks off by screwing a grease-monkey carnie. The rougher and dirtier you were, the more they liked it. I remember one girl sniffing my leathers after a show and saying, "God, I love the way you sweat!"

I glanced down, the filled rubber still hanging from my dick, my clothes scattered across the floor. I'd done what she wanted. We'd gotten whatever *it* was out of our systems. I was free to go.

I watched her fingers twitch softly next to her open mouth and the urge to leave, to stay, to leave was confusing. I was tired and it had been a long few days. With Tera's body wrapped around me, her sweet lips on mine, I'd felt something like ... peace.

Yeah, that's what it was—comfort.

I pulled off the condom and tied a knot in the end, then dropped it onto the floor. I'd find a trashcan later.

I lay back and I could smell her perfume on the pillow, on the sheets—hell, it was all over me, as well. Subtle, probably expensive.

I couldn't give her that: designer clothes, big houses and expensive cars. I couldn't give her anything except this: mind-blowing sex.

There must be a dozen guys in suits her dad had lined up. *What the hell is she doing with me?*

A cold thought twisted my gut—maybe I was just a giant *fuck you* to her old man. I didn't like that idea at all, but it fed on my doubts until it made me want to vomit.

Not that it mattered. It was a one-time thing. We both knew that.

Sighing, I closed my eyes. Just five minutes.

Tera

I woke up sweating, too hot and confined by the sheet tangled around me. I kicked with my legs, but the sound of a soft grunt next to me brought me wide awake.

The flood of memories rushed back as I stifled a groan. Holy shit, I was sore—damn near everywhere.

Tucker blinked up at me, and I felt exposed in more ways than one as his eyes widened in shock. But then he smiled— that killer smile that made his eyes sparkle with devilment.

It was a smile that said he was thinking of doing something shocking; his laugh meant he'd already done it.

I missed him and he hadn't even left yet. I forced myself to ignore the wild hammering inside me. This is what hooking up felt like. It was stupid to be emotional: stupid and dangerous.

I pushed it all away until it was safely hidden. I was too transparent, and Tucker was an enigma.

"Ugh, I'm all sweaty this morning," I complained, pretending to scowl at Tucker. "It's like sleeping next to a radiator."

He laughed softly.

"You didn't complain about getting all sweaty last night."

"Hence me mentioning 'morning'. That's what happens when the big yellow disc rises in the sky."

He narrowed his eyes, then reached down and threw the quilt over my head, sealing me into the damp sweaty sheets.

"Now you're a Tera burrito."

"Dork!" I laughed, struggling free.

I blew my hair out of my face. There were so many things I wanted to say, starting with: *Why did you stay last night?*

From the look on his face, I could tell he was expecting questions—but I *really* didn't want to hear the unpleasant truth of honest answers.

"Time to get up and face the day," I said instead, swatting his shoulder.

He pretended to flinch.

"I'm kind of comfy here. Sure you don't want to go for round two?"

His smile could have made an angel sin.

"Well, I..."

"I'd take it slow this time, sugar," he said, his eyes roving over my body, slow and lazy. "I could spend hours on those beautiful breasts, take my own sweet time touching and tasting you."

He patted the mattress next to him, the invitation in his smile as much as his gesture.

"They should call you 'layabout' not 'roustabout'," I moaned.

"I'm going for a shower—and if you were the least bit environmentally-minded, you'd share it with me to conserve water."

I staggered out of bed, hoping the sight of my round white butt in daylight didn't scare him too much. I turned on the shower then peed quickly, the running water drowning out the noise of, well, the running water.

I flushed, and hoped the shower water wouldn't go cold while I quickly brushed my teeth.

I hopped inside just as I heard the bathroom door open and Tucker took his turn to pee.

"You know that's kind of gross," I called out, "peeing in front of someone else."

"I figured you'd object if I pissed out the window," he said reasonably.

"Ugh, whatever."

He opened the shower door and stepped up behind me, pressing his hard body against my back as his arms wrapped around my waist, resting his chin on my shoulder.

It was such an affectionate gesture, but then I reasoned that it was just Tucker being Tucker.

Even so, I was determined to enjoy it.

I turned around too fast, slipping slightly, and Tucker clamped his long fingers around my biceps.

"Careful, sugar," he said, grinning. "Can't have you throwing yourself at my feet."

"Oh shut up," I said, using a vocabulary that my hundred-and-fifty-thousand dollar college education had paid for.

I pressed my lips against his, and he responded willingly. I was expecting the same rough passion of the night before, but he was gentle, sensual.

His mouth moved softly against mine, his tongue just hinting at the aggression I knew he was capable of, his fingers moving over my hips in soothing strokes.

I could feel his hard length pressing between us, but he didn't seem in any hurry.

Then he pulled away from me and reached across for the shampoo. I was surprised and touched when he started to massage my scalp, his thumbs making me sigh with pleasure before his strong fingers slipped to my neck and shoulders.

"I didn't know you could use shampoo for that," I hummed happily.

"One of several off-label uses," he chuckled, nudging me with his hard dick.

"Well, I approve," I said, at the same time thinking of reaching back to stroke him. "They could re-brand it as shower-lube."

"Hey! I didn't say anything!" Tucker laughed. "It was your mind that went straight to the gutter."

"Hmm," I murmured, my tone noncommittal even though he was dead on.

He turned me around and rinsed my hair under the showerhead, then repeated the whole process with conditioner.

"By the way, what's with the tattoos?"

His hands stilled for a moment, then he shrugged.

"Too much to drink—woke up with those," and he jerked his thumb over his shoulder.

Four stars outlined in thick, black ink cascaded from his shoulder to the middle of his back, decreasing in size. They were neat, but not beautiful, and I could tell that he didn't like them.

"I have a feeling there's more to that story," I teased. "I'll make you tell me one day."

He laughed deeply. "Miss Hawkins, you're wet and naked in the shower with me. I'm fairly certain you could make me say my name was Daisy Duke and I'd do it with a smile."

My hands were hot and slippery when I reached out to

touch his erect dick. He sucked in a deep breath and stepped away from me.

I looked up at him, puzzled.

"Shower sex is a bad, bad idea," he chuckled, shaking his head as he leaned against the tiles.

"I think it's a great idea," I said, pressing my breasts against his chest and reaching up to kiss his lips lightly.

He kissed me back briefly, then let his head thud against the wall.

"Man, shower sex is not all it's cut out to be. You get shampoo in your eyes, and your arms feel like they're about to drop off while you're holding her up, and my legs always start to go in the last minute…"

I sniggered quietly. "Sounds like you need to hit the gym," and I slapped my hand against his rock-hard stomach.

He winked at me, but didn't take the hint.

I tried again, pressing against him, sliding his dick between my legs, enjoying the firm pressure.

But he grabbed my shoulders and pushed me away, a serious look on his face.

"I don't have any more rubbers, TC."

I stood on tiptoe and licked his ear. "That's okay, I'm on the pill and I'm clean."

A pained look passed over his face. "I haven't gotten tested in … a while."

That got through to me.

"Oh."

"Fuck," he muttered quietly, fisting his hands against his thighs.

"Oh well, there's other stuff we can do," and I stroked him again.

"TC…"

"Shh," I said, and this time he didn't argue.

. . .

Tucker

Damn it all to hell. This woman was going to be the death of me.

I was propped up against the tiles in the shower, trying to remember how to breathe as she washed my cum from her hands and stomach. My legs were shaking and I'd pretty much lost the power of speech.

She smirked at me over her shoulder.

"You really shouldn't argue with me, Tucker."

"No, ma'am," I wheezed.

I stuck my head under the hot water and shook like a dog, flicking wet hair out of my eyes.

Tera laughed happily as she stepped out of the shower, her eyes smiling, and I knew: *this* was why I'd stayed—for that look.

Because I didn't want her to think I was an asshole even if I was, even if this was the first time I'd stayed the night because I wanted a woman to think well of me. I was fucked. I had to finish this now. I had to tell her that...

"Do you want to do something later?" she asked.

"Later?"

She raised her eyebrows, a smirk pulling at her softly swollen lips.

"Yes, later: the time that comes after now."

"TC, I don't..."

Her smile dropped. "I know. One night stand and all of that. But honestly, Tucker, if casual sex is always as great as that for you, I'm really envious."

I thought about her words as I dried myself with a thick, white towel that spoke of luxury I could never afford.

No, sex was never so ... intense. Yeah, that was the word—fucking intense.

"Look," she said, her voice no nonsense, "Like I told you, I'm in town because I'm helping my dad with a couple of things, as well as seeing Kes and Aimee. So I'd definitely be up for some more mind-altering sex. Not right now, because like I said, I have some appointments. But I can be free after dinner if you want round two."

I should say no. I should definitely say no. But those weren't the words that came out of my mouth.

"Aw, sugar, are you begging me again?"

She slapped my butt with her wet towel. *Man, that stung!*

"Don't be an ass, although I know that comes naturally to you."

Then she turned to a chest of drawers and pulled out a pretty lace bra and panties that were dark pink and looked silky.

My mouth watered, and I watched with hungry eyes as she continued dressing.

She glanced over her shoulder, watching me watching her.

"A gentleman wouldn't have looked."

"I never said I was a gentleman."

"Yes, you did!"

Damn—she had me there.

"That was last night," I grinned at her.

"Oh, go play with your porn collection," she muttered, then smiled at my stunned expression. "Aimee told me," she said with a grin.

"It's a complete misunderstanding," I lied, shaking my head.

"Oh wait, let me guess ... you were studying anatomy."

Her phone rang, interrupting whatever I might have said—not that I had a whole lot of thoughts in my head once she mentioned porn. And how the hell did Aimee know about that? I was going to have words with Kes when I got back to the carnival.

"Yes, Jeffrey, I'll be there," she sighed impatiently into the phone. "Fine. Fine. Yes, okay."

She tossed her phone onto the bed.

"I have to go."

"Work?"

"Yes, breakfast meeting. Can you show yourself out?"

"I can be ready in ten seconds, sugar," I said, reaching for my clothes that were still in a pile on the floor. But then I glanced up and saw her worried expression. "Oh, right—I'm not supposed to be seen with you." I kept my voice deliberately casual. "Don't worry, beautiful. I'm trained in stealth and evasion." *And I've crept out of a lot of women's rooms.*

"I'm sorry."

I shrugged. "Don't be. I've been thrown out of worse places."

She shimmied into a tight-fitting skirt that made her ass look like a ripe peach.

"So, are we on for tonight?" she asked, slipping on a sleeveless shirt that looked like it might be made of silk as well.

"Well now, I don't recall agreeing to that," I teased.

She didn't bother to reply, but tossed her damp towel at my head.

"You sweet-talked me into it," I laughed, catching it one-handed. "Where do you want to meet? Wait, I'll give you my cell number," I offered, breaking a cardinal rule. "You could call me?"

She threw me an amused look at my hesitant tone.

"And if I don't?"

"I'll feel used and abused," I deadpanned.

Tera laughed out loud, and the sound made me smile.

"Poor baby." Then she pointed at her phone. "Put your number in. I'll call you later."

And she disappeared to the bathroom to fix her makeup.

I punched in my number, knowing I'd broken about all of my own rules with this woman, but I couldn't stop myself smiling while I did it.

When we were both ready to leave, I slipped out of her room first and headed to the Duke.

CHAPTER FOUR

TUCKER

It was midmorning by the time I rode back to the fairground. I could still taste her on my lips, and just thinking about Tera was making me hard again.

I had to push the thought away before I got in a wreck.

But when I drove up to the RV, Aimee was waiting outside and as soon as Kes heard the Duke, he appeared behind her.

Shit! Already? How the hell had they found out?

I stood my ground, waiting for Kes to throw the first punch. But he didn't. Instead, there was a weird expression on his face and Aimee looked downright upset.

"Tucker, your phone's off. I've been trying to call you."

I shrugged. "I was getting a lot of random calls so I turned it off."

Kes nodded slowly then shot a look at Aimee who was chewing her lip.

"We were worried about you," she said softly. "You don't usually stay out ... um, you usually come home after, so..."

She blinked, looking helplessly at Kes.

"Yeah, well those calls weren't that random," Kes continued

as he reached out to take Aimee's hand. "They called Zach instead and he called me."

What?

"Yeah?" I said casually, my heart beginning to race.

To hide my thoughts, I turned away to start getting ready for the day.

Kes laid his hand on my shoulder.

"I'm sorry, man. It was your brother calling. He wanted to tell you ... your mom died."

I waited, waited to feel something. A soft tug at my memory, then ... nothing.

Kes was still staring at me.

And what? Did he think I'd give a shit?

I looked straight ahead. "Okay."

Kes's grip tightened on my shoulder. "Did you hear me, bro?"

"Yep."

I shrugged him off and went to collect my leathers from the RV.

Aimee's voice was hesitant behind me.

"Do you think ... do you want to call your brother?"

"Nope."

There was a pause while they muttered behind me.

"Just leave him," Zef said quietly. "He'll deal with it when he's ready—his way."

We walked over to the showground in silence, working steadily under the hot sun while my numb brain swirled uselessly.

I'd done set-up so many times, that I didn't need to think about what went where. Which was just as well, because my mind wasn't on the job.

We finished mid-afternoon, then did a run-through of the show. The fair didn't open until tomorrow, so I was officially finished for the day. Most people used a day off to do chores, but my only intention was to get shit-faced.

Zef wiped the sweat off his forehead and slapped my shoulder. "Let's take a break. There's not much left to do. I can finish up later."

I ignored him and carried on checking that the wingnuts on the rig's wheels were as tight as they should be. I'd noticed one was loose.

Zef walked up and grabbed the wrench from my hand.

"You make a mistake, and we're all fucked," he said flatly. "Come on, Aimee called chow time 20 minutes ago."

I stood up and stretched my back and neck.

"Broccoli pizza?"

Zef laughed. "Yeah, maybe."

"Son of a bitch stew, that would be fucking funny, wouldn't it?" I grinned at him.

Zef frowned but didn't answer. No sense of humor, some people.

Aimee had put some beers in a cooler outside the RV, so I grabbed one as soon as I arrived then collapsed onto a patch of grass. I drank deeply, letting the heat of the day and the tiredness leach out of me.

Ollo was there, sitting in the doorway of the RV, his legs dangling.

"You smell like a whore's bedroom," he grinned at me, wrinkling his nose.

A flare of anger shot through me but I hid it behind a smile.

"Damn, Ollo, how'd you get so short? Jeez, you could sit on the edge of carpet pile and swing your legs."

"And you're so tall, your blood doesn't get all the way to your brain, which explains why you're so dumb."

"As long as my blood gets to my dick, I'm good."

That's when Aimee smacked me upside the head.

"Ow! What the hell's that for?"

"I could give you a long list of reasons," she smirked, "but really, do I need one?"

"No," laughed Ollo. "Hit him again, Aimee. It's like watching whack-a-mole, but more fun."

Aimee ignored us both, dishing up something that may or may not have been meatloaf. I was too hungry to care.

I'd only taken a couple of mouthfuls before she started on me.

"Did you call your brother yet?"

"Stepbrother," I said, without looking up. "I'm not related to that asshole."

"Okay, stepbrother: so, did you call?"

Kes shot her a look, but she ignored him.

I'd been working hard all day to forget that Asshole 1 or Asshole 2 had been in touch. Unfortunately, not answering didn't work.

"Did you?" she persisted.

I threw my fork down and stared straight back at her.

"Hey, Aimee, you're a teacher: how do you spell o-bitch-uary?"

I laughed at my own joke. It was pretty funny for spur of the moment. Hmm, looked like I was the only person who thought so.

"Wait, I got another one for you," I said, tipping a second beer down my throat and wiping my mouth on the back of my hand, but Aimee's wounded expression made me shut the hell up.

I immediately regretted the lame joke, but she had no idea what she was talking about.

"That's enough, man," Kes said quietly.

My appetite was officially done, so I left my plate of food on the ground for Bo who dropped the piece of pineapple he'd been eating and dove in.

I envied the hairy little dude: eat, sleep, shit, repeat.

I grabbed a bottle of Johnny Walker and a six-pack, ignoring the loaded looks. Whatever—we didn't have a show tonight—and I headed out.

I didn't know where I was going—somewhere people weren't talking at me all of the time.

For a second, I was tempted to call Tera. But hell, she didn't need my shit, and she'd made it damn clear that all she was offering was sex. Of course she wouldn't want to get mixed up with a guy like me—or the shit that my life had been before I joined the carnival.

I was halfway across the fairground before I knew where I was going.

Jade was one of a pair of trapeze artists that traveled with us. I'd hooked up with her a couple of months back and she'd let me know that she'd be up for another go-around. She was cool, and the only reason I was prepared to make an exception to my rules was because she wasn't interested in a relationship. And I really needed to get laid right now. I needed to stop thinking, stop feeling. I needed to be me, the Tucker McCoy who didn't give a shit about anyone else.

She was doing stretches outside her RV when I walked up, her body bending and flexing in some seriously crazy ways.

"Hey, Tucker! Aw, you brought whiskey. You might just be the ideal man."

She grinned, and relief flowed through me. I wouldn't have to talk, wouldn't have to think about anything else tonight.

I crouched down next to her and pulled her lips toward me, kissing her hard. I ignored the voice in my brain that said she didn't taste as good as Tera.

"Someone's eager," she said breathlessly. But then she pulled away. "Jeez, Tucker, you stink. When did you last shower?"

"Earlier," I mumbled against her neck. "Morning."

"Yeah, well I'm not going to fuck you smelling like that. Go take a shower."

"Come with me," I said, pulling her to her feet.

I didn't have to ask twice.

I fucked her in the shower and twice in her bed. Hours later, as the carnival sank into silence, she snored softly. For me, sleep was as far away as ever. I needed the distraction of a show, needed the concentration of a performance, because that meant there was no space in my head to think of anything else.

But now, with the too quiet space around me, I couldn't even close my eyes, because when I tried, I saw Tera's beautiful face staring at me, disappointment pullings the sides of her mouth downwards.

Why the hell did I feel guilty? She wanted a hookup and that's what she got—no strings. But that didn't stop the acid pooling in my gut. Tired and frustrated, I scrubbed at my eyes.

If sex didn't work, I'd try booze.

I rolled out of her bed quietly and headed back to the RV. I checked my phone, seeing two missed calls from Tera, but she hadn't left a message.

We were supposed to hook up again tonight, but I couldn't use her like that. She was sweet, decent. And she was Kes's sister. *What the fuck had I been thinking?*

Zef was sitting outside the RV drinking from a bottle of bourbon. He handed it to me without asking where I'd been, and we sat there quietly as the bottle passed between us.

Eventually, he spoke.

"You gonna carry on ignoring this?" he asked.

I took another swallow, beginning to feel numb at last.

"Yep."

Zef raised an eyebrow. "Real mature, Tucker."

"Yep."

He took the bottle out of my hands and took another long slug. "You never asked me why I was in prison."

I looked at him sideways. "None of my business, bro."

"Yeah, I used to think that was the reason, but it's because you didn't want anyone to ask questions about you, isn't it?"

I didn't answer, but he didn't expect me to either.

"If I'd dealt with my shit earlier, maybe I wouldn't have gotten arrested," he said. "Maybe I wouldn't have let down my little brother and gotten sent away when he needed me. Maybe..."

"Is this your bedtime story now?" I asked, leaning back on my elbows. "And the moral of this story is...?

He replied evenly, "you've gotta sort your shit. Sooner rather than later."

He stood up and screwed the lid back on the bourbon before taking it with him. *Douche.*

I rubbed my hands over my face and stared up at the stars, listening to the sounds of the sleeping carnival.

Nearby I could hear one of the rodeo horses snickering quietly. Creaks and groans from wood and cooling metal sounded loud in the night. Smoke drifted on the air, our ritual bonfire burning the final embers. Somewhere I could hear a guitar playing, one of those sad fucking songs that Luke always liked. I guess that was because he knew his boyfriend Zach had a permanent hard-on for Kes. I didn't understand why people did that—be with someone when they were in love with someone else. Being second-best sucked. Maybe I wasn't the only person who needed to get their shit together.

This was my home. This was where I belonged, where I felt free. But it wasn't where I'd started out.

My world had been small, dark and cruel and there was no fucking way I was going back.

I wondered if it was Jackson or Jason who'd called, then decided I didn't care. They were both assholes.

I must have fallen asleep because the next thing I felt was the toe of Kes's boot in my ribs.

"Morning, fucker."

I squinted up at him and grinned. "I keep telling you my name is Tucker, but I guess that's too complicated for you."

"Aimee's making pancakes. Better apologize to her or she'll burn yours."

I sat up slowly, groaning as my body protested at the hard ground and the two mean little men stomping around inside my head.

I needed wake-up water: coffee, hot and strong.

"Yeah, okay," I said. "Sorry, man."

"Tell her, not me," he said, shrugging as he walked off.

I shuffled into the RV's kitchen. From the stiffness in Aimee's shoulders, I could tell she knew I was there.

"My two favorite things," I said, "a beautiful woman who's cooking me breakfast."

She turned around and glared at me while I smiled back. When she turned away, she stabbed at the pancakes with her spatula. *Yeah, I was going to have to try harder.*

I walked across and wrapped my arms around her waist, leaning my chin on her shoulder.

"I'm sorry, Aimee. You know me—if my mouth was any bigger I'd have a foot in each cheek at the same time."

"You're such an asshole," she said, but I could tell she'd accepted my apology.

"But a cute asshole?" I prompted.

"No, you smile too much," she snapped.

"I can't help it. I was born smiling and they had to smack my cute ass to see if I really could cry."

"You're so full of shit, Tucker," she said, laughing reluctantly.

"Run away with me, Aimee," I begged, falling to my knees and holding my hands up in front of me. "Leave that loser behind and..."

My throat closed up as Kes grabbed me in a headlock and wrestled me to the ground. He wasn't being any too gentle either.

"Hands off of my girl, fucker," he growled.

Seeing as I couldn't breathe too well, I tapped out 'uncle' admitting that he'd won, and Kes grudgingly let me go.

Aimee stood over me shaking her head and smiling.

"You can take that as a no, Tucker."

"I know you want me really," I wheezed, and Kes gave me an angry stare.

"Just eat your pancakes," Aimee sighed, throwing a warning glance at Kes.

Zef arrived just as I was forking delicious hot pancakes with sweet syrup into my mouth.

He tossed his cell phone on the table.

"They've started calling me now, bro."

I didn't have to ask who he meant. Suddenly the pancake tasted like old cheese and I had a hard job swallowing past the brick in my throat.

Aimee sat down opposite me. "You have to go, Tucker. She was your mother."

Kes frowned.

"It's up to him what he does."

"This isn't just about him," she pressed quietly. "His family needs him, or they wouldn't be calling all of us."

"I'm not going anywhere," I said fiercely. "We've got a show tonight. The show must go on, right?"

"We can do a two-man show," Kes said carefully. "You guys did that all last season to save my ass." He shrugged and met my eyes. "Just do what you gotta do, Tucker. We're cool either way."

Zef pushed his phone toward me. "Call them."

I looked at his cell phone the way I might look at a rattlesnake.

"I always wondered what an intervention was like," I muttered, only half joking.

Kes cracked a smile but nobody laughed. I sighed—tough audience today.

"Fine, I'll make the call, but you fu—" Aimee glared at me. "Um, never mind."

I picked up Zef's phone to call the number, reluctant from the soles of my feet to the tips of my fingers. But maybe they were right; maybe I needed to deal with this shit once and for all.

Or maybe this was the worst decision I'd made in a lifetime of bad decisions.

I dialed and it was answered on the second ring.

"Did you talk to him? Did you speak to Tucker?"

When I heard a woman's voice, I nearly dropped the phone.

"Hello?"

I strode away from the RV. I didn't want anyone to hear this conversation. Hell, I didn't want to hear it myself.

"Hello?"

I steeled myself so no emotion showed.

"Hello, Renee."

There was a sharp intake of breath. *"Tucker?"*

"Yeah."

"Jackson is in the shower, so I answered his cell. We've been waiting to hear from you…"

She was with Jackson?

She'd spoken rapidly as if she was nervous, but now her voice tailed off and we listened to each other breathing down the line.

"How are you?"

"I heard Momma died."

There was a pause.

"Yes, I'm sorry for your loss."

I laughed harshly but didn't answer.

"I'm sorry for everything," she said softly.

I rubbed my forehead, the ache worsening with every word.

"Are you coming home?"

"This is my home."

She sighed. "

Are you coming back to Tennessee? The funeral is on Friday and I ... we ... your brothers would really like to see you."

"Stepbrothers. And I doubt it."

"Please, Tucker," she said quietly. *"You need to come."*

"No, I really don't need to," I bit out.

There was another long silence.

"For me?"

I shook my head even though she couldn't see me, but words wouldn't come.

"Please, Tucker," she begged, her voice breaking on my name.

She knew I hated that. I was furious to find it still worked.

"I'll be there," I said, and ended the call.

I needed a minute before I faced my friends. It had shaken me to hear Renee's voice after all this time. I'd never thought she'd still be living there, let alone answering my stepbrother's cell.

I slumped onto the bottom step of the empty carousel and leaned back against the black-and-white stripes of a wooden zebra, staring at the sun reflecting from gold hooves. His painted mouth seemed to laugh as he gazed at the short tail of the giraffe in front of him.

"You have it easy, man," I said, scrubbing my hands over my unshaven jaw. "You just got to stand there and look pretty, and..."

"...and travel in circles all day long with screaming brats sitting on your back."

I squinted into the sun as Jade stood in front of me, her hands planted on her narrow hips.

"Were you having a moment with the zebra?" she smirked. "Because you might be in more trouble than I thought."

"Sweet cheeks, I was born trouble and just got bigger."

She grinned and sat down, stretching out her long, tan legs.

"So, what are you doing talking to a wooden zebra?" she asked. "It's not like you to be introspective."

"Intro— what?" I grinned at her. "Can't even spell the word."

"Hmm," she said, arching one eyebrow. "Seems to me like you're taking life too seriously. What blew up your ass?"

I gave her a shocked look.

"You think I'm being serious? Say it ain't so!"

She laughed and pushed my shoulder.

"That's more like the Tucker McCoy I know. I could use a repeat performance tonight. I get so sick of guys who want to talk to me when I just want to fuck. At least with you I know you won't want a conversation. Thank God. See you after the late show."

I opened my mouth to tell her I wouldn't be around, but then she stood up and walked away, swinging her hips, her long black hair glossy in the morning sun.

I shrugged. Jade wouldn't care one way or another. If I wasn't around, she'd find some other guy.

Zef caught up with me in the RV as I tossed clothes into a bag and dragged an old quilt out from under the bed. I didn't know where I'd be sleeping once I arrived in town. I'd bet a dozen quarters that the old motel was still in business, but I'd only stay there if I wanted to get bitten to death by bedbugs. I'd rather take my chances outdoors.

Zef leaned against the door, his arms folded as he watched me.

"This is your damn fault," I grumbled, hunting down my toothbrush. "Being so chatty with a bunch of Butternuts."

He cracked a smile.

"I've never been accused of being chatty before."

It was true: while I made the ladies laugh all the way to the bedroom, Zef just did the brooding thing. Whatever works—we made a good team.

He continued watching me as I finished packing but didn't say anything else until I was sitting on the Duke, everything I needed was stuffed into my backpack. The storage space was just about big enough to take a toothbrush. Yeah, I could have bought saddlebags, but you don't buy a racehorse to pull a cart.

"Easy on the bends," said Zef.

I nodded, raised my hand in a silent salute then pressed the starter button, loving the roar of the engine as I slowly released the throttle, bouncing over the dusty, uneven ground.

The roustabouts had finished erecting the Ferris wheel and carousel, and were working on the fast rides. I watched Carl shin up the framework of the rollercoaster and my mind spun back into the past, to the days when I first joined the carnival as one of the small army of itinerant workers who made up the laborers, the roustabouts.

The tents and kiosks along the midway were taking shape, the skeleton frames sharp against the clear blue sky, the faded canvases dressing the bones, like an old woman in her Sunday best. It was tricks and lies, all designed to part the rubes from their money, but it was honest, too. No one pretended it was anything more than a good time. Maybe that was why I fit in.

I paused by the grandstand, watching as Kes did a walk-through, checking the ground before he took the bikes over it. Aimee waved from the bleachers, Bo clinging to her shoulders.

Tera was standing next to her, arms folded across her chest, her face unreadable.

Ignoring the twist in my gut, I glanced into my mirrors, a glimpse of yellow dust that followed my tires. The air shimmered with summer heat and I had to squint through my sunglasses as sunlight bounced from the straggling lines of silver trucks and trailers.

Aimee was always going on about finding the magic here. I don't know about that, but it never got old, not for me. The carnival was my home—the first one that ever meant anything to me. Twelve years ago I'd been a kid on the verge of manhood in Tennessee. If I'd ever really been a kid.

And now I was going back.

I was fucked.

CHAPTER FIVE

TERA

I stood and watched as Tucker rode away. I knew he'd seen me but he didn't show any sign, no acknowledgement. That stung. I thought we were at least good enough friends to...

No, I was lying to myself. Tucker and I weren't friends. We'd hooked up, it was fun. And I thought we were going to meet again last night, but both my calls had been ignored.

I now knew why: Tucker's mother had died.

I felt terrible that I hadn't been able to say something, to comfort him in some way, but from what Aimee said, he'd preferred to crawl into a bottle of whiskey instead.

"Are you okay?" she asked, as we walked back to the RV together.

"Yes, why wouldn't I be?"

She gave me a quick, penetrating look.

"I don't know. You seem ... distracted."

"I was thinking about Tucker," I admitted, hurrying on as she raised her eyebrows. "I mean, it's terrible about his mother, isn't it?"

Aimee nodded.

"Yes, and he was so weird about it, making all these horrible jokes. I've never seen him like that before. It was as if he was trying to prove that he didn't care. Kes has known him four years and he's never heard Tucker mention his family, *ever*."

She looked sad.

"And now this."

"Do you think ... do you think he'll be okay by himself?"

"Honestly, I don't know. I used to think Tucker was shallow: just drinking, biking, and screwing around with skanks."

Ouch.

Aimee didn't notice that I was cringing. Probably just as well.

"But there's more to Tucker, I know that now. But he wouldn't even talk to Kes, and they're closer than brothers. We don't even know where he's from in Tennessee." She laughed without humor. "Until yesterday, I thought he was from Kentucky."

She shook her head sadly.

"Poor Tucker. He's obviously not close to his family, but this has to have hit him hard."

I spent the rest of the day with Aimee and my brother, but my mind was on Tucker. I wanted to help him, but I had no clue how. I doubted he'd even want my help, but no one should be alone and dealing with something like this.

Tucker needed a friend, whether he knew it or not.

Tucker

Two days and nearly a thousand miles later, I slowed the Duke to a crawl as I hit the main drag through town. Boarded up shops looked gray and dingy against the sharp outline of the mountains behind. Sunny days were supposed to make things look better, although there are always exceptions. The town where I grew up being at the top of the list.

I was surprised to see a bunch of flags crisscrossing the street. They looked out of place, just painting the misery in brighter colors.

I had to stop when I saw a large crowd forming in front of the town hall and two police cruisers blocking off the whole area.

I found a spot at the side of the road and pulled over to take a look. I'd planned to rest up in town anyway, fixing to get some food and maybe see about a room.

I stood up stiffly, stretching to work the kinks out of my spine, thanking some good Italian engineering and my decision to get the comfort seat rather than the race seat for the Duke. Even still, a thousand miles on two wheels was no joke, but at least the slip resistant surface had stopped the twins—my balls —from sliding against the tank on the twists and turns or whenever I braked sharply.

I pulled off my helmet and gloves, running a hand through my damp hair. The heat was more intense now that I'd stopped, and not even the faintest breeze stirred the candy wrappers and scraps of paper lying in the gutter.

I frowned at the thick dust covering the Duke, the red wheel trim almost black and the white engine casing a hazy gray. I'd have to clean that. Daisy was too pretty to leave crusted in dirt.

I peeled off my jacket, relieved that I hadn't worn my one-piece race leathers. In theory, they were more robust—safer— than pants and a jacket. I used the one-piece when I was performing, but not for a road trip. You come off of the road anywhere remote, and you could bleed to death while someone tries to get through the body armor and a quarter of an inch of leather.

A woman with a baby on her hip, gripped another child by the wrist, almost dragging her along the sidewalk. She slowed as she approached, and I could see the hunger in her eyes as she stared at the Duke. She might not know what kind of bike it was, but she knew enough to guess it would feed her family for a year.

Her eyes narrowed as she looked up at me, then her shoulders jerked back and her mouth went slack with surprise clearly written on her worn face.

"Tucker? Tucker McCoy?"

I flipped through my memory, but nothing came to mind.

"You know me?"

Her teeth snapped together and she nodded once. "Mary Dunne. I was in the same year as Jackson and Jason."

I shouldn't have been surprised that I didn't recognize her. She was only two years older than me, but looked ten. Women's lives were hard around here.

Her kids stared at me with accusing eyes.

"Sure, I remember you," I said, smiling. "You were on the cheer squad."

It was hard to believe looking at her now, with the angry lines carved around her mouth and the permanent frown that hardened her once pretty face.

"Heard your momma died," she said, not attempting to offer condolences.

I nodded my head at the crowd. "What's going on?"

Her eyes had drifted back to the Duke and she twitched a shoulder.

"Big wigs. Politicians liking the sound of their own voices. Where you stay these days?"

A guy in a suit who was sweating worse than a whore in church tapped the microphone, drawing my attention. He'd tried to dress upscale, but his accent was pure East Tennessee.

I'd let mine drift away as soon as I left. But Aimee said I still had an accent, which surprised me.

Feedback screeched through the mic and everyone winced. The guy flushed even redder then started babbling on about 'honored guests' and shit.

The bigwig was from the Senator's office in Nashville. He kind of reminded me of the online photos I'd seen of Kes's dad: sharp suit, sharp hair, white shark-like smile. He had a young blonde woman with him, probably some sort of assistant. She had the same glossy poise as Tera, the same air of being classy without trying.

I shook my head to clear it. Coming back here was really screwing with me—I needed to forget about Tera and focus on the clusterfuck that was sure to be heading my way.

After the short speeches, the crowd began to clear and the police cruisers reopened Main Street. I said goodbye to Mary and climbed back on the Duke, slowly heading toward where the old family-run motel had been. It was still there, but not quite the dump it used to be. I took a room, bargaining with the guy at the desk from $40 a night, the price he probably reserved for tourists, down to $35.

I dumped the leathers in a corner of the room, then tested the full-size bed, bouncing slightly on the well-used mattress.

Despite being ass-naked, sweat was trickling down my spine, the summer humidity sucking the life out of everything. I cranked up the AC, wincing as the unit rattled and wheezed, banging so loudly I was afraid it would shake itself apart.

The water in the shower was lukewarm, but I was so damn hot and sticky, I didn't care. I *did* care that being alone with soapy water had me thinking all things Tera, but then I remembered why I was here and my dick deflated faster than a birthday balloon.

When I couldn't put it off any longer, I climbed back on the

Duke and rode out of town, turning off at the dusty path that led up the mountain and more than a decade into the past...

...Don't bite the hand that feeds you.

That's what my momma told me my entire life while I was growing up, which was pretty damn funny, considering I was hungry every single day. It was the kind of gnawing hunger that would shrink your belly so bad, it'd feel like it was trying to tie itself into a knot. I wouldn't be surprised if the first word I learned was 'food', although it might have been 'hungry'. I spent a decade fantasizing about eating. Momma seemed to think that filling us up on soda was enough. I'm surprised my teeth didn't fall out, the gallons of Mountain Dew we used to drink. My stepdaddy told her that the bubbles took up more room so you didn't need to eat as much. Maybe she believed it, maybe she just pretended to, but I can tell you for sure that it's bullshit. Thank God medical and dental was covered through welfare.

By the age of three, I'd learned not to cry because it didn't do any damn good—no one ever came ... or Momma smacked the shit out of me until I was quiet. That was the year my father died in a car accident. I don't remember him, and any photos were hidden away. Maybe that's when Momma started drinking, maybe not. All I know is that I couldn't remember a time when she didn't stash a bottle in her purse and another under the bed.

She used to cry and say that the people you loved always left you. Guess she was right.

Anyways, Momma replaced my pa a couple of years later. Randolph came with his kids, twins who were two years older than me.

I learned not to ask for more or to question the way things

were after my stepfather answered with his belt across my backside, or my stepbrothers spoke with a fist to my face.

I was as skinny as piece of string, just a tall streak of nothing. I stole what I needed and I knew not to get caught.

Renee lived at the next place over, a half-mile down the mountain. I knew her from Junior High, just another too-pretty, too-young girl who was a woman at 13 with eyes of an old lady.

Those eyes had seen things. It was something we had in common.

"Guess you're pretty hungry, huh?"

That was the first time she ever spoke to me.

I cleaned off my mouth with my hand and carefully placed the bowl back down on the porch by my feet.

"You must be if you're eating dog food."

My gaze was stony, but I didn't answer.

Her old Bluetick coonhound threw me a mournful look, but was too gentle to complain. The ole fella ambled over to lick out the canned dog food that I'd left—which wasn't much. I couldn't help my eyes following, envying that damn dog.

A flash of pity in her pebble-hard eyes sent a burn of humiliation through me, making my gut squirm and my cheeks flush.

We stared at each other across the porch: her in cute little cut-offs, smelling sweet from the shower; me in torn shorts and dirty t-shirt.

I wanted to beg her not to tell anyone, but I guess I must have had some pride left. Who'd have thought it? Dog-food boy still had some pride. I figured I could laugh it off if she told anyone at school—say I done it for a bet. Everyone already thought I was the class clown.

I turned and was halfway across the yard when she called after me.

"You want pancakes? I'm just fixing a batch."

I turned to stare, wary now.

She stood there, poking at a weed that was growing up through the deck, her bare toes painted candy pink. When I didn't answer, she looked up.

"Well, come on in if you're coming."

I followed her inside and ate everything that she put in front of me.

We didn't talk much; I guess I was too busy shoveling food into my mouth.

It was nearly dark when I got home. Lights were shining through the window and I could hear Randolph's voice as he yelled at Momma, and her slurred replies. Then there was a sharp crack, the sound of flesh hitting flesh, and she started to cry; long, soul-breaking sobs. I crept away before they reached the part where flesh started slapping flesh in a different way.

I got between them once, trying to protect her from Randolph. But there's not much a kid can do against a grown man. I lost a tooth from my stepdaddy's fist.

You know what my momma said? "It's just a milk tooth."

When she still didn't kick him out, I stopped trying.

Sometimes you've got to want to be saved.

I stretched out on the porch, wrapping an old blanket around me, and wondered what it would be like to be anywhere but here. Were there places where it didn't hurt to see the stars shining in the blackness?

I started hanging out at Renee's place when school was through. She'd give me food, then I'd give her what she wanted in her bedroom before she kicked me out to do her homework. She liked school, saying it was her ticket out.

She was my first, but I wasn't hers.

We dated, kind of, for the next four years. I reckoned that when we graduated, I'd get a job in the distillery. That's where the men from town worked—the ones who were lucky enough to have a job, however shitty. Renee would get over wanting to leave, and take a part-time job until she popped out a couple of kids. I thought I had it all figured out: life was shit and you did what you had to do to get by. Sex was the only thing that was fun and free. If there was more to life out there, I knew I'd never have enough money to go look for it.

We understood each other and in our own way we looked after each other. She fed me and fucked me; I kept the sharks off of her at school. Because Renee grew up pretty, which wasn't always a blessing.

I was an average student, not smart like Renee, but there was one thing I was good at—dirt bike riding. Most kids messed around on BMXs, but my buddy Brandon had two parents working in office jobs, which made him rich by the town's standards, and he got a Honda 80 when he was 14. He took me with him, and we tore up the mountain trails. I think he did it because it was something to do, but I loved it. We learned some stuff in shop and then taught ourselves to strip the parts and understand the basics of how a two-stroke engine worked.

Brandon got a car when he was 16, so the bike was pretty much mine after that.

I swore I'd save up to pay him back the $300 bucks it was worth. I had a job after school sweeping up at the distillery and hauling whatever shit needed hauling.

But it was because of that bike that my eyes were opened.

Our last summer before senior year, a bunch of us had been hanging out at the dried up riverbed. There was a place where the bank sloped upward at the widest point, making a natural ramp.

Everyone said it was impossible to jump the gully, but I knew I could do this. I'd gotten plenty banged up jumping that bike all over, and no one could touch me. I liked that. If I'm honest, I liked it a lot. Renee thought it was kind of childish. Maybe it was, but flying through the air was the closest I'd ever been to being free. I could look across the whole town and see further, imagining a world just out of reach—one that I'd only seen on Renee's TV.

Brandon pulled me to one side and slung his arm around my neck.

"You don't have to do it, man. Just walk away—it's not worth getting busted up."

I grinned at him. "You chicken?"

"Hell, yeah!" he said sharply. "And if you had more brains than guts, you would be, too!"

I shrugged. I knew the jump was a monster, but I could make it. *How* I knew, was something else: I just knew.

Adrenaline was surging through me, making everything pinhole sharp. I could *see* the jump in my mind, knew how it would go and the exact patch of dirt where I would land. I backed up a good ways, then revved the engine hard, the wheels spinning before I let her fly. The wind was hot in my face, and my eyes were squinting against the angle of the sun that sent up shards of light from the glittering sand. The bike hit the highest point on the ramp and I tensed my thighs, rising above the seat like I was on a galloping horse.

Higher, higher, higher we flew, arcing out over the dusty riverbed, and it felt like I could see everything in slow motion: my past, my present, my future—all laid out like the town in the distance.

And then I was hitting the dirt hard, the bike bouncing and bucking like a wild stallion. I wrestled the handlebars, working to keep her upright. Behind me, I could hear shouts and screams.

And then I was braking, turning the bike in a slow curve as the adrenaline rush spiked and began to ebb away. Looking back at my friends, I waved, a huge shit-eating grin stretching across my face. As I looked at the riverbed, my eyes widened. *Holy hell! That is a long way down!*

I rode back slowly across the rickety wooden bridge, enjoying the moment of triumph, feeling like a goddamn gladiator. I shook my fists in the air and howled.

"Man! That was freakin' epic!" Brandon yelled as I stopped the bike next to him and cut the engine.

"I could hardly look!" screeched Mary Dunne, her painted nails digging into my bare arm.

I grinned and winked at her.

Her boyfriend pulled her away and scowled at me.

"Huh," he said, trying to look unimpressed. "Any fool can do that. Watch me!"

"Don't be a butthead," groaned Brandon. "Tucker is the only one who can make that jump!"

He didn't listen. Harley Law's dad was floor manager at the distillery so he thought that made him something special. Maybe it did, but not out here.

Harley looked pissed. "Don't you know that my word is Law?"

We all rolled our eyes—we'd been hearing that joke our whole lives.

Harley wasn't a bad guy, just kind of self-centered. Guess he couldn't help it. But when he started revving his engine, getting ready to let it burn, I was already cringing: no way he'd make it.

Some part of him must have agreed, because when he hit the ramp, I saw him hauling on the handlebars till the bike tipped over and skidded as he landed in the dirt.

Mary screamed, but I could already see that he wasn't hurt. He came limping back, a wry expression on his face.

"Hope you can fix this, McCoy," he grimaced, pointing at his bike's bent metalwork, "or my ole man will be handing me my ass."

"Man, you landed on your butt so hard, I thought you might have broke that too, the way you're rubbing it!"

When I'd stopped laughing, I agreed to go home and pick up some tools so I could hammer out the dents.

The rest of the afternoon is a blur, a twist in my gut when I think about it—which isn't very often—but some moments stand out in my memory.

I remember being surprised that my stepdaddy's truck was in the driveway. He wasn't usually home this time of day. Momma had just gotten herself a job stocking shelves in a small grocery store so there was food on the table for the first time in months. I knew it wouldn't be long before she went back to drinking, and lost her job again. Even when she did manage to earn something, the bastard spent her money at the bars in town and then came home and beat the shit out of her, or me. I could never figure out why she didn't leave him, but she just said that I was too young to understand.

I understood well enough, but if she didn't want to admit it, I wasn't going to force her. She thought a drunken abusive bastard who beat up on her and her kid was better than no man at all. My guess is he married her just to have someone look after his own kids. I've heard people say that indifference is worse than hatred, but it's not true.

My whole life, home was a three room shack. Momma and the bastard slept in one bedroom, and my stepbrothers shared the other. I slept on the porch in summer, or on the couch when the cold chased me indoors.

I'd lie awake and listen to the bastard fucking my momma, and then I'd listen to her cry while he snored.

The place was a dump. There were holes in the floor that could trip you up if you weren't paying attention. I needed to steal some timber to fix them. There were holes in the roof too, and newspaper plugged the gaps in the walls and around the windows. The fridge had stopped working years ago, so we kept milk and beer in a bucket by the backdoor.

I was the only one who ever fixed anything around the place

—when you have no other choices, it's amazing what you can learn to mend. My stepbrothers were useless wastes of space— drinking and stealing cars, cutting school until they were old enough to leave for good. But I had some pride and I kept our place almost respectable. Which meant I cleaned the trash from the front yard, and sometimes the back; and when I could steal enough money from Momma's purse, I'd buy glass to fix the windows instead of plastic bags and cardboard. Until the next time one of the assholes decided to toss a chair through it.

That day, my pride was broken on the rack of reality.

I don't know why I walked into the living room, because the tools I needed were in the shed. But I did, and that chance decision, what I saw next, it changed the path of my whole life...

...And here I was again, 12 years later.

I cut the engine, letting the silence wash over me. Insulated inside my helmet, I could hear myself breathing. I turned my head slowly, looking around at the place I swore I'd never see again.

Leaving the hotel to come here was one of the hardest things I'd ever done.

I parked the Duke fifty yards in front of the shack, not wanting to get any closer. I swung a leg over the saddle and took a deep breath. Then I pulled off my helmet and made the rest of the way on foot. I'm not sure why: maybe I didn't want my Ducati associated with all the shit I left behind.

The place had changed; a small addition had been tacked on the side, but overall it was neither better nor worse. I stared at it critically—I could guarantee that roof leaked like a bastard.

There were no vehicles, unless you counted the rusting carcass of a Chevy, its wheels long gone, the windowless cab a home for squirrels by now.

A shudder ran through me, the raw anger that I'd been running from suddenly caught up—I wanted to burn that shithole shack to the ground. I wanted to see flames licking over the roof. I wanted...

I shook my head slowly—that wasn't me anymore. I'd put it all behind me. I had.

It was a bad idea coming here and I sure as hell didn't want to run into my bastard of a stepfather.

I decided to leave. Seeing him at the funeral would be more than soon enough.

As I stood there, tamping down the angry past, the door opened and Renee was in front of me, one hip resting against the door jamb, her arms crossed. She looked different but familiar. Same straight hair the color of corn; same cold blue eyes; but there were harsh lines around her mouth and she was too thin. She didn't smile when she saw me.

"Renee?" My voice was hoarse as I spoke, and my body was frozen to the spot, unwilling to enter.

She raised her eyebrows. "You gonna come in?"

"You ... you live here?"

She glared at me impatiently. "Where else would I live?"

That was a good question. Why the hell had she stayed? To be with my asshole stepbrother? It didn't make any sense.

She opened the door wider and stepped back, and I wasn't sure if it was an invitation or a challenge.

I nodded, forcing a weak smile onto my face, and followed her inside. The same sagging couch was in the corner, but the other furniture had been moved around and an enormous flatscreen took up most of one wall. Someone had made an attempt to put up wallpaper, but now it was stained and peeling. The room smelled musty, although the place seemed clean enough and dust-free.

"Nice ... TV," I managed.

She gave a harsh laugh. "Our pride and joy."

I was silent, the memories weighing too heavily. I kept smiling as I met her impassive face.

"You look well..." I began, but she interrupted me.

"Cut the crap, Tucker. You don't have to charm me. I know how I look."

I glanced down and noticed that she was wearing a wedding ring.

"So, you and Jackson?"

Her hard eyes glittered as she stared at me coldly, her hands rigid at her side.

The door was flung open suddenly.

"Momma! Did you see the motorcycle outside? It's a Ducati! That's Eye-talian!"

A skinny kid of about 10 or 11 skidded into the room, his eyes narrowing when he saw me and his shoulders tightening defensively. His child-sized hands balled into fists.

"Who are you?" he demanded, his chin jutting out as he spoke, his gaze hard.

Renee answered. "This is your Uncle Tucker." She wrapped her arm around him and her voice softened. "This is my son Scotty."

I stared in shock. *Renee had a kid?* I don't know why I was so surprised. All the women around here had kids before they were 25, most before they were 20, and I'd been away a long time.

The kid groaned and rolled his eyes.

"Momma! I told you about a billion times! It's *Scott!*"

I hid a smile and held out my hand. "Hey, man, good to meet you."

He stared at me warily then tilted his chin up. "That your bike outside?"

"Sure is."

His eyes flashed with excitement, but then the sullen look reserved for strangers was back.

I let my hand drop to my side. I wasn't offended—I'd been just like him at his age. Strangers didn't usually mean anything good.

"Scott, go do your homework," Renee said briskly.

He shot her a venomous look but didn't argue, walking into the addition with dragging steps.

"I didn't think you'd come," she said at last, hostility closing her face. "Mr. Big-shot bike rider, too busy for his own family."

I gave an ugly laugh. "That shit don't fly, Renee. You know why I left."

She stared at me impassively, and I felt like she was weighing something in her mind. "So it took your momma's funeral to bring you back to Tennessee—is that all?"

I'd been asking myself that question.

I shrugged. "You made it sound important."

"Your momma's funeral isn't important?"

A thread of guilt pulled at my gut. Probably not as much as it should, but still, I felt it.

And I couldn't help feeling that Renee wasn't being upfront with me. I used to think we didn't have any secrets from each other, but I'd been shit wrong about that. So when she asked about Momma, I wasn't ready to answer that question yet. I changed the subject.

"Where's Jackson?"

"Out," she said, without much interest. "Drinking with Jason is my guess."

I nodded uncomfortably at her answer. "And ... Randolph?" Even his name tasted bad in my mouth.

She smiled coldly. "Bumming drinks from Jackson and Jason. They'll be home later."

"Shit ... *all of them?* They all live here?" *Still?*

She flicked her hair over her shoulder. "This is their home. Where did you expect them to live?"

I really didn't want to get into this with her but... "I'm surprised you're still here. In town, I mean, not..."

Her shrug was impatient, dismissive. "I didn't have too many choices when my momma threw me out."

"What did she do that for?" I frowned, feeling again that there was something missing from her reasoning. "Why come here?" Then I answered my own question. "Because of Jackson."

She didn't answer.

"You want a drink?"

I sighed. Renee wasn't in any hurry to say whatever she had to say. And it looked like I was stuck in town till Friday.

"Sure. Water would be good."

A harsh, amused smile stretched her thin lips. "You turn into Snow White while you were away?"

I decided to fight fire with fire, and grinned back coldly.

"You're the one living with the seven dwarves—or maybe just three: Grumpy, Dopey and Sleazy."

Her eyes glittered dangerously, but then she let out a sharp bark of laugher.

"Ain't that the truth!" Then she smiled a real smile. "C'mon out the back and sit a while."

In the kitchen, she ran a glass of water from the tap and passed it to me.

"Bottled water costs too much," she muttered, before pushing her way through the screen door.

I wasn't expecting a lot from the backyard, but I was surprised to see flowers and a vegetable patch.

Renee saw the direction of my gaze and a dull red crept up her neck to her cheeks. She gave an embarrassed laugh.

"Gotta do something to keep me sane."

"When does it start working?" I grinned at her, raising an eyebrow

"Hey!" she laughed, swatting my shoulder.

We were silent for a moment while I sipped my rusty-tasting water, and I remembered all the times she'd taken care of me, fed me. And yeah, fucked me. We were kids. What did we know about anything?

I sat down on the deck, stretching my legs out onto the steps. Renee did the same as I stared out at the familiar landscape, the mountains rising up in the distance, sheathed in haze that looked like smoke, the sprawl of trees taller than I remembered.

There were too many memories here—most of them bad.

"How did she die?" I asked at last.

Renee sighed. "The drinking. Her liver gave up, that's what the doctors said."

I nodded slowly.

"She wasn't all bad, Tucker."

I laughed harshly.

"She wasn't," Renee sighed. "She took me in when no one else would. And it wasn't like she needed the trouble. When she was sober..."

"And how often was that?"

"Not often," Renee admitted. "She missed you."

"I'm surprised she noticed I'd gone," I said bitterly. "Or maybe she noticed when the roof start leaking, or when something broke or needed fixing. When she ran out of money for booze."

Renee gazed at me. "She was a drunk and a lousy mom," said Renee. "But it didn't mean she didn't love you..."

"She just loved to drink more."

Renee grimaced, but didn't disagree.

"Scotty seems like a great kid," I offered, needing to say something.

Renee smiled and her hard face relaxed one degree. "He is. Best thing I ever did. What about you? Got any kids?"

"Hell, no!"

The words exploded out of me, making her laugh again.

"You sure about that?" she asked, elbowing me in the ribs.

"I always package the goods!" I replied quickly.

Her smile faded. "Yeah." Then she looked away. "Got a girl waiting for you, Tucker?"

Without permission, my thoughts strayed to Tera. I shook my head.

"Nope. Happily footloose and fancy free."

Renee nodded slowly. "Ever?"

I glanced across at her. "There was a girl. But it was a long time ago."

Her lips compressed into a bloodless line. "Don't."

"Renee..."

"I mean it, Tucker. Leave it."

And that was it. If you don't keep moving, your past catches up with you sooner or later.

I stood up slowly, my heavy biker boots sounding loud on the wooden deck.

"Reckon you're right, Renee," I said.

I didn't want any part of whatever was going on here. I'd left once; I'd moved on.

I stared out at the trees, the low angle of the sun slanting through the thin branches like fingers—all pointing at me.

"See you at the funeral."

Her mouth turned down. "Always running away, aren't you, Tucker?"

Even though my gut was churning, I smiled at her and winked. "Best way of not getting caught."

CHAPTER SIX

TERA

I was still cringing from the confrontation with my father.

It was because I'd decided to find out where the funeral for Tucker's mother would be taking place. Yes, I could have just called him, but I had the feeling that he wouldn't be answering his cell. Besides, my last two calls had gone unanswered. He hadn't even sent so much as a text message before blowing me off. I really should have taken the hint and walked away. But after what Aimee had told me, I just couldn't do it.

Finding the right funeral parlor wasn't as easy as I thought it would be. It turned out that a lot of women in their fifties or sixties had died in Tennessee the same week as Tucker's mother; I just hadn't been able to pin it down, especially as there weren't any deaths registered in the name of McCoy.

Defeated, I'd asked my father's personal assistant for help.

I'd known Marjorie almost my whole life. She was a sort of honorary aunt and I'd grown up playing in her office when Dad had taken me to work. She was a whizz at finding things out and I swear the CIA had nothing on her.

When I'd told her what I was trying to do and that it was

because I was worried about a friend, it hadn't occurred to me that as well as finding out the information, she'd tell my father.

I was standing in the living room at my parents' house in Minneapolis reading Marjorie's email.

"Who's this friend you're trying to help?"

I nearly jumped out of my skin when my father touched my arm.

"Dad!" I yelped, clutching my chest.

"Marjorie said something about a funeral? Is it a college friend?"

"No, just a friend."

"A guy friend?"

I rolled my eyes. "Dad!"

"A girlfriend?"

"The friendly kind of friend. Does it matter?"

"Well," he said, settling onto the couch and leaning back, "seeing as you had Marjorie working overtime to get you the information, let's just say I'm curious."

I sighed, knowing that he'd get his answer one way or another: sometimes it was just less hassle to tell him.

"It's the mother of my friend Tucker. He works with Kestrel."

My father's face remained smooth, but I heard the steel in his voice. "One of those carnies."

"He's a lot more than that," I said defensively. "He's a very skilled motorcycle stunt rider." *Like my brother.*

"Did your … did Kestrel ask you to help?"

"Not exactly…"

"Then why *exactly* are you interested?"

"Tucker lost his mother. He's all by himself and … he's a friend."

"And you couldn't just ask your friend where the funeral is taking place?"

"He's ... I haven't been able to reach him. I was worried, so..."

My father's voice remained calm, but I could see his jaw ticking.

"He must be a close friend for you to go to all of this trouble."

"No, I ... you know what, it doesn't matter. I'm just going to send some flowers."

He nodded, a smile relaxing his whole face.

"That's sweet of you, honey."

"Thank you, Daddy," I said, as I kissed him on the cheek and left the room.

What I didn't tell him was that I planned to deliver the flowers in person.

~

Second-guessing myself the entire time, I bought a flight to Nashville, then took a cab the rest of the way.

If I hadn't been so preoccupied, questioning my motives and actions, the scenery would have been impressive. The Smoky Mountains rose in the distance, clouds gathering around the peaks, swirling like smoke; tall trees grew thickly in the valleys, and Tennessee glowed under the scorching summer sun, lush and beautiful.

As I stared out of the window, the town where Tucker had grown up passed before me. Crowds of people lined the road, and red, white and blue flags were strung along the street. Even so, I couldn't help but notice the empty lots and boarded up shops—it looked like a town that was struggling.

My hotel was on the outskirts and newly built. It contrasted with everything else that I'd seen, and I wondered if it was a sign that the local economy was on the up. But then again, its location pointed more at tourists who'd come to explore the mountains.

When I checked in, I asked if Tucker was staying there, but the friendly receptionist said they didn't have anyone by that name.

Five minutes of googling places to stay on my phone brought up only one other alternative nearby—a cheap motel on the road out of town.

And this time I struck gold—Tucker had checked in an hour ago.

I sat back on the bed and wondered what to do next. I'd come all this way, and now I had no clue how to approach him or what to say without sounding like some creepy stalker. I really hadn't thought this through.

I took a quick shower, washing off the dirt and grime of travel, then dressed casually in a light summer skirt and tank top.

Heat shimmered in a haze as I waited for yet another cab to take me back into town. I fiddled with my hair nervously, then thought about what I was going to say.

Hi, I was in the area. Thought I'd drop in ... lame.

Fancy meeting you here! Pathetic.

I was worried about you, so I flew 900 miles to follow you to your mother's funeral even though you didn't return my calls ... too needy, too stalkery.

When the cab dropped me off, I was no nearer to a decision and...

"TC? Is that you?"

Tucker's astonished voice stopped me in my tracks outside the rundown motel.

Oh God! This was so embarrassing!

He stared at me, his eyes narrowed, a frown hovering.

"Wow, I thought I was imagining things? What are you doing here, sugar?"

Tucker stood in front of me, a confused smile crinkling his eyes.

"Um, hi!"

He leaned forward and kissed my cheek lightly, his lips soft, his stubble rough.

"Are you ... on vacation?" he asked, looking around him as if he was searching for someone, my traveling companion.

Seeing no one else, his confusion increased.

"Are you by yourself?"

"Yes, I..."

His frown faded.

"You're here on business? Your work sent you?"

"Actually, no. I'm here for you."

Tucker's eyebrows shot up. "For me?"

"Look, I promise I'm not a stalker," *much* "but when I heard about your mother, it just felt wrong that you were here by yourself having to deal with everything. So ... I'm here as a friend. If you need ... to talk ... or anything."

Tucker looked stunned. Confused, astonished, amazed—all those words that meant he had no clue why I'd come to be with him.

"You ... you came here for me?"

"Yes."

"Why would you do that?"

Good question.

"No one should be alone when they bury a parent."

His mouth twisted, as if he'd tasted something unpleasant.

"I don't want to be here, believe me, let alone anyone else." Then a thought occurred to him. "How'd you know where I was?"

"I, um, phoned a couple of funeral parlors."

"Oh."

He still looked puzzled.

"That's really nice of you, TC, but..."

He paused.

"It's okay," I said softly. "I can go. I don't want ... I just thought you might like a friendly face to talk to. But you've probably got family, so that's fine. I didn't think about that. I'm sorry, I'm sure you're really busy."

I was babbling, embarrassed, feeling stupid having come all this way, but then Tucker grabbed my hand.

"Thank you for coming, TC. Damn if that isn't the nicest thing anyone has ever done for me. Ever."

I smiled shakily.

Then he frowned. "I'm sorry about the other night."

I shook my head. "No, it's fine. Aimee told me that you'd just found out."

He nodded, but didn't look convinced.

We stared at each other awkwardly until Tucker spoke.

"Can I buy you dinner? To say thank you?"

I smiled at him. "We've already had sex, Tucker. You don't have to take me out on a date."

He laughed lightly. "It doesn't have to be a date, TC. We can just have dinner. As friends, like you said."

I smiled, hugely relieved.

"Okay, that would be great. So ... I'll see you later? Dinner-that-is-not-a-date."

I felt the need to clarify, but Tucker nodded, a small smile pulling at his lips.

"I'll check out a few places and text you, okay?"

"Sounds good," I smiled.

Tucker

My mind was totally spun that Tera had come all this way because she was worried about me. I wasn't used to someone caring like that. It hadn't happened in a while.

I knew that Kes and Zef were on my side, but that was different. Having Tera here—it felt personal.

We'd have dinner and a couple of drinks and then I'd call her a cab and she'd go back to her hotel. I'd be a liar if I said I wasn't thinking about taking her back to my room and losing myself inside her soft body. But I couldn't do that to her—she was decent, good, and she didn't deserve to be treated like that.

Besides, the motel was a roach-infested shithole.

Shaking my head at the weirdness of the day, I turned around and headed back up Main Street, wondering where would be good enough to take a woman like Tera.

Two hours later, I'd just left my motel to meet Tera when the cherry red glow of a cigarette caught my attention and the harsh scent of smoke hung in the warm air.

"Nice evening," said the man as he stepped from the shadows.

I was immediately on edge. I scanned him quickly, trying to work out why his innocent greeting seemed like a threat.

"Sure is," I said easily, keeping him in my peripheral vision as I turned to walk away.

He was wearing a suit, which was unusual in these parts, and he had the close-cropped hair of someone who was military or ex-military.

"She's pretty," he said, drawing hard on his cigarette.

His words stopped me in my tracks. I clenched my jaw but kept my voice calm.

"Who is?"

"Nice rack, too."

"Sounds like you're having one of my dreams, buddy," I said, trying to laugh it off.

"Well, the Senator doesn't like you having dreams about his daughter. It could be bad for your health."

What the fuck?

I glanced around, but couldn't see anyone else—whoever he was, and I had a pretty good idea *what* he was—he seemed to be alone. Maybe this was a private message.

I stood lightly on the balls of my feet, ready to move if he decided to take a swing. But instead, he seemed relaxed, sucking on the end of his smoke.

"Bad habit," he said, gesturing with the cigarette, "but I can't seem to give it up. Ah well, a man's got to have a few vices."

He looked straight at me as he said that.

"You should know all about that, Mr. McCoy. Vices."

I tensed, waiting for the punch line—maybe literally.

"You fuck women once and toss them away."

I didn't argue, because it was true.

"The Senator won't allow his daughter to become one of your statistics," he said, his voice calm, confident.

"Seems to me that she's a grown woman and can make her own choices," I pointed out.

He tossed the cigarette away.

"Stay away from her, McCoy. This is your last warning."

He turned to walk away.

"I've got a question for you," I said. "If Senator Hawkins told you to take it up the ass, would you?"

His back stiffened but otherwise there was no reaction from him.

"Last warning," he repeated, then disappeared back into the shadows.

I was stunned.

How the hell had the douche found me? How long had he been watching? The thought creeped me out. I wondered if I should tell Tera. Was this standard practice for her old man?

I shook my head. *What a fucked up evening.*

Looking over my shoulder the whole way, I headed to the bar where I'd arranged to meet Tera for dinner.

After encountering the Senator's goon, I didn't know how I felt about seeing her. I didn't know if he was following me or her. Either way, he'd know I'd ignored the warning.

But as soon as I saw her smiling from a booth at the back, I felt like I was in the right place at the right time for once in my sorry ass life.

We talked easily over dinner, nothing too heavy, and thankfully she didn't ask any questions about the funeral or my so-called family.

But at the end of the meal, she seemed to get more nervous, and it wasn't long before I found out why.

"I was wondering," she said quietly, "Would you like me to help you with the funeral arrangements?"

I closed my eyes with a sigh before meeting her gaze, compassion glowing in her beautiful eyes.

"Look, I really appreciate your offer, TC, but this is something I've got to handle by myself."

"But why? Friends help friends—let me help you."

I shook my head.

"Honestly, TC, I don't want to be here; I sure as shit don't want you getting mixed up in all of it."

"I'd like to help ... but I understand." She paused. "Do you ... do you want to stay with me tonight?"

God, yes!

"It's probably not a good idea, TC."

Her face dropped.

"No, you're right. You've got lots of other things to do, I get it."

I sighed. "It's not that..."

"Then what?"

I shook my head ruefully. "I'm trying to do the right thing here."

She cocked her head on one side. "And I'm the wrong thing?"

"No! I mean, fuck, you're a really nice girl, TC, and..."

She shuddered. "Ugh! 'Nice.' That's the kiss of death."

I couldn't help smiling. "Okay, fine. You're sexy as fuck and I want to kick myself in the balls for turning you down..."

"Then don't. Take me to your hotel."

I shook my head. "It's a shithole."

"I don't care."

"Bed bugs," I muttered, smiling as she shuddered.

"My hotel then," and she slid her hand up my thigh as she said the words, and I couldn't think of a single reason to keep on saying no.

And right now, I'd blow my load if she so much as smiled at my dick.

The only thought going through my brain other than the need to get her naked was this: *being weak has its advantages*.

I followed her cab back to a fancy upscale hotel, parked in a dark corner, then waited nearly a minute before climbing off the Duke.

Her door was ajar when I got there and I slid inside, closing it firmly behind me.

The room was enormous, a suite rather than a simple bedroom. There was a separate dining area and living area, with a huge picture window.

She was waiting, trying to look relaxed, but her breathing was rapid and a flush of pink had risen up from her chest to her neck and cheeks.

She turned toward the bedroom, but I caught her around the waist and she stumbled, tripping on the three steps that led toward the bedroom and landing on her knees.

"W-what...?

I slid my hand around to her stomach, unbuttoning her jeans and pulling them down over the curve of her ass.

"Right here?" she gasped.

"Yeah," I growled, my voice harsh with want. "Right here."

We didn't sleep much that night, and it was just as hot as the first time we'd fucked, maybe hotter. I'd come so hard, my ears rang and I thought I'd gone blind, until she kissed my eyelids and I realized that my eyes were closed.

All I needed was to lose myself with her, but I made damn sure that Tera got all of my attention. I'm not the kind of guy who has to ask if a woman has had an orgasm—there are some things you can't fake, and I've made it my business to know the difference. I don't have anything else to offer except sex—so I'll damn well make it something she'll never forget.

Tera looked so beautiful laying there asleep, and I felt a reluctant sense of shame that she had to wade through my shit.

I'd never met anyone like her—so soft and kind and caring; so sassy and sexy. The woman made my head spin.

I took one last look, my eyes tracking up the soft skin of her thigh, the dip of her waist, the soft curve of her tits, her honey-blonde hair spread over the pillow—damn, she was sensational.

Tearing my eyes away, I scrawled a note in my ugly handwriting saying that I'd call her so we could make dinner plans. The thought of seeing her later made me feel a hell of a lot better, especially after reading the text I'd had from Renee earlier.

 9AM FUNERAL PARLOR

I shoved the cell into my pocket and slipped out of the room.

Heat made the air shimmer as I stepped into the parking lot. I squinted at the morning sun and pulled my shades over my eyes. I couldn't see anyone looking at me. I should have checked last night that the goon hadn't seen me. But being with Tera made me feel ten feet tall and to hell with the consequences.

I mounted the Duke and rode into town.

Renee's text had brought me back to earth and the realities of why I was here in this shithole.

I stopped at a diner and ordered biscuits and gravy, then sat and drank the bitter black coffee that must have been brewed a couple of hours ago. Sweat trickled down my back and dampened the armpits of my t-shirt as a noisy fan rattled overhead. The plastic seating was cracked and worn, the mug I drank from was chipped, and the smell of grease hung in the air.

I couldn't imagine bringing Tera to a place like this. My reality was truck stops and living like a gypsy. Hers was limos and guys in suits.

For the first time in a long time, I tried to imagine my future, any sort of future. But it was a cloudy nothing. Where was Madam Sylva when I needed her? That old gal was plenty spooky when she started with her fortune-telling. But damn if she didn't call it right more often than not.

I glanced at the clock on the wall and realized I couldn't put it off any longer.

I left the Ducati by the curb and walked the fifty yards to 'Friendly's Funeral Parlor', the sun burning the back of my neck.

A beaten up Dodge Ram was parked outside and I wondered if it belonged to my asshole stepbrothers. It would be like them not to fix the oil leak that I could see staining the dirt below the engine casing, or the bent wipers that probably didn't work.

I took a deep breath and pushed open the door.

The air conditioning raised goose bumps on my arms immediately—either that or the shock of seeing Jason and Jackson.

They were sitting on a black pleather sofa looking bored, with Renee in an armchair. Jason wore bib overalls and Jackson was wearing faded jeans. Only the scar on Jason's face clued me in to which of them was which—I'd put that scar there when I was 12. Scotty was messing with a brick of a cell phone and ignoring his parents and uncle.

I scanned the rest of the room, but thankfully Randolph wasn't there. Even I knew you shouldn't start a fight in a funeral parlor.

Renee looked up as I walked toward them.

"Didn't think you'd come," she said.

I shrugged. "Didn't have anywhere else to be."

We all stared at each other in ugly silence. Then Jackson got to his feet and held out his hand.

"Tucker."

I hesitated for a second before shaking his hand.

"Jackson."

Then Jason hauled himself up, grabbing my hand briefly. "Reverend," he smirked.

I'd forgotten he had that lame nickname for me. Just because Renee was the only girl I slept with and I used to try to look after Momma.

I gave his hand an extra hard squeeze and had the extreme fucking pleasure of seeing him wince.

Before things got more awkward, a man in a tired suit clapped his hands together, capturing our attention.

"Good morning, folks. I'm Bob Friendly. You're here for the Foster viewing?"

Renee nodded and the man smiled quickly, before leading us into a room at the back.

Reluctantly, I eyed the body lying in an expensive looking casket, a vase of cut flowers next to her head.

The woman who'd brought me into the world.

If I hadn't already known who she was, I wouldn't have recognized the heavily-made up face or dyed hair that was blonder than mine. She was wearing a flowery dress that made her look as if she was going to a wedding.

But it wasn't her. It was just a body, the empty shell. The person she'd been was long gone. I felt weird, like I should feel something more. I'd hated her for so long, but it seemed pointless now.

She looked decades older than her age.

We all stared at the corpse and I could see Scotty's eyes flicking between us, wondering what he was supposed to do.

"Kiss your grandma," said Jackson.

Scotty looked appalled. "I ain't kissin' a dead body!"

Jackson cuffed him around the ear and I couldn't help wincing as the sharp sound echoed around the sterile room.

Scotty stumbled, rubbing his ear, then leaned forward so his lips almost brushed his grandma's cheek: almost, but not quite.

Jackson narrowed his eyes, but then Renee moved forward, touching the back of the dead woman's hand.

"Goodbye, Maggie. Thanks for taking me in." Then she looked up at me. "We'll leave you alone with your momma."

Silence settled over the room as the door closed behind them. I wished they hadn't left me here. I wished I could hear a clock ticking, anything to tell me that time was passing.

I didn't know what to say. I felt like I ought to say something, but the words got stuck in my throat. Dust was getting in my eyes, making them water. Or maybe it was the damn flowers.

"You were a shitty mother," I said at last, my voice too loud in the tomb-like room. "You never stood up for me against Randolph. Not even once. Why didn't you leave him, Momma? We could have gone away, started again someplace else. But I guess there's no point blaming you now. I hope it's better where you are. Did you find my pa?" It felt weird talking to the empty room, but I carried on, the words tumbling out. "I'm doing good now—stunt riding in a carnival. Maybe you know that. Yeah, I'm ... I'm good."

I stared down at the familiar unfamiliar face and shook my head. This was too weird.

I wiped my hands over my eyes and took a deep breath, looking for the last time at a woman who should never have had a kid.

"Bye, Momma."

They were all waiting on the sofa, Scotty listening to music through his ear buds, the tinny music sounding loud in the quiet room. Jackson looked bored and Jason was taking a nap. Renee sat apart from them, staring out the window.

As soon as I appeared, the guy in the ugly suit came back, and Jason jerked awake.

"Was everything to your satisfaction?"

It seemed liked a strange question, but Renee answered immediately.

"That wasn't the casket I picked out."

"Ah no," Bob smiled at her, showing a missing tooth in his lower jaw. "That's our viewing casket. We like to make it nice. For the family, you know?"

"Uh huh," she said, her cold gaze unwavering.

The man gave her a professional smile. "I have your invoice for the cremation and..."

"Cremation?" I said, surprised. "Didn't she want to be buried next to ... next to my father?"

Momma never visited his grave; didn't care that it got overgrown with weeds. Even so, I'd just assumed...

Renee barked out a laugh. "Sure, if you want to pay $10,000 for a burial and a memorial service."

Bob Friendly looked at me appraisingly. "I'd be happy to make the arrangements if you'd prefer a..."

"Save it, Bob," Renee said coldly. "Tucker won't be paying out for that."

"If you folks would like to discuss it further...?"

Renee stood up suddenly and dumped an envelope into his hands, making Bob back up. "Here's $500. We'll pay the rest later," and she threw me a look.

Bob Friendly cleared his throat. "I'll need the balance tomorrow. We wouldn't want any delay to the service."

Renee narrowed her eyes. "No, we wouldn't want that, would we, Bob?"

She swept out of the room and the rest of us trailed behind her.

At the truck, she stopped and looked at me.

"The ceremony is at the crematorium. Ten o'clock." Then she smirked. "Bring the other $500 with you."

At least now I knew why she'd insisted I come to the damn funeral.

Renee climbed into the truck and Scotty jumped into the flatbed at the back. Jackson cleared his throat, his eyes shooting to his brother.

"You have $500?"

I turned my head slowly to stare at him. "Looks like I'll have to find it."

He nodded quickly. "We're a little short this month after all the, um, expenses. Kid needs supplies for school, you know?"

I laughed out loud. "I'll bring $500, but that's it. Where's Randolph?"

Jason answered. "Dad wasn't feeling too good this morning."

I nodded, not needing to hear more. "If he starts anything tomorrow..."

I left the words hanging in the air.

Jason snickered, his scarred face folding into a scowl.

"You think you're something special with your fancy motorcycle, but the only thing you were ever good at was taking a beating."

"It took two of you when I was a kid," I grinned at him. "You want to try now, feel free," and I held out my arms from my sides, inviting him to take a swing.

When he didn't, I laughed out loud.

"You're yeller, Jason, just like you always were. And man! You're so ugly that when you were born, I heard that the doctor slapped your momma."

His eyes narrowed and I tensed my body, waiting for his attack.

But Renee leaned on the horn angrily and Jason muttered something under his breath.

I watched them climb into the truck and drive away, dust clogging the air long after they'd gone.

That went better than I'd expected.

The nearest ATM was across the road, so I walked over to draw out five hundred bucks. I winced when I saw that my account had less than $800 in it. Damn, it could be a few weeks till next pay day. I'd have to ditch the motel, even if it was cheap. The weather was warm, I could sleep outside.

Or I could sleep with Tera.

I shook my head. I couldn't keep thinking like that.

Feeling weirded out by the whole day, I drove back to the motel, paid my $35 for a room I hadn't used, and packed up my shit. I'd almost convinced myself to leave the money and get the hell out of town when my cell rang.

"Hey, sexy! Miss me yet?"

I couldn't help grinning, even though she couldn't see me.

"Is that Miss Manning, my old high school teacher?"

Tera laughed. "

It wouldn't surprise me at all to hear that your teacher was crushing on you." She paused. "*You like picnics?*"

"Uh, I guess?"

"*Good. Meet me in the hotel parking lot in thirty minutes. Don't be late!*"

And with another laugh, she hung up.

I stared at the phone. For the billionth time, I wondered what the hell I was doing.

CHAPTER SEVEN

TERA

I expected Tucker to balk at the idea of going on a picnic with me—a picnic was much more date-like than dinner and a booty call. But I was trying to think of ways to take his mind off why he was here. I could tell when he was thinking about the funeral, because he'd start frowning and that distant, detached look would be back in his eyes.

Inviting Tucker on a picnic was far more calculated than asking him to come to my room last night. But if he really didn't want to go, he was smart enough to invent an excuse. Now though, I was a little nervous that he'd expect more sex every time we met up—including right now; not that I was averse to it, but I was still a senator's daughter. Being caught having sex outside was a big no-no, it was also a misdemeanor, not to mention the shitstorm that would rain down on my father because of me.

I heard the Ducati pulling into the hotel's parking lot, wondering what it would be like to ride behind Tucker on that beautiful bike with its white frame and sexy red wheels, but I wasn't dressed for anything like that and anyway, he'd never asked me. Last night he'd followed my cab back to the hotel. Well, he probably wasn't traveling with a spare helmet. Probably.

Today, I'd decided to rent a car—I thought it would be good for both of us to get out of town for a few hours.

He swung a long leg over the bike and strolled toward me, smiling broadly.

"You're a sight for sore eyes," he said, and for a moment I thought he was going to kiss me, but then he seemed to think better of it and pulled back, glancing around him quickly.

I gave him an amused smile.

"Hello, dear, how was your day?"

"Better for seeing you," he grinned.

"Oh my God! That was so cheesy! Do you get all your lines out of a Cracker Jack's box?"

"Only my best ones."

I shook my head sadly. "That's what worries me."

"Aw, you worrying about me again, darlin'?"

"Only the same way I'd worry about vaginal warts."

Tucker winked at me. "I won't tell if you don't."

"Get in the car before I come to my senses."

He tossed his helmet in the back, then slid into my passenger seat.

"Where are you taking me?" he asked. "Or is it a secret?"

"Yes, they'll find your body wrapped in plastic in a ditch about six months from now."

"Wrapped in plastic, huh? I didn't know you were so kinky, TC, but I kinda like it."

"Kinky? That's not kinky."

He glanced across and smiled. "Well, what's your definition?"

"I think of it this way: erotic is ... when I use a feather."

"Yeah?"

"Kinky is when you use the whole chicken."

He laughed out loud. "Damn! Why does it sound hot when you say it?"

I tried to stop my grin. "Does everything come back to sex with you?" I huffed.

"Here's hoping," he said with an easy smile.

"Aren't you ever serious?"

"Nope, it's against my religion."

I shook my head—maybe Tucker should go into politics. My father never gave a straight answer either.

There had been a time when I was desperate to follow in my father's footsteps, hence the Master's in PolSci. But losing my belief in him, for the way he'd treated Kes since the secret of his paternity came out, as much as the previous 26 years.

Our father's disdain for his youngest son's career was clear. I didn't understand why he couldn't be proud of what Kes had achieved. Maybe he was, but he didn't think it would help his political career.

That had been the final blow to any ambitions of my own in that direction.

Tucker leaned back in the car, watching me as I shifted gear.

"Damn, that is sexy," he grinned, licking his lips. "A woman who can drive a stick."

I smiled at him and raised an eyebrow. "I like being in the driving seat."

He started to reply, but when he noticed I was heading up the mountain, his words tailed off and he seemed uneasy.

"You know where you're going, TC?"

"I was told there's a really pretty view from up here—you can look down and see the whole town. Somewhere near a..."

"...a dried up riverbed," he said, staring out the window.

I glanced over at him. His forehead was creased in thought and he wasn't smiling.

"You know it?"

He nodded.

"Yeah, I used to live a ways over there."

He jerked his chin toward a thickly wooded area. I could see a dirt track heading further up the mountain. Was that Tucker's home? The place he'd grown up?

"Thank you for telling me that." *I wish you'd tell me more.*

He gave a small nod, then cleared his throat. "We're here."

Tucker was right: we'd run out of road. I pulled the car to the side and opened the door, missing the cool air as soon as I stepped out into the furnace.

"There's a blanket in back—can you get it?"

"Sure, because it's blowing a blizzard out here," he laughed, his good humor seeming restored.

"Oh funny. Well, I'll be the one laughing when poison sumac makes you swell up."

"I thought you liked it when I *swelled up*," he said with a wink.

"Oh, grow up, Tucker!"

He froze, and the blood drained from his face.

"What's wrong?"

Tucker

Grow up, Tucker.

The memories play like a horror movie behind my eyes.

The day Harley Law crashed his bike on this very spot, the day my life changed...

I shook my head to clear the ugly pictures and saw Tera's worried eyes looking up at me.

"Tucker! Are you okay? What just happened? You looked like you saw a ghost."

I laughed awkwardly. "Yeah, something like that."

She edged closer and laid her hand on my chest.

"Your heart is racing," she murmured, concern lining her forehead.

"I'm fine," I said, stepping away.

She looked at me sadly. "You're not fine—you just don't want to tell me."

"Nothing to tell," I said firmly, and I grabbed the blanket from the backseat and pulled out the cooler next to it.

"That's garbage," said Tera, her eyes narrowing in on me. "If you don't want to talk about it fine, but don't give me some BS excuse that it's nothing."

"Right again," I snapped. "I don't want to talk about it."

She sucked in a deep breath and I felt like such an asshole.

"Sorry," I muttered. "I didn't want to come back here, and it's fucking with my head."

She touched my arm lightly. "No, I'm sorry. I shouldn't have pushed you."

"Does that make us a sorry pair?" I asked, trying to laugh it off.

"I think that's a given," she smiled.

Tera took the blanket from my arms and laid it out in a patch of shade, close to the thick trunk of a towering redwood.

"The view is everything they said it would be," she said calmly, kicking off her shoes and settling onto the blanket.

"Yeah."

She looked at me critically. "I think the view would be better if you took your shirt off."

My shoulders relaxed and I grinned down at her. "That goes for you, too."

"Um, no!"

"A little hypocritical, Miss Hawkins?"

"Probably," she laughed. "But I'm not going to get caught half-naked by some passing lumberjack. I'll leave that to you, bucko!"

I pulled my t-shirt over my head, kicked off the heavy biker boots, and got rid of the socks. Then I slumped next to Tera, leaning up on one elbow to look down across the valley.

Just like that day, the riverbed was dry, not even a trickle of water to lay the dust. The air was hazy with heat, and from this distance, the town was just a straggle of ugly buildings in the valley. It didn't look as if much had changed—I wondered how much I had changed.

Despite the heat, I shivered when Tera traced her fingers over my shoulder and back, her nails lightly scratching against my ink.

"You were going to tell me how you got those tattoos."

I groaned. "You really want to hear how dumb I was when I was 17?"

Tera smiled. "You're a guy, so you can't help being dumb, especially at 17. So, tell me."

I rolled onto my stomach and propped my head on my hand.

"I got so drunk on tequila that I woke up with a Mexican accent and those tattoos."

She laughed disbelievingly. "Tucker! Tell it properly!"

I shook my head. "That's the truth! That's how it happened. I'd left home and it was my first night of freedom."

Tera

He was pulling away again, but I was beginning to understand him better now. Anything that was difficult or upset him, Tucker covered it with a joke. It didn't take a genius to figure out that where he grew up wasn't a happy place.

I lay on my back and stared up at the shimmering sky and light dappling through the patchwork of leaves and branches.

Maybe if I told him about my childhood, he'd open up a bit more. Maybe.

"My childhood was picture-book perfect," I said, my voice

drifting to the past. "I had two parents who loved me and I grew up in a beautiful house—several beautiful houses, in fact—and had private schools, my expensive education paid for. My father was successful and my mother stayed at home. Our family had staff: private chef, maids, bodyguards..." I laughed lightly. "I thought it was normal to have men with shaved heads in dark suits talking into microphones in their collars."

I looked across at Tucker. He was watching me closely, as if my poor little rich girl story fascinated him.

"All my life, I wanted to be like my father—that's why I studied politics. I'm not stupid, but I was oblivious. I could see my parents trying to ignore the cracks in their relationship, but I figured that's what married couples do, you know? Try to make it work."

I paused, my eyes tracking across Tucker's expressive face. He wasn't smiling now, but listening intently.

"Finding out about Kestrel and Falcon—that was a turning point for me. I saw my Dad for what he is: flawed, human. I don't blame him for that, but I do blame him for the way he treated their mother, the way he treated them. Even now..." and I shook my head. "Even now, he won't accept Kes for who he is. A carnie doesn't fit the image. Kes doesn't *fit*. Falcon is a different story, but he won't give Dad the time of day—not without his brother." I sighed. "I'd always wanted siblings. I'm glad I've found them now, but we've missed out on so much."

Tucker looked down. "Your dad isn't too happy that you're friendly with us carnie folk."

"No, he isn't," I said honestly. "But he doesn't get a say in it either."

Tucker stared at me skeptically. "You sure about that? Because you flew all the way out here and you're driving a pretty fancy car, and I'm guessing a junior PR executive doesn't make a ton of money." He smirked at me, "...or maybe enough to pay for designer clothes."

I laughed and elbowed him lightly in the ribs.

"God, I'm so shallow! You're totally right. I *could* live without dear old Dad's handouts, I just don't want to." Then I frowned. "But if he pushes me, I *will* make my own choices."

I turned my head to look at Tucker, hoping he'd read the message that was clearly written on my face.

But he rolled onto his back and closed his eyes.

"Why are you here, TC? I don't mean in this shitty little town ... why are you here with me?"

"Because I like you."

He waited, obviously expecting something more. Then he scrubbed his hands over his face in frustration and turned his head to look at me.

I studied him, treating myself to a long look at those gray-green slate-colored eyes fringed with thick lashes, the too-pretty face, strong jaw and sensuous lips always set in a soft pout. His lean muscled body, sculpted by work and play. I reached out to touch him gently, intrigued by the muscles of his stomach dancing under my fingers.

"You could have any guy you wanted," he said, his voice low and rough, not realizing that his bewilderment was part of the charm. "I don't get it."

"That's a long way from true. And anyway, surely I can't be the first woman who likes you just for you?"

Or maybe I am ... because you've never given anyone else a chance to get to know the real you.

"What about you, Tucker? You could have any woman you want—you have, you do. And from what I understand you don't do dates and you don't do repeats, but you're here with me now. Maybe I should ask *you* to explain."

He leaned up to grin at me.

"A hot, sexy woman invites me for a picnic—I'm supposed to turn her down?"

I gave him a small smile.

"I'm not expecting you to be serious with me all the time, Tucker, but you don't have to make everything a joke either. Not for me. I'm just trying to get to know you—but that's what you *don't* want, isn't it?"

He looked out across the valley, his eyes following the winding path of the river, a silver thread in the distance.

"There's not a lot to know, TC. I'm a high school dropout and I work in a traveling carnival. I have no home, no savings, nothing to offer anyone. I'm not so dumb as to think a woman like you could be interested in a guy like me except for..."

His words trailed off and an unfamiliar pink tinged his cheeks. I laughed softly.

"Oh, Tucker! You think I'm using you for sex!"

He smiled sheepishly. "Yeah, when you say it like that, what am I bitchin' about?"

"I *like* you," I stated. "I *like* like you."

He raised an eyebrow. "You *like* like me?"

I smiled at him and turned away, my eyes closing. Slowly, I let my hand creep towards his, our fingers twining together.

"Yes, I like you," I repeated simply.

There was a beat of silence, then he said, "Your Dad isn't going to like..."

"No, he isn't."

"And Kes isn't going to..."

"Probably not."

"And I'll be traveling..."

"I know."

"And you'll be in San Francisco..."

"Tucker," I sighed. "Do you like me?"

His fingers tightened around mine compulsively.

"Do I like you, or do I *like* like you?" he teased.

I pinched his waist and he just about jumped out of his skin.

"Ticklish?" I laughed.

"No," he lied, tentatively rubbing the reddening section of skin.

"Then answer the question: do you like me?"

"Yeah."

I couldn't help smiling. I knew it was pointless to ask for more than that; I needed my hopes and dreams to stay small, realistic, but being with Tucker was an explosion of hope in Technicolor. It was terrifying.

"Why do you like me?" I asked shyly.

He closed his eyes and shook his head, but he was smiling.

"Always with the hard questions!"

I gave an exaggerated sigh. "It can't be *that* hard, Tucker! There must be a reason that you like me!"

"Well, you kinda told me to," he laughed. "Jeez, I don't know, TC. You're not like other women."

"I've got boobs, an ass and a pussy—how am I different?"

He didn't answer so I turned to look at him. His jaw was clenched and his eyes were squeezed shut.

"What?" I whispered.

"Don't. Say. That!" he bit out.

"Which part?"

I could almost hear him grinding his teeth.

"Don't say ... pussy!" he hissed.

I laughed out loud.

"What do you want me to call it? My tunnel of love? Pussy! Pussy! Pussy!"

My laugh ended in a gasp as his heavy body rolled on top of me, pressing me into the blanket. His mouth was on mine, his teeth nipping at my lips as the buckle of his belt bit into my waist.

One hand was at the hem of my skirt, his rough palm pushing the material up my thigh; the other was in my hair, gripping hard as he kissed me feverishly, his tongue driving into my mouth as if I was his last supper. He was intense, passionate, control gone—and I couldn't get enough.

With a hard yank, my skirt was up to my waist and Tucker was fingering me under the lace of my panties. My surprised gasp turned into a moan as my brain warred with my body.

When my brain lost, my hands tightened on the denim covering his butt and I squeezed hard. Tucker growled against my throat and hooked my leg over his hip, grinding his erection against me.

Yes! This is enough! This is what I want! To be desired, needed like this.

I was lying to myself. I was falling for him. And I had absolutely no clue how Tucker felt.

"Holy shit!"

It wasn't Tucker who'd spoken and it sure as hell wasn't me.

He shot upright, his body tense.

Embarrassed and beyond turned on, I struggled to sit up. The speaker was a skinny kid, a boy, maybe ten or 12 years old.

"Jeez, Scotty!" Tucker huffed out. "You training to be a stalker?"

"I was just walkin' by," the boy said defensively.

Tucker muttered something under his breath and reached for his t-shirt, pulling it over his head, leaving it untucked. I guessed that was to cover his hard-on. After all, the boy was probably scarred enough already.

"Yeah, okay," sighed Tucker. "You go on now."

The boy nodded, but his eyes were on me. Feeling horribly self-conscious, I tried to tug my skirt down to a decent length.

Tucker's eyes narrowed and he folded his arms across his chest. The boy caught the movement and flushed red.

He turned quickly, then called over his shoulder, "See you tomorrow at the funeral, Uncle Tucker."

I gasped, my eyes snapping to Tucker. "Wait, he's your nephew?"

Tucker grimaced. "Yeah."

I waited for him to expand his answer, but there was nothing. No expression on his shuttered face. A lifetime of smiles and now he'd run out?

Disappointment banked by fury ignited inside me.

"Just talk to me, Tucker!"

His lips tightened to a thin line.

"Tell me!" I cried out. "Your mom, your dad, how you grew up? Tell me something!"

Stupid tears stung my stupid eyes as the silence billowed out between us.

I grabbed my shoes and the blanket, and strode to the car, wincing as sharp splinters of rock dug into my bare feet.

I flung everything in the back and jumped into the driver's seat—Tucker could find his own damn way back to the hotel. I was too humiliated to...

"Tera, wait!"

My vision was blurry as I glared at him, hands bunched into fists as I gripped the steering wheel.

"I didn't know I had a nephew until yesterday," he said quietly. "I hadn't spoken to my momma or anyone in my family for the last 12 years."

I deflated as air whooshed from my lungs.

"Oh! Tucker, I..."

A huge sob hiccupped out of me as obstinate tears leaked from my eyes.

He shook his head. "Don't cry, sugar. She's not worth it."

"I'm not crying for your mother," I gulped, my voice wobbling.

"I don't understand," he said gently, pulling me into his arms.

"I'm crying for you!"

He buried his face in my hair.

"Don't," he said softly. "Don't ever cry for me."

"Someone has to," I whispered, but I don't think he heard me.

He held me against his chest and I could hear the rapid beat of his heart slowing, easing. I felt foolish, regretting my outburst. It wasn't how I'd been brought up.

"Sorry," I muttered, pushing away from him.

His arms dropped to his sides and he gave me a half smile that faded quickly.

I wiped my eyes and hoped I didn't resemble a panda too badly.

"I'm sorry about your mother," I said quietly.

He shrugged and looked away. "Like I said, we weren't close."

"Do you ... would you like...?"

He looked at me curiously as my words tumbled out. I took a deep breath to compose myself.

"I could go with you, if you like."

He frowned. "Go where?"

"To your mother's funeral ... if you like."

He looked stunned and I could see him already starting to shake his head.

"Don't decide now," I said quickly. "But if you want I could ... or if you don't want to go by yourself..."

"Jesus, TC," he laughed uncomfortably. "Hell, *I* don't want to go—I wouldn't ask a friend to go with me."

I swallowed the bitter pill.

"That's what friends do," I said quietly. "Friends help you through the bad days."

He smiled and pressed a dismissive kiss to my forehead.

Tucker

Tera confused the hell out of me, and being around her was a rollercoaster ride.

I saw the hurt when I called her a friend, but I didn't know what else to say. We'd fucked twice—stuff I'd done with a lot of other women. But dinner together? A goddamn picnic?

That wasn't normal—not for me. I felt relaxed around her, but jittery and on edge at the same time, and I didn't know how that was possible. She was hotter than hell, sweet and funny. Smart, too.

She likes me.

I teased her when she said that, but it felt good hearing it. And that made me nervous.

As for what had happened after Scotty saw us, I had no idea what that was or what it had to do with Momma's funeral. And she'd offered to come with me...

Hell, I knew I was rusty, but I didn't remember funerals being places to take a date. Unless you were Marilyn Manson.

I pulled my boots on and scooped up the cooler, wondering what Tera had packed for us. My stomach rumbled, reminding me that I hadn't eaten since breakfast. But one look at Tera hunched over a compact as she tried to cover up the blotches from her crying jag, and I lost my appetite again.

I hated women crying. I'd do anything to avoid that.

Anything except stay.

"Do you want me to drive?" I offered.

"I thought you only drove things with two wheels," she snorted.

"Yep, those and the eight-wheeler rig," I reminded her with a grin, relieved that the sass was back.

"No, I'm fine, thanks."

"Okay, well if you could drop me at the parking lot, that would be great. I don't really want to hike down the mountain in motorcycle boots; they're about as comfortable as concrete blocks for that, especially since these are pretty new."

Tera gave me a strange look.

"Oh, do you have to be somewhere?"

I shrugged, not wanting to explain that I'd be looking for a place to camp tonight.

"I've got all this food, if you're hungry," and she jerked her head at the cooler.

"We didn't have too much luck having a picnic," I pointed out.

She smiled and raised an eyebrow. "That was embarrassing. It's been years since I was caught making out. I hope your nephew wasn't too upset."

"Seeing you will have given him plenty of spank bank material for years to come. You probably did him a favor."

Tera looked horrified. "Oh gross! I can't believe you just said that!"

"What? It's true. Anyway, he'll be finding out about women for himself soon."

She gaped at me. "You're kidding! He's only, what, twelve?"

"I'm not sure exactly, but probably 11. I've been gone 12 years."

I shut the words off quickly, but Tera had already caught them.

"Why didn't...?"

She mashed her lips together as if that would hold back the questions.

"Well, I think he's got at least five years before he's really interested in girls."

I shot her an amused look. "I had a girlfriend when I was 13."

She huffed in disbelief. "Oh sure, sharing snowcones and slushies at the Dairy Queen."

I laughed out loud. "Damn! Did you grow up in the fifties? Because I gotta say, TC, you look pretty good for a 70 year old."

She smacked my arm.

"No! I'm just saying that having a *real* girlfriend is different."

My smile faded.

"They start 'em young around here."

Tera didn't answer and maybe she was thinking what I was thinking—that we came from different worlds.

At the hotel, we went through the same game of hide-and-seek as the night before. Tera headed to her room carrying the cooler, and I snuck in later.

I'd snuck into a lot of girls' rooms, but this was different.

When she opened the door, I could see the picnic spread out on the floor behind her.

"Surprise!" she said, her cheeks turning pink. "Are you hungry?"

"Yeah, I am," I said, not looking at the food.

Tera

Tucker spent the entire night in my bed. Again.

He was affectionate and funny, but didn't share anything else about himself.

The problem was I saw a lot to like. He was sweet and surprisingly thoughtful, given his insistence that he was as shallow as a summer puddle. He was unselfish and marvelous in bed—my God! More than I could have imagined. I felt as if my body had been awakened for the first time, felt him worshipping every inch of me, seeing every part, every blemish, all the small defects that I hid with clothes: the orange-peel skin on my thighs; the white stretch marks on my hips and stomach from when I'd been somewhat chunky, gaining the freshman ten and more in college; the scar on my knee that I'd gotten falling over when I was ice skating; the birthmark on my neck that I hated because a boy had once laughed and said it was shaped like a dick. Mom said it was shaped like Florida, but that's another story.

He kissed every part of me from the soles of my feet to the

tips of my fingers, sweet and slow and sensual kisses that made my body blaze.

And in between the haze of lust, the thick fog of sexual expression, we talked.

And although he reminded me more than once that he was an uneducated hick—his words—I found that he was well informed about national affairs and even world news. He grudgingly admitted that in private he was addicted to Fox News.

I kept getting glimpses of hidden layers and it frustrated and intrigued me.

I fell asleep with my head on his chest, soothed by that slow, steady beat.

In the morning, I woke up to the feel of his rough fingers sweeping gently across my shoulders and back.

I glanced up, but he was looking into the distance, as if his soft strokes were simply absent-minded. As I shifted in bed, he noticed I was awake and flashed a brief smile.

"I gotta get going," he said, carefully moving me away from him.

"Okay," I nodded, trying to sound normal—whatever that was since Tucker had become my new obsession.

"Is it alright if I shower?" he asked cautiously, pointing toward the bathroom with his thumb.

"Of course, go ahead. I'll ... I'll order some breakfast."

He pressed a quick kiss to my forehead and slid out of bed, his muscles flexing in the slanting morning light, his tight butt and long legs a sight that made my mouth water. But it was clear his mind was elsewhere and I couldn't blame him for that.

The previous day, I'd had one idea that would show I was thinking of him.

Making sure the bathroom door was shut, I grabbed the small bag and placed it on top of the bedside table.

The night before, Tucker had put out a clean pair of jeans

and a new shirt to wear—a white button-up still in its shop packaging. It didn't seem as if the man owned a pair of dark slacks, even for a funeral. Either that, or it didn't make much sense to wear them when he was riding the Ducati.

He emerged from the bathroom in a cloud of steam and smelling of my bodywash. He was freshly shaven, his smooth cheeks making him look younger than his 29 years.

Unselfconsciously naked, he dressed quickly, frowning at the white shirt as he stripped off the cellophane.

I took my turn in the bathroom, washing off the sweat from our night of love-making, washing off the scent of Tucker. I didn't have time to blow-dry and style my long hair. Besides, Tucker had already seen me looking less than stellar, so there was no point trying to shovel on the makeup either.

I'd just pulled on a fluffy bathrobe when room service knocked on the door. Tucker opened it, and I wished he hadn't, because the server's wide eyes as his gaze shuttled between us made me think the news would get back to Dad somehow. Sooner rather than later. I could do without that particular scenario.

Tucker ate quickly, but he didn't comment on the food and I doubt he even tasted what he was putting in his mouth.

He swallowed the last morsel of bacon and washed it down with coffee before immediately standing to leave.

"I'd better get gone, TC," he said quickly. "Probably shouldn't be late to a funeral, unless it's my own."

I tried for a weak smile, but it got lost around the corners of my mouth.

"I ... I have something for you," I said hesitantly, beginning to feel certain this was a bad idea.

He paused at the door, his impatience to be gone painful.

I held out the small bag and his eyebrows drew together as he peered inside.

"You got me a necktie?"

His eyes were questioning as he looked up, but he didn't seem upset.

"I thought maybe ... maybe you'd like to wear one today?"

He stared at the tie, and I regretted my presumption. But then his eyes softened and he smiled.

"Thanks, TC. Will you put it on for me? I never learned how to do that shit."

I gave a relieved smile and stepped toward him.

As I took the soft black silk from his hand, our fingers touched and the same strange flash of heat passed between us, and his pupils seemed to dilate.

I lifted the collar of his shirt, passing the sliver of silk around his neck, knotting it carefully and smoothing out the ends over his broad chest.

"There," I said. "You're ready."

I looked down at my bare feet, the disrespectful toes bright pink, hardly the color for a funeral. They butted up to the heavy leather of Tucker's biker boots and he shifted carefully, cradling my feet between his.

I felt his finger under my chin as he lifted my head up gently.

"Thank you," he said, whispering the lightest kiss across my lips.

And then he was gone.

I paced up and down, wondering what to do.

Friends don't let friends go to their mother's funeral by themselves, I told myself.

But I'd offered to go and Tucker had all but laughed at me. Would he want me there?

Second-guessing was tiring, so I combed my hair into a neat French pleat and pulled on a dark gray linen suit that I had with me just in case.

I ignored my cell when it chimed with my father's ringtone, then called for a taxi. While I was waiting, I

Googled the local paper to check out the announcements for Margaret Foster.

She must have remarried after Tucker's father. Another piece in the puzzle.

The crematorium was a single-story white building with trees on one side and a wide asphalt driveway. The parking lot had only a few older cars and battered looking trucks. Tucker's bike stood out like a sore thumb.

Taking a deep breath, I paid the taxi driver and asked him to wait until the service was over. He didn't seem unhappy when I said I'd pay him for his time, and he hunkered down with a flask of coffee and the radio tuned to a country station.

I slipped into a seat at the back, hoping to be unseen by the thirty or so people who were there, but I saw Tucker's nephew turn in his chair, already bored. His eyebrows lifted when he saw me, then he nudged the woman sitting next to him. I assumed she was his mother, which made her either Tucker's sister or sister-in-law. I prepared a smile of condolence, but when she turned to stare at me, or rather glare at me, her thin lips pulled into a sneer.

I slumped back in my seat, more than a little surprised. I couldn't imagine what I'd done to upset Tucker's family. Maybe being here was a bad idea.

Tucker was sitting off to one side by himself, his eyes fixed on the cheap looking coffin covered in flowers. I recognized the spray of white lilies that I'd ordered from a local florist.

The minister droned on without a drop of emotion, describing Tucker's mom as a hard-working woman who'd taken on two stepsons that she loved like her own boy. It all painted a very rosy view of a family Tucker could barely bring himself to speak about. But I suppose that's what we do at funerals—whitewash the truth that's too dirty to mention.

I didn't really learn much more except that Margaret McCoy-Foster née Sutton had been born in the town 51 years ago and had never left. She'd have been very young when she had Tucker.

Maybe that's why Tucker was a roamer, to do what his mother never could. Either that, or he couldn't wait to leave home.

I gathered that she'd been widowed young, and I wondered what had happened to Tucker's father.

An older man sitting in the front row started intermittently cursing and drinking from a bottle of whiskey, only partially hidden by a paper bag. I guessed he was the widower, which made him Tucker's stepfather. The two burly men next to him seemed uninterested in either stopping his drinking or quieting his cursing. Tucker didn't even turn his head.

It was the strangest, most oddly dispassionate funeral I'd ever been to.

As the service ended, I slipped away quietly and waited outside for Tucker.

He looked surprised when he saw me, his expression quickly becoming upset. He glanced uneasily at the blonde woman, then started walking toward me, but before he could say a word, the woman caught up to him.

"This her?" she said, her voice a tough bark. "This the one you were up at the creek with? Scotty told me you were screwing some rich girl with a fancy car."

Tucker scowled at her. "Scotty has a big mouth—and he's not good friends with the truth either." Then he turned to me. "What are you doing here, TC?"

"I thought..."

"He's with his family," the woman spat. "He doesn't need you and I sure as hell don't want *our son* to see a slut like you."

I gasped, my eyes darting to Tucker as he swore softly.

Had I heard that right? Tucker and this woman?

"You have a son?"

I could hear the shock and disbelief in my voice, and I didn't know which weighed the heaviest.

Tucker was staring at me. Then he scowled, his eyes turning to ice as he looked at the woman.

"What did you say?"

She didn't reply, just stared at him, a grim smile on her face.

My voice was trembling and broken as I asked again.

"You have a son?"

Tucker shrugged, still not looking at me, and that indifference almost killed me. *What does that mean—a shrug?*

I'd believed I was beginning to know this man, but I was wrong.

Tucker's lips pulled into a cold smile. *I really hate the way he smiles. How can he smile at me? How dare he?*

"Looks like," he said easily. "TC, you should go."

Then he gripped the woman's arm and pulled her toward the parking lot, his voice a low, angry rumble.

He didn't even look at me.

I stumbled back to the taxi, falling into the back seat.

The driver looked at me with sympathetic eyes.

"Sorry for your loss," he said.

CHAPTER EIGHT

TUCKER

The look on Tera's face just about killed me.

"Why did you have to say that to her?" I all but snarled at Renee.

She tugged her arm free and threw me a hard look.

"She got no business being here!"

"Is that right? She's my best friend's sister. *You* got no business talking to her like that."

Renee laughed coldly. "Your best friend's sister? A stuck up bitch like that! You're a liar. She's that northern senator's daughter—I seen her picture in the paper, Miss Tera Chastain Hawkins. That's right, isn't it? Your *friend*." She smiled again. "Strangers in a small town are big news, Tucker. You should know that."

"What the fuck, Renee? You tell me two minutes before the service that Scotty is my kid, and the next minute you're telling everyone!"

What a complete mindfuck. My son! I had a kid—all this time and I'd never known. I only had to look at his dirty blond hair and know that he was mine. Fuck! FUCK! FUCK!

I tore at my tie. Other than the minister, I was the only man wearing one today. The knot felt like it was strangling me.

"What about Jackson? Does he know?"

Renee shook her head, her chin jutting out, her scowl defiant.

"No, he doesn't."

"Why?" I asked furiously. "Why are you with him?"

She pressed her lips together in a flat line.

"There aren't too many choices when you're 17 and pregnant."

My stomach lurched and I felt a cold sweat break out all over my body. Renee sneered at me.

"Jesus, Tucker! Don't look so shocked, we'd been screwing since we were 13. Guess it caught up with us."

"Yeah, but I wasn't the only one," I bit out. "What about Randolph?"

"Scotty doesn't look anything like him. Wake up, Tucker! The kid is the spitting image of you."

"Why didn't you tell me?"

She shrugged. "I didn't get the chance. You were away and gone; didn't exactly leave a forwarding address, did you?"

I gave an angry laugh. "Are you surprised? The last time I saw you, Randolph was..." I couldn't even bring myself to say it.

Renee shook her head bitterly. "You were always such a dreamer—head in the clouds. Everything was just a damn joke to you. Well, life has gotten serious."

I had to look away. "You never did get me, Renee."

"What does that mean?"

I sighed and rubbed my eyes. "Doesn't matter. Where does Jackson fit into this?"

She shrugged. "Scotty needed a father and he was a better bet than Randolph. I told Jackson it was him. He believed me."

Jesus! Had she been screwing my whole family behind my back?

Maybe Jason, too? I shook my head, not wanting to think about it.

"So why are you telling me now?"

A cold gleam glittered in her eyes. "You've done well for yourself; got out of this dead-end town, didn't you? I read about you on the internet, riding with that famous stuntman."

I met her stare. "So this is about money?"

She licked her lips. "You owe me. I was the one who was supposed to leave."

"Well, you're shit out of luck because I'm broke."

"Bullshit! You ridin' that fancy foreign motorcycle. Tell me that isn't worth thousands of dollars!"

She was right, but it was also the only thing I had.

"I want a paternity test," I said. "If Scotty's mine, I want to know it for sure."

Renee grimaced. "I can't afford that kind of money."

"What about Jackson? You're married to the douche—he must be down on Scotty's birth certificate?"

Renee looked away.

"We're not married. Jackson gave me a ring, but we never made it legal."

Sounded like Jackson.

"Well, whose name is down on the birth certificate as Scotty's father?"

Renee lifted her chin and glared at me.

"No one."

I frowned, not sure what to believe.

"You've known where I was for a year now—you could have filed a paternity suit. The Courts would have come after me for child support."

Renee glared. "Oh yeah, sure. Right after Jackson had beaten me black and blue."

An ache filled my chest. *Just like Momma.*

I tamped down the growing feeling of guilt.

"Get the test, or you won't see a penny from me."

"Mom, what's going on?"

Scotty's worried voice interrupted us.

Renee grabbed his shoulders and pulled him into a tight hug. There was no doubting her love for the kid—I just doubted everything else that came out of her bitter mouth.

"Get the test, Renee," I said in a low voice. "I'll stay in town for two more days, after that, I'm gone."

Randolph lurched out of the door toward the truck, drunk and cussing up a storm.

He was smaller than I remembered, and it seemed unbelievable that he'd terrorized me for most of my childhood. I waited for the hot flash of hatred, but all I felt was disgust. He didn't even recognize me—or he was too drunk to care.

I walked back to my Duke in a daze. I didn't know what to believe. Rationally, I knew that Renee had lied to me before, but damn it she was right—Scotty was the spitting image of me. Jackson was dark haired and dark eyed. But then again, Renee was blonde, as well.

My mind twisted and turned, and on top of the whole clusterfuck was Tera. What the hell must she think of me now?

Maybe it was just as well. I was no good for her, a no-good guy with nothing to offer.

But I had to at least try and explain. She deserved that much.

I rode back to her hotel slowly, trying to find the words that would make her listen, practicing what I needed to stay.

I rode the elevator to her room and took a deep breath before knocking on the door. There was no answer.

"TC, it's me. Please, sugar, let me explain."

Silence.

"Tera, I just need five minutes."

I leaned my head against the door, my thoughts weighing

heavily. I waited another ten minutes before I decided to give her some space.

I walked outside into the blazing heat, feeling the sun beating down from the hard blue sky. I figured maybe I could wait for her. Maybe if I gave her time to cool down, she'd talk to me. It wasn't much of a plan, but frying my brain in the sun wouldn't help either. I wandered toward a thick tangle of pines where the shadows were deep and the air was a couple of degrees cooler.

From here, I could just see the hotel's entrance as well as the window of Tera's room. I'd wait.

I was so deep in thought, that I didn't hear them until they were nearly on me.

The soft rush of rapid footsteps behind snapped me out of it and I was already turning when a hard fist landed square in my gut.

The breath whooshed out of my lungs in a painful hiss as I jack-knifed over.

"You were warned. Stay the fuck away from her, McCoy. She doesn't need a loser like you in her life."

Thud.

The next fist landed on my cheek and I reeled backwards. I had just enough presence of mind to fold my body over as kicks rained down on me. I managed to grab onto someone's foot and take the fucker with me. I got in a few good punches before two other men grabbed my arms and hauled me upright, and another kick was aimed at my stomach. I tensed my muscles as much as possible, but the guy's aim was solid.

My body sagged as two heavies held my arms and another one used me as a punch bag. My left eye was swollen shut, my jaw was throbbing like a bastard and I could taste blood in my mouth. The knuckles on both of my hands were split, which meant the assholes holding me hadn't gotten away without some damage.

I looked up at my attackers, my vision blurring as I tried to focus.

The two men holding me had the type of short haircuts that made them look military, and the one beating the shit out of me had a radio mic in his ear which told me exactly what he was. So I wasn't surprised to see Senator Hawkins leaning casually against a tree. He'd come to make good on his threat himself—this was personal.

Another man flanked him. This was one fight that I wasn't going to win. Not five against one, when four of the dudes were probably security services, and the other hated me more than Satan.

"Are you listening, you fucking piece of shit, because next time I won't say it so nicely."

A fist hit my temple and everything went black for a second.

I shook my head, trying to clear it.

"Stay away from my daughter!"

The Senator's mouth was peeled back from his teeth and his eyes blazed with rage.

I laughed at him through split lips, pausing only to spit out a gob of blood.

"You think this will make a difference? You can't get me fired; you can't do anything to me ... and I can take a beating."

"Is that what you think?" The Senator stood upright and smiled coldly, then he nodded to his men. "Break his legs."

Oh, shit! That got my attention. I stared at the Senator, seeing no hesitation in his eyes.

I started struggling harder, lashing out with my feet and catching one of the goons in the shin.

He swore loudly and leaned down on my trapped arm. I heard a faint 'pop' as my shoulder dislocated and I landed face first on the ground.

One of them kicked me in the ribs as I tried to roll, pain shooting through my shoulder as my right arm hung limply.

"Tucker!"

I heard Tera scream, the sound coming from above, from her window.

"I called 911," she shrieked. "The police are on their way."

Immediately, the goons melted into the shadows and the Senator's voice was a hoarse rattle by my ear.

"Touch her again and it *will* be your legs."

Then he was gone.

I lay bleeding in the dirt, my whole body on fire.

Then I heard Tera's voice as she skidded to a halt next to me, falling to her knees, her hands fluttering over me, afraid to touch.

"Oh my God! Oh my God! Tucker…"

I groaned and tried to sit up, cradling my useless arm."

"W-what happened?"

I had less than a second to make a decision.

"Muggers," I said, my voice strained. "Probably after the keys to the Duke."

"Oh my God," she said again, her eyes darting back and forth. "Look at your shoulder!"

"Dislocated," I muttered with a grimace.

"How do you know? Are you sure? It could be broken! Don't try and move it!"

Her hands trembled as she tried to brush my hair out of my eyes.

"I don't know where to touch you—you're all hurt and bloody!"

I almost laughed, but my shoulder spasmed and I thought I was going to pass out.

"Oh God, Tucker! Don't die!" Tera gripped my hand so hard, I groaned.

"I'm not dying, TC," I grit out, "but I might if you cut off the blood supply to my hand."

"Stop joking!" she cried out. "This is serious!"

Blood dripped down my forehead from a gash over my eye. I could feel my lip swelling and knew I'd look like Donald Duck. I hoped Tera liked the pouty look. Then I remembered that we weren't together and never would be. Bile rose in my throat.

After a moment, she pulled a tissue out of her pocket and dabbed at the blood on my cheek.

"You're such a mess," she gulped, trying to swallow as the tears ran down her cheeks.

I was a mess—and in more ways than she meant. My body was a mass of pain, but seeing her tears, that was worse.

In the distance, I could hear the sound of the police and an ambulance, and after a moment blue lights turned the parking lot into an incident area. People were staring out their windows and a crowd began to gather, edging toward us.

The two police officers climbed out of the patrol car. One kept the crowd back, while the other cleared a path for the paramedics, an older guy and a girl who looked as if she'd just graduated high school—possibly.

"Got a dislocated shoulder," I said helpfully. "Done it once before and it hurt the same."

"We'll just take a look," said the guy, holding my arm at the elbow before he tried to touch me.

"How did this happen?" asked the police officer.

"Tripped," I said, and at the same time Tera answered, "he was mugged."

The police officer and paramedics exchanged a look while Tera gave me a hard stare.

They didn't ask any more questions, but gave me a pillow to hold in the gap between the side of my body and my arm to support it. Then they looped a sling across my forearm to hold it in place across my chest. Fucking hurt, but I didn't say anything.

They situated me on the gurney, my head already throbbing like a bitch, and my left eye was closing.

"Are you coming with him, miss?" the guy asked Tera.

She pressed her lips together then nodded abruptly.

I was surprised, but I shouldn't have been—she had a big heart, even for a guy who'd just broken it.

The journey to ER was painful, and not just because my shoulder felt like someone was sticking knives in it and the tortured nerves kept sending electric shocks up my spine. I just about bit off my tongue trying not to yell. I could feel sweat breaking out all over my body but I felt cold, as well. I hoped I wasn't going into shock.

Tera didn't say a word. In fact she could hardly meet my eyes, but she didn't stop staring at the cut on my head or my fucked up shoulder.

The bright lights of the ER made my head throb even worse. There wasn't a part of me that didn't hurt.

But I couldn't tell Tera that her father did this, I'd hurt her enough already.

The police asked a lot of questions that I just laughed off or ignored: I hadn't seen or heard anything; I couldn't describe my attackers and had no idea what they wanted. No, I didn't want to make a big deal of it. Tera stared at the wall behind me, her arms folded across her tits.

Then the doc waved them away while he glued my head and gave me some ice to hold against my cheek and lip. There wasn't anything he could do for bruised ribs.

The police weren't happy, but finally left, reminding me to call if I thought of anything else. I thanked them for their time, relieved that Tera hadn't forced the issue. She told them that she saw four, maybe five men, but they'd run away when she'd shouted out. Which was all true.

When the doc took me away to x-ray my shoulder, my eyes

met Tera's, and I saw pain and disappointment mixed with longing. I sighed and turned away.

I sure as hell didn't expect to see her when I got back, but she was still there—waiting through what seemed like hours. I began to feel like she was haunting me and I actually started to wish that she'd leave. I'd have told her go, but I knew that this was the last time I'd see her like this ... when we could still acknowledge what we had between us, what we'd shared.

Instead, I saw a long future of meeting her at Kes's parties or at the cabin and not being able to touch her. Worse still, maybe seeing her with some other man. It hurt like hell to lose her, even though she was still sitting a few feet away from me. I considered leaving the act, leaving Hawkins' Daredevils, but then I'd be the nothing she already thought I was.

I tried to find the words to tell her how I felt, about how Renee had ambushed me, but my brain was all shook up and I was having difficulty focusing on any of the thoughts ricocheting around my head.

The doc gave me a mild sedation before they manipulated my arm back into place. While it was taking effect, some woman came by to collect my insurance information. I went to reach for the wallet in my back pocket and swore when pain lanced through me. I tried to reach it with my left hand, but Tera stood up and quietly worked it out of my pocket, then rifled through it until she found the details. When she was done, she pushed it back into my jeans. She didn't speak once.

When the doc came to fix me up, she watched as he rotated my arm at the shoulder joint, grimacing as it dropped back into place. They debated x-raying it again, but in the end decided it looked good enough for me to be sent on my way in the morning.

"You'll need to keep your arm in a sling for a few weeks," said the doc. "And make an appointment with a physical therapist. You'll need rehabilitation to strengthen your shoulder. He'll show you a few exercises and..."

"I got this, Doc," I said, still a little woozy. "I popped my shoulder out once before. It's all good."

He narrowed his eyes at me. "What is it you do for a living, Mr. McCoy?"

"I'm a roustabout, Doc. I work the carnivals."

Tera interrupted, surprising us all, after her hours of silence.

"He's lying: he's really a motorcycle stunt rider. He's quite famous."

The doctor looked surprised, his gaze flicking between us.

I stared at Tera.

"What? Nothing to say? No jokes? No funny come back? I'm disappointed," and she turned away again.

The doc ignored her outburst, I guess he was used to shit like that in his job.

"You won't be able to ride a motorcycle for a while," he said blandly. "In fact no driving at all—not even an automatic car— for two weeks. After that, you can resume most activities, but avoid heavy lifting and playing sports for three months ... and motorcycle stunts."

I nodded absently, already knowing the drill. I was pissed that I would be letting Kes and Zef down again. I hated not being able to pull my weight.

The doc gave us a professional smile and told me that a nurse would be by with some pain meds.

When we were alone, Tera finally looked at me.

"Are you going to tell me the truth now?"

I laughed uneasily. "Which one do you want?"

"What is that woman to you? Other than the mother of your child. Did you come back for her? Why, after all this time?"

I rubbed my forehead with my good hand.

"I didn't know about Scotty, I swear. I wouldn't have left her to ... I wouldn't have left."

"Why should I believe you? If that's true, why did you leave?"

Tera was still staring at me, waiting for an explanation. I didn't want to share the ugliness with her. She was too fine, too clean, so much better than all this shit.

"Things were bad at home," I said simply. "I didn't know she was pregnant."

Tera nodded slowly.

"So she told you and you came back."

I looked down. "Not exactly."

When she spoke again, her voice was soft and full of hurt, but the words cut deeply. "Don't be shy, Tucker. After all, you've had your dick in my mouth and in my pussy—no secrets between old friends."

Part of me wanted to remind her that she'd followed me here and I didn't owe her jack shit. But another part hated that I was hurting her.

"Why did you come back?"

"Because of the funeral."

Her eyes flicked up. "Is that true?"

I nodded.

She pressed her lips together and looked away briefly before her eyes darted away from me.

"Is there anything else I should know?"

I was still fixed on Renee and Scotty, so I shook my head.

I could see the disappointment in her eyes.

"I've been thinking about it," she said quietly. "And I realized: the men who attacked you ... they were wearing suits."

I tried to shrug but pain lanced through me and I ended up cringing.

"Better class of mugger in that part of town," I tried to joke.

It didn't work.

145

"They were my father's men."

Her voice was flat and expressionless—and it wasn't a question.

I didn't answer.

"I'm right. I know I'm right," she said. "I just don't understand why you didn't tell the police. I don't understand why you didn't tell me."

She took a shuddering breath.

I shook my head. "The dude gets what he wants."

"Is it because ... did he pay you off? Did he pay you to walk away from me?"

The vulnerability in her voice hurt more than the Senator's goons. I hated that she thought that about me, but I was letting her go and it was better that she hated me than hated her father.

"Did he offer?" she insisted.

I gave a bitter chuckle.

She straightened her shoulders, tossing her hair back as she did so.

"How much did it take? Ten thousand dollars? Five? Or maybe just one."

She stood up and stared down at me. "I must be cheaper than I thought."

And then she was the one walking away.

I wanted to call after her; I wanted to tell her that no amount of money would ever have bought me off. But maybe it was better this way. She'd leave and have no good memories of me—nothing to regret. I lay back in the hospital bed and let the pain wash through as my head thudded heavily against the hard pillow.

A few minutes later, a nurse approached with two small white pills and a cup of water, and helped me to sit up.

"These will help with the pain," she said. "You'll need to stay till morning, but then your girlfriend can..."

"I don't have a girlfriend," I said, interrupting her.

She glanced down the empty corridor and her eyes softened in sympathy.

"Keep your arm in a sling for at least two weeks, then speak to a physical therapist about gentle exercises to help build up the muscles again." She smiled professionally, maybe even kindly. "And don't be a guy about taking pain meds—they're there to help you."

I didn't even have the energy to do more than give her a weak smile.

"Sure," I said. "Thanks for everything."

She nodded and patted me on my good shoulder.

"Be well, Mr. McCoy."

CHAPTER NINE

TUCKER

Tera walked away and didn't look back, but that was the best thing for her. I'd brought nothing but trouble. She'd be better off without me.

Everything hurt until the pain pills kicked in, leaving me hazy and weak. The Duke was still at Tera's hotel, not that I could ride it for a couple of weeks. Not that I had anywhere to go.

I stayed the night at the hospital, lying awake despite the pain and overwhelming tiredness. Nobody bothered me, but the friendly nurse brought me a cup of coffee as she was going off shift.

"Do you have somewhere to go?" she asked, handing me the scalding black liquid.

"Yeah, just not sure how I'll get there with one wing clipped," I said, forcing out a smile.

"I'll take you to reception," she offered helpfully. "You can call a cab from there."

I nodded. "Thanks, I'll do that."

While we were talking, a nurse I hadn't seen before arrived with my discharge notes and meds in a paper bag.

"Take two every four hours," she said, scanning over the paperwork, "but no more than eight in a 24 hour period."

"Yes, ma'am."

"I'll take him to reception, Grace," said the friendly nurse. "I'm going that way."

She found a wheelchair and insisted on pushing me to reception, saying it was hospital policy. Honestly, I was too damn tired and sore to care.

I thanked her and thought she was going to leave, but she hesitated.

"Do you have far to go?"

Now there was a question.

"That might be a bit of an issue," I admitted. "My friends are in Minnesota at the moment and I rode here on my motorcycle."

"Oh! I thought you were from around here. Your accent..."

I laughed dully. "Yep, still got it even though I haven't lived here in 12 years."

She looked so concerned that I gave her my best smile.

"Hey, thanks for everything you've done. You've been great. Even the coffee," I said, raising the Styrofoam cup and winking at her with my good eye.

She smiled. "Hmm, well, you seem much better. Take care of that arm, Mr. McCoy. And don't be a guy about taking the pain meds."

As she walked away, I finished the bitter brew that tasted like old socks. My head was fuzzy from the meds and lack of sleep, plus breathing kind of hurt, so it was hard to concentrate on anything. I hoped the coffee would help.

I had two immediate projects: find somewhere to store the Duke until I could ship her back to the carnival, and I had to talk to Renee. I wasn't looking forward to either.

149

And leave Tera the fuck alone.

When I'd finished the coffee, I called a cab. I told the driver to take me to the Duke. It was fucking depressing to think I wouldn't be able to ride her for a while. My shoulder throbbed mercilessly, so I grabbed my backpack, trying to ignore the burning pain. I knew one way to distract myself: I texted Renee to meet me at the diner I'd visited on my first morning.

She didn't reply, but I knew she'd come.

The diner was nearly empty, but the server gave a shocked gasp as I walked through the restaurant. I washed up in the tiny bathroom and managed to get the blood out of my hair. The shirt was ruined so I shoved it in the trash. Then I realized that trying to wear a t-shirt when I couldn't move my arm wasn't going to work. The only other shirt I had with buttons was my funeral shirt, and that was creased as hell. Whatever.

Looking almost human, I ordered the breakfast special, but my appetite was off. I ate the eggs and chewed through one of the dollar pancakes, but everything tasted weird. I drank some more coffee and persuaded the sour-looking server to let me charge my cell phone.

I'd been there nearly an hour when I saw my stepbrother's rusty truck pull up. I rubbed my temples and really hoped that Jackson wasn't driving—I wasn't in any shape to kick his ass today.

I was almost relieved when Renee jumped out of the truck and strode into the diner, a determined look on her face. She did a double-take when she saw me.

"What the hell happened to you?"

"Cut myself shaving."

"Did Jackson do that?"

I threw her an amused look.

"That bucket of lard couldn't hit his way out of a wet paper bag. Although," I admitted, "he might have a shot right now."

"Then who?"

"Does it matter?"

"I didn't think you were that unpopular in town." Then she narrowed her eyes. "Unless it's to do with that stuck up bitch you were with at the funeral. Bet her daddy didn't like that she's being screwed by a piece of trailer trash."

I stared at her coolly. "You speak about Tera that way again and I'll walk out the door right now. You'll get nothing. You'll have to take me to court and prove that Scotty is mine."

Her mouth clamped shut and she looked like she was trying to burn my ass to ash with her glare.

"Okay," I grimaced. "Now can we have a conversation about our ... about Scotty?"

She nodded once, but didn't speak.

I rubbed my eyes and leaned back in my seat. "You want a coffee or something?"

"Sure."

I waved at the waitress, and I saw her small eyes darting between us.

"Renee?"

"Hey, Della. Can I get a coffee and blueberry muffin?" Then Renee jerked a thumb at me. "He's payin'."

I couldn't help grinning at that, and Renee allowed herself a thin smile in return.

"So, how are we going to do this?" I asked when the waitress had left, still casting suspicious glances at us. "Have you said anything to Scotty yet?"

Renee shifted in her seat. "He doesn't need to know."

I stared at her in amazement. "Are you fucking kidding me?"

She shot me a defiant look. "Unless you can give us enough money to get the hell away, we have to stay living here. You don't think Jackson would toss us out if he knew?"

I thought about that: yeah, he definitely would.

"How much money would you need to be able to leave?" I asked quietly.

She licked her lips, clearly working out how much she could screw me for.

"Forty thousand."

I laughed at her incredulously. "You're crazy!"

"It's not even four thousand for each year of Scotty's life," she snapped back.

"That's not my fault! I would have stayed."

I shook my head as I rubbed my sore shoulder absently.

"I don't have that kind of money, Ren." Then I thought of the Duke—and the fact that I wouldn't be able to ride for a while. "But..."

Her eyes lit up with hope.

"But I can get maybe half that."

"How soon?"

"Couple of days. But I'll need that DNA test."

She scowled. "I told you: I don't have money for that."

"Fine, then let's take a cab to the lab and get it done now. I'll pay."

"Scotty's busy today."

I gave her a hard stare.

"He can be un-busy. He's my kid—I want to get to know him."

"What am I supposed to tell him?"

"Jeez, I don't know! How about the truth?"

"I told you—I can't."

Something wasn't adding up here. If she wanted out that badly, she would do anything, wouldn't she? Yeah, she totally would. Anything. Including scamming me.

"I guess I owe him a few birthday presents," I said casually. "When's his birthday?"

She didn't answer immediately. Did that mean she was working it out?

"It would have to be before the middle of March, because I left in June," I said tightly. "Don't even think about lying—I could ask anyone who knows him and they'd tell me the truth. Even if you won't."

Her chin jutted out as she stared at me.

"You asshole! He was born March 13th. He's yours. You're just a shitty excuse for a father."

My lungs contracted and I had to get away.

I pushed out of the chair so fast it tipped over. Heads turned and the waitress tried to give me the check, but a red rage was firing through me. I kicked open the diner's door and let the fury burst free.

I wanted to lash out at Renee. I wanted to hurt her the way she'd hurt me 12 years ago and again now. *Twelve years!* I should have known about my son. I should have known. I shouldn't have left—definitely shouldn't have left him with fucking *Jackson* for a father.

I paced up and down the sidewalk, adrenaline making my whole body quiver with pent up fury.

Too late, I realized that Renee had followed me into the street.

I reeled around and yelled in her face.

"What the fuck did I ever do to you, Ren? Why do you keep shitting on me? You think I wouldn't have taken Scotty in a heartbeat if I'd known? You think I wouldn't have helped you? I have no one! Nothing! I got a crappy mom and a stepfather who beat the shit out of me every day and twice on Sundays. *You* were the only good thing I had, and you..."

I couldn't speak anymore and if I didn't get away from her I'd do something really stupid.

I turned and punched the wall, seeing the skin split and watching as blood ran from my knuckles for the second time in two days.

"Tucker, no!"

She tried to grab my arm, but I shook her off and swung at the wall again, slamming my knuckles against the rough brick and hearing a satisfying crunch.

"I'm sorry!" she cried out. "I'm sorry! Tucker, stop!"

Her words penetrated the red mist and I lowered my hand.

"I'm sorry," she said again, her voice dropping to a whisper. "I was young and stupid. That's not an excuse, I know. I was desperate ... I've been desperate for a long time."

I looked at her—really looked. The last 12 years hadn't been kind. Deep grooves edged her mouth and her forehead was set in a frown, her skin dry and dull-looking. Her blue eyes that used to captivate me were diamond hard, although anguished now.

I couldn't hold the anger inside me any longer—I knew what she was prepared to do to get out. And I couldn't blame her.

"Come on," she said softly. "Let me take care of your hand."

I stepped away from her.

"I don't need your help. Not anymore."

I walked back in the diner, ignoring the stares and muttered comments.

In the bathroom, I rinsed off the blood and watched as the flesh swelled across the knuckles and started to bruise.

Great, just what I needed—now I was even more banged up.

I leaned my forehead against the greasy glass of the mirror and forced myself to calm the fuck down.

After a few minutes, the cold water was running clear. Spent adrenaline and unfamiliar emotion had left me feeling exhausted and empty.

I decided to pay the bill, walk to the fleapit and get my room back.

But Renee was waiting for me.

"That wasn't too smart," she said, her hands on her hips.

"Well, no one ever accused me of that," I bit out. "Tucker

McCoy is everyone's fool. Line up! Line up! Let's drown the clown."

"I don't know what you're talking about but you need to calm the hell down," she hissed.

Folks were looking and I knew that she was right, but it didn't mean I had to like it.

"Come on," she said. "Let's get out of here."

And she tugged my good arm toward the door.

"Like I'd go anywhere with you," I snarled at her.

She just shrugged. "You got anywhere else to be? Didn't think so. Now get in the truck."

Defeated, in pain, and too damn tired to argue, I climbed into the truck and waited for her to walk around to the driver's side.

The engine coughed and hiccupped, protesting loudly. I suspected the filters were clogged, but, whatever—not my problem. Or maybe it was. I was a father now—I should fix stuff for my family. But what was Renee? How did she fit in? How did *we* fit?

I let my head rest against the seat and closed my eyes. I didn't know where she was taking me and I was past caring.

To a basketball court, as it turned out.

"Why are we...?"

I recognized Scotty playing with some older kids.

I watched for a few minutes while Scotty raced around the court, dodging, turning, spinning and beating out the older guys who towered over him.

"He's good," Renee said softly. "Really good. But he's got no chance if he stays here. Another year and it'll be booze and weed and girls—you know how it goes, Tucker, you lived here. *You know*.

"There's a program for kids like him in Richmond. Jackson isn't interested and just says we haven't got the money to waste."

Her voice softened from disgust to despair.

"It's his chance to get out of here, Tucker. Mine, too."

I watched the game for several more minutes, aware that Renee was staring at me the whole time.

I didn't speak because I had no clue what to say, and I couldn't find a joke inside me to break the silence.

Eventually, it was Renee who spoke.

"I never meant for you to find out about Randolph and ... well, you know. I wouldn't have deliberately hurt you." She sighed. "I know you think we were in love, Tucker, but we weren't. I did care about you. I know it doesn't seem like it, but I did." She paused, "I do."

I shook my head in disbelief and her voice became more urgent.

"When you left, no one knew where you'd gone. You just disappeared. I thought you'd be back when you cooled down. But days passed, then weeks and then it was months. Me and Jackson ... well, we got together. When I knew I was pregnant, I had to drop out of school before Scotty came along."

She sighed.

"I didn't know what had happened to you until a year ago. I caught a news program about how that famous stuntman you ride with broke his back—and they mentioned your name. I couldn't believe it. All I could think about was getting in touch with you."

"For money."

There was a painfully long pause

"Yes," she admitted at last. "Money for Scotty."

I shook my head again, incredulous, unable to look at her. Then Renee gently laid her hand on my arm.

"That girl, the Senator's daughter—you like her, don't you?"

It didn't matter what I felt about Tera. Not anymore.

"I could tell she likes you, too. I mean, hell, she came to your momma's funeral."

"Yeah?" I said harshly. "Well, she sure doesn't like me after what you said to her."

Renee sighed. "I could talk to her..."

"You've done enough already. Anyway, she probably already left town."

Renee stopped talking and closed her eyes for a moment, her shoulders slumped.

"Where do you want to go? I'll drive you."

"The Happy Eater Motel."

"That dump?" she said in surprise.

I glanced across at her. "I told you I didn't have money."

We drove in silence and when she pulled up outside the hotel, I had nothing to say to her.

"Tucker, I'm sorry," she said again as I started to walk away. "I'll ... I'll get the DNA test. I'll do it today."

I nodded, but couldn't look at her.

"I'm heading there now—I'll tell them you'll be along with Scotty later."

Life was changing so fast. I was a father. I had a kid. What the hell did I know about being a father? I straightened up and stared at the sky.

Time to get my head out of my ass and find out.

After going to the lab and letting them take a swab from my mouth, I holed up in my room for the rest of the day, playing a game where I counted how many roaches scuttled across the floor in an hour. The record was 16.

But I thought about a lot of things, too.

I thought about Kes and Aimee, the years they'd spent apart, and the love that brought them back together; I thought about Zef and his brother Daniel, and how the death of their parents had made them close; I thought about Zach and Luke; I thought about Ollo, and how tough life could be when you were different. All carnies—the people who made up my family.

I thought about Momma and the stories she used to tell me

about my pa and how he liked messing with bikes too; stories that stopped when she married my stepfather. I thought about Renee and Scotty, and what she was prepared to do for her kid. I thought about myself and the way I'd lived and was still living.

And I thought about Tera, who'd blazed into my life like a shooting star, and was gone just as fast.

Then I picked up my phone and made a call.

Satisfied with the answer, I took double the number of pain pills I was allowed and passed out.

When I woke up in the morning, my body ached, but not nearly as badly as it had the day before. Better yet, my head felt clear. I still looked like shit, but I didn't care about that.

I thought back to the call I'd made the night before and was still satisfied that I'd made the right decision.

Maybe Tucker McCoy had grown up at last.

I sent a text to Renee to meet me in the diner in four hours.

I thought about texting Tera, but I had no clue what to say, so I took the coward's way out—I did nothing.

When I arrived at the diner, Renee was slowly shredding a napkin, waiting for me with a wary look.

"We going to do round two now?" she asked, her lips pressed together in a thin line.

"Maybe, that's up to you," and I passed her the envelope.

"What's this?"

"Well, it's easier to find out if you open it," I said, leaning back and gazing at her.

Frowning, she opened the envelope, then her eyes grew big and her hand flew to her mouth.

"Tucker, I ... I don't know what to say."

"There's nothing to say. You said you wanted to get Scotty out of here—now's your chance."

"But ... there must be thousands of dollars here," she said, rifling through the money.

"Twenty thousand dollars," I confirmed.

"But how? You said you were broke?"

I shook my head slowly. "I said I didn't have any money, and I didn't."

"Then how?"

I looked down at my arm in a sling. "The doc says I can't ride a bike for a month—maybe more. Can't do stunts for three. I've got my stunt bike back at the carnival. That's all I need."

She stared at me as understanding sank in.

"You sold that fancy Italian motorcycle?"

"Yes, ma'am."

"For me?"

"For Scotty."

She frowned.

"You were right, Renee. You should have been the one to get away from here. You're smart and Scotty seems like a good kid. I shouldn't have run out on you. I should have stayed ... I didn't protect you and I should have. So this is me, saying I'm sorry. Please take the money. Make a better life for both of you. I'll get more when I can. And then maybe ... maybe I can be a part of his life?"

She looked down at the money and sucked in a long breath.

"Thank you, Tucker."

"I don't want him to think I was a deadbeat who couldn't give a shit about him. But I know that you need to get away first. So when you get ... wherever you're going to go, you'll let me know? And I can ... I don't know ... come see you ... get to know him?"

She swallowed and nodded quickly.

"Do I figure in this?" she asked quietly. "You and me and ... could we...?"

I shook my head slowly, meeting her steady gaze. "That ship has sailed."

She closed her eyes and nodded again.

"I know."

When she looked up her eyes were glazed with a sheen of tears.

"I'm sorry ... for the way things worked out. I ... if there's anything I can ever do for you..."

I nodded.

"You could drive me to the airport."

She smiled and reached across the table to squeeze my good hand.

"I can do that."

Tera

With what was left of my pride, holding the shattered pieces of my heart in my empty hands, I'd left Tucker in the hospital, dried blood on his shirt, and I walked away.

I walked away.

I told myself that I had too much pride to chase a man who lied to my face, who had a son he'd abandoned. A man who didn't want me. But the truth was that I lacked the courage to go after what I wanted. Too much pride, but too little courage. And everyone would say I did the right thing.

How ironic.

Dad came to my hotel. I didn't even bother to ask how he'd found me or why he was there. He probably tracked my cell phone. Yes, he pretended he had some business to take care of in Nashville, and he asked me to help him out with the PR. But I wasn't a complete idiot; only when it came to Tucker, it seemed.

I went to the meetings Dad had lined up with his

connections in the city, and he introduced me as his daughter and PR expert. Whatever.

For the next two days, I went through the motions. I found it hard to look my father in the eye and wondered about confronting him. But what was the point? He'd just deny it, and he was much better at covering up a lie than I was. Although I was getting in some good practice now. "I'm fine," were words that fell from my tongue every hour.

I was relieved when his work was finished so I could head back to San Francisco. Emotionally, I felt like I'd been run over by a Mack Truck.

Senator Andrew Hawkins shrugged into his jacket and turned to me. He didn't even have to ask me to straighten his tie: it had been my special job since I was a little girl.

I smoothed out the double-Windsor knot, pretending it wasn't already perfect.

"Thank you, honey," he said, brushing a kiss over my hair. "It means a lot to me that you've been here to support your old dad."

I resisted rolling my eyes. My father knew that he still had it. His thick hair was silver at the temples, and a few laugh lines edged his eyes and mouth, but he was a good-looking man and appealed to both female and male voters. Plus, he was fanatical about staying in shape, saying that a healthy body meant a healthy mind, something I knew for a fact was bullshit. After all, he'd been cheating on Mom from the start of their marriage, and I'd begun to wonder if he wasn't still cheating on her. I didn't think either eventualities constituted anything but a healthy dick.

The bottom line was that my father is a good-looking guy at 50 and could pass for ten years younger—and he totally knows it.

My smile came out a little tight. I'd made it very clear that I didn't want to be here, that he'd coerced me. Whatever the Senator wanted—he always got his own way.

The Senator smiled and winked at me, and my breath caught. My God, how could I not have seen it before? He looked just like Kes before he went out to do a stunt: adrenaline, the excitement of performing for the crowd.

I looked away from him and concentrated on keeping a professional smile on my face in front of the people seeing us off: the perfect daughter of a potential Presidential candidate.

He'd gained a 15 point lead against his nearest rival over the last year—the revelation that he had two children out of wedlock had made him seem human and relatable. People loved it, especially as Mom had decided to stand by him. I knew Dad would have liked to have my older brother, Falcon, shoulder to shoulder with him, in his Air Force uniform, of course. But Kes … no, a carnival stunt rider couldn't help my father climb any political ladders. I had a feeling that Dad would still try to use my burgeoning relationship with Falcon as a means to that end. So far, he hadn't made a move, but my father was a patient man.

I hadn't wanted to stay here after everything that happened with Tucker, but Dad had gotten his own way as usual. He didn't need me at all. The Senate's PR team was more than capable of handling his visit.

I fingered the edge of my jacket, a lightweight raw silk. It was supposed to be cool to wear, but the stifling heat of a Tennessee summer was too much. I felt a bead of sweat trickle between my breasts, and I shifted uncomfortably in my four-inch heels.

Taking a calming breath, I walked behind my father as he made his way to the waiting limousine, smiling the way I'd been taught for the two journalists taking their last chance of a picture.

Dad's driver was taking me to the airport at Nashville, although he had another meeting to get to.

"Well, I think this has been a successful trip, don't you, Tera? I've got to say, working with my beautiful daughter is inspiring. We must do this again, sweetheart."

In some ways it would have been easier to just smile and nod, but I couldn't do it.

I turned to look at him.

"I know what you did to Tucker, Dad. What you had done to him."

"Tera, I..."

I raised my hand.

"Don't say anything."

"I have to, sweetheart, but I'm not going to apologize for looking after my little girl."

"I'm not a little girl. I'm 27."

He shook his head. "You're my little girl and always will be."

Then he took my hand in his and held it lovingly. I jerked my hand free.

"Beating up my..." I stumbled over the appropriate word to describe Tucker. "Beating up a man like that is not looking after me. It's cruel and it's wrong. I should report it to the police."

He raised his eyebrows, giving me an amused smile.

"That would be a pointless exercise."

"I know, so I won't. This time."

He frowned, his lips pressing together into a hard line.

"I know what guys like that want, what they're after. Hell, for all I know, Kestrel told him to do it just to get back at me. You know that you're the most important person in the whole world to me."

I could see the love and concern in his eyes, but he was wrong. So very, very wrong.

"Was the beating enough? Did he agree to stay away from me?"

My father's eyes widened in surprise.

"Oh," I said softly. "He didn't."

"It's a cruel world out there, Tera. You don't know. You don't understand..."

I gave him a grim look. "That doesn't mean you to have to protect me from the world."

"Yes, it does," he said fiercely. "That's exactly what being a father means."

I looked at him sadly. "But I'm not your only child."

He stiffened and looked away.

"I'll always look after my little girl," he repeated firmly.

"I know."

I gave him a quick kiss on the cheek and slid out of the car as the driver opened the door.

I was relieved that I could wait at the airport by myself, alone with my thoughts.

I bought myself a coffee and a gossip magazine to pass the time, enjoying the normalcy of being anonymous.

Or not.

Of all the luck!

I recognized Tucker immediately, his height, his lean muscled body moving with confidence in my direction. But his right arm was in a sling, and instead of his usual graceful movements, he was walking with a slight limp. His face was a mess too, a scab on his lip and another over a very black eye. I could tell that he was in pain from the permanent grimace that tugged at his lips. He was trying to carry his backpack and helmet in one hand, and avoid getting his damaged arm jostled by the crowd.

He hadn't seen me yet, so I slid lower in my seat, peeking at him over the top of my magazine. He looked tired and he hadn't shaved, that delicious golden scruff covering his face that I'd felt three nights ago between my legs.

I grew uncomfortably hot at the memory, but the rational part of my brain convinced my body to stay put.

I watched him until he was out of sight, then let out a long breath.

I didn't know whether to be pleased or disappointed that he hadn't seen me. It was going to be so awkward next time we met at Kes and Aimee's. He'd definitely been right about wanting to avoid that particular disaster. I wish I'd listened. Hopefully, by the time it happened, enough water would have flowed under that particular bridge.

I'd been a fool. Played by the ultimate player.

I was of two minds whether or not he'd deserved the beating my father's men had given him. I could have quite happily kicked his ass myself. But still, four or five on one—hardly a fair fight. But the other thing was...

"Hey, TC."

I nearly dropped my paper coffee cup when I heard him say my name hesitantly.

I looked up slowly, my eyes roving over his battered face.

"Do I know you?"

He forced a smile. "Not sure I know myself at the moment. Can I sit down?"

"Will it make any difference if I say no?"

His smile vanished and he stared at me intently. "Yeah, it will. Say the word and I won't bother you again."

Say no! Say no! Say no!

"Take a seat."

Oh God, why did I say that?

He smiled with relief, then carefully lowered himself into the plastic chair, wincing as he jarred his arm.

"How's the shoulder?"

I saw a flash of the old Tucker when he grinned at me.

"Shitty with a cherry on top."

"You look awful," I said, bitchiness and honesty combined in one short sentence.

He grimaced. "Yeah, I know. You look great though."

I rolled my eyes.

"I'm serious, you look amazing. But then you always do." His eyes dropped to the lapels of my jacket. "Classy."

We lapsed into silence as Tucker studied the faint scratches on his helmet that he'd propped on his knee, and I drank my coffee.

The silence became unbearable, but talkative, laughing, joking Tucker remained mute, and I wondered why he'd bothered approaching me in the first place.

"Are you getting your motorcycle shipped back?" I asked at last.

Tucker sighed and looked up.

"Nope. Sold it."

I gaped at him. "You sold it? Just because you can't drive it for a few weeks?"

He shook his head. "Not exactly. I needed the money, so..."

I put two and two together.

"Backdated child support?" I said briskly.

His mouth twitched and I saw a spark of anger behind his eyes, and I regretted my bitchy remark. But this man had the power to hurt me even worse. He'd warned me he didn't do relationships so it would be my own fault. Maybe if I made him angry enough, he'd just walk away. Because even now, I didn't know if I could.

"Anyway, didn't my father pay up?" I said bitterly. "Surely you'll get something for staying away from me?"

"I never took any money from him," Tucker snapped. "He never offered, but even if he had, I wouldn't have taken it."

His voice burned with sincerity and his eyes begged me to believe him. And I did. Dad had looked surprised when I'd mentioned a pay-off.

"You could have taken it for your son," I said quietly.

Tucker shook his head.

"No. I'll figure something else out about that. I'll be making good money again—soon as my shoulder is fixed."

"So you're leaving them behind again," I said, my voice flat with contempt.

He froze, his eyes glaring at me, then he slumped in his seat.

"Not exactly. They're leaving anyway. Scotty has a chance at a basketball scholarship to some fancy school in Richmond. Renee is taking him there. When they're settled, I guess I'll go visit. Try and ... I don't know ... be a father or something. I have no fucking idea how, but I want to be part of his life. I've just got a few things to figure out first."

"So, you and...?"

"Renee. She was my first girlfriend. We'd started dating when we were 13."

"And you left home when you were 17 because of her?"

"Yes!" he snapped, loud enough to make people stare at us. "Yes," he said again, in a slightly more reasonable tone. "But I didn't know she was pregnant, I swear."

He looked straight at me.

"She told me about Scotty two minutes before the funeral. I sat there the whole time feeling like I'd woken up in a nightmare. I was so fucking shocked. And then, what she said to you..."

"So, you really didn't know about Scotty?"

He shook his head vehemently.

"No."

"Then why did you leave all of those years ago?"

His lips twisted and he looked down.

"She was ... seeing someone else."

"She was cheating on you?"

"I caught her with ... another guy."

"Your brother Jackson?"

I couldn't hide the horrified tone in my voice.

"Maybe," he said slowly. "Later, obviously," and he laughed without any drop of humor.

"Then who? Who was she cheating with?"

"I don't know if you could call it cheating exactly..."

Tucker

Grow up, Tucker.

The memories play like a horror movie behind my eyes.

The day Harley Law crashed his bike, the day my life changed...

I rode home to get my tools to fix the dents in Harley's engine casing. I should have gone to the shed, but something drew me inside the house.

I remember walking into the living room.

I remember the breath catching in my throat, my lungs freezing.

I remember the blood draining from my face.

I remember seeing my step-daddy's hairy white ass pumping away between a pair of creamy thighs.

She looked up at me, her eyes impassive as her tits jiggled with every thrust. She watched me watching them.

She didn't say anything.

She didn't do anything.

He groaned as he came and then pulled out roughly.

Renee winced and closed her legs, but not before I saw his cum spilling out of her. Randolph rolled over and grinned when he saw me.

"Nice piece of pussy you got there, boy. Not as tight as it was, mind you."

Ice cold, shocked and humiliated, I stared at my stepfather, and I didn't know if I wanted to vomit or hit that motherfucker. I tore my eyes away from his grinning face and turned to look at Renee, waiting for her to say something, tell me he made her, something.

Randolph narrowed his eyes.

"I can tell what you're thinking, boy, but me and Renee got an arrangement." Then he jabbed her in the stomach. "Don't we?"

She lifted one shoulder in a callous shrug, then sat up to pull on her clothes. The crotch of her panties stained darker as his jizz leaked out. If she noticed, she didn't care.

"Same time next week, sweet thing," he said, sticking a couple of bills into her bra and smirking while his eyes stripped her bare again.

She brushed past me on her way out the door, and I followed, dazed.

When the front door slammed behind us, I grabbed her arm.

"Why?" I asked, my voice hoarse.

She pulled her arm free and scowled at me.

"You weren't supposed to be here."

"Answer me!"

"I'm saving up for college," she said defiantly. "In a couple of years I'll have enough to..."

"A couple of *years?*" I roared. "You going to keep whoring yourself with him?"

Her chin tilted up.

"It's nothing and he pays real good."

Nothing?

I knew I sounded pathetic when I asked, "What about me?"

What I really wanted to ask was, did it mean nothing when she did it with me, but I was too weak to ask—or to hear the answer.

She shook her head. "Nothing has to change."

For the first time I could remember, I felt tears prick my eyes. "You think I could ... when he...?"

She huffed impatiently.

"Grow up, Tucker."

Then she walked down the road and out of my life...

Tera covered her mouth with her hand as her eyes crinkled with horror and disgust.

"She was ... prostituting herself with your stepfather?"

And probably both my stepbrothers, too. Renee hadn't said and I hadn't asked—but it explained a few things.

"Yep, that's about the size of it."

"Oh my God," she said sadly.

I looked up, seeing nothing but pity in her face.

"I'm sorry you got hurt too, Tucker. I can't imagine how ... what drove her to make those choices. She must have wanted to get out so desperately. Why didn't she apply for scholarships, a student loan? Anything but *that*."

I shook my head.

"I don't know. She never said anything to me. I didn't know. If I had..."

Tera reached out and took my free hand in hers.

I'd made my peace with the past, and now my son needed money from the Duke more than I did. I could always earn a living—assuming my shoulder wasn't too fucked up.

I looked down at Tera's hand, the skin paler than mine, although not by much, but way, way smoother. There were no scars or scabs to spoil it.

I reveled in the feeling of her soft fingers stroking over the back of my healing knuckles.

"Now she's got her way out," I said quietly.

Tera's hand stilled, and I wished she'd go on touching me.

"What do you mean?"

I glanced at my helmet, abandoned on my backpack.

"Oh," she said softly, leaning back. "Your bike. You gave her your Ducati."

I winced at the reminder.

"Yeah, well, I sold it and gave her the money. Most of it, anyway. She's taken Scotty and left. Dropped me off at the airport an hour ago."

I looked up at Tera and gave a thin smile.

"She said that if I saw you, I should tell you that she was sorry." Then my expression turned serious. "And me. I'm sorry too, TC. So damn sorry."

I could see tears gathering in her eyes, and hell, if I didn't feel like crying myself.

"You're forgiven," she whispered.

CHAPTER TEN

TERA

My emotions were in complete meltdown. Tucker's grim story appalled me.

I read the newspapers, I knew what happened when poverty and hopelessness combined, but it had never affected me personally. Until now.

Tucker sat there and told me every part of his life story, holding nothing back. The beatings, the near starvation, eating dog food to silence the hunger pangs, stealing to survive.

In some ways it was banal and pathetic, the mundane drudgery of everyday living, but the raw honesty in his voice cut me deeply. I kept asking myself, *how could this happen?* We had a welfare system, a society that was largely well-meaning.

How did whole families, whole towns slip through the cracks like this?

I had no answer, nothing easy to offer, but I looked at this bloodied, bruised man in front of me and wondered how he survived to smile, to laugh at the world? Yes, I knew that was his shield, but it seemed as if he'd simply chosen to be happy, in whatever way he could.

And it also explained the string of one night stands: not getting serious meant not being hurt again. An easy equation.

And yet...

And yet the moment he'd heard about his son, he'd done the honorable thing.

My flight was called and Tucker stood up at the same time.

"You don't have to see me to the plane," I smiled.

He raised his eyebrows, "Uh, that's my flight."

"You're going to San Francisco?"

"Yeah, then I'll get the bus to Arcata."

"Oh! You're staying at the cabin?"

He nodded. "I talked to Kes and he says I can stay there till my shoulder's fixed."

I picked up my carry-on bag and Tucker frowned. "I'd take that for you, but..."

I smiled. "I'm not a damsel who needs rescuing, Tucker. In fact..." I snagged his helmet from the table, "...let me carry that for you."

It was so cute seeing him protest, but I winked at him and walked to the gate where boarding was about to start.

"Where are you sitting?" I asked.

"Um, 37C," he said, studying his boarding pass.

"Not for much longer."

Then I turned to the two air stewards.

"Hi, I wonder if you can help my friend. I've just found out that he's on the same flight as me, and as you can see, he's badly injured. I'd be able to take care of him so much more easily if he were next to me. Do you think you could upgrade him? Oh, I'm a Gold Card Club flyer, by the way."

The stewards exchanged a look, then set their approving eyes on Tucker who was grinning from ear to ear.

"It surely would be a kindness, ma'am," he said to the woman, using a more pronounced version of his usual honey and molasses accent.

I withheld an eye-roll as he seemed to be having the desired effect without any further help from me.

"I'll see what we can do, ma'am, sir," said the man, glancing at Tucker from under his lashes.

Ten minutes later, we were both seated in First Class.

"What would you have done if they'd said no?" Tucker asked, leaning back in the comfortable leather seat.

I shrugged. "I have a ton of air miles that I would have used instead. But I knew they'd take one look at you, all banged up and pathetic, and feel sorry for you." *Or the fact that you're seriously hot.*

And a father. He's a father to another woman's child!

"I could get used to this," he smiled. "But not if I have to use my face as a punch bag."

"Hmm," I muttered, my mood darkening.

"Hey, I deserved it," he said quietly.

"What? How on earth did you *deserve* it?"

My voice was incredulous, but Tucker just gave me a rueful smile.

"Your dad told me to stay away from you. I didn't. Hell, if I had a daughter hanging with a guy like me, I'd want to beat the shit out of him, too."

"Wait, what? When did he tell you to stay away from me?"

Tucker grimaced and looked down.

"The first night in town, before we were supposed to meet for dinner. This guy was waiting for me. He said it was my first and last warning. I guess your dad was serious—the guy plays hardball."

All sorts of conflicting emotions were at war inside me: fury at my father, irritation that Tucker hadn't said anything before, surprise that he'd stood up to the Senator, annoyance that he thought he deserved to be hospitalized, and a growing sense of joy that he'd wanted me enough to fight for me.

"So ... he really never tried to pay you to stay away from me?"

"No."

"But you let me think that about you?" His gaze dropped. "Why?"

Tucker sighed.

"I knew you were better off without me. I didn't want you to hate your dad because he was taking care of you."

Stupid, honorable fool.

"You know," I said conversationally, "I'm kind of pissed at you for only telling me this now. I'd have talked to my dad and told him to leave you alone. We could have avoided all of this," and I gestured at his battered face and damaged arm. "I keep telling you I'm not a delicate princess—I don't need to be protected. I'm strong. I can take it."

Tucker's eyes were warm and his smile bright.

"I know you don't need protecting, but it doesn't stop me wanting to."

I rolled my eyes. "Such a guy."

He leaned across so his lips were almost brushing my ear.

"I thought you liked that about me."

"You have your moments," I conceded.

He grinned and looked around at the luxurious surroundings.

"So, this is what first class feels like."

I smiled. "It gets better: wait till they bring the snacks."

A few minutes later, we were in the air and the stewards immediately offered us a glass of champagne each. Tucker's eyes widened in surprise, but before he could say anything, I ordered him a soda.

"You're on pain meds," I said severely. "You shouldn't mix them with alcohol."

"Okay," he said, smiling at me.

"Okay?" I blinked at him in surprise. "You're not going to argue with me? That's a first."

He shrugged his good shoulder, but his cheeks were slightly flushed.

"What?" I asked.

"Nothin'."

"It must be something—the infamous Tucker charm never takes no for an answer."

He glanced at me sideways. "I'm not used to having someone look out for me—other than Kes and the guys, and now Aimee, I guess. I'm not going to argue when you try to do something nice for me. Again."

I was floored by his sudden honesty. All of the men that I'd been out with before would have argued that black was white just to make a point.

"Don't be mad at your dad," he went on, his voice dropping to a low murmur. "He's just looking out for you, sugar. Can't blame him for that."

"No one has the right to brutalize another human being," I said softly. "No one."

We locked eyes, but the moment was interrupted by the arrival of our food.

Tucker's eyes widened at the plate of baked salmon, steamed vegetables and potato au gratin. And then he proceeded to inhale it like a starving man.

"Damn! You weren't wrong about the food!"

I laughed quietly. "It's even better when you taste it."

He gave me a sheepish look. "Yeah, sorry."

I nudged his good shoulder gently and smiled.

For the next seven hours we chatted easily. Tucker had stopped trying to charm me into bed and/or keep me at a distance with his jokes; and I stopped trying so hard to be the kind of woman he might want.

It also helped that we didn't discuss anything serious, only talking in general terms.

In other words, we relaxed with each other, but beneath that, the pull of attraction still fizzed silently.

Tucker napped for a while after dinner. He looked worn out. He'd even admitted that after the attack, he'd laid wide awake at the hospital until daylight, thinking about everything that had happened. The second night, he'd gone back to the roach-infested motel.

I watched him sleep, his breathing deep and even, and I wondered again if we could have a future based on more than friendship. But the problems of distance remained...

He stirred in his seat, and his eyelids fluttered. He started to stretch and then yelped as he moved his shoulder.

"Are you alright?"

He gave me a wry look. "Sure, except for the whole forgetting my-arm-is-in-a-sling wakeup call."

He struggled to get out of his seat.

"Can I help?" I offered.

He bent down so he could whisper in my ear.

"Well now, seeing as I'm going to take a piss, I'm not sure what you could do ... unless you're offering to hold my dick, in which case..."

"Yeah, yeah," I growled. "Don't open the wrong door while you're there—you didn't pack a parachute, and only angels and birds can fly. You, my friend, are feather-free."

He grinned at me and made his way along the aisle, exchanging a few words with the attractive brunette stewardess. And those few words certainly ruffled my feathers.

By the time he returned to his seat, I'd made my decision.

"I've been thinking..."

"Uh oh, sounds dangerous," he said with a smile.

"Funny ... not. Why don't you stay at my place tonight? I

have to go to work Thursday and Friday, but on the weekend, I'll drive you up to the cabin."

He blinked, looking surprised.

"You don't have to do that, TC. I can take the bus."

"Tucker, you're all banged up and you look like shit. Just ... let me help you. Friends help friends, right?"

He tilted his head to the side. "Friends?"

"Never been friends with a girl before?"

He chuckled quietly.

"Not so much. Unless you count Aimee—and she gets violent on my ass if I leave wet towels in the bathroom." Then his smile gentled. "If you don't mind having me around, that sounds pretty great." And as an afterthought, "Thank you."

"You're welcome."

The light came on to tell us to buckle our seatbelts—time for landing.

I gripped the armrest tightly, my heart beginning to race.

Tucker gave me an enquiring look. "Are you scared of flying, sugar?"

"Nope, not at all. I'm scared of crashing and dying a horrible, flaming death."

His frown deepened.

"But you didn't look worried before?"

"I wasn't, but when it gets toward the end of a flight I feel like my luck is already used up," I said plaintively.

"Naw, my girl's too brave for that," he said, unclamping my fingers from the armrest and holding my hand, stroking my knuckles soothingly.

My stomach lurched, a feeling totally unconnected with traveling at 500 mph.

I gave him a weak smile and tried to ignore the sinking sensation and the buzzing in my ears. Maybe it was the airplane after all—it was hard to tell.

Finally, we landed, and as we left the plane, the stewards all wished Tucker a speedy recovery. If they noticed me, I couldn't tell.

We had to wait forever to collect our bags and it was a relief when we could climb into a taxi to take us to my loft apartment in Mission Bay.

"Have you been here before?" I asked.

Tucker smiled.

"San Francisco? Yeah, although I was in Berkeley rather than this side."

"Oh really? Did you know someone who went to school there?"

Tucker's expression was amused, and I waved my hand dismissively.

"Obviously a woman, in which case I don't want to know."

He winked at me then went back to staring out the window.

My smile slipped. Being friends with Tucker would be hard if I felt the stab of jealousy every time he so much as mentioned another woman.

When we arrived at my apartment, Tucker let out a low whistle.

"Nice crib, TC!"

He gazed around, taking in the large living room and balcony patio, with views over the ocean.

I looked at it from his point of view. Nine months of the year he lived in the RV with three other people, sharing 400 square feet. My apartment was just for me, I had over 1100 square feet, and the rent was $3,600 each month. He'd been right about my father subsidizing my lifestyle.

The sense of privilege washed over me and I felt uncomfortable. Even though I'd always been encouraged to work, the family wealth was inherited.

Tucker coughed. "Uh, TC, you only have one bedroom in your apartment."

My cheeks flushed.

"Um, so, I didn't exactly think this through," I said, staring at him in dismay.

"It's cool," he said, giving me a brief smile, "I can sleep on the couch. It's still a hell of a lot better than sleeping in a Greyhound bus—trust me on that one."

"You can sleep with me," I blurted out, my cheeks on fire.

Tucker looked at me carefully.

"You sure about that?"

"We don't have to have sex," I said quickly.

Tucker gave me a wry smile.

"Yeah, I really don't think that's gonna work for me, TC," he said, shaking his head. "Having you in the bed next to me, all soft and smelling so good, it'll be pure torture not to be able to touch you. I'll take the couch."

"You can touch me," I said quietly. "I like it when you touch me."

Tucker swallowed, and I watched as his gaze tracked down my body.

"I thought we were going to give this friendship thing a try?"

I sighed. "Yes, sorry. You're right. It was a bad idea."

"I didn't say that," he muttered, just loud enough for me to hear him even though I pretended that I hadn't.

I sighed remembering all the reasons why sleeping with Tucker again was a bad idea: *manwhore, distance, absentee father, my brother's best friend.* Repeat ten times.

The mantra echoed in my head. Nope, it wasn't working.

He was honorable, kind, sweet, funny ... I still wanted him.

I cleared my throat. "There are some takeout menus in the drawer. Choose something: we'll order in."

"Pizza okay?"

"Knock yourself out. I'm going to unpack. The bathroom is through there."

I dumped my suitcase on the bed and started sorting the contents: laundry basket, drycleaners, back in the closet.

I heard Tucker order the food and then there were several minutes of silence. I wondered what he was doing, but when I looked up, he was leaning against the door watching me.

"Oh my God! You made me jump! Creep much, Tucker?"

"I'm in a woman's bedroom, it's like an instinct," he grinned.

I rolled my eyes. "That makes you sound so appealing."

He winked at me. "I could use a shower, if that's cool with you. I won't mind if you want to creep on me a lil bit, or if you want to conserve water."

"Friends, remember?" I laughed.

"Can't blame a man for trying."

I frowned when he left. His flirting was confusing me. Just being around him was hard enough. And it didn't help that I was flirting back. Hell, I even invited the guy to sleep in my bed —talk about mixed signals.

Belgian chocolates, toast drowning in butter, boxed sets of 'Sons of Anarchy'—why do we always want what's bad for us?

I heard the shower running and it made me want to walk inside and watch Tucker getting all hot and wet. No: friends didn't shower with friends.

To block out the sounds, I plugged in my iPod and blasted out Nate Ruess, but it couldn't block out the images of my increasingly feverish imagination. I could almost see the water running over his back, his chest, his taut stomach and tight ass, cascading over his hard...

I only just managed to hear the door buzzer and had to rush out to the annoyed pizza deliveryman. I was going to tip him double, but the way he looked at my boobs was probably enough of a gratuity.

I snatched the pizzas and stomped back inside, dumping them in the small kitchen.

I heard the shower turn off and a minute later Tucker

strolled into my living room wearing nothing but a pair of jeans. His wet hair was slicked back and water was dewing on his chest and arms, lazy drops rolling down the ridges and dips of his abdomen.

But those weren't the only things that caught my attention: his ribs and back were covered in bruises, fading from purple to yellow.

"Oh, Tucker!" I gasped, my eyes filling with tears.

He looked down at his chest, his expression rueful.

"It looks worse than it feels, sugar," and he reached into his backpack and pulled out a crumpled shirt to cover up the worst of it.

"I had no idea..." I said helplessly.

"I'm fine," he said, shrugging it off. "I've had worse."

I was having trouble believing him, especially when he put the sling back around his neck and situated his arm with a look of relief.

"I'm so sorry ... about my father."

He shrugged. "It's not your fault, TC."

"No, but ... thank you for not reporting him to the police."

Tucker shook his head. "I wouldn't do that to you."

I felt humbled by his words.

"Thank you," I said softly.

He smiled briefly, seeming uncomfortable with my gratitude.

"That pizza smells good," he said, heading for the kitchen.

While we ate, Tucker kept up a steady stream of jokes, mostly aimed at himself, as well as stories about life with the carnival. I knew he was deliberately distracting me, but I let it go.

After all, I'd already spoken to my father and doubted it made a shred of difference.

When Tucker finished his pizza, he took a beer out to the balcony and spent several minutes staring into the distance.

I wasn't used to having someone in my apartment and I kept throwing glances at his unmoving form. It was slightly unnerving.

When I met my friends, we mostly went to bars or clubs. Sharing a takeout meal in my apartment felt almost more intimate than the moment he had me naked beneath him, my body wet and wanting, the second before he pushed inside and made me scream his name.

But maybe takeout pizza was nothing to a practiced player like Tucker who was used to communal living.

Thankfully, he was surprisingly easy to have around, cleaning up after dinner, despite only having one arm that worked. Aimee had told me he was a slob in his own room, but when you had four adults living in the RV, you had to keep the family areas tidy.

He stretched his good arm over his head then yawned.

"Are you all tuckered out?" I asked drily.

He snorted with amusement. "I haven't heard that since grade school," he smiled. "But yeah, I'm pretty tired. I think I'll call it a night; I just need to ice my shoulder first."

"Oh, of course!"

I jumped up, annoyed that I'd forgotten he should do that.

"Did you remember to take your pain meds?"

"Yep, sure did. They're what's making me sleepy."

I passed him a bag of ice wrapped in a towel and he eased it onto his shoulder with a sigh, leaning back on the couch, his eyes closed.

"Thanks, Tera."

I was so used to him calling me 'TC', hearing my full name sounded more personal. I wondered if he knew he'd done it.

I left him on the couch and hurried through my nightly routine, pulling on the only cute pair of pajamas that I owned.

Then I had to climb to the back of my closet to find sheets and pillows for my unexpected guest.

Tucker smiled gratefully when I walked back in, murmuring that he'd take his turn in the bathroom.

I made up the couch and waited for him.

"Are you gonna tuck me in, TC?" he asked with a cheeky grin.

"Don't push your luck, McCoy!"

I turned to walk away, but he caught my hand.

"Wait, TC! I just … thanks for letting my sorry ass stay at your place. After everything that went down, it's really nice of you."

He squeezed my fingers gently, sincerity shining in his eyes.

"You're welcome," I whispered, as he let my hand go.

"Tera," he called after me. "I don't know how it will be with Scotty. I don't know how to be a father…"

"You'll be a great dad, Tucker. I know you will."

He shook his head, his eyes defeated.

"I'm going to try, but…" and he looked up at me. "I'm not with Renee, and I'm not going to be. I just … I wanted you to know that."

I nodded, but didn't speak. If I had, I might have cried.

CHAPTER ELEVEN

TERA

I tried to sleep.

I needed to be at work at 8AM and it had been a tiring week. But even though I screwed my eyes shut and lay as still as a plank of wood, sleep eluded me. Instead, all my moments with Tucker ran like an erotic, pornographic movie behind my eyelids.

Frustrated, I opened my eyes, staring up at the ceiling.

The blanket of darkness left my eyes wide open, giving me too much space to think. Too much room to corral my wayward thoughts. Too much thinking, too many thoughts, and I tossed and turned restlessly.

The Pacific breeze set off the wind chimes that I kept on the balcony, a sound I usually found soothing, and even the quiet hum of the air conditioning seemed loud.

I was listening out for Tucker: a rustle of sheets as he moved around on the couch, soft footfalls on the floor that meant he was coming to my room. But there was nothing.

Silence.

Sighing with frustration, I tiptoed into the kitchen to get a drink of water. Yes, I *could* have gotten water from the bathroom, and yes, I *could* have walked through the bathroom to get to the kitchen. I just happened to walk through the living room instead.

I could see the bulky outline of Tucker's body on the couch. The sheet had slipped to his waist and I paused beside him, staring at his hard chest, examining the darker shadow of his bruises now that he'd removed his shirt again.

I jumped when he spoke.

"Can't sleep, sugar?"

"No," I whispered, then wondered why I was whispering. "No," I said again, more clearly.

"Me neither."

He sat up slowly, careful of his damaged shoulder. Then his eyes traveled across my body, pausing at my chest, before looking up at me.

"This 'friends' thing is hard," he said ruefully.

I flopped down next to him on the couch.

"Why did we decide to do this again?" I asked.

He shook his head and sighed. "Because we're on two different roads, TC. Crossing paths was an accident, but it's not meant to be."

I suppressed a giggle at his serious tone. "You've been hanging out with that old fortuneteller too much."

He smiled. "Yeah, probably. Doesn't make it any less true though."

"Can't we make our own road, choose our own path?"

"Do you want to?"

I nodded fervently, but Tucker looked away.

"I don't see how we..."

I placed a finger against his lips.

"Let's just try."

He reached for me and then hesitated.

"Fuck, Tera, if we start, I won't want to stop."

"I'm not asking you to stop."

I straddled his lap, lightly resting my hands on his shoulders, and pressed my lips gently against his. A low growl sounded in his throat and he kissed me back, deeply, passionately with an edge of reckless desperation.

"I've been wanting to do this since Nashville airport," he grit out, as his hands slid around to the small of my back, pulling me firmly against his fast-growing erection.

My hands wound into his hair, tightening roughly as our breaths grew ragged, and the way he held me bordered on the edge of painful.

When his hands slid under my pajama top, I could feel his rough palms on the smooth skin of my back, his short nails tracking over my spine. Then he tugged on the hem of my shirt and started to pull it over my body, but let out a curse as he raised his hands.

"Fuckin' arm!"

He slumped back against the couch massaging his shoulder, his lips peeled back in a grimace.

"Are you alright?" I gasped, laying one hand against his chest, feeling his heart pounding furiously.

He nodded quickly.

"Yeah, sorry. I just forgot..."

"It's okay. Let's go to my bedroom. We've got more room. And then I can ride you properly."

His eyes widened in shock. "Hearing you talk like that...!"

"I'm not a princess, Tucker. I'm a woman. I thought you knew that."

"Fuck, yeah!" he grunted, his voice husky.

I shuffled back off him, missing the hot press of his body against mine.

"Wait," he said standing up, his voice an intense rumble. "Your shirt..."

I yanked it over my head and he was on me instantly,

187

licking, biting, sucking, kissing, kneading my breasts with his hands, lowering his face to meet them.

"Bed—more room!" I gasped, tearing myself away before he took me right there.

But we didn't get that far. I crashed into the breakfast bar and Tucker hoisted me up awkwardly with one arm.

"Lift!" he ordered, tugging on the lower edge of my pajama shorts.

I held my weight on my hands as I lifted my butt and he yanked the material off. The granite counter was cold, making me shiver.

Tucker knelt in front of me, pushing my legs apart. I felt wanted and wanton, my head thrown back, my breasts jutting forward, my hands gripping the hard granite. Heat poured from my body, rivulets of sweat running down my back. He nuzzled my stomach, then spread hot kisses over my pubic bone before I felt his tongue pressing inside as he spread me out like an X-rated buffet.

I cried out and my knees shook.

Tucker licked and sucked the soft skin of my inner thigh, then his tongue disappeared inside me. In seconds, I was clenching around him, only his strong hands keeping me from crushing his head with my legs.

I felt Tucker's soft laugh against my swollen clit, the vibration sending a thrilling shock through my whole body. I gripped onto his hair with both hands, tugging hard.

He hissed as my knuckles whitened, pulling his hair harder, and he retaliated by biting at the soft flesh of my inner thigh.

"Oh, sorry!" I gasped, easing my grip.

He didn't reply, but slid one hand to my ass, pulling my mound closer to his face, burying himself in my short curls. Looking down, all I could see was the top of his head, but the sounds! I could *hear* how wet I was, and if I wasn't so close to coming, I would have been mortified.

Tongue, fingers, teeth—his furious attack, his focused concentration, his need to pleasure me regardless of his own arousal sparked my orgasm, catching fire as tremors ran up my body, finally igniting in a rush as my eyes closed and fireworks exploded through my brain.

Pushing me wider, he bit down on my clit, then sucked it hard as I came and came, trembling and groaning.

"I need ... I need..." he hissed, his voice sending a shudder through me.

The words were ripped from him unwillingly, Tucker reluctant to admit how much he wanted this, too.

"What do you need?"

He shook his head slowly.

"You're asking questions ... can't think ... no blood in my brain..."

A breathy giggle erupted out of me and I stood on Bambi legs. Tucker followed quickly, catching my hand in his and kissing me senseless all the way to my room. Against the wall, by the hallway, thudding against the door as we crashed into my room, mindless with need, eyes clouded with desire.

He was naked except for a pair of tight-fitting gray briefs that left nothing to the imagination. Besides, I'd seen Tucker fully erect before, and even now, the head of his dick was pushing out of his waistband.

I gripped hold of him, pressing over the soft material, and I felt the muscles of his stomach tense, his breath hitching at the same time.

Suddenly I wasn't moving fast enough, and Tucker all but dragged me with him.

As I hit the bed, my knees started to buckle and I fell backwards, Tucker's one good arm not enough to hold me up any longer.

Vaguely, I was aware of the soft rustle of cotton and the mattress dipping as Tucker climbed in beside me. I felt his aggressive tongue on my breasts, his teasing bites that had me gasping, and finally as he kissed me deeply, I tasted sweet Tucker and my own salty arousal.

"Don't stop," I muttered hazily, another orgasm hovering just out of reach.

"Wasn't gonna."

I felt the blunt head of his dick at my entrance, rock hard, patience gone as Tucker rotated his hips, ready to crash inside me, but I managed to think coherently and pushed him away.

"Condom!" I hissed, my voice urgent.

His eyes widened. "Shit! I've never forgotten that before. Please tell me you have some in your bedside drawer."

I laughed breathlessly. "I do, but I'm not sure you'll want to wear it."

"Why the hell not?"

"It's a novelty one that a girlfriend gave me. It, um, glows in the dark."

Tucker laughed hoarsely. "Hell to the yes, even if my dick is going to look like Dr. Banner getting his freak on."

I reached into the drawer while Tucker rolled onto his back, his chest and stomach rising and falling rapidly.

"Put it on, sugar," he said, his voice like gravel. "I want to see your hands on my dick."

"I can do better than that," I whispered.

I knelt down and pulled his dick toward me, the leaking head glistening. Sucking deliberately hard, Tucker's hips convulsed toward me and a string of impressive curses rolled from his dirty mouth. In one, long, swallowing motion, I took him inside me.

His tip hit the back of my throat and I moaned around him.

"God, Tera! That sound! You rock my world."

His hands grabbed my hair, pulling me in more firmly.

It didn't feel like friendship or even friends with benefits: it felt possessive.

And I liked it.

Tucker

This whole evening—hell, this whole day—had been a complete mind-fuck.

I'd woken up alone, my shoulder pulsing with pain, the owner of a $25,000 Ducati Panigale Super Sports motorcycle.

Now I was broke, bikeless, a busted flush, being given amazing head by the sexiest goddamn woman I'd ever met.

The only thing that hadn't changed was my fucked up shoulder. And the fact that my kid was out there in the world.

I was thrown, I admit it.

Nothing made sense, but at this moment, this wonderful crazy moment, everything made sense.

I looked down at the hotter than hell sight of Tera's blonde hair sweeping over my thighs, her red lips stretched around my dick.

As I watched, my mouth hanging open, my chest heaving, I thought I could see her eyes watering. The faint orange glow of street lights shining through her window made it hard to tell, but I gently eased her off of me anyway.

I pulled her onto my chest, kissing her hard to show my appreciation, then I grabbed the condom from the sheet where she'd dropped it and handed it to her.

She stretched out her neck and worked her jaw some. *Yeah, sugar, I'm a big boy.*

Watching her tear open the packet while her eyes were fixed on mine was enough to make my brain melt.

For the first time in a long while, I wondered if I was going to last. I was so damn horny, the odds weren't good.

Then she rolled the thin latex down my shaft ... and burst out laughing.

My dick was lit up like a fucking neon sign, glowing a

ghoulish yellow, the kind of thing you'd find in the Ghost Train ride at the carnival.

"Jeez, TC, you can't laugh at him—he's sensitive like that."

"I can't help it," she wheezed, "he looks so cute in his little jacket. Like a miniature Homer Simpson."

"Yeah? Well, Homey is looking for his Marge—come here, sugar," and I grabbed my glowing dick with one hand and guided her hips down with the other, at severe risk of passing out from the pain in my shoulder. It was the only thing that kept me from coming on the spot.

Breath hissed out of her in a long, sexy growl, and she arched her back, taking me in deeper. Then she grabbed her tits and started massaging them, and suddenly I was starring in my favorite porn movie—except that I wasn't going to get a strange girl deciding to sit on my face later. But hell, reality was better than any two-dimensional digital chick.

She kneaded those amazing tits together, working the nipples, her body writhing from side to side and up and down, drawing my dick in circles. I had to close my eyes and focus on my throbbing shoulder or I would have shot my bolt there and then.

But when her breathing started to quicken, I spread my hand over her belly and used my thumb against her clit.

She screamed out my name, *my name*, and tightened around me, drawing a powerful orgasm up my shaft that left me gasping beneath her.

Tera fell forward onto my chest as my body continued to pulse inside her, and soft arms fastened around my neck, her breathing harsh in my ear.

An intense wave of emotion rushed through me. How could I ever be enough for a woman like this? Beautiful, smart, funny, kind—and rich. I couldn't forget that. What chance in hell did I have to make a woman like this stay? She'd run from me. She *should* run from me. I had nothing to offer—less than nothing.

But for the first time in a long time, I wanted a woman to need me, to hold onto me and never let go. If only I could be the man worthy of her. But I wasn't.

And I had to accept that all I'd ever have would be this.

I had to live for the moment—whether I wanted to or not.

I'd nearly blown it by boning her without a rubber.

After the shitstorm with Renee and learning about Scotty, the thought of doing that to Tera was horrifying. I knew she was on the pill, but I couldn't risk fucking her without protection for her sake. Yeah, I'd always wrapped it, but some of the skanks I'd been with … not something I felt too proud of right about now.

I decided I'd make an appointment at the local clinic when I was up in Arcata and get tested for everything. It was the least I could do. The very least.

I lay on my good side in TC's enormous as fuck bed, sweaty from some really amazing sex. My shoulder hurt like hell, but she didn't need to know that and besides, it was so worth it.

Curled up beside me, she trailed her fingers over the top of the tattoo that started on my shoulder, her expression thoughtful.

"Are you ever going to tell me about the tattoos? Please, I'd like to know. You tell me what you think I should hear, but I want to know *you*."

I frowned. "It's not a pretty story, TC."

"None of them are," she said sadly, "but tell me anyway."

I sighed and closed my eyes. Even then I could feel her patient gaze as we laid facing each other. We'd been naked together for hours, but speaking these words stripped me bare. I had no defenses left with Tera.

I took a deep breath.

"After I'd seen Renee with Randolph ... with my stepfather ... I had to leave. I couldn't handle thinking about her like that. So I threw some shit in a bag and headed out on the I-40. I rode all night, only stopping when I needed to fill up the gas tank. I just kept going until my eyes were closing and I damn near drove off of the road."

I felt her drop a soft kiss on my shoulder and paused as she stroked the small of my back.

"Go on," she encouraged.

"You sure you want to hear this?"

"I want to know *you*, so yes; the answer is yes."

I sighed and rested my head on my hand before continuing.

"I didn't even know the name of the town or which state I was in. But I found myself downtown, drinking in a real sleaze pit. I had fake ID, but no one cared enough to even look at it. I bought a bottle of tequila ... and that was the last thing I remembered."

Tera pushed a lock of sweaty hair from my face, concern shining in her crystal blue eyes.

I craned my neck to kiss her lips lightly and she smiled.

"The tattoos?"

"I don't remember, and that's the truth. But I woke up with my sleeping bag glued to my back and the skin was sore and throbbing. Although to be fair, my whole body was throbbing in time with the mofo of all hangovers."

Tera laughed lightly.

"Exactly how much had I drunk the night before? I had no idea."

I rubbed a finger across my eyebrow, remembering.

But here's the thing that I've learned about drinking: it only numbs the pain, it doesn't kill it. And with the sun searing my eyeballs, every gut-wrenching memory poured back in Technicolor.

"Well, I managed to roll onto my side before I puked, so the day didn't start completely shit." I glanced at Tera but my lame joke seemed lost on her. "I squinted up at the sun, then immediately shut my eyes again, rolling onto my back. But the second I did, a bolt of pain shot up my side. That's when I looked over my shoulder."

I mimed the whole *what the fuck?* look that I must have had on my face, and this time Tera laughed.

"Jeez! Just when exactly did I get a freakin' tattoo? Man, that is ugly!"

Gingerly I rolled onto my front so Tera could more easily trace over the four stars spilling down my back, outlined with thick black ink.

"Why stars?" she asked.

I had no idea why I chose stars. Maybe because they seemed so distant, glittering, peaceful compared to how I was feeling.

I felt disgust and hatred toward Randolph, but it was Renee who'd damn near broke my heart.

I turned my head to Tera and gave her a small smile.

"Well, I was too drunk to remember talking about it with the tattoo artist, but thinking about it later, maybe I thought that if Fate or life or my own damn family was going to shit on me, I'd smile at them all. I'd keep smiling till my lips cracked, and I'd *never* let them know that they'd beaten me."

"I can understand that," she said softly. "The first time I saw you, standing by that bonfire, you were laughing. Wherever you go, people smile. I remember thinking, *Oh, that's him—that's Tucker—Smiling Tucker McCoy*."

She paused.

"You don't have to smile for me, Tucker, not unless you want to."

I held her small hand in mine and kissed her smooth skin.

"It wasn't all bad, sugar, because that's the day I joined the carnival."

. . .

I remember someone shouted at me in guttural Spanish. A short fat guy with thick black hair was standing over me.

When he saw my confused frown, he spoke in heavily-accented English.

"Hey, gringo! You can't sleep here."

I staggered to my feet, staring around me.

"Where am I?"

"A bad place, kid," he said, shaking his head. "You should leave. And get yourself an AIDS test after getting marked in a shithole like that—people piss in the alley where you were sleeping, and that *bastardo* uses dirty needles."

He threw me a sympathetic look as I gagged, my empty stomach spilling out what was left of the tequila I'd drunk the night before.

The tattoo parlor had a broken neon sign advertising its services, and was next to a toilet. I heaved again, then forced a smile.

"If I die young, at least I'll leave a good-lookin' corpse."

The man rolled his eyes and wandered away, shaking his head and muttering to himself.

I looked around me again. There was nothing that gave a clue as to where I was.

I stood up, reeling slightly as I tried to get my balance. Je-zus! What loony juice did I drink last night?

I patted my pants pocket, relieved to find my wallet and cell phone. But the battery was dead and I'd forgotten my charger when I'd slung a few clothes in my backpack and left Tennessee for good.

Maybe I could sell the phone because there was no one I wanted to call. I hesitated for a second, wondering if I should try to message Brandon, but then I shrugged off the idea. He'd always talked about going away to college, so he was leaving

Tennessee anyway. He'd understand, I hoped.

When I checked inside my wallet, my smile slipped for a moment—twenty bucks wasn't going to get me far. I had $237 in my checking account, but I'd have to be careful until I could get a job, because there was no way in hell I was going to turn tail and go back. I'd rather starve.

But first of all I needed water—a lot of it, and some greasy food to stick to the sides of my stomach. If I could force it down long enough to do some good.

My bike was in the alleyway where I'd left it, but it stunk of piss and I guessed that some asshole had drained the pipe without caring what he was doing. Hell, for all I knew, it could have been me. I smiled at the idea of marking my territory with my own piss.

Yep, I'd smile till my teeth fell out. Nothing would stop me smiling.

Talking to some locals, I learned that I hadn't wandered across the Mexican border in the dark. I was in Leary, Texas ... wherever the hell that was. I must have crossed the State line during the night.

Hot, yellow dust and jewel-blue skies; men with leathery skin and wide-brimmed Stetsons strolled in high-heeled cowboy boots. Where I came from it was more truckers' caps and work boots.

I pushed my bike to save gas until I could find an ATM. I found a cheap tapas bar first, and bought a tortilla filled with chili, while the cute Latina waitress brought me a jug of water and a clean glass. I smiled at her and winked, grinning to myself when she blushed.

Then the image of Renee came into my mind, and the smile almost choked me.

By midmorning, I'd pushed that damn bike across half the town and still couldn't find an ATM that would take my card. I was beginning to feel desperate when I heard the sound of tinny music.

I glanced up, wiping the sweat from my face with my arm, and saw the towering skeleton of a Ferris wheel with bright red and yellow buckets turning slowly through the scorching air.

Maybe I should just run away and join the circus. Well, I'd already done the running away bit. I could ask around if they had work.

An older woman with brassy blonde hair was sitting by the entrance selling tickets.

She looked me up and down, her hard eyes seeing right through me. Her eyeballs crawled along the bare skin of my arms, a feeling like ants were swarming all over. I had to stop myself from scratching.

"You can't take that motorcycle inside, kid."

"No, ma'am. I was wondering, you got any work? I'll do pretty much anything."

She squinted at me.

"Law after you?"

"No, ma'am," I answered, trying to look trustworthy.

"Family?"

"No one who'd care," I replied truthfully.

"Hmm..."

Her eyes skated over me again, making me shiver.

"How old are you?"

"Eighteen," I lied.

"Kind of scrawny for 18," she said, raising her eyebrows.

"Must be 'cause I'm a hard worker," I smiled at her. "Just all gristle and muscle."

She laughed, showing a gap where her front teeth should be.

"I like you, kid. Go see Landon. He might have something for you."

Walking through the archway into the fairground, the door to my old life slammed shut behind me. I'd found a new way to live.

. . .

I glanced at Tera who was listening intently, her face screwed up in a cute little frown.

"Is that where you met Kestrel?"

"Nah, I didn't meet him till much later. I spent six years as a roustabout, then mixed that up with a little stunt riding, Wall of Death, you know?"

Tera smiled. "I do now, although I'm finding it's a learning curve."

"Yeah, you gotta learn the lingo, sugar. So I did that for a while and then I met Kes."

She sighed. "You've known him longer than I have and he's my brother!"

I could hear the frustration in her voice.

"Don't think of it that way," I said gently. "It's not the length of time you've known someone that matters. I've known my stepbrothers since I was in first grade: they were shitty then, and they're fat and shitty now. But Kes is solid—you're his family and he'll do anything for you."

She nodded slowly. "The carnies are his real family though—you and Zef, Zachary, Luke, Ollo. And Aimee," she added with a smile. "She's a carnie now, too."

We stared at each other, each acknowledging the truth the other told. Family: that was a loaded word.

"So where does that leave us?" she asked, her voice quiet, hesitant.

My reply was reluctant. "I don't know."

It wasn't the answer she wanted to hear.

CHAPTER TWELVE

TUCKER

I woke when an alarm started ringing in my ear.

"Urgh, what?"

"Shh," said Tera. "I have to get up for work, but it's early, go back to sleep," and she silenced me with the briefest of kisses.

I was vaguely aware of the shower running in the bathroom as I dozed through a haze of meds and too little sleep.

When she came back into the bedroom and dressed, I woke up enough to enjoy the show, and my dick definitely wasn't behaving like a gentleman either.

Tera laughed when her eyes dropped to the sheets below my waist.

"Hold that thought; some of us have to go to work," and she sighed. "I'll try and get out early and be back by five. I've left a spare key on the breakfast bar and there are coffee beans in the fridge." Then she paused. "I *will* see you later, won't I? You're not going to run out on me?"

I shook my head and grinned at her.

"Nope. The lady offered me a ride—and I don't get an offer like that every day."

Tera smirked. "I bet you do, but never mind. I'll see you later."

"Hey," I called after her. "Don't I get some sugar before you go?"

She laughed and walked back to the bed, her tight skirt sculpting her ass, as she kissed me quickly.

"Get some rest!" she ordered, skipping away from my roving hands.

"Yes, ma'am," I sighed, happily sinking back into sheets that smelled like her.

I was surprised when less than an hour later, Tera returned.

I'd taken her advice and gone back to sleep, enjoying the wide, comfortable bed and soft clean sheets.

Her bedroom door opened and I sat up sleepily.

"Hey, sugar, you forget someth...?" and then I froze.

An older woman with silvery-blonde hair was staring at me, appalled shock written across her face, both hands clutching the string of pearls around her neck.

"Who...?" Then she collected herself and stood up straighter. "Good morning. You must be a friend of Tera's. I'm her mother, Catherine Beaumont Hawkins."

I felt my cheeks heat, reddening uncharacteristically. I suddenly felt very naked lounging in Tera's bed, as if she was some sugar mommy and I was a guy she paid by the hour to warm her sheets while she went to work.

"Tucker McCoy," I managed, my voice sounded like I was ten years old before my balls dropped.

Tera's mother took a step closer, extending her right hand, then glancing at the sheet that had slipped below my navel, and thinking better of it.

"Perhaps we can continue this conversation in the living

room," she said calmly, backing away and closing the door behind her.

I flopped back on the pillows, trying to convince myself that the last 30 seconds hadn't happened, that my first introduction to Tera's mother wasn't when I was naked and, oh shit, sporting a raging boner because I'd been dreaming about her daughter.

But then I heard the coffee machine in the kitchen and knew I definitely hadn't imagined anything.

I rolled out of bed, cursing my useless arm and weighed up how disrespectful it would look if I made her wait while I took a quick shower.

Nah, the minute it would take to get clean would be well spent—much better than drinking coffee with Tera's mother while I reeked of sex from the night before.

Showering in record time under a spray of cold water, I pulled on my jeans then searched through my backpack for something to wear. I had clean t-shirts, but I couldn't get them on, and my button-up shirt was somewhere in Tera's living room.

In the end I decided that Mrs. Hawkins had probably seen a man's bare chest before—maybe even the Senator's—and mine would be mostly covered up by my sling anyway. A quick check in the mirror told me that the bruises had faded, but were still obvious. Then I reasoned that it was her chickenshit husband who'd had his goons put them there—she could damn well look at them.

I felt her cool eyes assessing me as I walked out of the bedroom. I tried to look casual as I glanced around the living room, wondering if my shirt would materialize before her gaze froze me to the spot.

"Are you looking for your shirt?" she asked politely. "I hung it over the back of the chair—I do so hate wrinkled clothes."

Was she for real? Was I supposed to thank her?

I muttered something indistinct and shrugged my left hand into it, fighting with my sling as I struggled with the other arm.

"That looks awkward," she said. "Let me help you with that."

Her pale hands were gently easing the material over my shoulder before I knew what she was doing. It felt ... uncomfortable.

"My, those are some nasty looking bruises."

Damn right—thank your husband.

She even buttoned my shirt, bottom to top, which was all kinds of weird.

"There," she said, smoothing out the wrinkles on my arms and patting my chest. "All done."

"Uh, thanks. Thank you, ma'am," I spluttered.

"Oh!" she said, a bright smile on her face. "Are you Southern? How charming! I do love a southern accent. Where are you from?"

"East Tennessee originally, so not really sou—"

"My daughter was just there with her father. Is that where you met?"

"Yeah, but..."

"And what business brings you to San Francisco, Mr. McCoy?"

"I..."

"Or maybe this is just a vacation?"

"No, I'm..." *Reeling from all your goddamn questions!* I took a deep breath. "That coffee smells d— mighty fine, ma'am," I said, pouring a cup and smiling to myself as her eyebrows shot up. "TC didn't tell me that you were in town."

"No indeed," she said, her icy blue eyes fixed on mine. "My visit was a surprise," and she smiled coolly at me. "In more ways than one." She took a sip of her own coffee. "I didn't know Tera had a new friend."

I bristled at the word 'friend' but tried not to make it look too obvious.

"You were saying where you met my daughter."

No, I wasn't.

"Tera's at work," I said, hoping she'd take the hint.

"And you're not, Mr. McCoy. How nice for you to have some time off. You do work, I take it?"

Enough of this shit!

"I'm a motorcycle stunt rider. I work with Kestrel Hawkins, your husband's son."

She blanched and set down the coffee cup, unable to hide the tremor in her hand. But she was a cool customer and placed her hands into her lap, giving a light, silvery laugh.

"Goodness! What a small world it is. I've always thought it must be charming to live with so many people. And such a change to be in a cosmopolitan city instead of all those sweet little towns in the Midwest. And it must be so pleasant for you to visit a lovely spacious apartment like Tera's. Of course, this is small compared to the house where she grew up. Oh my, she did love to ride her pony across the grounds. Such a lovely environment for a child to grow up in, don't you think?"

"I wouldn't know," I said, gritting my teeth.

"No, I suppose not." Then she gave a fake sigh. "My daughter has had a very privileged life, but she wears it so lightly. She has a gift, the way she can talk to people of any class."

My chest tightened at her words.

"She must get that from her father," I retorted.

Her left eye twitched, but the smile stayed on her face.

"She's such a homebody, as I'm sure you've realized. I've always felt that when she meets the right man, she'll make a lovely mother. But of course, there's nothing wrong with having a little fun first." She laughed again. "Oh, forgive me rattling on like that: perhaps you have children of your own?"

I drank the rest of my coffee and placed the empty cup on the table and didn't reply.

"Oh well, I suppose the traveling carnival is a very difficult environment to bring up children. It wouldn't be fair on little ones, would it?"

"People manage," I snapped at her.

"Yes, I'm sure they do, but Tera can do so much better than just 'manage'."

We glared at each other across the kitchen table.

"Tera's a grown woman—she can make her own decisions."

"Well, of course she can," chuckled the Senator's wife. "But she's such a soft-hearted girl—it would be so easy for her to be swayed by a hard-luck story. I hate to think of people taking advantage of her. Being a parent, it brings out one's protective instincts."

She ran her eyes over my bruises and the cut above my eye, and I knew without any fucking doubt, she knew exactly who had put them there.

She smiled, and I could tell that she'd made her point: I was shit and Tera could do better.

It wasn't as if that was anything I didn't know already.

She glanced at her wristwatch then picked up her purse.

"Such a pleasure to meet you, Mr. McCoy. Have a safe journey back to the circus."

And then she left.

I slumped in my seat, feeling like I'd just gone ten rounds with Floyd Mayweather's scarier mom—and lost.

Tera

I was in a Tucker-induced daze at work. Good sex will do that to you ... great sex seems to suck out rational thought completely. And I was speaking from recent experience.

Which wasn't good when I was snowed under. My desk was

covered in a flurry of paperwork, and I could barely see my computer screen for post-it notes stuck all over.

My manager, Lorraine, wanted a blow-by-blow account of every meeting I'd been to in Tennessee, demanding reports in full immediately. She was making the point that just because the client was my father, that didn't mean I could get away with being unprofessional. I didn't need the lecture, but I smiled through it anyway. Bitch.

I headed back to my desk to start on the paper mountain. But first, I checked my cell and was dismayed to see two missed calls from Tucker. I was about to call him back when Marie interrupted.

"You have a visitor in reception, Tera."

"What? There's no one on my schedule. Okay, I'll go down, I just have to make a call and…"

"It's your mom," said Marie. "I got the impression that she doesn't like to be kept waiting."

I groaned. "What does she want? Never mind! I just need to call…"

Lorraine appeared around the corner, chatting animatedly to my mother.

"You're on your own," Marie whispered, disappearing into her cube.

"Mother!" I said, smiling. "This is a lovely surprise."

Her gaze raked over my outfit, from hair to shoes and back again, a small frown on her face that I recognized as irritation.

"Tera, darling!" She patted my arm and kissed the air beside my cheek. "I do hope you have time to take your mother out to lunch. I've found the most divine place overlooking the ocean."

I looked helplessly at Lorraine, but she was on my mother's side; or rather on the side of the wife of one of her most prestigious clients.

"Of course, Mrs. Hawkins! We can spare Tera for a couple of hours."

She saw the annoyed twitch on my mother's face and interpreted it correctly.

"In fact, why not take as long as you want—you deserve it."

"It's not even lunchtime," I muttered, but no one was paying any attention to me.

My mother scooped me up and a minute later we were in a cab on the way to Benu, an upscale restaurant with a galaxy of Michelin stars. So like her. It used to be like me. I think.

Once we were settled at the right table, by which I mean not the first, or even second table that the host offered us, but the *right* one, she ordered herself a glass of champagne and water for me.

I raised my eyebrows.

"Darling! You're working. I can't send you back inebriated."

I gave a polite smile. "I don't think one glass would have done that, but never mind."

She returned my smile and squeezed my fingers, her pleasure in seeing me genuine for once.

"How did you enjoy working with Daddy?"

I wished she wouldn't infantilize like that.

"It was fine, but honestly, he didn't need me—his team knows what they're doing."

"I'm sure you helped."

Why did that sound so patronizing? But I did what I'd been taught to do and simply smiled.

The drinks arrived and we ordered our food. I was just beginning to feel relaxed when my cell rang. It was Tucker—and I hadn't returned his two previous calls either.

"Aren't you going to answer that, darling?"

"Just a work thing—it can wait," I lied.

Mom smiled at me.

"I spoke to Josh Hartington's mother this morning," she said. "And guess what? He wants to ask you to the Memorial

Day fundraiser in November. I told her that you'd love to go with him! Isn't that wonderful?"

I groaned, not bothering to hide my feelings.

"Mother! I can't believe you did that! You know I can't stand him. He doesn't talk to me, he talks to my boobs..."

"I'm sure that's not true!"

"It definitely is! I think he's waiting for them to talk back."

Mom laughed. "You do exaggerate. He'll call you to arrange the details."

I frowned. "No, Mother, he won't. I can arrange my own dates, thank you very much."

"Don't be petulant. That young man is going places. You'd be a fool to turn him down now."

I stilled and forced myself to speak calmly.

"Regardless of that, I am *not* going anywhere with Josh Hartington. You shouldn't have offered me up like some sort of sacrifice."

"You can't turn him down, it will look horribly rude."

"Then *you* shouldn't have set it up without speaking to me!"

She patted her lips delicately with her napkin.

"I'm your mother: I always have your best interests at heart."

I sighed.

"I know you do and I appreciate it, but I'm old enough to make my own choices."

"Are you though, Tera? You've led such a sheltered life."

"Really?" I said briskly. "You think maybe the last year and a half hasn't opened my eyes to one or two things?"

"There's no need to be vulgar."

"I wasn't: I was being honest."

She took a sip of her champagne and I knew she was just refueling for her next angle of attack.

"I dropped by your apartment this morning," she said, smiling up at me, her eyes glittering.

I cringed internally, but kept my expression impassive.

"Oh, yes?"

"Imagine my surprise when I found a strange man asleep in your bed."

Oh no. I took a much needed drink of water.

"He was tired?" I said lamely.

Her smile widened.

"Yes, he did look like he'd had a difficult few days."

Delicately put, Mother.

"Is he a friend of yours?"

I raised my eyebrows. "No, it's the new crime wave: naked men breaking into apartments to criminally rumple your sheets."

"Don't be facetious, dear. I was only asking if you had a new ... friend."

I smirked at her. "Yes, I have a new friend."

"Such a lovely accent. Tennessee, he said."

My smile fell. *Oh God! They'd had a conversation?*

"Originally."

"Is that where you met, in Tennessee?"

"No."

She seared me with a look. "Where did you meet him?"

I inclined my head to one side.

"Why are you so interested?"

"Darling! You're my daughter—I'm interested in everything you do. When I find a man in your bed in the middle of the day..."

"Hardly the middle of the day!"

"...I can only assume that you're a little more than friends."

"We are," I said, my cheeks coloring.

"And when were you going to introduce him to your family?"

Try, never.

"Or maybe he's just a passing interest. I would understand," she said, dropping her voice conversationally.

Well played, Mother! A body blow followed by an uppercut.

"I don't know what we are yet," I said, peering thoughtfully at my water. "It's very new."

Her eyes narrowed. "Tera Chastain Hawkins! Are you telling me that you just met this person and you're already sleeping with him? You were *not* raised like that!"

"Oh, for goodness sake! It's the twenty-first century," I clipped out, stung. "But no, I didn't say I just met him. In fact I met him in the spring. At my brother's."

Twin red spots of anger appeared on her cheeks.

"You do *not* have a brother!" she snapped.

"I have two half-brothers, Mom." I spoke as kindly as I could, knowing how much the proof of my father's infidelities hurt her.

She drew a breath.

"So this ... this *Tucker* person works at the circus," she sneered.

"He's a stunt rider, yes."

She sat upright, her nostrils flaring.

"What on earth could you see in someone like that?"

Her voice was tight with dismay, but I sensed that her question was real, too. And I wondered if she'd asked my father the same thing when she'd found about his relationship with Kes's mother.

What could I say to her? How could I answer so she'd understand when I barely understood myself?

He makes me laugh. I enjoy his company. And the other inconvenient truth: *He's hotter than hell in the summer.*

He was beautiful, charming, funny and thoughtful. He didn't need to be the center of attention, even though attention usually sought him out.

But when we were alone together, I was starting to crave that brief, unguarded moment when he lost himself inside me, the clown's mask gone for once.

There was no way my parents would accept him; no way they'd ever think Tucker was *one of us*—and truthfully, he was a lone wolf, like a wild creature, did and said what he wanted without a filter.

"I enjoy his company," I said weakly.

My voice trailed off. I couldn't explain, couldn't tell her *why*. Instead of words or explanations, I had memories. Maybe it was the possessive way he settled himself between my thighs, unembarrassed, adjusting the angle of my hips to suit himself, his strong, powerful body pressing over me, pushing into me, his rough hands grazing my flushed and heated flesh.

I didn't want soft hands, manicured nails. I wanted a man's hands, roughened from labor. I wanted Tucker's hands sliding over my skin.

"Well, I hope for *your* sake that this is just a passing fancy," said my mother, interrupting my increasingly carnal thoughts.

I glanced up sharply.

"As I said, I don't know what it is yet."

"Never mind," she said, patting my hand. "If you don't want Josh Hartington to take you to the fundraiser, we can find someone else suitable."

"I *have* a date," I lied. "Tucker is taking me."

She laughed out loud.

"Don't be ridiculous, darling. Do you really think a man like that would be comfortable wining and dining with the finest families in California? If you like him, as you say you do, it would be selfish to embarrass him like that."

I had no words. None.

Was she right? Horribly wrong? My thoughts were too confused to tell.

"Besides," she sniffed, "he's barely housebroken."

"This conversation is over," I said, throwing down my napkin and walking out of the restaurant.

I flagged down a taxi and jumped in, ignoring the driver's

grumpy tone when he bitched about how bad the traffic was in Mission Bay.

I tried to call Tucker, but his phone was switched off.

When I reached the apartment, it was silent and empty. The coffee cups had been washed up and the bed remade.

For a moment I thought Tucker had left, but I felt my lungs relax when I saw his backpack in the corner, his red helmet perched on top.

He'll be back.

I settled down to wait, drowning in a box of cookies and a gallon of ice cream, a tried and tested solution to a bad day.

Tucker

After Mrs. Hawkins cut me off at the knees with her sharp tongue, I sat at the kitchen table shell-shocked. In her own way, she was just as ruthless as her husband. How the hell they managed to raise someone as sweet as Tera was beyond me.

Once I got tired of feeling rattled, I cleaned up and called Tera's cell. She didn't answer so I guessed she was busy at work.

When my second call was missed, as well, I began to feel uneasy.

Maybe this was a conversation that needed to happen in person.

It was easy to find her name on the internet, and not much harder to find where she worked. I frowned, wondering how safe that was for a Senator's daughter.

It took me less than 40 minutes to walk to her office building. I hesitated, staring up at the sleek tower of glass and chrome.

You don't belong here.

I caught sight of myself in the plate glass window and shuddered. Wrinkled shirt, ripped jeans, face marked, arm in a sling—I looked like hell.

I pulled out my phone to call Tera, but she still didn't answer. Then remembering that I owned a pair of balls, I walked into the building.

I flashed my best smile at the receptionist.

"Hi, I'm here to see Tera Hawkins."

"Oh! Was she expecting you?"

"No, I thought I'd surprise her."

The receptionist's lips quivered as if she was holding back a smile. "It seems to be a day for that."

"Excuse me, ma'am?"

"You just missed her. I'm sorry. Her mom came to take her to lunch, as a surprise."

Damn! Her mom had gotten to her first!

"Can I take a message?"

I smiled briefly and shook my head, then wandered back out into the busy street. My hand twitched, wanting to call her again, but I didn't. Instead I headed further into the city until I found a sports bar, the kind of chill place I could relax. Somewhere I could think.

Tera's mom had aimed her words straight, the poison tip of the arrow hitting true. She'd pointed out every reason why a guy like me didn't fit into her daughter's life. But somehow, in some crazy way, we did work.

And despite all the times I'd tried to push Tera away, she kept coming back. She'd crashed through all my barriers and forced me to care about her. It was scary as fuck, but I couldn't ignore it any longer.

And maybe it wasn't all bad either.

She was less serious around me, we had fun, but I was different, too. People change. They grow up. Maybe I wasn't good enough for Tera, but I was going to try to be the best man that I could. It had started with Scotty and Renee, but for Tera, I'd try harder.

I couldn't give her the life fit for a Senator's daughter, and maybe I was kidding myself that she'd want a guy like me. But Tera didn't look down on the carnies, she never had. Maybe there was a chance?

I'd been judged and labelled by people my whole life: clown, poor kid, loser, carnie. But why did I allow them to reduce me to a single label? That was down to me. If I wanted to be with a woman like Tera, I'd have to be the man worth having her. Financially, materially, I had next to nothing to offer. But with Kes back in the game, the stunt riding was taking off again. Just before I left for Tennessee, we'd gotten the promise of a big booking in LA over Thanksgiving. Those gigs made decent money.

On the other hand, it was a risky life. I could pop my shoulder out again or break a leg and be out of the game for months, even permanently.

I had no education, although I might just about make it as a mechanic if I got certificated. Maybe a carpenter. It was a thought. But hardly enough to keep a woman like Tera. And fuck, I'd miss the carnival.

I sighed and rubbed my eyes.

Wanting to be with Tera was the dumbest, most senseless, ridiculously reckless act possible for a man like me—and I jumped stunt bikes for a living.

CHAPTER THIRTEEN

TUCKER

My phone had died again. Piece of shit couldn't seem to hold a charge longer than half a day. It was time I replaced it. What a joke—it would be months before I could afford that.

I wandered through Haight-Ashbury and found a hotdog vendor in Golden Gate Park. The leftover money from selling the Duke needed to stretch a long way, so fancy meals were out.

I didn't like thinking about Daisy—damn, she was beautiful. I wondered when I'd be able to ride something as amazing again. My thoughts dived to the gutter and the image of Tera's knockout body riding mine was a little too triple X for being in public during daylight hours. I forced my thoughts away and spent the afternoon being a tourist. That alone was a novelty— despite the many miles I'd traveled with the carnival, I'd always been working. Hard work and long hours.

I missed it.

When I figured it was late enough that Tera might be home from work, I walked back to her apartment.

I used the code to buzz myself into the main entrance, but before I could get a key into Tera's lock, the door flung open.

"Where have you been? I've been waiting for hours!"

She looked like a disheveled librarian, all tight skirt and classy shirt, her hair coming loose from some fancy hairdo.

"Whoa! Slow down. I thought you were at work?"

Tera huffed and rolled her eyes.

"Yes, but then my mother told me that you and she had met. Oh my God! Were you really naked in bed?"

I grinned at her. "Yep. Guilty as charged."

Then I leaned forward and whispered into her hair.

"And you know what, sugar? It's a good thing I had the sheet over me, because I was dreaming about you."

She laughed and groaned at the same time. "What did she say to you? Was she awful?"

I pulled her into my chest with my good arm and kissed her lightly on the lips. They were cold and tasted sweet.

"Can a man get a drink first? I'm dying on my feet here."

She frowned but strode into the kitchen.

"Beer or water?"

"Beer sounds great."

I slumped onto the couch, rubbing my sore shoulder. It ached constantly—I was so over it.

Tera appeared with two bottles of beer and handed one to me.

"So, what did she say?"

"Nothing to stress about, sugar."

She glared at me while I took a long drink, closing my eyes and enjoying the cool slide of artisan beer.

"Well?"

"It was nothin'."

"Tucker! Sometimes you're so laidback you're practically horizontal. Just tell me what she said!"

"Well, she complimented me on being such a fine-looking man, and was happy to hear that her beautiful daughter had finally gotten a good lay."

Tera's mouth dropped open and then she punched me in the arm.

"This is serious!"

"Okay, okay! No need to get violent on my ass!"

"Tucker! I've been waiting here for over four hours! I've eaten a whole packet of triple chocolate cookies and two pints of ice cream."

That explained the cold, sweet lips.

"To be fair, TC, I did try and find you at your office, but you'd already left with the Wicked Witch."

Tera giggled. "Careful! That's my mother you're talking about." Then she frowned. "Really? You went to my office? How did you know where I worked?"

"I Googled you."

Tera's surprise irritated me for reasons I didn't want to examine too closely.

"I can use the internet, TC. I'm not completely dumb."

"No, I never said ... I know you're not dumb, Tucker. It's just, I've never even seen you check messages on your phone."

"That's because I don't know anyone who would call me."

Except maybe you?

Her laugh was self-conscious. "No messages from a string of heartbroken women?"

"Only three women have my number," I said patiently. "You, Aimee, and ... Renee."

"Oh."

"Yeah."

Tera looked away, embarrassed.

"Are you going to tell me what my mother said?"

I sighed and leaned back against the couch.

"She said that her beautiful daughter deserved better than some guy who worked in a carnival."

Tera sucked in a long breath. "Mom said that?"

"She was very polite."

Tera stood up suddenly and started pacing up and down the room.

"I am so *sick* of them interfering in my life! This stops right now."

Then she spun around and stared at me.

"Come to the Memorial fundraiser with me."

"Come to what?"

She shook her head impatiently.

"It's this big fundraiser for the Semper Fi Fund in San Diego. Dad's father was a Marine. We go to it every year in November."

"Yeah? And what happens at this fundraiser?"

She waved her hand around vaguely.

"The usual: a load of people dressing up and paying a thousand dollars for a place at the table, charity raffle, drinking, dancing."

Holy shit! How much?

"Uh huh. And who's going to be there?"

"My parents, for a start!"

I'd already figured that out.

"Not really my scene, TC. And I don't have that kind of money."

She rolled her eyes. "I'd pay for you, silly! It's in San Diego, so I'll book the flights and hotel and we can..."

"I mean it, TC," I said, quietly interrupting her. "It's not me."

"But ... I want you there ... as my date. Then my parents would see that we're together."

My lungs squeezed painfully.

"We're not together, TC." *We have now, but we can't have a future.*

Her eyes widened but she didn't reply, and that by itself told me everything I needed to know.

I shook my head.

"It's really great of you, sugar, but I wouldn't fit in there. I'd say or do something wrong and just embarrass you. Thank you for asking me—I appreciate it more than you know. You're an amazing, beautiful woman and any man would be proud to have you on his arm. But you can do better than me."

"Why does that sound like goodbye?" she whispered, her words cracking and splintering.

My throat ached and awkwardness sat in ugly silence between us.

Then she walked toward me, staring down, hands on her hips, her expression hard and determined.

"You're doing it again, Tucker: you're trying to push me away because you somehow think it's the right thing to do. Yes, I want us to be together—but only if you want it, too. And I *don't* think I can do better than you. Have I ever said anything to make you believe that I did? Ever?"

A warm thread of hope slid through my blood.

"Let me show you how wrong you are, Tucker McCoy."

Tera

His wide shoulders were slumped and he passed a hand over his face wearily. For once his smile was missing. He looked exposed. Well, if Tucker had a problem believing my words, I'd have to find another way to show him.

His protest died on his lips when I took off my blouse and dropped it to the floor. Then I unbuttoned my skirt and wiggled it over my hips. His eyes darted between my breasts and my descending skirt, unable to fix on either for more than a second.

Standing in my bra and panties, I felt fierce, sexual, powerful.

I wasn't the woman he'd met in the spring, the one who'd regretted not taking what she wanted that night. Then, I'd only seen the happy-go-lucky roustabout, the free-spirited carnie who loved to laugh.

Now I knew the real person, I wanted him even more. He was a good man, an honorable man, a man who gave his last dollar to a woman he'd once cared about because it would help her and the child he never knew existed.

How could I not want a man like that?

He didn't see it himself—he only counted the material things that he didn't have, but if the last eighteen months had taught me anything, it was that my life so far was a house of cards, built on lies, and life was so much more than the right clothes and the right zip code.

The man in front of me had more integrity than my father, the Senator; and a moral code that he lived by, whether he knew it or not.

I unhooked my bra and slid my panties down my thighs, watching as Tucker licked his lips.

When I leaned forward to untie the sling from around his neck, he took the opportunity to press hot, wet kisses to my breasts.

I pulled back and smiled at him, tossing the sling to one side as I slid to my knees on the hard floor.

My bare flesh pressed against his jeans and the buttons of his shirt. I undid them one by one, stroking my hands over warm, satiny skin. His breathing sped up as I reached down to unbutton the worn denim of his jeans.

When I pulled his hardened dick from his pants, his body shuddered and his eyes squeezed shut.

When I licked the head of his dick, a low growl rolled out from his chest.

When I swallowed his long, thick cock in one go and palmed his balls, the breath hissed out of him in a stream of curses.

When I worked him around and around and up and down,

over and over, the muscles in his thighs trembled and his stomach tightened.

And when I could tell he was close to coming, he grabbed my hair, twisting it almost painfully as he pulled me away from him.

"Christ, Tera!"

And he stood up in one fluid motion, his good arm holding my entire weight as his mouth crushed my lips and his tongue drove into my mouth.

I gasped with pleasure and pain as he roughly handled my body, grunting as we thudded against the table, a flurry of old newspapers, books and takeout menus flying to the floor.

I wrapped my legs around his waist, his heavy dick pressed against my stomach, almost bursting with need.

With teeth and tongue and bruised lips, I rained kisses on his cheeks and neck and shoulders, biting his skin and pulling from him savage growls and hisses of pain and desire.

Crashing into my bedroom, Tucker lost his balance and we landed on the floor. He rolled at the last moment so I ended up on his chest and wasn't crushed by his weight. My head thudded against the bed; we were only inches short of our goal.

His kisses were hot and hard and demanding as he tasted every part he could reach while I used his body to climb free and crawl onto the bed.

When he knelt between my legs, his strong hands holding my thighs open, pleasure rippled through me.

When his supple fingers stroked my clit, I moaned wantonly.

When his hot tongue teased and tasted, then dove inside, I rode his face hard.

When I came in his mouth, I screamed his name; I wanted to cheer and beg him to do it again.

And when he pulled me up the bed and pushed himself inside me, I cried with gratitude.

And finally, when he came, his face ferocious, his jaw clenched, he kissed me with a violent joy that made me determined to never let him go.

He rolled onto his side, breathing hard. I couldn't move. I lay splayed out on my back, legs open, breasts heaving as I struggled to draw in breath to my burning lungs.

It was several minutes before either of us could speak.

"What..." I began, then had to stop to take another deep breath. "What *was* that?"

Tucker shook his head, his chest still rising and falling as he fought to regain control of his lungs.

"I have no fucking clue. Let's do it again."

"Right now..." I gasped, "that is the most..." *wheeze* "asinine comment I ever heard."

"Ass-what?" he laughed. "Yeah, your ass and my nine inches. Works for me."

I tried to smack him, but my hand was like a limp fish.

"Why are you still dressed?" I asked, when my hand landed on crumpled cotton.

"This wild woman wrestled me to the bed—I never stood a chance."

I ran my hand down his sweating chest.

"Are we together now, Tucker?"

Don't say no. Don't hesitate.

He hesitated. "Tera..."

"Don't say my name like that! Don't rule us out before we've even started. I like you; you like me. Isn't that enough?"

"I want it to be," he said quietly, "but we come from different worlds and we're traveling in different directions."

I wanted to grind my teeth with frustration.

"Won't you even try?"

He closed his eyes, a pained look on his face.

"Is that really what you want, Tera? A guy like me?"

I shook my head. "No, Tucker. I don't want a guy *like* you: I want you. Are we done arguing now?"

He swallowed and took a deep breath.

"Yes, ma'am, I'd say we are."

I felt the rush of warmth through my body, the pleasure that comes from being wanted. The fool's gold of love.

But it was Tucker who voiced the words.

"I don't know if I can be the man you need, Tera," he said, his voice dropping to a whisper. "I don't know how to do relationships. I don't know anything about the kind of upbringing you've had. And now I'm a father as well. I don't think I'm enough for you, but fuck it, I'm going to try."

I wound my fingers into his and held on tightly.

"Your mother might have messed up, got it wrong so many times, but Tucker, you're a good man. And somehow, in all the chaos, she raised a decent human being. There's nothing else I want."

He sighed heavily. "I want that to be true."

But I didn't know which part he meant.

Tucker

I jolted awake suddenly.

After Tera had shocked me from the insides out by her words as well as her actions, we'd fallen asleep in a sweaty, tangled heap.

The morning light was filtering through the window and Tera was still sleeping soundly next to me, the thin sheet clinging to her gorgeous body.

I had the memory of hammering into her the night before. It had been incredible. Her anger had turned her into an Amazonian warrior. But she'd made me forget the basics—I hadn't worn a rubber. The thought made my heart trip. I knew she wouldn't get pregnant; she'd told me she was on the pill, but

... I needed to get tested. It choked me up to think I could have...

Nope. Not gonna go there. Yet.

Making sure I didn't wake her, I slunk into the shower and got cleaned up.

Tera was just opening her eyes when I strolled into the bedroom in a towel.

"Spoilsport! I wanted to watch," she said. "Or better yet, video you showering."

I couldn't help laughing. "Got a bit of kink going on there, Miss Hawkins?"

"Maybe," she grinned. "Would it bother you?"

"That's a hell no!"

"Good. Now come back to bed and show me what I don't have to go on missing."

"Sure thing, sugar. I'll just get a rubber and..."

"We didn't use one last night," she said calmly.

"I know, but I should have. I'm ... I'm going to get tested today, so..."

Tera closed her eyes. "Wow. Way to kill the mood, Tucker."

Irritated, I stomped out of the room. Why was doing the right thing so goddamn hard?

I heard her bare feet padding after me, and then she wrapped her arms around my waist.

"I'm sorry. That was bitchy of me. Do you know where you're going to go? Because I'm sure my doctor would..."

"No, I got it. Thanks."

Fucked if I was going to let my girl pay for this.

Then Tera giggled.

"Oh my God! Imagine if I did get pregnant and we had a little boy like you! Holy shit!" and she tickled my ribs, making me screech like a girl.

"It could be a she-kid," I pointed out, panting from her

assault. "And if she looks like her momma, I'd have to stake her first boyfriend out in the yard as a warning to others."

Tera laughed loudly. "Hmm, that could work. Maybe we can practice *not* making babies after you've been tested." Then she winked at me and headed for the shower.

I watched her walk away, her stunning heart-shaped ass and long, long legs. Everything about her shouted she was something special.

Would she really think about having kids with a guy like me? After all the fucked up things she knew about me? Even though I already had a kid?

An unfamiliar and unwanted pain drummed through my chest, and it felt like my heart had started beating to a new rhythm.

Luckily, Tera was in too much of a hurry to get to work to wonder at my sudden weirdness.

Once she left, the apartment was too quiet. At the carnival, I had a role, a purpose. Here ... I had to find a fucking STD clinic.

As it turned out, there were a ton of walk-in places in San Francisco.

I picked the nearest to Tera's apartment and sat in a waiting room with a bunch of other shifty looking people. Yeah, you don't make eye-contact in a place like that. It just feels weird knowing that we're all there for the same thing: piss in a cup, blood test, lecture from a nurse.

Thinking your dick might be diseased is a leveling experience.

When it was my turn, a guy in blue scrubs led me into a small room and took the bottle of piss.

"I need to ask you a few questions about your sex life."

This was the part I hated. In the past, mostly I'd just had to fill out a form. That was bad enough—but doing it face to face with some dude: yeah, not cool.

"Don't worry," he said with a sickeningly upbeat smile. "These are all standard questions and no one is here to judge you."

Yeah, right.

I threw him a skeptical look, but he just smiled reassuringly ... which was probably worse. He looked like he was used to delivering bad news—also known as cock-sick shock.

"Anything you say will be completely confidential, except on the very rare occasion when we need to inform someone for their own protection."

My mouth suddenly went very dry and getting the hell out didn't seem like the worst idea I'd ever had.

"Results will be in about a week, and until then, we recommend that you use barrier protection, condoms, or safer sex alternatives."

I frowned at him.

"What's safer than rubbers?"

He looked like he was trying not to laugh.

"Well, condoms aren't 100% effective, so alternatives would be manual stimulation, for example, or abstinence."

I could guess what the expression on my face was like.

"When was your last check up?"

I tried to think back.

"When I changed my insurance—so about 18 months ago."

"And how many sexual partners have you had since then."

"Um..." *Shit! I had no idea.*

"Approximately?"

"Forty, or, um, fifty?" I hedged, sounding uncertain.

His eyebrows raised, even though he tried to hide his reaction.

And now I'm with Tera and she doesn't deserve this shit. Last night, I didn't use a condom.

Again, I felt a sense of unease, of shame.

"I see. And do you partake in any higher risk practices?"

Other than shoving my dick in every available hole for the last decade?

"Like what, Doc?"

"Oh, I'm not a doctor; I'm a nurse practitioner, but you can call me Alan." He smiled again. "Higher risk practices would include having multiple partners or being with someone who has had multiple partners, not using a condom..."

Goddamn, I'd checked all those boxes and he was just getting started.

"...intercourse with a prostitute..."

Clear of that one, thank fuck.

"...intercourse with a person who injects drugs..."

God, I hope not.

"...anal sex outside of a long-term relationship..."

Shit!

He paused and looked at me.

"Yeah, some of those," I admitted.

"And is there anything in particular that you're worried about?"

Yeah, dick rot.

I shook my head.

"So, no special reason for your visit today?"

"Um, I met someone. Someone special."

Stop fucking smiling at me!

It wasn't the most fun way to spend a morning—or the fact it cost $800 to get the full range of tests.

For the cut-price of $175, I could have gotten chlamydia and gonorrhea tests by themselves, but I figured I should get the boxed set. Luckily, my insurance covered it.

I sent up a silent vote of thanks to Zach. As the Daredevils' manager, he'd insisted that we didn't scrimp on insurance. Ever since Kes's accident, we'd all paid an arm and a leg to get full coverage: no pun intended. It was definitely paying for something now.

At least the nurse didn't bother with the lecture, which was a relief.

"If you don't hear back from us after a week, it means your tests came back negative."

"Okay, thanks."

"Sure. And if I give you a bunch of leaflets on sexual health, will you read them?"

"Probably not," I said honestly. "But like I said, I'm just with one girl now."

"One is all it takes, honey."

I grinned at him.

"I hear you, but I'm a reformed man."

Especially after today.

We shook hands and he sent me on my way.

I spent the rest of the day haunting the thrift stores and buying half-a-dozen button-up shirts. And then I found a tuxedo that looked like it was the right size.

I thought about Tera's invitation to the fancy party. Common sense told me it was a bad idea—but I'd never let common sense stop me before.

Tera

"How'd it go at the clinic?" I asked.

Tucker winced and dropped his hand from my ass, which had been part of the welcome home when I walked through my front door after work.

"Um, yeah. Fine. I have to wait a week for the results."

He stalked into the kitchen. I watched him for a moment, then followed, sitting on one of the bar stools as he pulled two beers out of the fridge and offered one to me. I shook my head, so he shoved it back inside, rattling the bottles.

"Okay, why are you acting so weird?"

I saw the tension in his shoulders, then he turned around to face me.

"We didn't use a rubber last night."

"I know. We talked about this. Did the doctor say something to you?"

Tucker couldn't meet my eyes.

"The guy was a nurse, but, uh, yeah."

I waited with a growing sense of unease.

"What did he say?"

Tucker took a deep breath and stood up straight. "That my sex life is pretty fucked up."

I blinked a couple of times. "You're going to have to explain that."

He blew out a breath. "I've had a lot of, um, partners. They class that as risky behavior. I mean, I *always* used a rubber, TC, I promise! You're the only girl I've ever ... *fuck it!*"

He paced back into the living room.

I followed again, pulling him into a hug, and he buried his face in my hair.

"I'm sorry, sugar."

"Listen to me, Tucker: you've done the sensible thing—you've gotten tested. I know I'm clean and you've always used a condom before. The chances are you're fine. Quit worrying about what you can't change. In a week, you'll know one way or another."

His good hand tightened around my waist.

"Yeah, okay."

I hesitated. "Tucker?"

"Yeah, sugar?"

"Uh, I was wondering ... what's *a lot* of partners?"

He groaned.

"TC, you're killing me!"

I let it go. And maybe it was double standards or being a hypocrite, but I made a mental note to get myself tested, too.

Welcome to the wonderful world of relationships.

He stood up straight so he could look at me. "Still want to be my girl?"

His voice was subdued.

"Tucker McCoy—are you asking me to go steady?" I teased him.

He laughed quietly. "Yeah, I guess I am?"

"Then yes. The answer is yes.

He smiled with relief. "Good."

"So, I was thinking?"

"Yeah?" he said, looking wary again.

"I know we were going to drive up to the cabin tonight, but now we're ... well ... together, why don't you stay here until your shoulder is better."

"Ten seconds ago we started going steady, now you want me to move in? Hey, you're one of those 'fast' girls that I heard about, aren't you?"

I punched him in the arm—his good one, although if he kept annoying me...

"You're the one with the sick dick," I pointed out.

His expression changed and his eyes narrowed.

Then he chased me across the living room, and I let out a loud shriek as he threw me onto the couch where we made out for the next 30 minutes. When we'd had as much foreplay as either of us could take, our clothes disheveled, our lips bruised, we went to my bed.

And yes, he wore a condom.

CHAPTER FOURTEEN

TERA

I got used to having Tucker around. I loved coming home to him after a long day at work. I loved how he took me places that he'd discovered in the city, places I'd never explored before, quirky cafes, strange shops in hard-to-find corners, thrift stores with weird and wonderful collections that he'd found. He chatted to shop keepers, homeless people, café workers—always a smile, always a joke. He didn't moan about what he didn't have —which was money, mostly—he found ways to enjoy himself regardless, and always made me smile, always knew how to make me laugh. He had a way of engaging with life.

When we went grocery shopping together, it was like having a barely domesticated wolf at my heels; his intense energy, his charisma obvious as he loped down the aisles, standing out from the men in suits and women in office-wear. I swear the woman at the deli counter looked as if she wanted to rip his clothes off every time she saw him. I knew how she felt.

After another week, he discarded his sling and started doing exercises for his shoulder. I made him find a therapist who could help with rehab as his insurance would pay for it, but mostly he exercised in the apartment or went for long runs.

In the evenings, he'd ice his shoulder, and then we'd have fun with ice cubes. Turned out I wasn't the only one who had a bit of a kinky streak.

We were both relieved when his STD tests were all negative. I think he knew he'd dodged a bullet there. But I couldn't persuade him to give up condoms either, even though the wistful look on his face told me that he'd really like to.

I knew that he'd texted Renee several times and even tried calling her, but she hadn't replied except to say that they were in Richmond and they were okay. Nothing else, no address. Not even her home phone number, or an update on the basketball program. Tucker didn't even know if she'd told Scotty about him. It must have hurt, but he didn't say much.

But each day that he grew stronger was a day closer to him leaving. The carnival was calling, louder every moment.

I didn't know what to do or what this would mean for our relationship.

Neither of us had said the 'L' word or dared to look too far into the future.

My parents were subtle in their attempts to break us up— certainly more subtle than the thuggish attack on Tucker back in Tennessee. Mom bombed my phone with texts about 'suitable' guys to date. I deleted them all. Dad used the company I worked for to send me out of town on projects. As soon as I realized what he was doing, I put a stop to it.

But separation was coming, whether I wanted it or not.

Four short weeks had flown by when Tucker told me he was leaving.

"You're going?"

I sat down on the couch, my knees weak.

"I gotta get back to work, sugar."

"But it's too soon! The doctor said no stunts for three months—at least!"

"I know, and I won't—probably. But there's more to it than showtime. Setting up the ramps, driving the rig and the RV, it's a lot of work. And I've been leaving it all to the guys. I've got to do my share."

I shook my head. "It's too soon," I whispered again.

"I need to start earning money."

"But the doctor said..."

Tucker pulled me into his arms and kissed my forehead.

"I can't stay here and live off you forever."

I wanted to ask, *Why not?* But I didn't: he wasn't that kind of man and it wouldn't do any good.

"I was getting sick of you leaving your wet towels on the floor anyway," I huffed.

Tucker raised his eyebrows and smirked at me.

"That happened one time! And you severely chastised me for that, Miss Hawkins."

"Oh, that's right," I said, a reluctant smile creeping over my face.

I'd snapped the wet towel against his bare butt which made him yelp. That turned into a tickling match which turned into Tucker bending me over the kitchen table and making my knees shake.

And I was late for work.

My smile faded.

"You're really leaving me?"

An exasperated sigh rattled out of him. "I'm not leaving *you!* I have to work, TC. If I don't, I'm ... nothing."

"You're not nothing!" I grunted angrily. *You're everything.*

And then I had to wipe away a pathetic tear.

He rocked me gently, as if we were dancing to an unheard tune.

"Don't cry, sugar. We'll figure something out. And December through February the carnival goes to winter quarters. If you want me, I'll come and stay here. You'll be sick of me."

I wrapped my arms around him more tightly. I wanted to beg him to stay, but I couldn't do that.

"Maybe..." he said tentatively. "Maybe you could fly out some weekends to wherever we've got a gig?"

I sniffed and wiped my eyes on my sleeve.

"I'll check my schedule—I think I'm having a manicure. I *might* be able to manage it." *I'll hate it. I want you here.*

He looked relieved.

"For a minute there, Tera, I thought you were going to tell me..." He shook his head.

"Will you miss me?" I asked, my voice plaintive.

"Well, damn! Is a frog's ass watertight?"

I snorted unattractively, hiccupping and laughing at the same time. "Is that a yes?"

He nodded and kissed my trembling lips. This kiss was soft and it broke me wide open.

"Yes, sugar. I'll miss you so fucking much."

And this time there was no joking.

Tucker

Leaving Tera was the right thing to do—so why did it feel so wrong?

I'd been waiting in the departure lounge at San Francisco Airport for an hour before I figured it out: it hurt. Something that had been fun and sexy as hell had turned into a sharp ache. It was like repeating the decade old pain to a different tune. But what else could I do? All the time I'd spent in San Francisco, I was checking my options, finding out what sort of jobs a guy like me could get. I talked to everyone, asked everywhere.

Turned out there aren't too many opportunities for a high school dropout.

Half the servers were in college or had degrees—I might have gotten work bussing tables, and one of the fast food joints was hiring for $7.75 an hour. Either way, it was a lot less than the thirty grand I earned last year, or the sixty-five thousand the year before. I wanted to kick my own ass for not saving any of it —and now I really needed it. The twenty grand I'd given Renee wouldn't last forever. Kids grew and needed new clothes; even I knew that.

I had to get back to the only thing I did well—even if it meant leaving Tera. I thought about all the crazy shit Kes had said and done when Aimee left him. I understood it now—their lives were traveling in different directions. Aimee had to give up her world to make it work for them. But she seemed to be able to do her online teaching job just fine while she was on the road, and she was tutoring carnie kids in the summer.

That wouldn't work for Tera. Her job was flying all over the country doing the PR shit for politicians and lobbyists, which I barely understood. It seemed to involve a lot of being nice to assholes. And I definitely included her father in that.

I figured she'd fly in a few times to see me and catch up with Kes. Then, gradually, the visits would be shorter with longer gaps between them. I'd seen it happen. Roustabouts met a small town girl and they'd promise to keep in touch. It would work for a while, and then the relationship would be gasping for breath, and then it would die. Once or twice, a guy or a gal would go live like a townie and give up the life. We'd see them getting fat and happy when we breezed through the following year, but there was always a look in their eyes that said they missed the crazy ride. Sometimes, a girl or a kid would travel with us for the summer, but more often than not, they'd be back home by Labor Day.

Tera would stay in touch because of Kes.

Not me.

God, I hope I'm wrong.

The Coconino County Fair was held at Fort Tuthill, a couple of miles south of Flagstaff. My flight got in just before the carnival finished setting up, and I'd messaged Zach to see if he could give me a ride from the airport.

He was waiting by his truck when I walked out of the low-rise building that was Pulliman Airport, blinking in the harsh white light and arid air.

"Damn, Tucker! It's good to see you, man! What the hell happened to your hair?" He laughed, flicking his hand at the shaggy mess.

"You going into hairdressing now?" I asked, raising my eyebrows.

"You wish."

Then he slammed me into a hug that had me wincing.

"How's the shoulder?"

"Fine, until you steamrollered over it," I said, rubbing the sore muscles.

"When did the doc say you can be back at work? And don't bullshit me."

I shrugged. "I'm fine to roustabout, but no stunts for another month."

"Hmm," he said, narrowing his eyes. "I'll check."

"You don't believe me?" I whined. "I thought we were buddies."

"Just because I said you had a cute ass, doesn't mean I'm falling for your act, Tucker," he laughed.

"Yeah, but my ass is cuter than Kestrel's?"

Zach shook his head. "Not going there, man!"

"Cuter than Zef's? Aw, come on, dude! It's gotta be cuter than Zef's!"

"Get in the damn truck before I decide to leave you and your cute ass at the airport. Jeez, Tucker, you don't change."

I laughed because that's what he expected, but I felt sick inside: I *had* changed.

I tossed my backpack into the truck, and placed my helmet on the bitch seat.

"You really sold the Duke? I can't believe that."

I gave him a crooked smile. "I told you—I needed the money. But whatever, I'll get another someday."

Zach eyed me curiously.

"What did you need that amount of money for?"

"Family stuff." I grimaced. "How's Luke?" I asked, wanting to distract him.

Zach smiled. "He's good. You'll see him later."

"He still roustabouting?"

"Sure, but doing a regular stint on the Dodgems." Then he grinned at me. "The girls like him."

"Pah! If I bossed that ride, he'd have no chance."

Zach laughed. "Yeah, well, it helps that you actually want to sleep with them."

I cringed internally, but it was my own fault. His description was fair: it was what I'd done for years.

"Kes thinks Luke could make a good stunt rider," he said, looking sideways at me.

"Yeah? We could use another man. Especially if one of us keeps getting fucked up," I sighed.

Zach nodded in agreement.

"Kes and Aimee good?"

"Yeah, arguing like crazy   crazy in love. The same."

"And what's that fucker Zef up to?"

"Same ole same ole. He misses his wingman. He'll be glad when he's got someone to party with now Kes is off the market."

"He's not hanging with Mirelle?"

Zach shrugged.

"I don't know what's with those two. It's intense when they

meet up, like they can't get enough of each other, and then ... nothing. She goes back to the East Coast. It works for them." He reached over to turn on his iPod. "How was the cabin? Everything okay there?"

Time to come clean.

"I never went."

Zach shot me a surprised look. "How come? Where you been staying?" Then a grin crept over his face. "You hooked up with some girl, didn't you? You dog!"

"It wasn't like that," I muttered.

"What was it like then? Was she a nun?"

"Come on!"

"A grandmother?"

"Hell, no!"

"Then what, Tucker? You going to tell me you spent the last five weeks keeping it in your pants, because I won't believe you."

He was starting to piss me off.

"Give it a rest, man. I met someone, okay?"

He didn't reply, and when I glanced at him, he was staring at me with his jaw hanging.

"Watch the road!" I yelled, as his truck started to veer off to the right.

"Shit! Sorry, man. But, for real? You met a girl?"

"Yes! Jeez! I met a girl. I stayed with her. We got ... close. Okay?"

From the look on his face I thought he was going to break out into show tunes.

"I think I just witnessed a miracle!"

"Fuck off!"

I stared out the window, knowing I'd get worse from Zef. As for Kes, when he found out I'd been boning his sister, it was entirely possible that he'd dislocate my other shoulder. Or maybe both of them. It definitely went against the code.

I sighed and leaned my head against the seat.

Zach was still grinning at me.

"Wow, you really like this girl? Is the one-and-only Tucker McCoy off the market? Hearts will be breaking wide open all over the world tonight."

"What part of *fuck off* didn't you understand?"

He grinned and slapped my arm.

"I'm happy for you, man. It's about time you dropped those skanks and got yourself a real girl."

Then he laughed.

"She's not a skank, is she?"

I turned to stare at him.

"Yeah, it's all very funny, so laugh it up while you can. But don't you ever fucking talk about her like that again. We clear?"

His laughter cut out immediately.

"You're serious?" He cleared his throat. "I'm sorry, brother."

I nodded, accepting his apology.

"So," he said after a moment. "Tell me about her. Where did you guys meet?"

I looked straight ahead.

"You were there—at Kes's breaking camp party back in the spring."

"You mean Rona, the snake girl? I thought she was traveling with Carters' Carnivals?"

I closed my eyes, remembering that I had hooked up with Rona that night. She'd let her python watch while we got it on. Freaked me the fuck out.

"No, man. I didn't hook up with Tera then, I…"

"Holy fuck! Are you talking about Kestrel's sister?"

I groaned, and Zach looked horrified.

"Yes, alright! Me and Tera … she was in Tennessee when I was there and … we got close. She's really great. She's … great."

Zach scratched his head.

"I don't know what to tell you, bro. There's a good chance Kes will beat the shit out of you."

"I know."

He blew out a breath.

"So ... you and Tera, huh? I didn't see *that* coming."

Nope, neither did I.

He glanced at me out of the corner of his eye.

"Is it ... serious with her?"

I shrugged. "I like her. I like her a lot, but she's this hotshot city girl and I'm ... fuck it, Zach, you know what I am!"

I heard the frustration in my voice.

"Tucker, you're a good guy. I mean that. Just ... treat her right."

Treat her right? I didn't even know what that meant. Surely treating Tera right didn't include asking her to share a tiny room in an RV where three other adults lived while we traveled from small town to small town?

Fucked if I knew. I just wanted to see her again.

Zach was silent for the rest of the short ride, every now and then throwing puzzled glances at me which I ignored.

I sat upright when I saw the poster advertising the carnival.

Fort Tuthill fairground was set in the woods, where narrow pine trees pointed toward the empty sky. Orange dust spewed up from the truck's tires as we bounced along the unmade road, and the whole landscape looked parched.

Some of the bigger rides were already being erected, and I watched as Luke and another couple of roustabouts wrestled the buckets for the Ferris wheel into place.

He turned and grinned when he saw Zach's truck, and Zach waved back at him.

It brought an unfamiliar rush of jealousy: Zach and Luke traveled together. It was a reminder I didn't need of how tough things were going to be for me and Tera to be a couple when we were apart more than we were together.

In the end, it didn't matter what I wanted, hoped for, dreamed about: what did Tera want?

Zach parked the truck next to Kes's RV and I climbed out, grinning when Aimee ran up and hugged the crap out of me.

"Hey, sweet cheeks! I knew you'd miss me. Finally decided that I'm the better man?"

The hug ended with an elbow in the ribs.

"If Kes heard you say that, you'd be wrestling around on the floor right now," she laughed.

"True, but I'd let him win because I know how much his pretty face means to you." I paused and looked around. "Where is the ugly douche?"

"Zef arrived with the rig twenty minutes ago. They're unloading by the grandstand."

"I'll go help," I said immediately.

"Are you sure you should?" Aimee asked, looking worried.

I winked at her. "I'm indestructible."

"You mean indescribable," she replied, rolling her eyes.

Zach laughed out loud.

"She's right about that, man. Come on, I'll drive you over. I've got to see the site manager anyway."

I hauled my backpack and helmet out of the truck and walked into the RV's living area, seeing the familiar, homey space. I went to throw my shit on the bed in my room when I saw a tiny ball of tan and black fur.

"Bo! What you doing in here? You've got your own crib."

His big black eyes looked up at me and his mouth opened in a toothy grin. Then he shrieked loudly and jumped up onto my shoulder, tugging gently on my hair, using it like reins.

"Miss me, buddy? Aw, I missed you too, little brother."

I glanced around the room as I walked back out. It looked tiny compared to the luxury of Tera's apartment. *She'll never live in here with you*, said the voice in my head.

Before I had the chance to worry even more, Aimee came

and stood behind me, gently taking Bo from my arms, ignoring his soft protests.

"Zachary said you met someone!" she gasped, her eyes wide.

"Dude has a big mouth," I snarked.

She laughed. "I think he was so shocked, he couldn't help himself. Come on, spill."

"Nothin' to say." *Especially not till I've spoken to Kes.*

"Ooh! A secret!" Then Aimee frowned. "She's not married, is she?"

Her question irritated me. "When have I ever been with a married woman?"

She scrunched her eyes up.

"What about that redheaded woman with the tattoos?"

I shook my head. "That doesn't count—I didn't know she was married! She didn't even wear a ring, goddamn it!"

My reputation was coming back to bite me in the ass—I only had myself to blame.

"Fine, don't tell me. But I'll get it out of you eventually." Then she cast her eyes over my button-up shirt. "You're looking spiffy, by the way. Is it the new girl?"

I didn't want to admit that it was because I still struggled to get a t-shirt on.

"This is my fancy city get-up."

Aimee smiled. "Sure, okay. Broccoli pizza tonight?"

I gave her shoulders a squeeze as I passed. "See, I knew you loved me really!"

Her laughter followed me out to the RV where Zach was waiting.

I punched him in the arm. "What the fuck, bro? Why did you tell Aimee that I'd met someone?"

He rubbed the place where I'd hit him, his expression wry.

"It won't be a secret once you tell Kes. You are going to tell him, right?"

"Of course I'm going to fucking tell him!" I grit out.

Zef and Kes were still unloading the rig when we got there. I couldn't help grinning when I saw them—I'd missed the assholes.

Zef saw me first.

"The prodigal returns! How you doing, man?"

We shook hands then he pulled me into a hug before Kes slung an arm around me.

"Good to see you, bro. How's the shoulder holding up?"

I nodded and grinned at them.

"Yeah, getting there. No stunts for another week or so, but after that I should be good."

Kes frowned. "That soon?"

"Yeah, pretty much."

I wasn't going to tell him that the doc at the hospital had said no stunts for three months. Fuck that. But Zach looked skeptical.

"You sure?"

"Maybe two weeks, but soon." I changed the subject. "So, looks like you guys need a hand?"

And just like that, I was part of the carnival again.

I got to work hauling heavy pieces of jump ramp out of the rig, ignoring the spikes of pain shooting up my arm.

Kes noticed that I wasn't firing on all cylinders and set me to work giving the bikes a tune-up. I'd always been better at maintenance than the others, and saw that the oil filters needed cleaning.

I worked away quietly, glancing up every now and again as the ramps grew higher, feeling a pang of regret that I wouldn't be jumping when the show opened tomorrow.

After a couple of hours of hot, dusty, sweaty work, Aimee dropped off some bottles of water and reminded us we had two hours before supper.

When she left, Kes walked over and kicked my foot.

"What's this about you and some broad?"

I tried not to cringe.

"I met someone is all," I mumbled reluctantly. "I don't know why everyone's making such a damn song and dance about it."

Kes smiled. "'Cause it's you, mothertucker. Who is she?"

This was the moment that I'd been dreading since my first night with Tera.

"I didn't go looking for this," I began by way of explanation. "It just happened."

He shrugged. "That's how it usually goes."

I stood up and took a long drink of water as Kes eyed me curiously.

"Look, there's no easy way to say it ... so I'm just gonna say it. It's ... I ... we..." *Fuck!* "I met TC when I was in Tennessee. We got close. It's Tera ... I've been seeing Tera."

I closed my eyes, waiting for Kes to punch out my lights. But after a second, nothing had happened, and I opened one eye.

"Aren't you going to take a swing at me?"

Kes frowned. "Do I need to?"

"Um..."

"Tucker, you're sweating like a bitch. Just chill. I know you'll treat her right, so there's no problem."

"You do? There isn't?"

He sat down on the grass, wincing as he stretched out his back.

"You wouldn't be this nervous if you didn't care about her."

"Jesus, Kes! I slept with your sister! You're not even a little mad?"

Kes scowled. "You don't need to draw me a fuckin' picture. I'd rather not think about that. But if you screw around on her, I'll rearrange your face."

I sat down next to him, more than a little stunned. "Fair enough."

"So, how's this going to work between you two?"

I shook my head. "Fuck knows. I mean, she's going to fly out in two weeks and meet us in Denver, but..." I shrugged helplessly.

Kes nodded.

"I get it. When me and Aimee..." and he couldn't help smiling just saying her name. "When we got our second chance ... or maybe third chance, we had to really want it, you know? It hasn't been easy—for either of us. But if it's worth having, it's worth work."

I frowned, thinking about what he was saying.

"I really thought you'd want to beat the shit out of me."

Kes laughed. "I still might if you fuck this up. Love is rare, my friend. And I know what it looks like. Don't be a chicken shit. I know you'll treat her right."

I sat there stunned while he stood up and walked away.

Tera was the woman who rocked my world like no one ever had before. But was Kes right?

Shit! Is that what this was?

Love?

I shuddered at the thought.

But maybe that was why it hurt so bad. Did I love Tera? Did she ... could she ... love me back?

I carried on working, my mind somersaulting as Kes's words rattled around inside my head.

When the guys were busy, I snuck off to call her. I knew she'd be at work, but I needed to hear her voice.

She answered on the second ring.

"Tera Hawkins speaking."

"Hey, sugar!"

There was a short pause, then she replied formally.

"If you could hold the line one moment, I'll check that for you right away."

I heard her apologizing to someone, then the sound of her footsteps and her breath in my ear.

"Sorry about that—my boss is so nosy. How are you? How was the flight?"

"Shitty—you weren't there."

She sighed. *"I know. I'm dreading going home to an empty apartment."*

My heart lurched. "Shit, Tera, I..."

"Don't apologize," she said softly. *"We both knew this would be hard. I miss you, that's all. I'm not trying to make you feel guilty for ... for doing your job."*

I hated not being able to hold her in my arms. I leaned my head against the side of the grandstand.

"Are you still there?"

"I'm here, sugar."

"How is everyone?"

I swallowed and closed my eyes. "I told Kes."

"You did? What did he say?"

"He was cool about it."

"Really?" she sounded as surprised as I'd been.

"Yeah."

"Well, what did he say?"

I smiled at the annoyance in her voice.

"He said that if I screwed around on you, he'd rearrange my face."

She laughed lightly. *"Yes, he obviously took it very well. But don't worry, Tucker. If you screw around on me, I'll rearrange your face myself."*

I had a feeling that she meant it.

"Tera, that's not going to happen. You know that, right? You're my girl. I don't want anyone else."

When she replied, her voice was resigned.

"I know. I don't want anyone else either." She paused. *"Which is why I'd really like you to come to the Memorial Day fundraiser in November. Please, please don't make me go with one of my mother's horrendous date choices."*

I gripped the phone so hard, I was in danger of cracking the screen.

"Don't go with those douches, Tera."

"Then come with me."

I sighed and thudded my head against the wall in frustration.

"We've got a show."

"Kes would give you the night off if you asked him."

I wanted to grind my teeth in irritation.

"You know I won't fit in there," I said sharply.

When she replied, I could hear the frustration in her voice at this old argument.

"You could fit in anywhere, Tucker."

"TC…"

"Alright, alright," she grumbled. *"Tell me what Aimee said about … us."*

"I haven't told her yet, but I'd guess that Kes is telling her about now."

"Okay, look, I have to get back to work. Call me tonight?"

"Sure thing, sugar."

She hung up, and I walked back to the arena, feeling like I'd been torn in half.

An hour later when the ramps were up and I was wiping my oil-stained hands on a rag, I walked back to the RV with Zef and Kes. Zef gave me a cheesy grin.

"Heard you're boning the boss's sister. Nice!"

I beat Kes to him by a split second, throwing Zef to the ground while he laughed his ass off.

"Last time you get to joke about it," I snapped, sitting on his legs and mashing his face into the dirt.

"You're shit out of luck, Tucker," he laughed, spitting out mouthfuls of dust. "This is just too damn funny."

Disgusted, I smacked the back of his head and stood up.

Kes idly kicked him in the ribs as he walked past, making Zef cough up dust. *Why didn't I think of that?*

I turned back and gave Zef another kick for good measure.

He lay in the dirt laughing and coughing until his eyes watered.

"One day he's gonna really piss me off," I said darkly.

Kes gave me an amused smile. "You realize that if it wasn't my sister we were talking about, I'd be ripping the piss out of you, too."

"Yeah, I know," I muttered.

We took our two-minute turns in the shower and I had to admit that I missed the long, lazy showers that I'd shared with Tera.

And I *really* missed the sex.

A small bonfire was blazing in the fire pit when I stepped out of the RV, and the usual crowd of carnies was grouped around it. I slumped down in a deckchair and helped myself to pizza, looking around and nodding at familiar faces.

I remembered the first time I saw Tera, back in the spring, sitting alone by Kes's bonfire, her hair gleaming in the firelight, one side of her face thrown into shadow. And then she glanced up at me and I remember thinking that there was a damn fine woman.

"Holy shit, Tucker McCoy looks like he's thinking!"

I looked up, grinning at Ollo.

"Hey, man!" I said, standing up and holding out my hand.

But quicker than a sober man taking a piss in the snow, he yanked my arm behind my back and had me on my knees. My bad arm.

"Fuck!" I yelled, my eyes watering from the pain.

Ollo laughed and let me up.

"You've gotten soft," he grinned.

I stood up slowly, pain throbbing through my abused body.

"What the fuck you do that for, dude?" I asked, massaging my shoulder.

He took a step closer.

"Tera Chastain Hawkins is family. You fuck her over and you'll answer to me," he said, his voice hard and menacing."

"I know! I know! Jeez, Ollo, you couldn't have just said it without ripping my damn arm off?"

The little man shrugged. "You need to know I mean it."

He walked away without saying another word.

I got it, I did, but it kind of sucked that everyone assumed I was going to fuck this up with Tera.

Sighing, I picked up my pizza from the ground, dusted it off and finished eating. A few other carnies came over to shoot the breeze and catch me up on the news, which wasn't much.

Everyone always wanted to be around Kes's fire—he was the closest thing there was to carnie royalty. But it was more than that—people were drawn to him, just wanting to be near. For the first three years I'd known him, he used that as a way of getting as much pussy as he wanted, but ever since he'd met Aimee again, he'd barely looked at another woman.

I wondered if it was easy or if it took a lot of willpower.

"Hey, lover!"

I looked up just in time to catch Jade as she dropped into my lap and kissed me enthusiastically.

"I heard you were back," she whispered, grinding her ass against me. "Want to come over later?"

"Damn, that's a good offer," I smiled, "but I'm going to have to say no."

She laughed in amazement.

"Why the hell not? You got religion or something?"

"Or something," I said, winking at her. "I met someone and we're kind of dating."

Jade looked stunned. "Seriously?" And she looked around. "Where is she?"

"She lives in San Francisco. She's flying out in a couple of weeks."

Jade's laugh rang out over the campsite.

"She's a thousand miles away and you're *kind of* dating? Well, I'm *kind of* not caring, Tucker," and she tried to kiss me again.

"Not interested," I said firmly, gripping her hips tightly.

"Yeah?" she smirked. "Well, your dick tells me something else."

Fuck! She was right. I couldn't help it—a pretty girl was grinding on my lap. My dick didn't know any better and was up for whatever action he could get.

I shifted Jade off of my lap.

"You're a great girl, Jade," I said soberly, "and we had some great times, but I'm with someone now."

She raised her hands in a gesture of defeat, but the glint in her eyes told another story.

"So you're housetrained now—I can take a hint. But if you get bored of waiting for Ms. Whitebread, you know where I'll be."

And she walked off swinging her hips.

I rubbed the heels of my hands over my eyes before the image was burned into them.

Zef nudged me.

"How's it feel to be a one-woman man?" he asked, his voice hovering between amused and curious.

"Right now it sucks," I admitted and Zef gave me a knowing smile.

I closed my eyes and leaned back in the deckchair. The weekend after next couldn't come soon enough.

CHAPTER FIFTEEN

TERA

Damn planes! Damn airports! Damn rental cars that weren't where they were supposed to be!

A two-hour flight and a short drive had turned into *six hours* of infuriating sitting on my ass.

It was one snafu after another and I was horribly late. I was nervous enough about seeing Tucker again—I really didn't need any extra stress.

We'd only managed one long conversation a week ago; everything else had been scattered texts, missed calls and hurried words while one of was rushing somewhere else. He'd even called me at work a couple of times, but I'd been stuck in boring meetings. Our schedules didn't match at all.

I hoped it wasn't an omen.

But I sensed a distraction when I did speak to him, a shadow in the distance that chilled me.

And now, instead of arriving in time to see the evening show, light was fading from the sky and the carnival was winding down. I was dirty, dusty, and my stomach was growling—not a good combination.

It took a while to weave my rental through the steady stream of traffic leaving the fairground, and then I had to convince the surly carnie at the campsite entrance that I wasn't just some rube trying to go where I didn't belong.

Finally, finally, hot, tired and tense, I parked my car catty-corner and lugged my suitcase across the campground, looking for Kes's RV.

Aimee spotted me first, followed by Bo, who shrieked happily and scampered across the open ground before climbing me like a tree.

"Hey, baby boy! Did you miss your Aunty Tera?"

Aimee grinned at me, squeezing my waist and kissing my cheek.

"Tera! How are you?"

"I'm good!" I said, smiling. "It's great to be back."

"To see us or to see a certain reformed manwhore who's awfully pretty to look at?"

My cheeks flooded with color as I grinned at her sheepishly.

"Can I say 'both' without upsetting someone?"

Aimee laughed. "Probably not. But I will say he's been like a cat on a hot tin roof waiting for you to show up. He's over there, on the other side of the bonfire."

We both turned to look and my heart skittered to a halt.

It was so much like the first time I saw him. He was surrounded by a group of people who were smiling at him while Tucker's intoxicating laugh rang out the loudest.

Tall and slim, his long lean build was easy on the eyes, and his oil-stained t-shirt clung to his arms and chest. The bonfire's flames turned his dirty blond hair into a fiery halo, his eyes dancing with happiness.

And, just like last time, a woman with glossy black hair that reached to her waist was hanging onto him, her short nails digging into his arm in a possessive way.

"Oh..." Aimee whispered, glancing at me nervously.

"Oh," I echoed, torn between fear and anger.

But then Tucker looked up, as if he sensed me watching him and a shadow passed behind his eyes. And this time I didn't have to wonder, I knew—the clown's mask hid something deeper, something darker. And possibly something dangerous.

Maybe he was a man to stay away from.

And if I was smart, that's exactly what I'd do.

A slow smile turned the corners of his mouth upwards, and I felt the intensity hidden in his lazy gaze and laidback smile.

He brushed off the woman's arm as if it meant nothing, and I didn't miss the irritation on her face. I *loved* the irritation on her face.

Tucker strode toward me, his fierce stare purposeful.

The angry, hateful words died in my throat as he wrapped his arms around me tightly and kissed me with certainty.

I could taste both tension and relief in his kiss, and I let myself sink into his arms gratefully, soaking up the warmth of his solid body.

The same passion fizzed and crackled between us, and I could feel his growing need against my thigh. But then he pulled away and stared into my face, examining every inch, as if searching for change or doubt or reservation.

Finding nothing, he smiled again, his beautiful face glowing as he grinned at me.

"Fuck, you're a sight for sore eyes, sugar!"

"Sweet words from such a gentleman!" I snorted, laughing and smiling at the same time.

"Let's go to bed," he whispered, nuzzling my neck.

I was nodding against his chest when he was ripped away from me.

"Hey!" he yelped.

"Back off," grumbled Kes. "That's my sister you've got your goddamn hands all over. Hey, Tera!"

Kes gave me a rib-crunching hug, casually elbowing Tucker out of the way as he led me toward the bonfire.

I threw a rueful smile at Tucker and mouthed the word 'later'.

He pretended to catch it with his hands, then winked and blew me a kiss.

This man made me completely crazy. It was a rush, a fairground ride that spun me around and flipped me upside down, leaving me dizzy and grinning like an idiot—the Tucker McCoy effect.

This dusty campsite and a State I'd never visited before—it felt like home.

I took my place at the bonfire, my brother on one side, my lover on the other. But when the woman with the black hair sat down on Tucker's other side, I was *not* happy.

"You looked good today, Tucker," she said, nudging his shoulder and smiling at him from under her lashes. "But then again, I always like you in leather," and she gave a husky laugh.

Tucker glanced at her appraisingly then smiled widely, and I had the feeling he knew exactly which game she was playing.

"Thanks," he said, as he slung his arm around me and nuzzled my cheek. "Tera, this is Jade—she's got a flying act, trapeze. Jade, this is Tera—my girlfriend." And as an afterthought, "She's Kes's sister."

Tucker might have missed her annoyed pout, but I didn't. I leaned against him, enjoying the closeness that wasn't about proximity; it was about him showing her and everyone else that we were together. Although I admit that Aimee's words about Tucker being 'reformed' were music to my ears.

Did I trust him? I wanted to, but we'd been apart for 13 days. It was good to know that a couple of weeks couldn't break us, but what about four weeks or six? What about when the miles between us were too far?

I didn't like to think about it, and for tonight, I'd put it out of my mind.

"I like you in leather, too," I smiled. "But isn't it a bit hot for that? Not that I have any objection to you getting all hot and sweaty."

He groaned softly.

"You're killing me, TC."

I laughed at his pained expression while he shifted uncomfortably.

"So how was your day?" I asked, letting him off the hook.

He shrugged. "The usual. Walked the ramps, checked the arena for oil patches, changed a chain and sprocket, fitted a set of braided steel brake lines."

He grinned at my lost expression.

"Sounds, um ... technical?" I muttered.

Tucker laughed, but before he could reply, Jade butted in.

"Aren't you going to tell her that you were practicing jumps?"

Tucker stiffened and I turned my head to look at him. "Jumps? You've been riding already?"

I could tell that Tucker was annoyed: with me, with her, I wasn't sure.

He drank from a can of beer and nodded.

"Yeah, felt good."

"The doctor told you three months," I said carefully, trying to navigate the minefield of being a protective girlfriend and being a nag. "It's only been seven weeks."

Tucker's lips flattened into a hard line.

"It was fine, and I..."

Jade interrupted. I could tell that she was enjoying herself, her smile spiteful.

"Aw, are you guys arguing already? That's so cute—just like an old married couple," and she laughed again. "The princess and the pauper. Too funny!"

I wanted to smack her, but Tucker gave her a fake grin. "My woman worries about me—not hating it, that's for sure," and then he tightened his arm around my shoulders as Jade raised her lip in a sneer.

Bitch.

Kes nudged me. "Don't worry, TC. He wouldn't be doing a show if the doc hadn't passed him on a physical."

"Why didn't you tell me?" I asked quietly, hurt that he hadn't mentioned something that was so important to him.

Tucker raised his eyebrows. "You checked your voicemail since you got off the plane?"

"Oh! I forgot! I was so annoyed when I got to the rental place and they couldn't find my reservation. You left me a message?"

He gave a serious look. "You were the first person I called, Tera."

I dug my phone out of my purse and listened to the voicemail. I could hear the excitement, his happiness shining through.

"Sorry," I said, leaning my head against his chest.

He kissed the top of my head. "I wanted you to see me perform tomorrow, so I made the docs do the physical exam today."

"You're sure it's not too soon?" I repeated hesitantly.

"He's fine, sis," said Kes. "Believe me, I wouldn't have a man on the show who wasn't fit, including myself."

Aimee threw him a skeptical look, but Kes grinned at Zach who'd been listening to the conversation. "Isn't that right?"

Zach nodded, a glimmer of humor in his eyes. "Yep, but we didn't make Tucker take the mental test 'cause he'd have no chance of passing that."

Everyone laughed, including Tucker, and it broke the tension.

"Well, I guess I've gotta be crazy to do this shit and live with you guys!"

Ollo tossed a toasted marshmallow toward us, and Tucker caught it in his mouth.

"Some are born carnies," said Ollo pointing at Kes. "Some are born crazy," and he pointed at Zef, "and some were dropped on their heads at birth," and he pointed at Tucker.

"And some are born with mouths too big for their short-ass bodies," grinned Tucker.

Without warning, Ollo dove across, knocking Tucker backwards and into the dust, landing on his ribs with a thud that made me wince.

Aimee pulled me out of the way, shaking her head with an amused smile as they rolled around, kicking up quite a dust cloud.

I could tell that Tucker wasn't trying very hard to shake Ollo off of him, and after a minute, they'd both had enough and sat up in the dirt, out of breath.

"Don't you go tracking all that dirt and dust through the RV, Tucker McCoy," Aimee warned.

"No, ma'am. I'll take my clothes off outside," and he sent a wink in my direction.

My libido, dozing peacefully, woke up.

Naked Tucker.

Yes, please. And now.

Aimee smiled at my expression and raised an eyebrow. "I got first dibs on the shower."

She walked away and Kes followed immediately, lifting her into his arms, making her squeal in surprise.

Tucker stood up and attempted to brush some of the dust from his clothes, although it didn't seem to do much good. He must have had the same thought, because he lifted up the hem of his t-shirt and wiped his face with the worn cotton.

Even while I was appreciating the hard lines of his body, and beautiful, small, flat, masculine nipples, I realized that he was able to wear t-shirts again. Obviously his shoulder was healing, although I was still annoyed that he was risking his health doing jumps so soon and...

"Enjoying the view," he grinned, catching me with my eyes fixed on his chest and stomach.

"Yes," I said, raising my gaze slowly. "Lovely scenery around here. Lots of ... trees."

"Yeah, they sure got a lot of ... trees," he agreed, his smile turning wolfish.

"I think they've got some ... trees over there that I haven't seen yet," I murmured, glancing toward the forest.

Tucker laughed. "God, I've missed you."

And if the night wasn't warm enough already, his words were a comforting blanket around me.

"Come on," he said. "Let's go see some trees."

Hand in hand, we walked into the woods, the bonfire's flames flickering and fading into the distance.

"I've never had sex outdoors before," I said absently. "Have you?"

Tucker threw me a quick, amused look. "Yeah."

"Of course you have," I laughed. "Is there anything you haven't done?"

He nodded. "Oh yeah. I haven't done you in a forest. I haven't done you in my bed. I haven't done you on the top of the Ferris wheel. I haven't..."

"The Ferris wheel?" I tried to imagine what that would be like, the bucket swinging, and then swinging some more. Hmm. "I'm getting the idea," I said, squeezing his fingers.

Tucker stopped next to a tall pine, then pulled his t-shirt over his head, wincing slightly as he lifted his arm. Then he laid the worn cotton on the ground carefully so I had something to sit on.

The t-shirt was old and tattered with oil stains down the

front, and it was still the sweetest gesture a man had ever made for me.

I sank down onto it, pulling him with me.

The bed of pine needles was soft beneath us, and I lay down, my hands stroking Tucker's warm skin and muscled shoulders.

His eyes were heated as he hovered over me, his breath rapid, his mouth slightly open.

I licked his throat, tasting salt on my tongue, and his body trembled.

And then all his attempts to be slow and gentle fell apart.

With a frenzied growl, he tore open my jeans and assaulted my mouth with hot, hard kisses. My nails raked down his back, making him hiss as he dove in deeper, possessing my mouth.

I palmed him over his jeans, feeling the heavy heat as his dick throbbed under my hand. He ground his body into me, his eyes wild.

When my jeans snagged on my sneakers, I thought he was going to burst with frustration, but instead he hooked his arm around my waist, depositing on my knees. Satisfied with my position, I heard the jingle of metal as he unbuckled his belt and sheathed his dick.

"This is going to be hard and fast, sugar," he muttered, his voice tight.

"God, *yes!*" I whispered.

And then he rammed into me and we rutted like wild animals, hot and thrilling and intense.

And when I came, I called out his name and tears pricked my eyes.

And when he came, his hot breath whispered, "Tera."

And when we lay together after, his hands and lips were drawn to my body, refusing to leave me for even a second.

And when we made love again, under the endless stars, the pink and yellow Ferris wheel lights glowing in the distance, I finally understood what Aimee was talking about—the carnival was truly magical.

～

Even though I hadn't seen Tucker for two weeks, there was no chance of enjoying sleeping in and catch-up sex. Instead, I'd been woken by the insistent thump of a headboard against the paper thin walls as my brother proceeded to fuck Aimee, very thoroughly, judging by her increasingly loud moans.

Tucker opened one eye and grinned at me.

"That's nothing—we can take them, sugar. Easy," and he trailed his callused fingers down my stomach.

I grabbed his hand quickly.

"I don't think I can—not if everyone's going to hear!"

He laughed drily. "No one will hear."

"How can you say that?"

He started stroking my stomach, drawing slow circles around my bellybutton.

"Because that's the way we do it here: no one hears anything, no one sees anything and no one says anything. The RV is our castle, sugar."

"My *brother* is right next door!" I hissed, as the banging and moaning got even louder.

"Trust me, TC. He's too busy to notice," and Tucker's fingers slid up the inside of my thighs.

I clamped my legs together, trapping his hand.

"I *can't!*" I repeated.

Disappointed, Tucker rolled onto his back. And that's when I noticed that he was 100% hard and erect, the veins on his shaft standing out.

As he followed my gaze, he looked at me half hopeful, but then sighed as I shook my head, and he rolled out of bed, searching for a towel.

"Wanna join me in the shower?"

That sounded more promising. Running water would cover up any ... noises.

"Okay, I'm in!"

Tucker grinned, but before we could move, we both heard Zef's voice right outside as he called out an obscene greeting to Ollo. Then he banged on Tucker's door.

"Get the hell up, you lazy bastard! Walk-through in ten!"

I looked at Tucker hesitantly. "Maybe later."

"Aw, he's just ornery 'cause he isn't getting' any. Come on, sugar."

I shook my head. "No, you've got to eat and get to work."

Tucker's grin wilted. I kneeled up and pressed a promissory kiss to his soft lips that did nothing to help his erection that strained between us.

"We've got the whole night ahead of us," I whispered. "I don't want to wear you out before your big comeback."

"Something to look forward to," he said with a wink.

Then he grabbed the towel and held it in front of him but didn't bother wrapping it around his waist before he left the room. He must have reached the bathroom a second before Aimee because I heard her yelling at him.

"Tucker! How many times do I have to tell you? I do *not* want to see your butt before breakfast!"

"Aw, you love my butt, you just won't admit it."

And then the bathroom door slammed.

"A gentleman would let a lady shower first!" she shouted.

"I would if I knew one," he called back.

She stomped into the living area, grumbling quietly.

Tucker was back in the bedroom in seconds, water dripping all over the floor, the towel covering his dick and nothing else.

"You might wanna get in there before..."

But then we heard the bathroom door slam and the shower started again.

Tucker gave me a rueful smile.

"Shouldn't be too long."

I smiled back weakly, somewhat desperate to pee.

Tucker kissed me firmly then pulled on a pair of ragged shorts and running shoes.

"You don't want to miss out on Aimee's breakfasts—they're awesome."

It was another ten minutes before I could get in the shower behind Aimee, Zef and Kes. The relief when I finally had a chance to pee!

It was only the second time in my life that I'd shared a bathroom—the other being my first year in college when I lived in a dorm. But even though I washed a gazillion times quicker than normal, everyone had finished their food as I hurried in to breakfast, only Tucker was still at the tiny table, with Aimee feeding pieces of banana to Bo.

"Damn, Aimee! I love your banana pancakes, woman!"

Bo seemed to agree as he snatched one from the pile in the middle of the table and scampered off shrieking.

Tucker grinned at Aimee while shoveling the last vast piece into his mouth, syrup smearing his chin.

A sharp spike of jealousy shot through me. I didn't have an act and I couldn't cook. I couldn't do anything useful here.

Then Tucker gulped down his coffee, kissed me quickly, his tongue warm and sweet and tempting, before quite literally running out the door.

Aimee raised her eyebrows.

"He seems happy. Well, Tucker always *seems* happy, but today..." and she reached out to squeeze my hand. "*You* make him happy."

"Do you think so?"

She stared at me quizzically. "You really can't see it?"

"See what?"

"That man is crazy about you."

I smiled. "I know he's crazy, but..."

"No 'but' about it."

I hesitated to ask the question that was burning on my tongue; it just seemed too needy.

Aimee cocked her head on one side. "What?"

"Ugh, I can't believe I'm asking this ... but has Tucker...?"

Her smile twisted to one side. "You want to know about other women?"

"Women? As in ... plural?"

"No! No, I didn't mean that at all. I told you—he's reformed. And it's not like he hasn't had offers..."

"You're talking about Jade."

"Oh, you know about her?"

"Well, she made it pretty obvious last night."

Aimee looked away. "He hasn't hooked up with her since he came back from San Francisco. I don't mean to upset you—he's turned them all down. For you."

Her wording was careful and I wondered if she meant more than she was prepared to say out loud. I shook my head: I was being paranoid.

"Thank you for telling me that," I said sincerely. "But I don't think Tucker is the type to cheat on me..." *Not after what he went through with Renee.* "He'd just tell me it was over and smile."

Aimee raised her eyebrows. "I can't see that happening anytime soon."

But one day?

She loaded pancakes onto my plate and we chatted over her delicious food and strong coffee. I really liked Aimee, but I wasn't ready to discuss my feelings about Tucker with her—not until I knew what they were myself. When he left San Francisco, I thought I'd been pretty clear how I felt, but now being at the fairground and seeing Tucker's happiness radiating from him, his joy in being able to perform stunts again, everything was more confusing.

I offered to clear up after breakfast, but Aimee said I was a guest and should just enjoy myself.

That was easier said than done. Everyone was busy. The carnies were getting ready for their working day, checking rides, feeding the horses, restocking games on the midway. Even the kids had their designated jobs. I was the only one on vacation. This was the machine behind the fantasy: hard, gritty work.

I wandered over to sit in the grandstand, watching Tucker and Kes pace over the ground, studying the ramps, concentrating hard. I didn't want to distract them, especially when they were going to perform tonight, but waiting around for Tucker made me feel like the nerdy high school girl pining for the quarterback. Pathetic.

When he saw me, Tucker waved and jogged over.

"Hey, sugar."

He kissed me sweetly, his lips gentle against mine. It was so hard to believe that those lips could lie to me.

"Have you slept with Jade?" I blurted out.

His body stiffened and he sat down heavily next to me.

"Yeah," he said at last, leaning forward and resting his elbows on his knees. "We've hooked up."

"That's what I thought. Since ... since me?"

He closed his eyes and tilted his head forward. "Not since I got back."

"But...?"

He turned to look at me. "The night I found out about my momma ... we hooked up then."

He'd gone from my bed in the morning to hers in the evening. That hurt.

"Thank you for telling me," I said slowly, pulling away.

"TC, I..."

I waved my hand. "No, it's okay. We weren't together then."

"No!" he said angrily. "I was a fuckin' idiot. I ... I wasn't thinking straight. You were the only person I wanted to talk to when I heard, but I didn't want to drag you into my crappy life. I wanted to get shit-faced and forget everything..."

"But Jade was there."

"Something like that," he sighed.

I hated it.

Jade was always going to be there when I wasn't. And if not Jade, someone just like her. I had to trust Tucker, but it wasn't easy. His history was against him, and the fact that he'd built up so many barriers tos intimacy. The short time we'd had together, was that really enough to change the habits of a decade or more?

I had to hope so, but it was hard.

"I'm not mad at you," I said quietly. "Disappointed, I guess. But we weren't together. You didn't owe me."

"Don't be so fucking nice about it," he growled. "I was a douche. You *should* be mad at me."

"I'm hurt more than anything," I admitted quietly. "Yes, angry too, even though I know I have no right to be."

"Fuck," he muttered. "You're the last person I want to hurt, Tera."

I waited for more: an apology, an admission of how he felt, but there was nothing. Instead he held my hand and played with my fingers.

"I don't know how to do this," he said at last. "But I'm trying."

"Me, too."

I leaned against him, breathing in the smell of his clean sweat and warm, earthy body. It was soothing and arousing at the same time. I couldn't blame him for being confused when my thoughts and emotions were equally haywire.

He started to say something, but then Zef called him over.

"I gotta go, TC. Will you be okay?"

"Sure, sure. Go do your crazy stuntman thing," I said, kissing him quickly.

He grinned at me, then jogged over to Zef, and he was lost in conversation again.

I slipped away, wandering down the midway, chatting to anyone who would stop for a moment. The carnies were polite, but not over-welcoming. And besides, they were all busy.

I understood and I didn't blame them: I was in the twilight world, neither entirely rube, but not one of them either.

Eventually, I walked back to the RV to see if I could help Aimee with lunch, but of course she already had it under control and didn't need my help. She reminded me that they only ate a light snack before a performance, saving the carb-heavy food for the evening.

"I've been working on a diet plan for them," she explained seriously. "They need to ensure a steady and regular supply of glucose to maintain optimum performance. So I use energy foods that are unrefined complex natural carbohydrates. They're low GI, so they release their sugars in a more regulated and continuous manner and avoid the insulin spike and..."

She smiled at me sheepishly.

"Sorry—TMI! It's just since ... since Kes's accident ... well, you know."

I nodded and gave her a quick hug. *I did know*.

She must have felt sorry for me, because she let me contribute by putting out the silverware. That took all of two minutes.

I could have sat down with a book. I could have caught up with some reading from the office, but I couldn't just sit around while everyone else was working their butts off. Instead, determined to be useful, I headed toward the horses and ponies who made up the rodeo outfit—at least they were pleased to see me. I stood rubbing their warm noses and feeding them pieces of carrot, chatting to them and wishing I had a currycomb so I could get some of the thick dust out of their manes.

"Hi, there!"

I turned around and saw Zach's boyfriend.

"Hi Luke," and I gave him a quick kiss which turned his cheeks pink. "Do you need a hand with anything? I'm feeling like a bit of a spare part around here."

He looked around him helplessly.

"I don't know. Is there anything you can do?"

I arched one eyebrow, and his blush deepened.

"Well, I can groom the horses or I can muck them out. You choose."

He seemed stunned. "Kes would have my hide if I got you shoveling shi— manure."

I rolled my eyes. "You can say 'shit', Luke. I won't faint. I just need to do something useful."

"Do you know anything about horses?" he asked skeptically.

"Riding lessons from the age of seven," I replied, raising an eyebrow.

Luke grinned. "Yes, ma'am! This way."

And for the next two hours until lunchtime, I brushed the horses until their coats gleamed and their tails and manes were free of knots, and I shoveled shit until my hands began to blister.

Hot, sweaty and smelling like a horse, I limped back to the RV, my muscles screaming, but full of a sense of achievement.

Kes laughed out loud when he saw me. "What the hell happened to you?"

"Looks like she's been rolling in the hay," Zef said with a calculated glance at Tucker, who frowned.

"Just helping out with the rodeo horses," I smiled, flopping down next to Tucker and kissing the scowl off his face.

He kissed me back enthusiastically, despite my equine odor, only stopping when Kes kicked his leg

"My *sister*, man!"

I raised my eyes to the sky. *Cockblocked by my own brother.* I liked that he looked out for me, but sheesh, couldn't a girl catch a break?

"Later," I whispered to Tucker, for the second time today, and he winked at me.

I caught Kes looking away, a pained expression on his face.

~

After lunch, the atmosphere changed. There was a tension in the air, an electrical charge that zapped along the midway and out to the grandstand, and then at 2PM, the gates to the fairground opened.

Showtime!

Children, families, teenagers, couples, groups of guys and girls poured into the fairground, the happy noise filling the dusty air. I could smell hotdogs and onions frying, and already people were enjoying the sugar rush of blueberry cotton candy, staining their tongues purple and catching it in their hair.

It was strange to think my brothers had grown up with this: one of them loving it, one of them hating it. Falcon never came near the fairground now, except on rare occasions or when Kes was doing a big event.

It was chaotic and loud, and a part of me sympathized with Falcon who had gone into the Air Force, seeking a more ordered way of life.

The Daredevils' first show was at 4PM, plenty of time for me to get nervous. I'd seen Tucker perform stunts before, but not since we'd been ... dating or whatever it was called ... and not since he'd dislocated his shoulder.

My stomach twisted with anxiety and I thought I was going to throw up.

Aimee pulled me to one side when she caught me pacing restlessly as the guys changed into their leathers.

"I know exactly what you're feeling," she said quietly. "I sort of hate this part. I love how excited Kes gets—this is his life—but I can't help feeling a little sick inside. That never changes."

I nodded and tried to swallow.

"I've found that the best thing to do is to stay away until they're ready to perform. They need to get in the zone; seeing us worrying about them doesn't help."

I listened to her advice carefully. She'd been through this so many times.

"How do you stand it?" I asked her, the tension making me twitchy and irritable.

She smiled a little sadly.

"I don't have any choice. But when I see Kes flying through the air, everyone in the crowd standing on their feet and cheering, I know he's doing what he was born to do. They're all like it: they're addicted. They don't know how to live without it."

Her words hit me hard. Tucker would never leave this life, couldn't leave it. So the question was: where did that leave us?

The closer the hour drew to four o'clock, the thicker the crowds of people were around the grandstand and lined along the fence that made up the arena.

As music pounded out across the PA system, I stood with Aimee, our hands locked together. With a roar, three motorcycles zoomed out in a cloud of dust, charging to the center, looking as if they were certain to collide. I gasped, and heard a soft, "Ow!" as my fingers clamped down around Aimee's arm.

"Sorry," I whispered, forcing myself to watch.

The bikes met in the center with barely an inch to spare, dust pouring from their tires as the bikes swerved in dizzying loops, and then they took off, the air filled with the smell of motorcycle fuel, noise and fumes.

I cringed and the crowd roared approval.

"They're fine," Aimee chanted. "They're fine."

The bikes circled the stadium like gladiators, or maybe like men jousting on horseback in days gone by: charging at each other, daring each other, until eventually they were ringed around the outer fence, each preparing for their first jump.

Zef blasted off the ramp, followed a split second later by Tucker in the opposite direction, and I was so certain they were going to crash in the middle, I screamed and closed my eyes.

Aimee squeezed my hand hard, causing me to wince. I opened my eyes just in time to see Kes leaping through a circle of fire, the flames glancing off his helmet.

On and on it went, higher, faster, closer. Sweat trickled down my body, pooling under my armpits, leaving me drenched and weak.

The engines revved and hummed, and then they all charged together, a flying tower of men, with Kestrel cartwheeling over the top of them.

The crowd screamed and clapped and cheered, and Aimee and I stood up, shrieking with them.

"Oh my God!" I yelled over the noise. "I nearly had a heart attack!"

Aimee laughed and wiped her eyes.

"Every time," she whispered, her voice shaky. "Every time."

I followed her back to the RV where the guys were peeling off their sweat-soaked leathers, standing in their underwear, huge smiles plastered across their faces.

Tucker scooped me up in a sweaty hug, his hot skin slick to the touch.

"You are amazing!" I said honestly, a relieved laugh breaking out of me. "Stinky, but amazing!"

He laughed loudly, his head thrown back, his eyes crinkling with happiness, and then he kissed me, deeply.

When I pulled back gasping, his eyes were black with want.

"Is it later?" he whispered.

I nodded, and he grabbed my hand, hauling me behind him as we hurried to the RV.

We crashed into his tiny room and Tucker ripped my clothes from my heated body, frustrated by the knotted belt that held up my shorts.

I heard a tearing sound, and a moment later, my body was naked and Tucker was focused on sliding a condom down the length of his hard shaft.

He muttered something I couldn't catch, then crawled between my thighs, slinging my legs over his shoulders and nearly folding me in half when he plunged inside.

I cried out, all thought wiped from my mind, feeling only the intense connection between us.

It was hard, fast, raw fucking, releasing every tension that I'd felt during the day. I clutched him tightly inside and out, overpowered.

Tucker came first, his hard body turning rigid, and with a muffled groan, his dick pulsed, hot and desperate.

When he slid his thumb over my clit, I exploded, flying upwards then crashing back to earth, breathless and spent.

And then in the quiet space, Aimee screamed Kes's name, and I couldn't help giggling quietly.

A beat later, Zef's aggrieved voice rang out.

"You guys are shitty friends!"

Tucker burst out laughing, but my cheeks were already too flushed from the last couple of minutes to show any embarrassment.

I turned to look at him accusingly.

"What?" he laughed. "Nobody heard a thing."

I laid back, slumped across his heaving chest, smiling to myself.

But we couldn't stay there long. The guys needed to eat and refill all the calories they'd used up, and then to prepare for their evening show.

I frowned when I saw Tucker rubbing his shoulder and wincing, but I managed to bite my tongue. He was an adult, and this was his choice, his work, his life.

The evening show was at 7.30PM, and I wasn't sure I had the stamina to watch another performance. My nerves were already shredded, but I guess seeing it through to the bitter end —that's what the supportive girlfriend does. It honestly made me appreciate past boyfriends who were bankers or lawyers. Being with an adrenaline junky was tough; much tougher than I'd realized.

Aimee and I watched from further away this time, but it made no difference—it was just as hair-raising. The only benefit was that we could get away faster and Aimee had food ready for the guys when they left the arena, howling like a pack of wolves.

Tucker tried to haul me off to his bedroom again, but I insisted that he eat first, and gradually they all calmed down, turning back from barbarians into rough approximations of civilized human beings.

Afterwards, Kes and Aimee walked over to Zach's bonfire where Ollo was drinking whiskey from a bottle and telling drunken stories about the good old days.

I smiled at Tucker and he grinned back. We had the RV to ourselves; we were definitely going to make the most of it.

CHAPTER SIXTEEN

TUCKER

Four weeks. Four long-ass, fucking weeks. A whole month since I'd seen Tera. She'd had to cancel our last weekend because of some work thing that came up. I couldn't complain —it was what I'd signed on for, but I sure as shit didn't like it.

Now I was staring at my cell phone wondering about the Universe's sense of humor.

We were at the Washington County fairground in Utah and Tera had just sent an email saying that she'd had a meeting cancelled and would be here in time to catch the evening show.

That wasn't what bothered me. Nope, it was the fact that Renee had emailed this morning to say that Scotty had a long weekend and had been bugging her to see the show. I'd hoped that he'd want to come and see what I did for a living, so I'd sent her the money for the flights. But did it have to be this goddamn weekend?

I wondered why it was suddenly so urgent. Had she told Scotty about me? She didn't say anything in her message. The only thing that made sense was if she wanted us to tell him together.

I hoped that's what this was about—I was getting tired of her giving me the runaround.

But the timing sucked.

I groaned and rubbed my eyes. The last time Renee saw Tera, she called her a slut. Yeah, she'd apologized since, but only to me. My experience with women told me that they weren't all that forgiving about things like that.

"Problem, bro?" Zef asked as we did a walk-through around the small arena where we'd be doing our show.

I looked up and realized that I'd paced half the area and hadn't seen a thing. Being distracted was not a good idea.

I sighed and rubbed the sweat off my forehead with my t-shirt.

"You know I said that Renee emailed? Yeah, well Tera just texted. She's flying in. Tonight."

Zef's eyebrows flew upward and then a huge grin stretched across his face

"Oh, man! Wouldn't want to be in your shoes."

"Thanks," I said sourly.

"What are you going to do?"

I blew out a breath. "Nothing I can do. They're both on their way already. But if Renee starts anything..."

Zef gave me a serious look. "I thought maybe you still cared about her."

I frowned. "I do, but not like that."

Zef shook his head. "Man, you can be so dumb! This chick cheats on you, lies to her husband about the kid being his, tells you he's yours even though she hasn't proved shit, and you send her off with a pat on the head and twenty grand! Gotta say, buddy, she'd have every reason to think she still has a chance with you."

"No way. I told Renee I wasn't interested—and she knows about Tera."

Zef shrugged. "Guess you'll find out."

The conversation left me feeling uneasy and I wondered if Zef was right. This was why guys like me didn't do relationships —too many ways of fucking up.

I tried to clear my head as show time neared. There were a few kids hanging around waiting to get their programs signed, so the three of us were talking bikes and stunts, and giving them the don't-try-this-at-home message—which was bullshit, because I knew when I was their age, it was exactly what I'd do. But we had to try. Zach was really clear about being on-message with the whole health and safety thing. To be honest, I used to think it was a bit of a joke, but after Kestrel nearly being paralyzed ... let's just say it focused the mind.

"Hi, Uncle Tucker!"

'Uncle'. So she hasn't told him yet.

I looked up from the program I was signing and found Scotty standing with Renee, grinning his head off.

I had to do a double-take. Renee looked way different from last time I saw her.

She'd cut her hair and had highlights put in, but the way she was dressed surprised me more. Instead of baggy jeans and a shapeless t-shirt, she was wearing a short denim skirt and tank-top. She looked good—I really hoped she hadn't dressed up for me.

"Hey, my favorite basketball ace!" I called out, walking toward Scotty and shaking hands before pulling him into a quick hug. "How you doin'? How was the flight?"

"The food was really neat," he said, his face lighting up. "It came in these lunch trays but it was way better than school food."

"That sounds cool," I laughed. Then glanced at his mom. "Renee."

"Hey, Tucker."

She gave this weird, simpering smile that set my teeth on edge.

Ah, hell. Zef was right.

"Good to see you," I said, forcing myself to smile.

"Even better to see you," she purred.

I frowned and glanced across at Scotty who just looked excited to be here. I'd have to get Renee alone later and find out what the hell was going on.

I introduced Scotty to Zef and Kes, and I could see them studying my son curiously. Then they showed him the stunt bikes and explained how they differed from a road bike.

Scotty's lips twisted a bit and he squinted at me nervously.

"Momma says you sold your Ducati motorcycle to help us get to Richmond."

"Yeah, best money I ever spent. When you make the NBA, I'll come see your games. But I want the good seats. Deal?"

"Deal," he said with a huge grin as we did a fist bump.

Renee watched us with a smile on her face. Whatever else, she loved the kid. But I wasn't going to let Renee spin this her way either. When I introduced her to my brothers, she gave a quick nod, sensing that they weren't her biggest fans.

Zef caught on pretty quick, and took Scotty off to look at the rest of our equipment. I turned to face Renee.

"What's going on?"

"What do you mean?"

"Why the sudden urgency to fly out here? Are we telling him this weekend?"

She relaxed slightly. "Yeah, I thought it was time."

Relief mixed with anxiety rolled through me.

"Okay, let's do it."

"Not now," she said, gripping my arm.

"Why wait?" I asked, irritated.

"He just got here. Let him get used to you again. Let's enjoy being a family," and she laid her hand on my arm suggestively. "We'll tell him tomorrow."

"What are you doing, Ren?"

"I don't know what you mean," she said, smiling at me from under her lashes.

"You know I'm with Tera."

"Really? You're still with her? I thought..." She gave a small, embarrassed shrug. "I thought you might have moved on."

"Nope. I haven't. I don't want to either. And just to be clear, Renee, I'm doing this for Scotty, not you."

"Very clear," she said, a tinge of bitterness in her tone. "But are you sure? You think a woman like her will stay with a ... with a carnie?"

Yeah, Renee still knew how to get under my skin.

"That's none of your business," I said sharply.

She shrugged again, a lopsided smile pulling at her lips, and she dropped her hand from my arm.

"Fair enough. Thought I'd ask."

I really hoped that was the end of it.

Tera hadn't arrived by the time we went to do the evening show, but she'd messaged to say that she was on her way.

Scotty and Renee had ringside seats in the tiny grandstand, and I was trying to focus, to get in the zone.

We were all in our flame-resistant leathers waiting for the countdown to start. Kes raised his hand in the air, his eyes glowing with the adrenaline, with the buzz. The music slammed through the PA system, and we could feel the vibration of the crowd stamping their feet.

"Gentlemen!" Kes yelled. "Let's kill it!"

We slapped hands, snapped our visors shut and shot out into the arena.

I felt calm, utterly focused, and utterly revved up at the same time. There was *nothing* better than this: not even sex. Although ...

Fuck, no!

Not the time to be thinking about Tera. I lined up for the first stunt, dropped the clutch and...

Showtime!

~

An hour later, I was dripping with sweat and my weak shoulder was burning. When we did a show, we put everything into it. We trained as hard as any athlete, needing to be at the top of our game. Throw a measure of danger on top, and it really focused the mind and honed the body.

Tera said I was just gristle and muscle, but I have to say, I got a huge kick out of the way her eyes drank me in.

Right now, all I wanted was a hot shower, but Scotty was waiting outside, his enthusiasm brimming over.

"That was so freakin' cool, Uncle Tucker! When you did that handstand and you were flying through the air—that was epic! This woman next to me screamed. It was awesome!"

His eyes were lit with enthusiasm and I couldn't help grinning at him.

"Yeah? You liked the show?"

He nodded furiously. "The best part was when Kes went through the flames! That was sick!" Then he looked contrite. "You were really good, too."

I laughed loudly.

"You got good taste, buddy. That's my favorite part, as well."

He grinned up at me, but then his expression changed and he frowned.

"I wish you were my dad," he whispered, an angry scowl on his face. "My Dad's an asshole."

His comment felt like a punch to the gut and Renee shot me a guilty look.

I didn't know whether to laugh the comment off or to roll with it now Scotty had brought it up.

"The thing is..." I began, but Renee interrupted me.

"Scotty! No cussing."

Scotty just stared.

I sighed and sank down next to him on the grass, stretching out my abused muscles.

"Look, man, you're right: Jackson *is* an asshole. I grew up with him, so I know what I'm talking about."

Scotty gave a shy smile.

"But you got your momma, and she isn't an ass— what you said before. So you're ahead of the game compared to a lot of kids, right?"

Scotty glanced at Renee and gave a quick nod.

"And you got this athletics scholarship and you got a new start..."

"You could be Momma's boyfriend," he said quickly, looking at me hopefully. "I know you used to date ... she told me. Then you could be my Dad for real."

Fuck, this was hard.

I glanced at Renee, but she shook her head and threw me a warning look.

I didn't like lying to him, but she was probably right—we should tell him when we were all calm, not hyped up after a show.

"Scotty, dude. That was a long time ago. We were hardly more than kids ourselves. Your momma and I are friends and..."

"But you could!" he insisted.

"I've got a girlfriend," I said firmly. "Her name is Tera. You met her."

His face closed down.

"I hate her!"

"I'd be really sorry if that's true," I said carefully, "because she's going to be around for a long time."

I glanced at Renee again, hoping that she'd give me some backup. But her mouth was pressed into a flattened line that matched Scotty's.

I stood up and looked at both of them.

"You'll always have me, Scotty. I promise I'll do whatever I can to help you and you'll always be a part of my life. But I hope that Tera will be, as well. You'll have to decide how to handle that."

I walked away, wondering if I'd said the right thing, wondering if Scotty would deal with it.

I was pissed as all hell at Renee, but maybe now she'd get the message.

I took my turn in the shower, wishing for once that I was back in San Francisco and enjoying Tera's spectacular friggin' shower, and not a one-minute, lukewarm wash.

But the evening got a whole lot better when I walked outside and saw Tera sitting by the bonfire talking to Aimee.

She was dressed casually in jeans and a t-shirt and she was still the sexiest woman I'd ever seen. And she was here for me.

I was one lucky mothertucker.

Tera smiled, then stood up and walked toward me.

There were no words as she wrapped her arms around my neck. Her breath was warm on my cheek and then my lips were on her mouth, and I kissed her hungrily.

"Goddamn! You are a sight for sore eyes," I murmured against her jaw.

She smiled at me and pressed a soft kiss to the dip at the base of my throat, then licked across my chest with her tongue.

"Sugar, if you keep doing that, I'm going to have a problem," I groaned, glancing down at the front of my jeans.

She laughed lightly and took my hand as we strolled toward the bonfire. I slumped down on the grass and she situated herself in my lap.

"You look stressed," she said, brushing a soothing hand along my shoulder and down my arm. "Aimee told me that you were with Scotty. How's it going?"

I shook my head in frustration. "Shit, I don't know. He was pretty upset."

Tera looked surprised.

"What's he upset about?"

I side-eyed her, wondering how much of the truth she needed to hear.

"Just tell me, Tucker," she said patiently.

I took her hand in mine and stared down at our fingers as I wove them together.

"He said he wished I was his dad and that if I was with Renee I would be." I shook my head in frustration. "I thought it would be the perfect time to tell him, you know? But Renee wants to do it tomorrow. Fuck's sake."

Tera gave a small smile. "I'm not surprised; he idolizes you and..."

"Hell, no!"

"Of course he does, Tucker. Look at it from his point of view: he feels stuck in a rut, the man he believes is his father doesn't care about whether or not he has the chance of a basketball scholarship and has no interest in bettering his son's life; you ride into town and make it all happen. Plus, you're a stunt rider, for goodness sake. Of course he's going to say things like that."

It was a version of what Zef had said to me before Scotty and Renee had arrived.

Then she gave a small smile. "He'll be so excited when he finds out that you're his father."

"Wow, I nearly fucked up, didn't I?"

"Tucker, no," she said soothingly. "How could you possibly know he'd say that? Tomorrow you can sit down together and tell him. It'll be fine." She paused. "What was Renee doing while Scotty was saying all this?"

"Not much. She just made it clear she didn't want me to tell him there and then."

Tera pursed her lips.

"Do you think ... has Renee let him get carried away with this idea of you and his mother...? Oh, I see."

"See what?"

"She wants you back."

I shifted uncomfortably, hoping that she'd drop the subject. But this was Tera, so no way that was happening.

"I told her straight that I'm with you. And Scotty. I said that he's got to deal with you being part of my life."

"You said that?"

"Yeah, I did."

Tera smiled at me, then ran her hands along the side of my jaw, pulling my face toward hers.

"You need to be kissed for that."

And before I knew it, the evening was a lot less shitty than it had been ten minutes ago.

I was at the point of taking her back to the RV, when she pushed on my chest and eased away from me.

"Someone's here to see you," she whispered.

Scotty was standing awkwardly, uncertain whether to approach or not. When I waved at him, he took a pace nearer, then stopped again.

"Hey, man! Come and sit down," I said, pointing at the space next to me.

He shuffled forward, casting nervous glances at Tera.

"Hi Scotty," she said kindly. "I have marshmallows. Want to get them toasted?"

He nodded, then reluctantly added, "Yes please, ma'am."

"You can call me Tera. Okay, let's get Kes to show you how they toast marshmallows in the carnival."

Kes grinned at Scotty from across the bonfire, held a stick in front of him with a marshmallow impaled on the end, then a jet of flames shot from his mouth, turning the edges a warm brown.

"Whoa!" yelled Scotty, his eyes wide. "Freakin' awesome!"

He turned to look at me. "I want to live in the carnival when I grow up. I'm going to be a stunt rider just like you." Then he glanced back at Kes. "And I want to learn to do that."

We grinned at each other, then Tera tossed him the rest of the packet of marshmallows.

Tera

Tucker and Scotty were enjoying themselves, eating toasted marshmallows, then burgers, then more junk food, in that 'I'll eat anything' guy-way. Seeing them together showed me another facet of Tucker, and I could see that for someone who'd been alone for much of his life, family was important to him.

Which was why I waited until his back was turned to hunt down Renee.

She stiffened when she saw me coming.

"Hello again," I said.

She nodded briefly.

"Scotty seems like a great kid," I began.

Her eyes narrowed warily.

"He is," she said, her words edged with suspicion.

"It's good to see him getting on so well with Tucker, with his father."

She put her hands on her hips. "Say what you've come to say."

"I'm not trying to come between Tucker and his son. I wouldn't do that because I care about Tucker and I can see what Scotty means to him..."

Renee opened her mouth to say something but I didn't let her interrupt me.

"...but I won't let you come between Tucker and me either."

Her lips thinned and she leaned forward, poking her bony finger in my chest and causing me to stumble backward.

"You have no idea, *no idea*, what we've been through. Me and

Tucker. Together. We've got a history; we shared everything. I understand him in ways you never can."

I flinched because I knew she was right. Renee saw it, arching her eyebrows at me in triumph.

"You'll never have that!"

I swallowed and looked her in the eye.

"That's true. I don't have that. But Tucker and I have a future together. And I promise you this—if you hurt Tucker again, you'll regret it."

Her eyes widened.

"Are you threatening me?" she asked, her voice amused and incredulous.

"I'm making a promise."

She laughed out loud.

"Honey, I grew up hard, same as Tucker. You wouldn't stand two minutes in a fight with me."

"We'll have to agree to differ on that because I have something worth fighting for."

I let that sink in first, measuring her surprise that I wasn't backing down.

"Tucker cares about Scotty and I can see you love your son very much. You owe it to both of them to tell Scotty the truth. I'm just saying don't try to come between them ... because you have no idea what I'm capable of. I'm sure you know who my father is. And if you think for one second that I won't do everything I can to protect Tucker, you're even more deluded than I thought."

Her mouth clamped shut.

"That's the first smart thing you've done," I said.

She nodded slowly.

"I did what I had to do for my son," she said, staring at me without flinching. "I never wanted to hurt Tucker. He's a good man."

"Something we can agree on," I said, folding my arms across my chest.

She looked like she wanted to say something else, but then changed her mind.

I watched her walk away, my heart racing.

~

The next morning, Tucker was on edge.

"It'll be fine," I said calmly for the twentieth time. "Scotty adores you. He'll be really happy about this."

"I don't know," Tucker said, shaking his head. "He'll be mad that we've been hiding it all of this time. Fuck, I would be."

"He'll come around. It's what he wants—you said so yourself. He's more likely to be mad at Renee than you." I sighed. "Look, I'd offer to go with you, but I think this is something you and Renee need to do yourselves."

"I know, I know. Okay, wish me luck!"

I kissed him lightly on his lips and waved him off. Then I slumped down onto one of the deckchairs. I hated that I'd sent him off alone to deal with that woman. I didn't trust her.

Aimee came out of the RV with Bo in her arms and sat next to me.

"Did he go to tell Scotty?"

"Yes. I just hope everything is alright."

Aimee nodded.

"He seems like a nice boy. I can't say I warmed to Renee."

"God, no! Me neither. I didn't want to come off like the jealous girlfriend, but I just wanted to bitch slap her smug face!"

Aimee grimaced and laughed. "Probably not the best thing to do. But hopefully you won't have to see that much of her."

"I know. I just hate the thought of Tucker being around *her*."

Aimee gave me a reassuring hug.

"You don't need to worry. Tucker loves *you*."

But did he? He'd never said the words.

Tucker

I stared in disbelief at the hotel receptionist.

"They checked out? Are you sure?"

"Yes, sir. Mrs. Foster left this for you."

She pushed an envelope across the desk with my name scrawled on the top.

> *Tucker,*
> *Something came up and it's not the right time to tell Scotty. I'll call you.*
> *Renee.*

I turned the piece of paper over, certain there must be something more, but that was it.

What the hell was Renee up to?

I pulled out my phone to call her, but surprise, surprise, it went straight to voicemail.

Frustrated, I shoved the phone in my pocket and headed back to the fairground.

When I got there, I found Tera with the horses.

"Hey, you! That was quick. How did it go?"

"I have no fucking clue," I grunted. "They weren't there."

"Where were they?"

I shook my head.

"They just up and left. Renee left me this."

I handed her the envelope and she read the short note.

"Oh my God! This is all my fault," she whispered, a guilty expression on her face.

I stood up straight.

"What the...? You want to explain that?" I asked, my voice calm despite a sudden rush of anger.

"I ... oh, Tucker! I just told her that if she messed with you, she'd be messing with me. I never thought she'd run away."

I stared at Tera in disbelief.

"You *threatened* her?"

"I could just see the way she was flirting with you, trying to use Scotty to get you back," she said hastily.

I was still staring, speechless. Tera swallowed, looking more nervous by the second.

"I ... I got scared. Because you have all this history with her, so..."

It didn't add up. Renee was tough, she'd had to be. If anything, Tera getting possessive would make her push back.

"That's it?"

"Pretty much," Tera said, biting her lip. "I'm sorry. I didn't think she'd run off like that."

I shook my head.

"I'm not blaming you. I'll talk to Renee when they land."

Tera

I felt awful. I never meant to drive Renee away like that. No, I didn't trust her, but I didn't want to stop Tucker from having a relationship with his son—I'd been trying to help, hadn't I? Or had I just been horribly selfish? Oh God, what a mess. It had backfired—badly.

I felt so guilty. And I felt ashamed, too. Tucker should have been telling Scotty this morning that he was his father, and I'd robbed him of that.

Worse still, Tucker couldn't reach Renee by phone and she wasn't answering texts or emails either. She and Scotty had dropped off the radar, and it was all my fault.

The only positive was that Tucker was more annoyed than upset.

"Fuck it," he said wearily. "Scotty's waited his whole life to hear the truth—another couple of months won't matter. I'll fly out to Richmond after Thanksgiving and tell him myself, whether she wants to or not."

"I feel really bad about this," I sighed.

Tucker pulled me in for a hug. "I'm not blaming you, Tera. Renee should have called me. I don't want to make a big deal of it with her because I know she's dealing with a lot right now. Yeah, it pisses me the hell off, but like I said, after the holidays, I'll go see my kid."

"I'm sorry," I muttered again.

I didn't really feel like company, and maybe Tucker felt the same way, because after the last show that evening, he wrapped his arm around me while we strolled down the midway, enjoying being spectators instead of part of the show.

"Where are going?" I asked.

"Ferris wheel," he answered, his full lips turning up in a sly grin.

"I hope you're not thinking what I think you're thinking, bucko!"

"I don't know, sugar. What are you thinking?"

I tickled his ribs and he danced away laughing.

"We can't have sex on the Ferris wheel," I said pointedly.

"Why, Miss Hawkins! I'm shocked! A gentleman would never assume such a thing from a fine lady like yourself."

"Huh. I'm as much a lady as you're a gentleman, but I'm still not getting arrested for public indecency."

Tucker smirked at me. "It's the moonlit ride, sugar. They turn off the lights in the buckets. Anything goes."

I paused. "Really?"

"Yeah."

Just then his phone buzzed with an incoming text.

Tucker checked it automatically, frowning at whatever he saw.

"Problem?"

"Not sure. It's from Renee. She says for me to check my email."

We left the midway and sat behind the helter-skelter, listening to the loud shrieks of people spinning down from the top of the tower.

Tucker's fingers drummed against his thigh as he waited for the email to download.

I saw him open the message, and then his body froze. He scanned the whole email, the lines edging his mouth tight with some deep emotion.

Then he threw his phone to me and stalked off without saying a word.

"Tucker...?"

I stared after him in surprise—I'd never seen him like this before and I didn't know what to do. But if he wanted to be alone...

I read the email on his phone, my concern softening to pity.

CHAPTER SEVENTEEN

TUCKER

Tera found me by the horses. There was something soothing about being with them ... maybe their unconditional acceptance, their simplicity. They didn't fuck you over—only people did that.

They snickered softly when Tera walked up, greeting her like an old friend.

I didn't need to ask if she'd read the message, I could tell by the look on her face.

"I'm sorry, Tucker."

I didn't answer. There was nothing to say.

"I'm so sorry," she said again.

She wrapped her arms around me, leaning against my chest. Having her there, giving me comfort because I'd had a shitty day, it felt good.

"I knew Renee was a liar," I said at last, reveling in the way Tera felt in my arms. "I just didn't think she'd lie about the kid. Not like this."

"Scotty definitely isn't your son?"

"No, the DNA test is 99% conclusive... he's not mine. I

don't know if that means he's Jackson's after all..." I frowned. "The email from the lab is a month old—she's known all of this time. Maybe she always knew."

"Then why...?"

"Why did she do it?" I shrugged. "Because she wanted the money, because he could have been mine."

She met my eyes without flinching. "Why aren't you angry? After everything Renee has done to you...!"

"Scotty could have been mine," I repeated, my voice so quiet it was amazing that she heard me over the noise around us. "We were together ... like that. So it could have been me. Just luck, right?"

She hesitated. "Are you ... disappointed?"

I rubbed my eyes tiredly.

"Scotty seems like a great kid, and I'd started thinking that we..." I paused, struggling to find the words that explained the confusing mix of emotions swirling through me. "Renee loves him, I know that. Maybe she's a good mom. But if I had kids, I'd want to be a part of their lives. Hell, I'd want them to know I existed!"

I let out a long breath.

"At least Renee didn't say anything to Scotty. I just don't know why she changed her mind. Why go through that whole charade and then leave? It doesn't make any sense. Maybe she had a conscience about it after all."

Tera winced.

"I think I might have an idea about that."

"What do you mean?"

"Um, well, don't get mad, but I didn't tell you everything I said to Renee last night."

I crossed my arms over my chest.

"Yeah? What did you say?"

Tera took a deep breath and met my gaze.

"I told her that if she ever tried to hurt you again, I'd make her regret it."

I waited, but Tera was silent.

"That's it?"

"Yeees," she said, her eyes flicking away from me.

"Fuck's sake, Tera! What else?"

"And um, I reminded her who my father is. I may also have said that she owed it to both of you to tell Scotty the truth."

"You said what?"

"I'm sorry," she said hastily. "I know it was none of my business, but I just had this *feeling* that something was off. It was all so odd."

Some of the anger drained out of me.

"Guess you were right about that," I said bitterly. "But, dammit it, Tera! The *Senator?*"

Her chin jutted out. "I'm sorry, I am. I just wanted her to know ... to know that you're not alone. That she had to deal with me, too."

Her lip trembled, and angry as I was, I couldn't bear to see the tears glistening in her eyes. I pulled her into a tight hug, resting my chin on her shoulder.

"My girl, looking out for me again," I whispered.

She sniffed and nodded at the same time.

"I'm sorry," she said again.

"Yeah. So am I."

There was a pause. "What will you do about Scotty?"

I shrugged. "He still thinks of me as his uncle. Whatever, I promised I wouldn't let him down, and I won't. But yeah, it changes things. Again."

"Do you think you'll ever want to have children?" she asked carefully.

I gave her a long, penetrating look, trying to figure out if this was some sort of test. I had no idea what the right answer was.

"I'd never really thought about it before this summer," I replied honestly. "I spent my whole life making sure I didn't have to."

"That's not an answer," she said thoughtfully.

"Yes, no, maybe. Right time, right place," I said, watching her beautiful face. "Right woman."

She nodded slowly.

"What about you, Tera. You want kids?"

She gave me a small smile and looked away.

"Children? I don't know. That's definitely a game-changer. But sure, why not? One day."

What did that mean?

I waited until she looked my way.

"With me?" I asked quietly, shocked at myself for even wanting to ask the question.

She sighed, her expression sad.

"Tucker, whatever you think, whatever demons you have chasing you, I know you'd make a great father. But not yet. Let's work on *us* first."

She wasn't saying no, but her answer wasn't as definite as I'd hoped. Can't say I was surprised though.

She ran her hands gently down my face, gazing into my eyes.

Was that what I wanted? I had to check to see if I'd gone completely freaking crazy. Nope: heart rate normal, anxiety levels … low. The thought of Tera carrying my child … I wasn't hating the idea. In fact...

"Are we okay?" she asked, her voice soft with uncertainty.

"Yeah," I nodded slowly. "We're good. I just feel so fucking dumb for letting her screw me over. Again."

Tera shook her head fiercely.

"You have *nothing* to feel bad about. This was all Renee. You're a good man Tucker McCoy. It's time you realized that."

I wanted to believe her.

"I'll try," I said at last.

"Let's just forget about this weekend, or at least, put it behind us. We've still got tonight. Come on," she said, her eyes smiling. "I never did get a Ferris wheel ride—you owe me."

I held her hand as we walked to the front of the waiting line of couples, ignoring the grumbles and snarky comments as Joel gave us the first bucket for the moonlit ride.

As promised, the lights had been turned off, so we'd be all but invisible as the bucket rose through the night sky.

The moment we were situated and the safety bar had been dropped into position, Tera started kissing up my neck, her warm wet tongue snaking against my pulse point, teeth nipping and biting as she pushed me back against the hard seat. Straddling my hips, her weight resting on my thighs, she pushed one hand up under my t-shirt and the other over the zipper on my jeans.

My woman knew *exactly* how to turn me on, and I went from zero to sixty in half a second.

"You really want this, Tera?" I muttered into her hair, then pulled her head to the side so I could kiss her throat. "You want me to take you here? Knowing everyone will be looking up while we fuck?"

"Do it."

This woman took my breath away.

Then she pinched my nipple hard.

"Just don't rock the bucket too much or I might throw up."

A hoarse chuckle burst out of my mouth. "You sure know how to romance a guy!"

She smiled down at me. "Oh, do I have to? I heard that you were easy."

"I'm reformed," I said, biting her earlobe and making her squeal as my left hand stroked up her warm back, under her bra. "Only one pussy I'm interested in now."

"Sweet talker."

"That's 'cause you're my sugar."

"So, um, how are we going to do this?" she asked, peering over my shoulder and down at the crowds that were already 20 feet below us.

"You forget how since this morning?" I chuckled.

"Funny guy. I'm just slightly afraid of falling over the safety bar and dying with my vag on display. That would be embarrassing."

"Woman, the things you say! You sure have some strange thoughts in your head, Tera."

"I know, and you're one of the strangest."

"Meh. You only want me for my body anyway."

"True. And there's one part of your body that I'm particularly interested in right now."

"Oh yeah?" I murmured, letting my fingers drift over the teeny tiny thong she wore under her thin cotton skirt.

She muttered something incoherent then wrapped her hand around the bulge in my jeans, squeezing firmly and making me groan.

The bucket rose higher and I could hear the laughter of people below us, but here, only the stars were above, and it was just me and Tera.

I pulled her closer, kissing her hard, telling her with my mouth and with my body, the only things I had to offer her, how much, how fucking much she meant to me.

She strained against me, grinding and rubbing over my aching dick.

By now, we were inching toward the top of the ride.

"Gonna have to be quick, sugar."

"That won't be a problem," she said breathlessly as she arched upward and I slipped a finger inside her.

Her body shivered and she gripped me tighter, making me cuss.

I unzipped my jeans and sheathed up with shaky hands.

"Turn around and face forward," I instructed. "Hold tight to the safety bar."

She stood up, clinging on with both hands, her gorgeous heart-shaped ass in my face. I couldn't help biting her left cheek hard so she squealed.

"You want everyone to know what we're doing, that's the way to tell 'em," I teased her.

She threw me a scorching look over her shoulder and lowered herself quickly, taking just the tip inside her.

She hovered, teasing me, taunting me.

I threw my head back, staring up at the bright pinpoints of light above, taking deep breaths.

This was a memory I'd take to my grave: the Ferris wheel, the stars, Tera panting above me, and a sudden and terrifying knowledge that I loved this amazing, fearless woman.

There was no doubt, not anymore. I'd tried so hard not to let anyone get near me again, but she had. Tera owned me, body and soul, and there wasn't a damn thing I could do about it.

"Put me inside you," I whispered. "All the way."

Tera licked her lips, then closed her eyes as she slid down, all the way.

I started breathing hard as she pushed her body up to slide down my shaft, igniting every nerve end in my sensitized dick, faster and faster, over and over again. I was hypnotized, staring at the way we were joined together, my dick gleaming and slick with her juices. My hips rocked to meet her, and I gripped her waist with both hands, helping her move more deeply, my fingers digging into her soft flesh, keeping her close, keeping her safe.

The bucket started to rock and she wobbled on her feet, but I held her tightly.

She nearly gave me a heart attack when she let go of the safety bar with one hand.

"Tera! What the hell are you doing?"

She didn't answer in words, but shoved her hand into her panties, getting herself off fast.

Damn, that was so hot, knowing she was touching herself like that.

My balls started to tighten, and sparks of light flickered up and down my spine until a wave of hot pleasure rushed through my dick and I came hard, squeezing my eyes shut as she clenched around me.

Her thighs trembled and her soft gasps told me she was there, too.

"I've got you, Tera," I grit out. "I've got you, sugar. I'll keep you safe." *Always.*

Her body softened and I lifted her from me, straightening her clothes as I pulled off the condom and tucked myself in.

"That ... that felt so dirty," she laughed quietly.

I choked on a laugh.

"Um, you're welcome?"

The Ferris wheel slowed to a halt, the bucket dropping the last few feet until we were at ground level again.

Joel unlatched the safety bar, a small smile tugging at his lips. I didn't know if he'd heard what Tera said or whether he'd guessed what we'd been doing.

Tera wrapped her arms around my waist and snuggled into me. I loved it when she did that—it made me feel like I'd won the lottery.

Too soon it was Sunday morning, and I only had a few hours before Tera had to leave for the airport and her flight back to California.

The weekend had raced by, a blur of images: Scotty and Renee, Tera, the stunts, Tera, showtime, Tera, nighttime, Tera, the Ferris wheel, Tera, love and fear, Tera, Tera, Tera. Too much, too little, too fucking terrifying to understand.

But the thought of having to snatch moments of time like this, well, it didn't thrill me, that's for sure. I didn't want to lose her, so I'd take what she could give me—whatever that was. It was time to figure out where we were going with this; it was time to have *the talk*.

I couldn't help cringing at the irony. The words *we should talk* were what every guy feared, and here I was, ready to spit them from my mouth.

Tera must have been thinking along the same lines, because she'd woken earlier than usual, her tongue wrapped around my dick, and I got to take her slow and deep before my crazy day started all over again.

Our bodies were pressed skin to skin, hot and panting, the sheets kicked off of the bed, and laying together, a tangle of sweat-slick limbs. Her wheat-colored hair was spread across the pillows, across my chest, and I stroked her silky hair, wanting to wrap it around my fist and refuse to let her go.

I was still sporting a semi, although I was like that the whole time Tera was around. She said that was sweet, even though she seemed kind of doubtful, but it was just the way things were.

"Do you have to go back right now? Maybe stay a couple more days?" I asked, and I could hear that my voice betrayed a longing that I hadn't known existed until now.

It shocked me a little; terrified me a lot. So much easier not to want; so much safer not to need.

"You know I do—I have my job," she said gently, stroking her hand over my forearm, then turning my palm up so she could trace the rough calluses.

"Me staying—this isn't going to work, Tucker."

My heart started to gallop. I knew she was going to say it, but hearing the words spoken aloud was bitter.

"I know."

"I can't follow the carnival all my life."

"I know."

Her hand slid up my arm to stroke over my chest, those crystal blue eyes shining with truth.

"But this doesn't mean the end. Not if you don't want it to."

I turned my head to look at her, hating the flare of hope I felt.

"What else can it mean?"

"We do the long distance thing. I'll fly out every two or three weekends like I've been doing, and during winter break, you come back to San Francisco."

I tried to imagine it: weeks at a time without seeing her. Maybe a month or more if she couldn't get away. The idea sucked balls. But then I tried to imagine not having Tera in my life at all. And that was worse. Far, far worse.

"I guess we could try," I said, feeling the ache reaching my bones.

"That's all I'm asking, Tucker. Let's just try. What we've got ... it's too good to throw it away without giving it our best shot."

Her voice was hopeful and that made me feel a hell of a lot better because it didn't seem like a soft way of letting me down.

"It'll be different," I said, wanting her to convince me some more. "For both of us."

She laughed lightly. "That's our motto. Everything about us is different, but it works anyway."

Her laughter died away.

"You can trust me, Tucker."

"I know."

"We'll be okay."

God, I wanted her to be right so badly.

.   .   .

Tera

Sitting on the airplane back to San Francisco, I was conflicted. I knew that giving up my life and following Tucker and the carnival—that wasn't for me. I couldn't do what Aimee did, but I couldn't and wouldn't give up Tucker either.

I felt awful leaving him so soon after everything that had happened with Renee, but I needed to get back. I couldn't put my life on hold for him.

So we'd do the long distance thing. Tons of couples did that. It wasn't as if he was in the military and I wouldn't see him for half a year or more. He was only ever a short flight away. And now I knew that Renee wouldn't be able to get her claws into him again.

It was wrong of me to have threatened her, but somehow I couldn't feel bad about that.

My mind flashed back to the insane sex we'd had on the Ferris wheel. I still couldn't quite believe I'd done that. My body shivered as I remembered, grabbing onto the safety bar, staring up at the stars then down at the fairground, people strolling along the midway in a sugar haze while Tucker thrust slowly and then quickly from underneath me, wondering how my life got so crazy.

But he hadn't said he loved me. Nor had I. And for once, it wasn't about some stupid rule, waiting for the guy to say it first. Tucker didn't do relationships and frankly, neither of us knew if he could. If he wanted to commit to a long-distance relationship, I needed him to prove it. But damn him! Couldn't he have given me something to hold onto? Maybe I was reading more into it, trying to read lines that weren't there, inventing layers of meaning that were only in my head.

When I turned my phone on again after the flight, there were two messages. The first was from Mom, reminding me that she had a number of 'suitable' dates lined up for me in case

I needed an escort for the fundraiser. The thought set my teeth on edge.

The second was from Tucker.

"Hey, beautiful! Hope your flight was good. Call me when you get in so I know you're okay? I'll be doing the show, but leave a message, yeah?" Then his voice lowered. *"It sucks that you're not here. I keep thinking about the way I woke up this morning with your sweet lips wrapped around my dick. And that noise you make, just before you're about to come—you are so fucking hot. Sweetest sugar I ever had."*

Then he muttered something I couldn't catch and the voicemail cut out.

His short message left me with a wide smile on my face—and very hot and bothered.

∾

Tucker

Two more slow weeks had gone by without seeing Tera.

We'd talked some, but it wasn't the same. She hadn't been able to get away to visit again, and I'd gone from missing her and wanting her to feeling like I had a phantom limb—it wasn't there anymore but it throbbed painfully anyway … all of the time.

Since Renee and Scotty had flown back to Richmond, I hadn't spoken to her and I didn't want to, but I'd swapped a few texts with Scotty. I'd keep my promise to him.

Ollo was watching me prep for the afternoon show and sharing a piece of watermelon with Bo who was sitting on the grass next to him.

"So, big man, how does it feel?"

I threw him a sour look. "How does what feel?"

He grinned. "Tucker McCoy falling for a girl."

I ignored him, and carried on checking the brakes on the

stunt bikes. They didn't really need any work, but staying in motion kept me out of trouble—mostly.

I glanced back at Ollo, hoping that he'd go away and irritate someone else, but I wasn't that lucky.

"You better treat her right," he said. "She's only got one heart to break ... but you have 206 bones, my friend."

It still pissed me off that everyone expected me to fuck up.

"Is your ass jealous of the amount of shit that comes out of your mouth?" I asked without looking at him.

He laughed and then tossed a piece of watermelon rind that hit me on the back of the head.

I swore softly. "Fuck off and play with the traffic, Ollo."

He sniggered quietly. "You've got it bad, brother."

I straightened up and looked at him.

"Yeah, I have. Why is that so fucking funny?"

His smile dropped away and he sighed.

"She won't follow you. Tera is family, but she's not one of us. She won't follow the carnival."

I stared up at the Ferris wheel, a spidery silhouette against the gray sky of early November, remembering what it felt like being inside her, knowing that I'd fallen for Tera; fallen far and hard and deep.

"I know."

"So how's this going to work for you?"

I shrugged. "I have no freakin' idea. Tera wants to do the long-distance thing..."

"What do you want?"

I couldn't help smiling. "I want Tera."

Ollo nodded then gave a sly grin. "You sure about that?"

"Yeah, I am. What the fuck is that supposed to mean?"

He stood up and dusted himself off, then held Bo's paw as they ambled away.

"What?" I yelled after them.

Ollo turned and grinned at me. "This is the carnival, where magic happens … and dreams come true."

What the hell? I stood scratching my head.

～

We'd finished the final show of the day and I'd almost forgotten Ollo's cryptic words, but when Kes called a powwow, I could feel a change coming, like storm clouds were gathering inside me.

The bonfire was blazing, and Kes stood in front of it, hands on hips, staring into the flames.

Zef was already there, squatting on his heels, chewing a piece of beef jerky, and Zach was sitting next to Aimee, talking quietly. Luke was hovering in the background and I was sort of surprised to see him, because I'd understood that this was a meeting about the Daredevils.

Kes looked up when he saw me, his expression hard to read.

There was no preamble, he just dove right in.

"Pomona has offered us a deal," he said. "They've already got us for Thanksgiving, but now they want to book us for five months next year, from July through November. The money they're offering isn't bad—it's pretty good, but it would mean changes."

He glanced at Aimee.

"With the money they're talking about, we wouldn't need to go on the road after Easter…"

Zef frowned. "You giving up the road, man? You saying you want to give up traveling?"

Kes shook his head. "No, I'm not saying that." He squeezed Aimee's hand. "I'll still be traveling. It's in my blood, it's what I do, but if we take the Pomona contract, we don't *have* to travel." And he looked at me. "You guys could have a normal life … whatever that is."

Zef snorted angrily. "You think we'd bail on you?"

Kes gave a small smile, then glanced at me again. "Nah, I'm saying things change. Traveling all the time, it's not for everyone."

I thought about what he was saying.

I could be in Pomona for a chunk of time each year, which was only a five-hour drive from San Francisco. Tera and I could see each other most weekends. And for Winter break, I'd be with her; we'd only be apart for maybe 14 weeks in the whole year. Or not.

We'd have a chance...

"With Pomona offering us a regular slot, we can expand," and Kes glanced at Luke, "bring on another member so we can be more flexible if one of us needs time off. It would be $370,000 for five months work, 15% for Zach as our manager, then split four ways."

Zef pounded Luke on the back. "Congratulations, man! Welcome to the Daredevils!"

Luke grinned as we all shook hands, then blushed as Aimee wrapped her arms around his neck and stood on tiptoe to kiss him on the cheek.

"We've still got to vote," Kes said, smiling at her. "Do we take the Pomona gig?"

The vote was a unanimous, *Hell, yeah!*

"Who's going to tour with me from April through June?" Kes asked.

Zef, Luke and Zach raised their hands, then they all stared at me.

"I..."

I wanted to say I'd still travel with them, that I'd always have their backs, but if I'd learned anything from Kes and Aimee, it was that I should to talk to Tera first.

"I need 48 hours," I said.

Kes grinned at me and Zef rolled his eyes.

"Pussy whipped!" he pretended to cough.

Aimee just smiled.

CHAPTER EIGHTEEN

TUCKER

The next afternoon, Zach drove me the 25 minutes it took to reach the suburb of Brea, and pulled up outside the motorcycle dealership.

"Have fun with the other woman," he laughed.

"Dude, I'm going to have fun with both of them!"

"Tera will kick your ass if she hears you say that."

"Nah, she understands."

Zach grinned at me, then saluted and drove off.

I was picking up my new Ducati. I'd be paying it off for the next three years, but I didn't care. I was also putting aside $150 a month for Scotty: it was just something I wanted to do. For him, not for Renee. It wasn't the kid's fault that he'd gotten a shitty start in life. And that was something I knew a hell of a lot about.

After what Renee had tried to pull, I didn't want anything to do with her. But I'd promised Scotty that I'd be there for him, so the money was going into a trust fund that Renee wouldn't be able to touch. Scotty would get it when he was 18. It could pay for some of his college education. Something.

The season had gone well for us, and with the promise of a good contract next year, I decided to sign on the dotted line. I'd missed Daisy.

Kes had let me take a day off. I didn't like missing a performance, but it was something I needed to do. It had been a sudden decision, although one I'd been toying with for a while now. Tera had told me that in spite of her mom's best efforts, she was going stag to the big fancy fundraiser she'd told me about. I'd argued like hell when she tried to persuade me to go with her, listing all the reasons why it was a bad idea, but now the thought of her dancing with another guy was making me want to get violent on someone's ass. So I'd changed my mind.

I was about to gatecrash a black-tie party. How hard could it be?

Tera

The fundraiser was just getting started and I was already irritated with my mother.

"Darling, there's absolutely no need for you to be here by yourself. Frankly, I'm relieved that you didn't invite that rough young man from the circus..."

"He's a stunt rider in a carnival—there's a difference. And he's not r—"

"Really, darling," she interrupted. "Pedantry isn't very becoming. Look, Olivia Hartington is over there with Josh. Why don't you go and say hello."

I narrowed my eyes at her.

"I hope you're not trying to set me up, mother. I have a boyfriend. How many times do I have to remind you?"

She sighed faintly.

"The Hartingtons are old friends. It would be very impolite to ignore them."

I knew what she was doing. My mother was a master of

manipulation. I suppose she'd learned a lot being married to my father all these years.

"Hello, Tera dear," said Mrs. Hartington, raking her eyes over my outfit and assessing every stitch by the dollar, from my Chanel shoes, to my borrowed sapphire necklace, courtesy of my mother's safety deposit box.

"Hello, Olivia. Lovely to see you again. Hi, Josh."

He kissed my cheek, lingering a little too long as he pulled back, and I suspected he was checking out my cleavage while he was in the area.

"You look stunning, as ever, Tera." Then he looked around him theatrically. "No date tonight?"

I gave a practiced smile in return. "Unfortunately, he wasn't able to get away from work."

"Oh what a shame," said Mrs. Hartington. "Josh wouldn't miss it for the world, even though his brokerage firm could hardly run without him."

"Slight exaggeration, Mother," laughed Josh, who had the grace to look embarrassed, which made me like him a little more.

But only a little.

"Well, seeing as you're by yourself," he said, clearing his throat, "perhaps you'd like to join our table tonight?" Then he lowered his voice. "And a dance, Tera? You look so hot in that dress."

And yes, he was talking to my boobs. Any flicker of liking was extinguished.

Before I could answer, there was a commotion at the entrance to the ballroom.

My astonished eyes met Tucker's, as he stood on a chair waving wildly. But before I could get to him, two enormous security guards rounded on him, forcing him to the ground.

. . .

Tucker

The Fairmont Grand Del Mar was a swanky resort hotel 20 miles north of San Diego. When I checked on my phone, the description said it had four swimming pools and a golf course. Yeah, totally my kind of place.

It was less than a hundred miles from Brea, so it had only taken me an hour to get there on the Duke. Damn, it felt good to have her between my knees again.

When I arrived, I overtook a line of limousines heading for the entrance. I wasn't going to trust the Duke to a valet, so I parked in the furthest corner of the parking lot and stripped off the leathers. I didn't have saddle bags, so I tucked them under a yucca tree, hoping that the place was too ritzy for someone to rip them off.

I eyeballed the tux that I'd brought with me. I'd never worn anything like that before. I'd never even worn a sports coat or suit jacket. Never wanted to, but I was trying a lot of new stuff with Tera. For Tera.

I'll pulled it out of my backpack. I'd been careful how I'd packed it, so it wasn't too wrinkled.

I'd found the tux in a charity shop up in San Francisco. It had been cheap, but it didn't look it. I hoped.

I pulled on the slacks, a new white shirt, black socks and shiny shoes ... and had a total fail as I stared at the black bow tie. In the end, I tucked it under the shirt collar and left the ends hanging.

I took a deep breath.

Showtime!

"May I see your ticket, sir?"

The guy on the door held out his hand expectantly. But instead of giving him a ticket, I shook his hand.

"My girl has the ticket," I called over my shoulder, taking the steps two at a time.

"But, sir!"

That was easy. I wondered why I'd ever been worried.

But then out of the corner of my eye, I spotted two goons built like brick shit-houses making their way toward me. I stepped it up, dodging around a silver-haired woman whose wide ass and long dress made her look like a ship in full sail.

The goons were getting closer, weaving their way through the crowds, eyes targeted on me.

I sprinted across the polished floor, skidding to a stop as I tried not to crash into a line of men in Dress Blues standing at the double-door entrance. The Marines didn't try to stop me, instead giving a ragged cheer when they saw the security goons on my tail, and standing back so I could shoulder my way through the crowds of well-padded guys with skinny girls. I'd have to buy those dudes a drink later. I slid through the ballroom entrance and looked around desperately for Tera.

The goons were close behind now, and the only thing keeping them from catching up to me was the fact they didn't want to cause more of a scene.

There must have been upward of 500 chairs in the room, although only half of them were currently filled. I stood on the one nearest to me, ignoring the gasp of surprise from a woman sitting at the table.

"My goodness! Are you the entertainment?"

"No, ma'am, but the strippers will be along later."

"You're not one of them? How disappointing."

I winked at her, ignoring the craning necks and heads that were turning in my direction. But a sudden movement caught my eye. Tera was standing at the far end of the cavernous room, waving wildly.

I jumped down from the chair, narrowly missing Goon 1, who was snarling into his hidden mic. But I wasn't lucky twice, because as I tried to dodge around an elderly woman, Goon 2 grabbed my right arm, forcing it up behind my back.

I couldn't tell if it was the same guy that had fucked me up before—they all looked the same to me. But chances were they were the Senator's men.

"Dude, not the bad arm!"

I'd done a lot of healing since my shoulder had been messed up, but his actions made my eyes water. I could have tried to kick the shit out of him, but I didn't think that getting my ribs stomped on would be a great start to the evening.

Tera marched toward us, her eyes flashing with anger. Behind her, I could see her mom, grinding her teeth at the sight of me.

I grinned painfully at Tera. "Hey, sugar."

"What are you doing here?" she gasped as her lips rose in a wide smile.

That's why I'm here, I thought. *To see that smile.*

"You invited me," I pointed out.

She laughed happily as the other guests shook their heads in disapproval, and Tera's mother attempted to incinerate me with her glare.

Tera turned to the goon who was slowly forcing me to my knees.

"Would you mind not manhandling my boyfriend," she said frostily.

The goon's eyes widened.

"Excuse me, Miss Hawkins, but he entered without a ticket."

"Because I have it," she snapped.

He let go of me reluctantly, and I grinned at him. "No hard feelings, man."

He tugged at his collar, staring at someone behind me.

I turned to look.

Senator Hawkins was barely holding it together. I had to admit I felt a bit nervous staring at the man who could have me evicted and then get his death squad to break my legs for real this time, but Tera just raised her chin and spoke clearly.

"Daddy, I think you've met my boyfriend Tucker McCoy."

Tera's tone was challenging, and she hooked her arm through mine possessively.

"Yes," the Senator conceded, forcing a smile and shoving his hands in his pockets so he wouldn't have to shake hands.

"Hey, Senator," I grinned. "You probably didn't recognize me without the black eye."

Tera nudged me with her elbow, a silent warning not to poke the grizzly.

But the Senator continued to smile. "No, I don't think it's that—it must be the tuxedo. But if you had a black eye with the tux, yes, I think I'd recognize you."

It was a warning, a threat, but with Tera's arm in mine, I wasn't backing down. There was nothing he could do to me here without embarrassing his daughter.

Tera's back stiffened and she glared at her father.

"Well, thank goodness there's nothing dangerous about attending a fundraising dinner. I'm sure Tucker is safe here."

Her father shrugged, neither agreeing nor disagreeing.

I leaned down to kiss Tera's cheek. "You look beautiful, sugar."

Her angry frown melted and she smiled at me.

"Thank you. So do you."

"Your mother wants to see you," the Senator bit out, unable to hold his fake smile any longer.

"Yes, I do. Right now," snorted Tera's mom, closing her mouth with a snap.

Tera just smiled. "It can wait. I think Tucker deserves a glass of champagne after that."

She held my arm tightly with both hands as we walked away.

"I can't believe you're here!"

"Good surprise?"

"Amazing surprise!" she laughed happily. "You scrub up

well." Then she tugged at the end of my loose bowtie. "Want me to fix that for you?"

I smiled down at her. "Does it bother you that I have no clue how to do that?"

She cocked her head to one side. "Does it bother you that I can't cook banana pancakes like Aimee?"

"Well, now you mention it..."

"Shut up!" she laughed, slapping my arm before knotting the bow tie. "There. Perfect."

"Nah, not even close."

"Tucker, I'm quite aware that you'd rather pull out your toenails one by one than come to something like this. You did it for me—so yes, if I say you're perfect, just nod and agree with me."

"Yeah? What if I didn't do it for you, Miss Hawkins?"

Her eyes were questioning.

"Maybe I did it for me."

"Explain," she commanded.

"Because I couldn't stand the thought of you dancing with any other man except me."

She raised her eyebrows in surprise. "Really?"

"Oh yeah. And if these bootnecks don't get their eyes off of you right now, we might have a problem."

She laughed out loud. "Probably not the smartest thing, challenging a room full of Marines."

"No one ever accused me of being smart."

"Oh, I don't know. You're dating me—so you must be smart enough to know a good thing when you see it."

"Damn straight!"

I pulled her into my arms, kissing her the way I'd wanted to ever since I arrived.

"Tucker," she sighed, melting against me. "Thank you for coming tonight. It means a lot to me."

Something tightened in my chest. "There's nowhere else I want to be, sugar."

We spent the next hour sipping champagne and circling the room, Tera introducing me to a bunch of old folk that I guessed were friends of her parents. Most of the conversations went over my head as they talked politics and about people I didn't know. I felt like an overdressed bodyguard most of the time, but Tera held onto my arm, letting everyone know that we were together.

"And what do you do, young man?" asked a woman wearing the remains of a small mammal around her neck and enough diamonds to choke a horse. "You don't look like a young Republican."

I grinned at her. "No, ma'am. I'm a roustabout in the carnival."

"Good heavens!"

Tera rolled her eyes. "He's being modest. He's a motorcycle stuntman. In the carnival."

"My, how interesting! And such a change from the stuffy young men you usually date, Tera, dear."

Tera laughed out loud and grinned up at me. "Yes, I'd have to agree that he's an improvement. It's a work in progress, of course, but his training is coming along nicely."

The woman shook her head, smiling kindly at us.

"Oh my dear, if you think you can train a man like that, it'll be the work of a lifetime."

Tera's eyes were soft as she smiled at me, and that strange ache in my chest intensified.

"I hope so," she said.

The moment Tera left to go to the bathroom, the Senator made his move. I'd been expecting it, so it was almost a relief when he finally strolled over to me.

This time he came alone, no goons. The dude was mighty sure of himself; that put me on edge.

He settled comfortably into Tera's empty seat and leaned back, his hands behind his head, a professional smile masking his anger.

"She'll get tired of you eventually," he said conversationally, targeting in on my weak spot.

"Did Dono say the same thing to you about Kes's mom?"

His eyes flared with fury, but he tamped it down.

"Tera would never choose to live an itinerant life. Her naïve interest will wear off—sooner rather than later."

I shrugged. "Well, until then, I'll do everything I can to make her happy."

He gave a humorless chuckle. "My daughter is intelligent, well-educated and beautiful. What makes you think a dumb redneck like you could possibly make her happy?"

My chair rocked against the wall as I turned to face him.

"I'm uneducated, not ignorant. I know I don't deserve her, but I'm going to work my ass off to change that."

"You live in a trailer—a trailer you don't even own! You barely earned minimum wage last year! You think that's good enough for her?"

"I don't think a fuckin' palace is good enough for her!"

He applauded quietly.

"Well played."

"It's not a fuckin' game!"

He leaned forward, his eyes dark with dislike.

"When you fuck up, which you will, I'll…"

"Save it. Kes already told me what he'd do to me if I upset Tera. And what he says means a hell of a lot more to me than any bullshit you can spout."

The Senator looked surprised, as if it hadn't occurred to him that Kes would look out for his half-sister.

"You think carnies are trash," I said, my voice low and hard. "But that didn't stop you from fucking one, did it? Four years you were with Kes and Falcon's mom. You were just too chickenshit to choose that life. You made your choice a long time ago: let Tera make hers."

He leaned back again, his expression thoughtful.

"You're going to pretend that you care about my daughter, that you're not simply using her to get to me?"

I felt a flare of anger as I studied him, rich and entitled, telling everyone else how they should live and what they felt.

"Yeah, I fuckin' love her."

I heard Tera's gasp behind me.

"You ... you love me?"

I stood up quickly, catching her arms as her knees gave way.

"Tera..."

"Do you?"

I grabbed hold of her hand and led her away from the table, almost dragging her across the ballroom and hotel lobby, until I found an empty bench outside.

I sat down and pulled her onto my lap, running my hands over her bare shoulders.

Her eyes were inquisitive as she leaned against me, gently stroking my chest.

A warm bubble of happiness rose up inside me.

"Tucker, did you mean what you said?"

I swallowed, knowing it was time to tell her the truth.

"I didn't know what it meant," I said, speaking so softly that she had to strain to hear me, "because I thought I loved Renee and this—you and me—it felt nothing like it. This ... *feeling* ... is painful when I'm not with you. So I didn't know that it means..."

I paused, unable to get the words out.

"What does it mean?" she whispered.

"That ... that I love you."

She stopped breathing. Or maybe it was me who stopped breathing. Maybe all the oxygen had been sucked out of the world. I wasn't sure.

"And I didn't want to be in love with you," I continued, my voice rough, feeling as if my teeth would break on the words as I spat them out. "The people you love always let you down; they always leave you. That's all I knew. But you ... you kept coming back."

Tera blinked, then a slow smile spread across her face and her eyes sparkled.

"You love me," she said, raising her eyebrows as if she couldn't believe it.

"Yeah."

"Wow."

"Yeah."

"So ... what happens next?"

I shook my head impatiently.

"Why the fuck are you asking me?"

Her eyes blazed with sudden anger, but then she burst out laughing.

"What am I going to do with you, Tucker?"

I grinned back at her. "Whatever you want, darlin'."

She laughed happily, then wrapped her hand around my arm.

"Will you be my escort, Mr. McCoy?"

"I'll be whatever you want, sugar."

"Glad to hear it. And just for the record..."

"Yeah?"

"I love you, too."

Shock, relief, satisfaction, astonishment, disbelief, hope. Most of all, hope. So many emotions flowed through and over and around me. I drowned in them, drank them in, feeling unworthy, blessed, and determined not to fuck up.

We grinned at each other like two fools.

"Do you want to get out of here?" I asked. "Lose the stiffs?"

She nodded, her eyes glittering with excitement.

I took her hand in mine, feeling like the man, the proudest fucker in the Universe.

In the parking lot, Tera stared at my new white Ducati with red trim on the wheels.

"Another Duke, huh?"

"Yep."

"A Duke and a ball gown," she laughed, looking down at the midnight blue silk that hid and revealed those mouthwatering curves. "What are we going to do now?"

I helped her onto the bike, tucking the billowing silk around her carefully and passing her a helmet and my spare leather jacket.

"Other than be together? Does it matter?"

She shrugged her shoulders and smiled at me.

"Guess not."

Tera

My mother loved being of use. So I'm sure she was delighted that her determined, pointless, snobbish dislike of Tucker had opened my eyes. I was grateful to her. Between my mother's glares and my father's threats, I'd finally grown up.

Maybe 27 was a little on the late side to become an adult, but I'd done it at last.

I'd also given my two weeks' notice at work and spoken to my landlord about breaking the lease on my apartment. I had a new job to go to in LA—still working in PR, but with the emphasis on entertainers not politicians, although there were definitely similarities.

It hadn't been a hard decision. I liked San Francisco, liked my job there, liked my apartment that Dad paid for ... but I loved Tucker.

Officially, he was still living in the RV with Kes, Aimee and Zef. Unofficially, he'd packed a small bag and slept every night in our bed at my new place. I'd told him he could bring all his things, but he'd just shrugged and said he had everything he needed. *One bag*—it made me want to cry.

But it didn't escape my attention that one of the things he'd brought with him was a small framed photograph of Scotty with a basketball, and stuck in the back, a scrawled letter thanking his Uncle Tucker for helping him.

I asked Tucker about the boy's father, but he just shrugged and said that Jackson wasn't interested and didn't care. I left it at that.

As for Renee, I hadn't forgiven her and I definitely didn't like how she'd used Tucker, but I guess I understood. When you love someone, you'll move mountains.

Or just move.

I'd rented a sweet little apartment in the small town of Whittier, 23 miles from Pomona. It took me half an hour to drive there, but Tucker could make it in 15 minutes on his new Ducati (for which I now had my own set of leathers and matching helmet, although I was still too chicken to let him go more than about 50mph with me on the back).

I dreaded to think how much he'd be paying in speeding fines, but he was adamant that he wouldn't get caught.

I was also less than 20 miles from my new job in LA, and even though I hadn't started there yet, I'd already brought them a new client: Donohue's Daredevils.

Kes had decided on a major rebranding for next year. It made me a little sad that he was finally dropping the Hawkins part of his name because it was something we shared—but it was the right thing for him to do. He no longer cared what our father thought; instead he wanted to honor his grandfather's side of the family.

So the Daredevils were finishing off their season with a huge display at Pomona Fairground, during the Thanksgiving holidays.

I'd suggested that along with the new name, they change their racing leathers to a patriotic red, white and blue.

"No fucking way!" laughed Tucker when I suggested it.

"Why not?"

He rolled his eyes.

"Because it's totally douchy. Who'd end up with the white leathers? Fucked if I'd wear them!"

Kes smirked at him.

"They'd match the Duke: white trim and red wheels—are you saying that *isn't* douchy?"

Tucker scowled. "Make Luke wear the white leathers—he's the newest."

Which was true: Luke was still in training, and although Kes was happy about how it was working out, there was no way Luke would be ready to perform for the last show of the season.

Luke raised his eyebrows. "It's a bit seventies, the whole Evel Knievel vibe."

Tucker laughed loudly. "Yeah, and isn't it ironic that the colors red, white and blue are supposed to stand for freedom ... unless they're flashing behind you."

The guys laughed their asses off so I turned to Aimee.

"What do you think?"

"I like the black leather," she said, her eyes sweeping along Kes's body as he stretched out on the grass in front of the RV, grinning up at her. "But I think it would be a good idea for everyone to have a different color helmet so the crowd can tell them apart."

"I'll take red," Tucker said quickly.

"Blue!" laughed Zef.

"Guess you're stuck with the white, Luke," chuckled Zach.

"That means you get all black," I said to Kes.

"How come he gets the cool outfit?" grumbled Tucker, looking at me like I'd betrayed him.

"Oh, I don't know," I whispered, resting my hand on his thigh, "I think black leathers and a red helmet is *hot*."

I leaned down to plant a scorching kiss on Tucker's lips.

Kes groaned and shot an angry look at him. "My *sister*, fucker!"

Tucker winked at me and leaned back in the deckchair, hands stretched above his head a wide grin on his face.

Hmm, Kes wasn't getting over it, even though Tucker and I had officially been together for some time now.

Ollo sauntered over with Bo clinging to his back.

"Gates open in ten; rubes are lining up."

Bo leapt down and scampered across to Tucker, stealing a slice of his pizza before darting to Aimee and climbing into her arms, chattering excitedly.

Tucker muttered something under his breath, and both Bo and Aimee threw him a look full of reproach, which made me laugh.

I looked around, happy in the warmth of my new family, my crazy carnie family. I wasn't closing doors with my parents, but I wasn't letting them dictate my life either.

Ollo's words had unleashed that familiar quiver of anticipation, an edge of excitement and expectation that clung to Tucker and the guys before a performance.

I hated it because it meant that soon Tucker, my brother and Zef would be hurling themselves through the air, through flames, doing things ordinary humans couldn't, wouldn't and shouldn't do.

I shared a look with Aimee. She gave me a weak smile and stood up abruptly, murmuring about getting Thanksgiving supper ready. That was how she coped: doing *something*.

Tucker threw me a knowing glance.

"Come on, sugar. Let's go get you some cotton candy."

He held my hand as we strolled along the midway,

unembarrassed to show affection, perfectly at ease with the role of adoring boyfriend. He grinned down at me and winked.

I knew what he was doing: he was trying to take my mind off the upcoming performance.

I hadn't seen this side of Tucker before. He always seemed so reckless, so free; but there was another side to him, a thoughtful, caring side. And I couldn't help loving him a little more.

"Want some funnel cake and a carousel ride, Tera?"

"I'd love to, but I can't afford the calories, and you shouldn't eat something so heavy before a show."

"No *can't* with us, sugar. Do what feels good."

"I'll get fat and you won't want me anymore."

He chuckled quietly. "Just more of you to hold in my arms."

"Very smooth, Mr. McCoy."

"You're welcome, Miss Hawkins."

At that moment Jade walked past wearing the smallest shorts I'd ever seen and a strip of material covering her chest that might generously be called a bandage, maybe a Band-Aid, although I think it was supposed to be a tube top.

She glared at me, threw a look at Tucker as if to say, *see what you're missing*, then tossed her glossy hair over her shoulder and stalked off.

"I can see your eyes swiveling from here," I griped.

"I was being polite," he grinned at me.

"What? How on earth did you work that one out?"

"I only looked at the parts she's got covered."

A reply floundered on my lips as I took in his amused expression.

"Aw, sugar. She's got nothin' on you. I wouldn't say her tits are small, but they'd be pointless without nipples."

I settled for tickling the life out of him, but he dodged away laughing.

But then the PA announced that the Daredevils would be performing in an hour.

Tucker sighed.

"Gotta get going. Raincheck on the carousel?"

The smile froze on my face.

"Yes, of course," I said, my voice strangled.

Tucker's gaze softened and he pulled me into a hug.

"Nothin's gonna happen to me, Tera, I promise."

I nodded numbly.

God, would I ever get used to this?

On the short walk back to the grandstand and the guys' changing area, Tucker visibly shifted into performance mode.

He stood upright and walked with purpose instead of his usual easy-going slouch. His eyes were bright and focused and I could see the adrenaline beginning to pump through him.

He gave me a quick, wide smile, his eyes alight with anticipation.

My returning smile was watery but I forced myself to put some steel in my spine; I wouldn't be one more thing he had to worry about.

Tucker began to distance himself from me mentally if not physically, reaching that place of calm and confidence inside himself.

I'd seen this a dozen times before: each of the Daredevils found a quiet space to prepare themselves, speaking short sentences in muted voices.

Tucker told me once that he visualized the whole show, running it through in his mind, seeing all the jumps landed successfully.

That was the mental preparation. The physical preparation involved something that looked like a combination of yoga and Pilates stretches, and then 10 minutes before they were due to go on, pumping the adrenaline some more with shadowboxing, or in Zef's case, kicking the hell out of one of those wooden mannequin posts that they use in Martial Arts.

Encased in their leathers, they looked like gladiators, but I felt like the one going into battle. It was going to be a long hour.

Giving me a swift smile, Tucker fixed his helmet in place, then pulled on his thick, leather gloves.

Ollo was watching me silently with Bo in his arms. When the guys jogged out of the changing room, he followed.

"You're not staying for the show?" I asked, anxious not to be left alone with my thoughts.

"Not tonight," he grinned at me. "Bo doesn't like the flames."

"Where are Luke and Zachary?"

"Couldn't tell you." He jerked his thumb at the tiny monkey who was staring at me with wise round eyes. "I'm going to take him down to the Big Top. There's a performing dog act there that he really likes. He's friends with one of the stars."

"Oh," I said, smiling. "Who's that? Is it that girl with the curly brown hair?"

"Yolanda? No, his friend is Maverick—the Golden Retriever."

Ollo laughed at my expression. "See you later, princess."

I sat alone in the changing room, then got a grip of my nerves and headed out to the stands just as the pounding music of Ramstein filled the speakers. I could barely make out the roar of the bike engines over the crowd's screams and yells.

Three charging motorcycles burst into the arena and thousands of people stood up and cheered.

Pride flooded my chest, heating my whole body and slapping a huge grin on my face. That was my man out there. My man performing those harebrained stunts. My man who looked so incredibly hot in his racing leathers, so fearless as he flew through the air, a man adored by men, women and children, a man who would be in my bed tonight.

My heart started to race and I cheered with the crowd as three motorcycles flew into the air simultaneously, missing each other by mere inches, or so it seemed. I screamed and screwed my eyes shut as Tucker took off again, performing a handstand midair, only daring to look when I knew he must have landed.

Higher, faster, crazier stunts, through the air, through fire, my brother performing a complete somersault as Tucker and Zef freewheeled across the arena.

Suddenly, a tremendous explosion sounded behind us making me jump, and a pall of gray smoke poured into the air.

Out of the corner of my eye, I saw Zef fluff his landing, his bike skittering as he tumbled across the grass. Hardly anyone noticed, even though Tucker and Kes raced toward him.

Zef sat up, shaking his head and holding his left arm. Then he gave a quick thumbs up and relief rushed through me as I forced my way toward the safety barriers.

"Oh my God! The Big Top is on fire!"

I turned as the woman next to me screamed the words.

Shock. Complete shock. My heart thudded against my ribs. "Ollo!"

Kes saw me waving frantically and rode over, sending up a spray of sand as he skidded to a halt.

"What the fuck's going on?" he yelled as he flipped up his visor.

"The Big Top! There's been some sort of explosion. It was so loud. Kestrel! Ollo is inside! He was going there with Bo to see..."

Kes didn't wait to hear the rest of my words. He signaled Tucker to follow him, and they both roared out of the arena, leaving Zef kneeling on the grass while a First Aider talked to him.

As thick, black smoke started to drift over the grandstand,

panic rippled through the crowd. The ushers were trying to funnel everyone out through the emergency exits, but small fights were breaking out as people tried to push to the front.

There was no way I could follow Tucker through the pulsing, angry mob. Instead, I climbed over the safety barrier and ran to Zef.

He'd tugged off his helmet and the First Aider was gripping his arm and twisting his wrist.

"Christ, Tera! What's going on?" he growled, his face pale beneath his tan.

"I don't know! I don't know! There was an explosion—someone said it was from the Big Top. Ollo was going with Bo. Tucker and Kestrel, they've gone over there but I don't know what they can do."

The First Aider manipulated Zef's wrist again. "It's sprained, not broken. You were lucky, Mr. Colton."

"Thanks, man," Zef muttered as he stood up.

"Wait! I need to tape that for you!"

Zef shook his head. "Later."

Then he turned to his fallen bike and heaved it up.

"I'm coming with you!" I yelled, running toward him, ignoring his look of frustration.

"Fuck, okay! Sit on the seat and I'll stand on the pedals. Don't let your legs touch the exhaust or you'll get a burn. Hold on—it's going to get bumpy."

I could smell hot leather and bike fuel as he climbed on in front of me and sweat trickled through my hair and down my neck, but my body was cold and tremors rippled across my skin.

I gripped the handlebars as hard as I could, my knuckles turning white, and Zef kick started the bike again.

We skidded out of the arena, but it was soon obvious that we couldn't get through the streaming crowds.

"We'll have to go the long way around," Zef shouted over the noise of the crowd.

He took off again, skirting the rivers of people and heading behind the Big Top. The wind whipped my hair and I could smell acrid smoke that stung my eyes and caught in my throat. I could hear the sirens of fire engines and police in the distance—too far. Too far away.

Weaving and bucking, swearing at everyone who got in his way, Zef finally managed to get as close as was safe to the Big Top. Red and yellow flames roared loudly and the air was thick and choking.

People were still scrambling out, their faces blackened with smoke, coughing, their eyes streaming. I saw the two stunt bikes abandoned on their sides near the entrance.

"Stay here!" Zef shouted at me.

"But..."

"Stay!" he yelled, shaking my shoulders so roughly my head wobbled.

I nodded wordlessly as he darted into the smoke-filled tent.

I stood with my fists clenched, wondering what to do. My limbs unfroze as I realized that the wind had shifted and all three of the bikes were dangerously close to the flames. I strained my muscles to pick up Zef's bike, rolling if further away from the flames. Carl and Buddy saw me struggling, grabbed Kes' and Tucker's bikes and moved them clear.

Two ambulances had arrived and were already treating people for minor burns and smoke inhalation. I could hear more on their way, screaming sirens growing louder.

I strained my eyes to peer into the smoke-filled tent, there was no sign of the guys.

I stood and waited, watching, waiting, watching, waiting, breathing, holding in the desperation.

Please God, bring them out safely. Please God...

A team of fire fighters arrived, trying to usher me away.

"Please stand out of the way, ma'am."

"My boyfriend is in there with my brother and their friend Zef! They were trying to help people..."

Suddenly, a figure appeared out of the gloom, a figure dressed in racing leathers.

"Kestrel!"

He collapsed onto his knees and the small bundle that he'd been holding started to cry. It was a child, a little girl of about five, her face streaked with smoke and tears.

"There are others in there..." Kes gasped. "Trapped at the back. Maybe ten ... I couldn't see..."

I ran toward him and his eyes were wild. "Tucker?"

"I don't know!" he shouted, his voice filled with frustration and fear.

The little girl's cries penetrated my own terror and I scooped her into my arms, carrying her toward one of the ambulances. Her wordless cries and racking cough brought me to tears. One of the paramedics took her from me but she started to scream louder so I stayed with her, watching from a distance as Kes stumbled to his feet. He tried to go back inside, but a firefighter held him back. Then I heard Aimee screaming his name, throwing herself into his arms.

She was shaking her head and trying to drag him away, but he was standing firm. Then Zachary ran up, followed by Luke and they grabbed his arms and physically hauled him away.

A team of firefighters with breathing apparatus made their way inside, torches shining, then disappeared through the smoke.

We stood, watching, waiting, daring to hope, but as each second passed, my belief and hope leaked away as if they were carried on the stench of smoke.

I realized that I'd lost all feeling in my hand, and when I glanced down, I was surprised to see that the little girl was still gripping it tightly.

Two firefighters loomed out of the smoke supporting an

elderly man and woman. More lives saved, but where was Tucker? Where was Zef? Ollo?

It seemed impossible that anyone could live inside that inferno, and police began moving the crowds even further back. But all the carnies refused to move. Jade was there, tears in her beautiful eyes, her black hair bedraggled; the roustabouts Carl and Buddy were trying to organize a headcount; Rhonda was there with her rodeo family, reassuring her children that the horses and ponies were safe.

I saw Yolanda sobbing, heartbroken as the Big Top burned, her faithful dog Maverick beside her, but crying for her three other dogs who hadn't made it out.

My eyes stung. It was the smoke. Only the smoke.

And we waited.

"Fuck's sake!" Kestrel yelled, making us all jump. His hands fisted in his hair. "My brothers are in there! You have to let me go!"

Aimee was almost incoherent, her arms wrapped tightly around him, begging him not to go back inside; begging, pleading. Luke and Zach held his arms, their faces gaunt with fear.

And then a figure appeared out of the smoke, coughing and retching onto the grass. It was Zef, and the tiny figure of Bo, who wasn't moving.

Aimee gave a hoarse cry, ran forward, gathering the little figure into her arms. A harried paramedic didn't want to help her when there were so many human casualties, but something about that tiny form tugged at his heart, and Bo received oxygen, just like a human child. One breath, then another, and finally his innocent black eyes opened wide, and his fingers curled into Aimee's hair.

Zach and Kes raced to Zef, hauling him to his feet and dragging him clear.

"Tucker?" I whispered.

Zef couldn't breathe, but he shook his head, and I didn't know what he meant. Didn't know if...

Kes's face was tight. "Zef! Did you see Tucker in there?"

Another head shake.

"Ollo?"

Zef's head drooped and he passed out.

The paramedics got to work, pushing the carnies out of the way to clear a space.

Four more people were brought out by firefighters, but the heat was unbearable now and we reared back as fresh flames tore up the canvas side of the Big Top.

Surely no one could survive that? The pungent smoke grew thicker and we were all moved again as the wind shifted around, taunting us with lazy swirls of choking, acrid fumes.

I felt like I was splitting at the seams, tearing apart.

Almost nothing of the Big Top was left, just a blackened skeleton.

The Fire Chief was pulling his men out and I wanted to scream at him, *Not yet! They're still in there!* But the breath was ripped from my throat.

Please, God! Tucker!

Stumbling, almost blind from smoke, a figure appeared, hunched over.

Someone screamed and suddenly everything was happening in slow motion. Kes and Luke rushed forward, pulling the frail form of Ollo from Tucker's hands and carrying the unmoving figure to the paramedics.

I tore myself free from everyone who tried to stop me, running to Tucker as he stumbled and collapsed. I fell to my knees as other hands pulled off Tucker's helmet.

His face was streaked with smoke and sweat, his eyes were red and his lips were cracked from the heat. But he was alive. He was breathing.

"I thought I'd lost you!"

"Never," he gasped. "I'll always find my way back to you. Always."

I cried and laughed and cried some more as the paramedics led us away, insisting that Tucker, Kes and Zef go to hospital. Half the carnies followed, the other half staying to help with the fire investigation, staying to clear up, because although the Big Top was destroyed the show must go on.

Right?

I tightened my arms around Tucker's neck, not caring that my clothes were smeared with black and we both smelled like we'd been barbecued.

"I love you!" I cried.

"Love you, too," he croaked, gulping in air. "So much. So fucking much."

"Don't ever scare me like that again!" I yelled, tears running down my cheeks.

Even as I said it, I knew how pointless my words were. Tucker was a stuntman; a brave, fearless, honorable man—who was going to drive me absolutely crazy every day we shared. Life wouldn't be boring.

Being with Tucker was going to knock years off my life—but who wants to live forever?

CHAPTER NINETEEN

TERA

It was two weeks after the horrific fire that ripped through the Big Top. I didn't like to think about it too much, but the reminders were everywhere, and each night since, Tucker had shaken me awake from a nightmare where I was searching in the dark but couldn't find him.

Tucker was different, too. It was as if coming so close to death, he was determined to squeeze every drop of pleasure out of life and party like there was no tomorrow. It was exhausting trying to keep up. I hoped that we'd find some middle ground soon.

But today he was in a more somber mood; we were at the hospital visiting with Ollo.

He was sitting in a chair fully dressed, his short legs sticking out in front of him, and a few belongings stuffed into a grocery bag on top of the bed.

Kes strode forward, bending down low to hug him. They held each other for a long time and Kes whispered something to Ollo that we couldn't hear. Ollo nodded and when Kes stood up, the little man was wiping his eyes.

Tucker shifted uncomfortably, and I felt like I was intruding on the moment, but then Aimee stepped forward, giving Ollo a quick hug too, and promised to make his favorite banana pancakes when he came home.

"Yo, Ollo, you shrink again, man?" Tucker said when it was his turn, crouching down to shake Ollo's hand and slap him on the shoulder.

Ollo elbowed him in the chest and Tucker lost his balance, landing on his ass with a grunt.

"He gets dizzy," Ollo grinned at me. "No oxygen all the way up there."

We laughed and I smiled at Tucker, grinning as he lay sprawled on the floor. No one could be sad for long around my man.

"What's the news?" Ollo asked Kes. "Have I been eighty-sixed?"

I glanced at Tucker for a translation.

"Ollo wants to know if he's been barred from the fairground or if he's cleared to come home."

"Sure, man!" Kes answered. "We're here to spring you."

Ollo grinned widely, but then the door opened and a doctor in pale blue scrubs walked inside.

"Mr. Kolski, how are you this morning?"

It took me a second to realize that the doctor was talking to Ollo. I'd never heard him called by his surname before. I'd never heard it, period.

"Ready to roll, Doc," said Ollo confidently.

The doctor frowned.

"Mr. Kolski, I've explained to you that I'm concerned about the heart arrhythmia that we found. Untreated, it could be very serious."

Ollo stuck his lip out. "I'm not staying and you can't make me. Right, Kestrel?"

A silent conversation took place between the two of them

while Tucker stood with his arms crossed, a small frown drawing his expressive eyebrows together.

"We can take care of him at home," Kes said decisively, finally looking at the doctor. "Whatever treatment he needs, he'll get it."

The doctor was shaking his head before Kes had finished speaking.

"I can't recommend that. As Mr. Kolski doesn't have any family, he..."

"What are you talking about?" Kes said fiercely. "We're his family."

The doctor frowned, checking his notes.

"Not legally, so any decisions..."

"Fuck the law!" snarled Kes, and Aimee laid her hand on his arm.

The doctor seemed taken aback.

"A man of his age shouldn't be living in a trailer," he argued. "I can recommend a good retirement home not far from here where his disabilities can be catered for and..."

I heard a low growl in Tucker's throat. "Ollo doesn't have any disabilities," he said flatly.

The doctor's mouth dropped open.

Ollo slid from the chair, his dark eyes hard and cold.

"If I'm going to die, it won't be in a damn hospital. I was born on the road, not in a building. The carnival is my life. A rube like you can't understand it, but everywhere is my home and the sky is my roof. And you're wrong, Doc, there are thousands of people in my family. Thousands of them. And all carnies."

I felt so many emotions in those few minutes. Concerned for Ollo's health, relief that he was alive, moved by the connection between him and my brother. But most of all, I finally understood the word 'family'. It means doing the wrong thing for the right reasons; it means standing up for the people that you love; it means accepting their decisions and supporting their choice; it means loving them for who they are and not what you think they should be. It means a love that comes without conditions.

And I knew I had it here with my new carnie family.

Tucker clapped his hands together, a huge smile on his face.

"Nice shooting the breeze with you, Doc."

Then he scooped up Ollo's grocery bag and walked out of the room, chatting to Ollo who strolled along next to him.

Kes looked hard and dangerous as he handed the doctor a business card, staring the man down.

"Whatever Ollo needs, you tell me. Understand?"

The doctor nodded, a tight-lipped expression on his face as he tucked the card away.

Zach was waiting in the hospital's parking lot, leaning against his truck door as he idled in a tow zone. Bo sat on the truck's hood, clutching a soft toy in the shape of a pig. I recognized it as a prize from one of the sideshows.

Bo shrieked and chattered excitedly, dropping the toy to climb into Ollo's arms and cling to him as if he'd never let him go.

"Everything okay?" Zach asked, shaking hands with Ollo.

"Sure, no problems," Kes said.

I watched with a smile on my face as the four of them climbed into Zach's truck and drove away.

Tucker stretched his arms over his head, his washed-out t-shirt pulling taut over his lean muscles.

"Want to go back to the fairground with them?"

I shook my head. The place creeped me out a little. It had been closed for two weeks while the fire was investigated, but the twisted steel carcass of the Big Top hadn't yet been torn down, and just seeing it gave me shivers.

It turned out that a delivery driver had left a propane gas cylinder next to a hot dog stand. The Fire Department decided that the cylinder was probably leaking gas when it exploded.

It was sheer blind luck that there were no human casualties, but three of Yolanda's dogs had died. Tucker said he'd seen one of them—it had been too terrified by the flames to come to him, and he hadn't been able to reach it.

Yolanda mourned the loss of her friends, as did all the carnie folk. Just because a person has fur and paws, doesn't make them any less loved. Those dogs were her family. She still had Maverick, thank God, but they drifted around the fairground side-by-side and if Maverick was left alone for even a minute, we heard him howling in distress.

Bo was quiet and shaky for several days, spending most of his time clinging to Aimee, hiding his fearful face in her hair.

All of the guys had been treated for smoke inhalation and had been kept in the hospital for 24 hours observation, and Zef had a badly sprained wrist, as well. That was a long day. Seeing Tucker lying on a gurney again—I dreaded to imagine that it might be something I would have to get used to.

It was worse for Kes because we'd all been waiting to hear about Ollo. The little man had nearly died, and the two weeks of his hospital stay was the longest he'd ever been away from his carnival home. He'd hated every moment. Kes had taken it hard, wanting to believe that Ollo was indestructible. But nothing lasts forever. Even Falcon had come down to visit Ollo in hospital. He was their last link with the past.

Most of the carnies had left for their winter camp, but a few were still on site. In another week, Kes and Aimee were heading up the coast to Arcata with Ollo. Luke and Zach were going with them, planning to build their own cabin on Kes's land.

"Back to your place then?" said Tucker, raising an eyebrow as my gaze tracked across his firm chest and narrow hips.

"Our place," I corrected him automatically.

Tucker grinned and tugged me forward so he could zip up

my leather jacket. Oh, and cop a feel along the way. Hmm, well, he wasn't the only one who could play that game.

Soon, I was beginning to wonder if we'd make it out of the parking lot at all, but eventually, we had to come up for air.

I'd gone a long way from being the Senator's daughter, afraid of PDA and the possible ensuing publicity.

Tucker helped me onto the terrifyingly high pillion seat on the Ducati. I still hadn't gotten used to it, and it didn't feel particularly safe, but Tucker was careful when I rode with him. And I have to admit, the throaty roar as he started the engine was darn sexy. Just like Tucker.

As we neared my apartment, I sat up straighter, then clung to Tucker when I made the bike wobble.

Parked outside was a dark sedan.

Tucker cruised to a halt and kicked down the bike-stand then swung off the seat and turned to help me down.

The driver's door opened and my father climbed out. We stared at each across the sidewalk, until I felt Tucker's hands unfastening my helmet. He'd already removed his own and his expression was concerned.

"You don't have to talk to him, sugar."

I gave a small smile. "No, that's fine. But ... stay with me?"

He took my hand in unspoken acknowledgement and we walked toward the Senator.

"Hello, Tera," he said, flicking a gaze to Tucker before meeting my eyes.

"Hi, Dad."

Tucker stood silently next to me, his face unreadable.

My father cleared his throat. "Your mother misses you."

"I miss her, too," I said honestly. "But she knows where she can find me. Obviously."

He glanced at Tucker again, who had remained uncharacteristically mute.

"Can we go somewhere to talk?" Dad asked at last.

"Sure," I said evenly. "Come on in."

"Somewhere private," he said smoothly.

I cocked my head on one side. "What could be more private than our apartment, Dad?"

I saw him frown when I said 'our apartment', but the emotion was immediately cleared from his face. He changed his tactics, turning to Tucker.

"I'm sure you wouldn't mind if I spoke privately to my daughter, would you?"

Tucker gave a cool smile. "No, I don't mind, but Tera asked me to stay, so I'm staying."

Dad was too used to the political game to show his annoyance, but I could tell that he was more than a little irritated at our refusal to play by his rules.

I tucked my hand into the pocket of Tucker's leather jacket, and he smiled down at me, placing his arm around my shoulders.

Part of being a good politician is knowing which battles to fight, so Dad just smiled and waved for us to lead him inside.

The apartment was much smaller than the one I'd had in San Francisco, but it was light and airy and within my budget. Tucker had made little impact upon the décor, shrugging when I asked his opinion on colors or fabrics, seeming bemused by my questions.

The most obvious sign of his inhabitance was a set of racing leathers hanging by the front door like a sloughed off skin.

I watched my father taking it all in, his eyes resting on Tucker's leathers before moving to the small, framed photographs hanging on one wall. His eyes softened as he gazed at a picture of him with my mother and Arnold Schwarzenegger at some political rally. Next to it was one of Kes and Tucker flying through the air, mid-stunt; and finally, a photo of Tucker sitting on the Duke with me leaning into him. I loved that picture.

He stood by the window, his hands in his pockets. I knew he wouldn't sit down, because in a power negotiation, the person standing has more influence than the person sitting.

I perched on a bar stool and Tucker stood behind me so I could lean against his firm chest.

"How are you?" Dad asked. "You look well."

"I am, thank you." There was an awkward pause. "How's Mom?"

"Busy," he smiled. "The usual. But I meant what I said—she misses you."

"I'm not going back," I said firmly. "Not to Minnesota or San Francisco or D.C.. This is my home now."

Dad looked across at me, his eyes intense.

"It wasn't a wise decision to move down here," he began. "And I know you took a pay cut."

Tucker shifted behind me and I knew I'd be answering questions about that later, as I'd omitted to pass on that particular fact.

"It was the right decision and my new job offers plenty of potential," I said calmly. "Besides, I don't want to work with politicians anymore."

Dad flinched minutely. "You have a Master's degree in Political Science," he pointed out. "What use will that be to you if you stay where you are?"

I raised an eyebrow. "You'd be surprised how many actors go into politics."

He gave a small smile, conceding that I'd won that point.

I folded my arms. "Why are you here, Dad?"

He pursed his lips. "May I speak candidly?"

"That would be a nice change."

He gave an amused chuckle. "Old habits. I want you to come and work for me. Not as an intern, but as a paid member of staff. You'd have your own office, a six-figure salary, and..."

"Dad, stop. I've already told you. It's a great offer, but it's not for me. I'm happy here."

He shook his head, disappointment written on his face.

"You can do better than this, Tera," he said, looking over my head at Tucker. "So much better."

I felt Tucker tense behind me.

"Thank you for the offer, Dad, but the answer is no."

He stared at Tucker again.

"Is this what you want for her? Earning a fraction of the money she could, living in some non-descript suburb, waiting around for a guy who performs in the circus?"

"Dad!"

Tucker laughed.

"Do I think I'm good enough for her? Hell, no. Do I want her to give up her life to follow me around the country? No fucking way. But whatever she wants, I'll break every bone in my body to give it to her."

Hearing his words, so certain and sure, my heart expanded.

My father snorted with amusement. "It's so easy for you to say the words, isn't it? But I know your type: you'll never be satisfied with just one woman."

Tucker stood up straight and walked around to stand next to me.

"You'd know about that, wouldn't you, Senator? Having more than one woman? Kestrel's mom wasn't enough for you. So you had Tera's mom, too."

My father's eyes flashed angrily and he surged toward Tucker.

Tucker just grinned and held his hands away from his sides.

"We gonna throw down now, Senator? That could be interesting: one on one, without your goons to back you up. I'll give you a tip: my right shoulder is still fucked. That'll give you an advantage. Come on!"

"Stop it!" I yelled, pressing both hands on Tucker's chest

and pushing him backward. "There'll be no fighting! Do you hear me? Both of you?"

Tucker smiled and winked at me, but my father looked furious.

"For God's sake, Tera! He's barely more than a circus clown! Is that what you want out of life?"

"Yes."

He put his hands on his hips and shook his head.

I expected Tucker to look triumphant, but his face was hard.

"Why do you hate the carnival so much, Senator? Is it because you were too chickenshit to travel with Kes's mom when you had the chance? Too scared to follow your own road?"

I threw a surprised look at Tucker, but it was my father's bitter expression that caught my attention. His shoulders slumped and he looked torn.

"Maura was ... different," he said slowly. "You can believe me or not, but I did care about her. But I also had responsibilities to more than myself. My family had expectations, and I cared about that more." He shrugged. "Maura would never have given up the carnival—she didn't know any better."

I shook my head sadly.

"And my brothers?"

He sighed. "They've grown into fine men."

"Both of them?"

He gave me a small smile. "Yes, both of them." He paused. "I heard that Kestrel saved a child's life."

I felt a warm glow at his words, however much I'd forced them out of him.

"How's Ollo?" he asked.

This time I couldn't help my smile. "Doing better. Thank you for asking."

He nodded. "I'm glad. Ollo's quite a character."

I walked toward my father and he hugged me tightly, wrapping his arms around me.

"I'm not choosing the carnival, Dad. That's what you don't understand: I'm choosing Tucker. He's a fine man, too. And I love him."

My father blinked, then closed his eyes.

"I know. But I had to try."

He left soon after. He and Tucker would never gos for beers together, but I hoped that they wouldn't be inclined to punch each other either.

"Are you okay, sugar?" he asked, pulling me onto the sofa so we were snuggled up together.

"Yes, I am. Actually, I'm really good. Thank you for not hitting him."

Tucker laughed lightly. "I didn't think you'd let me sleep with you if I beat the shit out of your father."

I tickled his ribs and he yelped.

"Still think you're getting lucky tonight, mister?"

He looked at me seriously. "I feel lucky every night, sugar. Every damn night."

We were saying goodbye to our friends.

Zef was taking the rig up to Arcata, then flying east to see his on-again/off-again girlfriend, Mirelle.

Kes was driving the RV with Aimee and Bo, and Luke and Zach were going with them to start work on their own cabin.

I could tell that Tucker was torn: he'd promised to help his friends, but our relationship was still so new, we wanted to spend time together, as well.

We'd discussed it and decided together that we'd give ourselves two weeks, then Tucker would go up to Arcata and help with the groundwork and ordering supplies. He'd spend four days a week working on the new cabin while I went to my job in LA, then we'd spend weekends together. It wasn't ideal, but both of us were learning the meaning of a new word: compromise.

"You guys are welcome to come for Christmas," Aimee offered. "So long as you don't mind sleeping in the RV," and she threw me an amused look, knowing that I wasn't overly fond of it.

"Thanks, Aimee, but we're kind of thinking that we'd like to have Christmas just the two of us."

"Yeah," said Tucker. "I want to see my girl in her Christmas stockings."

Kes threw an apple core at Tucker's head. "That's my *sister* you're talking about, asshole!"

Tucker laughed and pulled me against his firm chest.

"Your brother has issues," he said in a loud whisper. "Maybe he isn't getting any."

Aimee spluttered, her cheeks going pink.

"You'll pay for that McCoy," she threatened. "And it *so* isn't true!"

She whispered something to Kes and his frown disappeared instantly.

Zef rolled his eyes. "We gotta hit the road. Lot of miles to travel."

I stood up and gave him a quick hug, then kissed Zach and Luke, while Tucker did the man-hug-shoulder-slap thing.

We watched as Zach and Luke's truck disappeared from the near-empty fairground, the rig following behind. Zef shouted something obscene at Tucker, who grinned and gave him the finger.

I could see that Kes was impatient to get going, too.

"Look after yourself, sis," he said, pulling me into a hug. "Let me know if anyone needs his ass kicking, 'cause I'm the man for the job," and he shot a hard look at Tucker, who just grinned at him.

Aimee quietly offered her own highly individual advice for keeping Tucker in line, which made me laugh and made both the guys frown as they wondered what was being said.

I hugged her, agreeing that we'd visit over New Year's. Then I bent down to kiss Ollo on the cheek.

"You're family, Tera Hawkins," he said sincerely. "Don't forget that."

"I won't, I promise."

His words made me misty eyed and I felt a tightness creep into my throat.

Tucker knelt down and hugged the little man, nodding at something Ollo whispered to him. Then Tucker held Bo in one arm as he helped Ollo into the RV, situating Bo on the bench seat. sAimee and Kes jumped in, and the massive engine started with a rumble.

Finally, Tucker and I turned and waved as the RV bounced across the ground, small dust clouds churning up beneath the huge tires. Tucker watched until they were out of sight, a slight frown on his face.

"Are you sorry you're not going with them?" I asked tentatively.

Tucker gave a small smile and wrapped his arms around my waist, resting his forehead against mine.

"My home is where you are, sugar. I don't have any regrets about that."

My man. My beautiful man with his rough hands and loving heart. My man was a roamer, a roustabout.

And he was staying here with me.

EPILOGUE

TUCKER

I'd never lived in a house that had bricks before.

Tera's new place was the top floor of an old colonial that had been divided into apartments. It had a yard with flowers and a white picket fence.

A picket fence.

I think having the Duke parked outside might have spoiled the homey image, but I was good with that—so was Tera.

No one knows what shit life is going to throw at them, except maybe spooky ole fortune tellers like Madame Sylva. You don't know when you'll meet someone and suddenly you're traveling in a different direction. It could be today, tomorrow. It might even have been yesterday and you just don't know it yet. Like me and Tera.

With everything that had happened between us, from those early, stolen kisses to the moment I admitted that I loved her and everything in between and since, I learned one important fact: it's okay not to have all the answers.

There was nothing about us that matched: she was from money, and I'd grown up dirt poor; she had a Master's degree and I was a high school dropout; she was a vegetarian and I liked burgers and steaks; she liked having manicures and girly shit, and I had motor oil under my nails. Hell, the woman even voted Republican—we had nothing in common, except Kes, I guess.

She didn't even love the carnival the way we did. There was nothing about Tera and me that should have worked, but somehow, we did. We just fit.

Being with her was a giant slice of happiness—that woman was my own starlight, someone who could brighten the darkest night. How did a penniless roustabout get to be so damn lucky? Time was precious. Life was precious. I wanted both with Tera.

She loved me and she held my heart. There would be times when there were miles between us and the hours would pass slowly. There would be bumps in the road and sometimes we'd lose our way, but always, always, I'd find my way back to her, my pole star shining in the dark.

Everything else? All the problems that life would throw at us? We'd figure it out along the way. Somehow.

Together.

THE END

Read on for the first chapter of Zef's story in *Carnival*, book 4 of the *Traveling* series

CARNIVAL

PROLOGUE

I was nearing Missoula when the phone rang. I'd covered a lot of miles today, driving the eight-wheeler across the rolling plains of Montana, the sharp silhouettes of the Rocky Mountains in the distance.

Our destination was the County Fairgrounds. It was one of the smaller places that we played, but I liked that. I got a buzz out of bringing our show to small-town folk. They always gave us a great reception when they saw Donohue's Daredevils roll into town. Well, except for the people who thought carnies were trailer trash. These days, I couldn't afford to get into anything with fucktards like that, so I walked away. Mostly.

The Western Montana Fair was a big date on the locals' calendar. We'd played there for the last two years, and I loved the soaring skies and wide open spaces.

Outside my air conditioned cab, the early June weather was hotter than a furnace, and the blacktop shimmered and danced like a mirage in the desert.

I glanced down as my cell started playing *Daddy Yankee* and Mirelle's name flashed up.

Damn, it was good to hear from her—it had been nearly

three weeks since we last talked, much longer since we'd managed to get together.

I took the call on my hands-free cell, in a cradle on the dashboard, grinning as her east coast accent with a Puerto Rican lilt filled the cab.

"Hey, beautiful! How you doin'?"

There was a short pause.

"I'm pregnant. It's not yours."

CHAPTER ONE

One week later...

I watched the flames leap and dance, sending a shower of sparks into the sky as one of the logs caught light.

Even though the daytime temperatures had soared into the nineties, it was considerably cooler now and everyone gathered around the circle of fire. It was a carnie tradition that went way back, signaling the end of another day.

Tonight was special because it was the penultimate night at this pitch, and our last chance to take it easy for a few days. The final night was always crazy busy because it was a jump day —which meant that all the roustabouts were taking down the carnival rides and packing everything back into the rigs, then driving through the night to get to the next town by morning, to set up for the following afternoon, when the whole cycle started over again.

In fact, the 24-Hour Man had already left. He was the guy who went ahead, signposting the way for the rest of us to follow. It may not sound important, but you don't want fifteen eight-wheelers getting stuck or ending up driving down a one lane road to the wrong field.

So tonight was our night—our time to kick back, relax, and visit with other carnies.

"Bro, you look like someone just kicked your dog. What's up with you? You've been a pain in my ass all week."

Tucker left the others by the fire and squatted down beside me, ignoring the fuck-off vibes I'd been giving everyone else.

"What's eating you, man? Tell Uncle Tucker all about it."

Tucker was a year younger than me, but sometimes he acted like a teenager and spoke like a California surfer, if you ignored his Tennessee accent. We were all like that in the carnival— mongrels who didn't call any place home, but everywhere was our kingdom and the road was our right.

I didn't reply and he threw an arm around my shoulder.

"I know about Mirelle. Tough break, brother."

I shot him an angry glance and he pulled a face.

"Mirelle called Aimee, Aimee told Kes, and well ... you know how it goes."

Yeah. I knew. Kes and Tucker were my family, my blood brothers—cut one, we all bleed. We didn't keep secrets. And since Mirelle was Aimee's best friend, I'd expected the news to circulate faster than it had. Perhaps she'd thought I'd tell them myself.

I should have, but I couldn't do it. I didn't want their pity.

"She wasn't right for you," Tucker said softly. "I like Mirelle, but she wasn't going to make it as a carnie. She has roots and that big ole Puerto Rican family back on the East Coast."

I knew he was right, but the sharp cut of disillusionment was hard to take. Aimee had lived out East and she'd followed Kes to the carnival; Tucker's woman flew out to see him every couple of weeks. Why couldn't that work for me?

I shrugged off his arm and stood up. I was ready to walk away when a thought stopped me in my tracks.

"Did she tell Aimee who the father is?"

"Yeah." He stared down at the dirt, idly pushing his fingers through the tough, brown grass. "Some dude who teaches at the same school."

Figured.

Suddenly Kes rose to his feet. Everyone stopped talking and we all turned to face him.

He stood with the fire at his back, the flames dancing behind as he faced us. His people, his family.

"I've got some news I want to share with you," he said. "Perhaps I'd better say that *we've* got some news to share with you."

He smiled at Aimee as she walked to his side, her eyes glowing with love as she looked at him, and he slid his arm around her waist.

"We're going to be parents. By January, there'll be a new little carnie joining the family."

Yells and cheers rose from the carnies around the fire, then Tucker called out,

"Oh my God! Does that mean you've been having sex?"

"No, it's an immaculate conception, dufus," I muttered, slapping him around the back of the head.

Aimee shot Tucker a look that said he'd be paying for his dumb joke later.

Everyone crowded around offering congratulations.

"A new little stunt rider for the family business?" asked one of the carnies.

Kes shrugged, his whole body lit with happiness as men slapped him on the back or shook hands, and women kissed him on the cheek. Aimee was surrounded with her own admirers, smiling and laughing, glowing with joy as she turned to look at Kes to hear his answer.

"Our kid can be whatever he wants."

"So, it's a boy?"

"Maybe. We don't know yet."

When the crowd around them thinned, I walked over to give Aimee a kiss on the cheek. Then I turned to Kes.

"Congratulations, man. That's great news."

"Thanks, Zef. I appreciate it. And I wanted to ask you—Aimee wants the baby to be christened, something old school, you know? So I was wondering if you'd be Godfather."

That was the last thing I'd been expecting. I wasn't the kind of guy that a kid could look up to.

Kes read the doubt on my face and laughed.

"I'm going to ask Tucker, too. So the kid will need at least one Godfather who's not completely crazy."

I grinned at him.

"Well, when you put it that way ... I'm the lesser of two evils?"

"Something like that." His voice sobered. "So, will you do it? If anything happened to me and Aimee..." he swallowed, a flicker of fear on his face, "if anything happened, I'd want to know that I could count on you."

"Fuck, man, nothing's gonna happen to you!"

"Yeah, but it could. We both know ... *we know* it could and ... I need you to say it, man. I need to know that you'd be there. If I hadn't had Dono to take care of me and Con, I'd have been in a fucking foster home. "

I rubbed my hand across of my face.

"Of course. Of course I'd do it—anything."

I stuck out my hand and he shook it before pulling me into a swift hug.

"Thanks, Zef."

I nodded, then asked the question that had been burning me since he'd made his announcement.

"Are you scared ... about being a father?"

Kes cocked his head to one side, thinking about it.

"Nah, I couldn't fuck it up as bad as Mom the alcoholic or

dear ole dad who barely knew I existed, or cared. Anyway, I've got Aimee to keep me straight."

He grinned and turned to accept more congratulations from other carnies.

I walked away, surprised by the emotions I was feeling.

Kes, a father!

That was some pretty serious shit. Coming on top of Mirelle's news, I was feeling off kilter. I tried not to picture her with a guy who wore a collared shirt to work, some nice, safe townie who'd give her security. But she deserved that. She deserved more than a tatted up wiseass who jumped motorcycles for a living—a man with a criminal record who'd served time in prison.

Someone walked over my grave and a shiver ran down my spine. I'd cleaned up my act since then and I wasn't *ever* going back.

And I meant what I'd said to Kes: if anything happened to him and Aimee, I'd take care of their kid. Fuck knows what kind of parent I'd be, but he'd asked me and I'd sure as hell try.

The breeze had picked up since sunset and I could see the tops of the distant trees swaying blackly against the rising moon.

The Ferris wheel was still and silent, a towering monument to man's desire for mindless pleasure. It didn't go anywhere, it didn't do anything—except give the illusion of movement. And wasn't that what the carnival was all about? Cheap thrills for a few bucks before moving on to the next small town. And yet, even with the existence of Netflix, tablets and smartphones, people still came, searching for a little of that stardust, that illusive magic, the freewheeling world of the carnies. Maybe that was what made it so unreal: we'd arrive in the half-light of dawn, and by the evening a world of bright neon and music erupted from an empty field. A few days of eating cotton candy and corndogs, a few moments of adrenaline as you were whirled around the Tilt-A-Whirl or rode the bumper cars, and then we'd vanish in the night, leaving patches of flattened grass and an empty field.

I pushed my hands into my jean pockets and stared up at the moon as if it had called my name.

How many years did I have before my body broke down, before my knees or ankles or spine couldn't take it anymore, when throwing myself through the air on 200 pounds of metal no longer seemed like a good idea? Then what? What would my life be then?

"The Cheyenne tell a story that the moon was held by a warring tribe, so a pair of antelope tried to rescue the moon and take it to a good village. But Coyote, the trickster, decides to make trouble, and the antelope chase him. Coyote tosses the moon into a river each night, just out of reach of the antelope."

I didn't turn around as Ollo spoke.

"Is that supposed to mean something to me, old man?"

I heard his soft chuckle behind me, a wheezing, hiccupping laughing cough.

"Nope, it's just a story about the moon."

"Great, thanks for that. Very educational."

He sat down behind me, ignoring the obvious message that I didn't want company.

I felt a soft tug on my pants leg as Bo started to climb me like a jungle gym, nestling into me and throwing his thin arms around my neck, chattering in my ear.

"Damn monkey doesn't know when he's not wanted," I grumbled, supporting Bo's tiny fury body as he snuggled into my chest.

Ollo laughed again.

"I'd say he knows exactly when he's wanted. Capuchin's are smart critters—smarter than most damn humans."

I sighed, knowing I wasn't getting any alone time tonight.

I sat down on the bone-dry dirt next to Ollo, smiling as Bo

took his chance to go scampering off into the darkness. For a moment, I listened to him rustling in the tall grasses at the side of the swing-boats and I leaned against the canvas backdrop of the Ghost Train.

When I was a kid back in Georgia, I used to try and sneak in under the canvas without paying when the carnival came to town. Sometimes I made it, and sometimes I got dragged out by a hard-faced carnie and sent packing with a smack to the back of the head.

It didn't matter how many times that happened, I always snuck back. I was fascinated by the mechanics, all of those big machines whipping you into the air or speeding around in circles. I hadn't heard of hydraulics or knew anything about the physics of gravity, but I loved the dirt and grease behind the scenes, and the rides that made people laugh and scream.

Now, I could take a ghost ride anytime I wanted, but I never did.

I sighed, wondering if the carnival would ever feel magical to me again.

"Good news about Kes and Aimee—new life. A child will keep the carnival alive."

I nodded, but I wasn't sure that Ollo was right. It was a hard life, the traveling carnival, and many of the smaller outfits had shut down or gone out of business. I knew as well as anyone that there were no guarantees in life, but I hoped Ollo was right.

"Yeah, I'm happy for them."

I watched a shooting star shimmer across the sky, wondering what the world had in store for me, wondering if fate was planning some new torture.

"She wasn't right for you, Zef."

Ollo's voice broke and squeaked like a twelve year-old boy, although his body was no taller than the average seven year-old.

Ollo was a dwarf and had lived his whole life in a traveling carnival. He'd done every job from clowning to tumbling, fire-eating and fire-breathing to knife-thrower and rodeo rider, fairground barker to roustabout, and everything in between. He was old now; no one knew how old, probably not even Ollo, but he'd been with Kes's family since the second world war, so he must be at least eighty.

He probably weighed no more than ninety pounds. I could have picked him up and tossed him over my shoulder without a problem, but I had too much respect for him to do something like that.

So I sat back and listened to what he had to tell me.

"You're the second person tonight to say that Mirelle wasn't right for me," I said, my voice wry.

Ollo spit a stream of tobacco juice onto the hard-packed soil, aiming at one of the iron tent pegs.

"Are you surprised? Her family has uprooted once—she wasn't going to do it again. Not for you."

"Feel free to sugarcoat it!"

"Aw, is the big, tough stunt rider feelin' sorry for hisself?"

I shook my head.

"Nah. Just pissed that she was seeing someone else and didn't tell me."

There was a long silence and in the distance I could hear the sound of Luke's guitar playing.

"I had a woman once," Ollo said softly. "Long time ago."

His voice was quiet and it sounded like a confession.

"She wasn't like me," he said. "She was a townie, a petite lil' thing. Delicate all over, tiny waist. Taller than me, of course. We were in Boise for the summer and it was the swinging sixties. She had long straight hair, golden brown, the color of corn. I was a rodeo clown in those days, and she'd come to see the ponies. We got talking and became friends. I'd wait for her to come for me at night. We'd hold hands and sit watching the stars from the top of the Ferris wheel. We fell in love."

"Sounds ... nice?"

"Yeah, it was. She was going to come with me at the end of the summer," he chuckled quietly. "Run away and join the circus."

"But she changed her mind?"

Ollo shook his head.

"I don't know. One night, she didn't come. I waited every night, knowing that soon we'd be moving on. I went to look for her. In the town."

I stared up at Ollo's stars, knowing that this story didn't have a happy ending. I imagined how brave he'd have to be, leaving the carnies—his people—to go look for this girl among strangers, among townies.

"I didn't find her, but her father found me. Gave me what they used to call a damn good beat-down, and told me he wouldn't let a deformed freak like me near his daughter. I don't know if she'd been sent away or whether she was locked in her room, listening to her father whip me with his belt as I kicked and screamed and tried everything to fight him off. I always wondered about that."

"Jesus, Ollo!"

My voice was quiet, shocked, and he was silent.

"You never saw her again?"

"Ah, but I did. Ten years later, we were in Boise again doing the northern circuit. By then, the music was louder and angrier. We were all trying to forget about Vietnam, and everything seemed a little wilder. Borders were breaking down, and even the townie boys were starting to wear their hair long. That's when I saw her. She was with a rube and they had two kids—a boy and a girl, maybe seven or eight years old. They had her eyes, I remember that. She saw me watching her and she stared back. She smiled at me, then she turned and walked away."

His voice disappeared, lost in memories.

"That was the last time I saw her. I never tried anything with a townie again."

"What was her name?"

"Jeanie. Jeanie with the light brown hair."

I heard the soft patter of Bo's footsteps, and he appeared out of the darkness, his tiny body curling into Ollo's arms as he chirruped quietly.

I watched Ollo stroke the soft gray-and-white fur.

"Am I supposed to take some deep meaning from that story?" I asked, hoping to lighten the mood.

Ollo coughed out a laugh.

"Nope, just a story about a boy and a girl under the stars."

And then, as silently as he'd arrived, he stood up and walked away, Bo still cradled in his arms.

I leaned back against the canvas, thinking about everything he'd said. If I was honest with myself, I'd known from the start that me and Mirelle wouldn't last, but it still stung that she'd obviously been with this other guy for a while. And that she'd picked someone who was the complete opposite of me.

I didn't have any trouble hooking up with women who wanted a one-night stand with a biker carnie, but even I had to admit that had gotten old. And now Kes was married and about to become a father, and Tucker lived half the year with his woman in LA. Everything was changing.

I'd had a family once—Mom, Dad, and a little brother. I still had my brother, but he was a man full grown now, successful and living his own life. He didn't need me anymore, and he definitely didn't need the shit I'd brought to his door. It was better that I kept moving, kept those wheels rolling.

The other Daredevils were my brothers too, but now they all had partners and I was on the outside again.

Sometimes it felt so damn lonely.

Download CARNIVAL now!

REVIEWS

Reviews are love! Honestly, they are! But it also helps other people to make an informed decision before buying my book.

So I'd really appreciate if you took a few seconds to do that.

Thank you!

MORE BOOKS BY JHB

Series Titles
The Education Series
An epic love story spanning the years, through war zones and more...
*The Education of Sebastian (Education series #1)
*The Education of Caroline (Education series #2)
*The Education of Sebastian & Caroline (combined edition, books 1 & 2)
Semper Fi: The Education of Caroline (Education series #3)

The Traveling Series
All the fun of the fair ... and two worlds collide
*The Traveling Man (Traveling series #1)
*The Traveling Woman (Traveling series #2)
*Roustabout (Traveling series #3)
*Carnival (Traveling series #4)
*Gypsy (Traveling series #5)

The Justin Trainer Series
The bodyguard and the billionaire

Guarding the Billionaire (Justin Trainer series #1)
Saving the Billionaire (Justin Trainer series #2)

The EOD Series
Blood, bombs and heartbreak
*Tick Tock (EOD series #1)
* Bombshell (EOD series #2)

The Rhythm Series
Blood, sweat, tears and dance
*Slave to the Rhythm (Rhythm series #1)
*Luka (Rhythm series #2)

Standalone Titles
Contemporary Romance
The Lilac Cadillac
Battle Scars
One Careful Owner
*Lifers
At Your Beck & Call
The New Samurai
Exposure

New Adult
*Dangerous to Know & Love
Dazzled
Summer of Seventeen

Paranormal
*The Dark Detective: Venator (Book #1)
*The Dark Detective: Paukúnnum (Book #2)

Novellas
Playing in the Rain

*Behind the Walls

Anthologies of Short Stories
*The Year Book Volume 1
*The Year Book Volume 2
*The Year Book Volume 3

Audio Books
One Careful Owner
(*narrated by Seth Clayton*)

On the Stage
Later, After: Playscript
Trailer

With Alana Albertson
Father Figure

* These titles are published in languages other than English.
Please check Jane's website for details—and receive **a free
short story every month** when you sign up for her newsletter

:)

QR code for Jane's website

ROMANCE WITH STUART REARDON

My love co-author with these titles

Two book series - contemporary romance

*Undefeated

*Model Boyfriend

Three book series - romcom

*Gym Or Chocolate?

*The World According to Vince

*The Baby Game

Standalone

Survivor Love Island *(romcom)*

*Touch My Soul *(novella)*

WRITING AS BERRICK FORD

Police Thrillers, UK

Dead Water
Dead Man's Dive
Dead Reckoning
Dead Shore

www.berrickford.com

www.ingramcontent.com/pod-product-compliance
Lightning Source LLC
Chambersburg PA
CBHW072113250626
47159CB00007B/2426